# TOMORROW'S EVE

*"To seek in the transient
for eternal tracks."*

Villiers de l'Isle-Adam

# TOMORROW'S EVE

translated by Robert Martin Adams

University of Illinois Press
Urbana   Chicago   London

First paperback edition, 2001
English translation © 1982 by
the Board of Trustees of the University of Illinois
All rights reserved
Manufactured in the United States of America
♾ This book is printed on acid-free paper.

Library of Congress Cataloging-in-Publication Data
Villiers de l'Isle-Adam, comte de, 1839–1889.
Tomorrow's Eve.
Translation of: L'Eve future.
ISBN 0-252-06955-2 (pbk. : alk. paper)
ISBN 978-0-252-06955-0 (pbk. : alk. paper)
PQ2476.V4E9213      1982
843'.8      82-13411

P 10 9 8 7

University of Illinois Press
1325 South Oak Street
Champaign, IL 61820-6903
www.press.uillinois.edu

# ❧ CONTENTS ☙

# TRANSLATOR'S INTRODUCTION

O<small>N THE BANKS OF THE</small> Oise a few miles north of Paris stands the little hamlet of l'Isle-Adam; the house of Villiers has been associated with it for many hundreds of years, if not quite from the beginning. The first Villiers of whom we have record was Seigneur de Villiers et Dormans— native, thus, of a district about seventy miles to the east of l'Isle-Adam. But in 1324, Jean de Villiers married Marie de l'Isle, and, the male line of de l'Isle dying out at that time, the formal style became Villiers de l'Isle-Adam. In six or eight centuries of unbroken nobility, a family may pick up a very respectable number of quarterings. During the Renaissance, members of the Villiers family are found making major donations to the ecclesiastical foundations of nearby Beauvais; one of the clan was a marshal of France, another was grand master of the order of St. John of Malta. These are not myths, but facts.

The traditions of the family were loyalist, Catholic, conservative; to families with such traditions, the revolution of 1789 was not kind. The Marquis Joseph Toussaint Charles Villiers de l'Isle-Adam and his wife were thus living under reduced circumstances in the remote Breton town of St. Brieuc when there was born to them, on November 7, 1838, a scion whom they named Jean Marie Mathias Philippe Auguste Villiers de l'Isle-Adam. This was the poet and author of our present novel.

That a handsome, talented, and ambitious son, sprung from the stock of a decayed nobility, should be looked upon as the restorer of the family fortunes is nothing new or surprising. Mathias (such was the poet's name within his family circle) was nominated for this role before he was into his teens. It was an article of faith with the father, the mother, the sisters, the adoring aunt: Mathias would by his literary glory restore the name of Villiers to its rightful place among the stars. More perilous was an associated delusion of the father's: he must and would build a scaffolding of immense wealth on which his son's rise to fame would be sustained. Not only did he think himself destined to make millions; even as he cast away the family's last modest possessions on ridiculous speculations, the infatuate old man was convinced that he was really accumulating the wealth of Croesus—not for himself, of course (nothing could have been farther from his thoughts), but for his glorious son. When he was dying at the age of eighty, he said to a friend, "It's all up with me, but I die at ease with the world: for I'm leaving Mathias a fortune to rival those of the great princely families." The friend, humoring him, leaped to the wildest extremes of imagination, and asked if this fortune might amount to as much as fifty million francs. The old man wrinkled his nose in disgust and said, "Pooh! Fifty millions; what penury!"

In fact, he left nothing but debts.

For his first thirty years, however, our poet was able to live a life of some elegance, about equally divided between high society and literary bohemianism. Thanks to the financial support of that devoted aunt, he even managed a measure of youthful debauchery. Formal schooling he despised, and never cultivated it, though in areas where his interest was aroused, he readily made himself a learned, sometimes an extraordinarily learned, man. He had presence not wholly distinct from the aura of mystery he always distilled; he could walk down a public thoroughfare like a man from another planet—remote, majestic, indifferent. Few men were his intimates, and he always seemed to reserve, from whatever society he was in, some crucial part of his life which was rooted elsewhere. Barely twenty, but with the proverbial slim sheaf of verses in hand, he came to Paris, introduced himself to the society of poets, and was received by them as a peer and destined luminary. But there were aspects of his life in which Catulle Mendés and Léon Dierx never shared; there were aspects in which nobody shared. And in this vacancy the myth of Villiers flowered like a tropical plant. Villiers retired for a season to live among the Benedictines of the Abbey of Solesme. It was as much a literary seminar as an ecclesiastical retreat, for among his fellow guests was Louis Veuillot, but legend invested the episode with mystic and occult trappings. Periodically Villiers disappeared from Paris altogether; in fact, he was often visiting his father and mother in St. Brieuc, but he had a way of intimating ancestral castles on mist-enwrapped peninsulas. More spectacular, though still a little speculative, was the episode of Villiers' candidacy to fill the vacant throne of Greece (1863). Technically, of course, anyone can apply for such a job, and that Villiers himself took his candidacy seriously is no guarantee that anyone else did. But apparently some others really did—though in the end the crown was bestowed on Prince William George of Schleswig-Holstein-Sonderburg-Glucksburg. On another level altogether, Villiers was the unquestioned friend, intimate, and admired colleague of men like Baudelaire, Mallarmé, and Wagner, who were lavish in their praise of his genius. If he was a legend, it was a legend based on some authentic substance—how much was anybody's guess, and uncertainty made the legend grow. His debauchery, his taciturnity, his mysterious comings and goings, his religiosity, his macabre jokes, his ferocious wit, and his fantastic showmanship all contributed to the Villiers phenomenon.

He was a performer on improvised stages, in cafés, in groups—yet always, on these occasions, it was as if only a fragment of his submerged life was showing itself. We have accounts of these hilarious, grotesque inventions which combined virtuosities on the piano with long, improvised narrations—extravagant and theatrical, yet hypnotically compelling, and funny, sometimes, to the point of tears. An outstanding figure

in these recitals was a grotesque character—rational, officious, complacent, sadistic, cowardly—the epitome of bourgeois common sense as Villiers perceived it. The dummy's name was Tribulat Bonhomet. The name,
and maybe even the character, may have owed something to Ben Jonson's
Tribulation Wholesome, but Villiers made of him a creation entirely personal. As Père Ubu would be for Alfred Jarry a few years later, Tribulat
Bonhomet became for Villiers a figure of nightmare and obsession; he
was also a vehicle for Villiers' demonic satire. At the home of Liszt in
Weimar, Villiers improvised on the story of Tribulat Bonhomet before a
glittering social gathering headed by the Duke of Saxe-Weimar, to such
effect that he reduced the entire company to convulsions of helpless
laughter.

He was an anomaly among the bohemians, if only for his aristocratic
pretensions, and another sort of anomaly in the aristocratic circles to
which he had easy entrée, though sometimes under awkward conditions.
He often had to borrow the suits in which he attended parties where frac
was obligatory, and at which he would be, in a way not altogether une-
quivocal, the star attraction. In literary cafés he was thought of as a man
from another sphere, out of place among the poets but in place nowhere
else, unless among his own reveries and aspirations. Men laughed at him
and plagiarized his recitals, ridiculing what they could not rival and then
turning it to their own profit. For these and no doubt other reasons,
Villiers lived at war with much of the world; and, having a keen tongue
and a talent for instant riposte, he made enemies. At an entertainment
where white gloves were called for, he appeared without, not having any;
a lady sarcastically congratulated him on the elegance of those he was
wearing. "Gift of my mother, madame," he said, turning on his heel. His
unworldliness was proverbial. "Eh, Villiers," said a fool, meeting him one
day, "are you still drifting around up there?"—waving at the clouds. "And
you," was the retort, with a contemptuous finger at the ground, "are you
still crawling around down there?" He made no friends that way, and not
many in any other way, at least not till he had learned the brutal lessons
of humility.

His dream was all but absolute. He thought himself, as he had always
been encouraged to think himself, a genius. "Go Beyond" was the family
motto, and he sought success only by the road of artistic integrity, high
and aloof, uncompromising. One curious byway to fortune if not fame
ran constantly through the minds of the poet and his family, in contrast
to their uniform hauteur elsewhere: it was the conviction that Jean Marie
Mathias Philippe Auguste was destined to make his fortune by marrying
an heiress. This project left its mark on our present novel, *L'Eve future*
*(Tomorrow's Eve)*, and has a bizarre interest of its own that justifies an
account of it. On December 23, 1873, Villiers de l'Isle-Adam entered into
a contract with the Comte de la Houssaye, by the terms of which the
party of the second part was to provide for the party of the first part a
wife worth at least three million francs; of this sum, two hundred thou-

sand francs would be the broker's commission. Following the Count's instructions, Villiers accordingly betook himself to London early in January, 1874, where with remarkable promptitude he fell in love with an appropriately wealthy young lady. (Modern scholarship seems to have identified her as a Miss Anna Eyre Powell.) If only from the outcome, we know that the courtship went badly, but tradition (i.e., gossip) tells us just how badly. Outfitted by his sponsor with the last word in polite attire, including a repeating watch, Villiers escorted his young lady to Covent Garden, and in the privacy of a box declared his passion. But he recited so much poetry, gave such a long reading from his next novel, and grew so frantically agitated that the young lady was frightened, thought him an escaped lunatic, and made her escape from his society as abruptly as she could. The broker accused Villiers of ineptitude, there was a quarrel in which the borrowed clothes were angrily taken back, and only with great difficulty was the poet able to make his way back to France. But of the whole episode what remained most strongly in Villiers' mind was the spiritless, blockish female who had been utterly incapable of responding to his romantic declarations, had not even glimpsed the world of his ideal values. Miss Alicia Clary, of *Tomorrow's Eve*, was a degraded female Tribulat Bonhomet, but she was also an actual person whom Villiers (in whom there is more than a trace of Lord Celian Ewald) had encountered in real life.

Already as this comedy was being acted out, Villiers was beginning to feel the harsh bite of financial distress. Bit by bit, his father managed to lose in ridiculous and visionary speculations the last vestiges of his own property, his wife's property, and that property which belonged to the once-inexhaustible aunt. The old man's last resort was apparently a knowledge of heraldry, picked up over the years by assiduous study of his own genealogy. Advertising himself as an authority, he proceeded (as the biographer neatly puts it) to sow on the most uncongenial of soils, and at very modest rates indeed, a forest of genealogical trees. Such agriculture paid poorly, however, and even had the Marquis been able to offer help to his son, there seems some doubt that the latter would have been willing to accept. Loyal as ever to the family traditions, the poet served in the miserable war of 1870 against Prussia and took part in repressing the ferocious episode of the Commune; but thereafter he fell on hard times, harder than his worst imaginings could have foreseen. Villiers became poor, not just ignobly decent, but houseless, fireless, foodless indigent. He had not clothing to keep himself warm. He had not a bed or a table. He missed meals, not just one or two, but for days on end. He slunk through the grim back-alleys of Paris, cadging food from garbage cans and begging for second-hand clothes with other derelicts. He took the most menial jobs wherever he could pick them up. We hear of him refereeing boxing matches in rough clubs, where part of the evening's humor was watching him get hit by the contestants. He worked for a medical charlatan, pretending to be distracted until fed a bottle of the quack's nostrum, which of course cured him instantly. He borrowed where he could. He tried to sell stories, and when he was lucky enough to do so, he got derisory prices for them. For some time one bitter winter he slept on the bare boards of a building under construction; one snowy night when he was huddled there, the night watchman, spying him, came over and deliberately ground his muddy boot on the poet's face. Yet these hideous years of dark squalor and degradation were lightened in some measure by the fact that Villiers was never more than half-aware of physical circumstance. As the fool said, he lived with his head in the clouds, lost in his own noble phantasmagoria. And from time to time there were incidents of glittering momentary sunshine, as when he visited Bayreuth to hear the operas of Wagner and to be hailed as a friend and fellow artist by the composer. Or again, there was a moment when he served briefly but dramatically as political secretary for the pretender to the throne of France. He even tried to run for public office on the royalist ticket—with predictable results.

He did not parade his poverty or beg for pity. He lived a dream, and it was more a noble than a ridiculous dream, though of course it was both. When his understanding friends met, Mallarmé tells us, and one had seen Villiers lately, the other would ask sensitively, "What did he say?" To ask how he *was* would only have been painful and demeaning. Infinitely more important was the state of his mind, with which his deplorable physical circumstances had nothing whatever to do.

He never ceased to consider himself a literary artist and to stand up for his artistic conscience, however petty the review for which he wrote, however paltry the sum of money involved. When he saw the name of an ancestral Villiers de l'Isle-Adam vilified in a cheap historical melodrama, he rose to a posture of bristling dignity and fought with all the weapons at his command in defense of his family and their principles. He even had to fight for his own name. During the great genealogical muddle of the Napoleonic era (when dukes, as the Baron de Charlus smartly remarks, were being named after bridges), authorities lost sight completely of the Villiers de l'Isle-Adam and allowed a collateral and secondary family of Villiers to assume the title. The poet was challenged to vindicate his name, and he nearly did so on the field of honor, except that his historical proofs were so overwhelming as to leave the challenger no choice but withdrawal—a withdrawal which he managed with grace and generosity. Still, family trees, however authentic, pay no bills, and Villiers continued wretchedly poor. It is said that *Tomorrow's Eve* was written in an unfurnished room, where the author, unable even to afford a table, crouched on the floor and penned his pages using the bare boards as a writing desk. And when things became too much for him, he simply disappeared. Rather than advertise his misery or appeal for help, he dropped out of sight for months, even years on end. We simply do not know what he was doing or how he survived during those periods.

That he came back from absolute destitution as from the grave, that he

began slowly to write again, to be published, to be recognized and even
admired in certain circles is a fact not easy to explain. A decisive episode
was Calmann-Lévy's decision, practically forced by Catulle Mendés, to
publish the collection of short stories known as *Contes cruels* (1883).[1]
*L'Eve future* appeared, first in a magazine (*La Vie Moderne*, 1885–86),
then in a volume (1886). Improvident and necessitous, Villiers had sold
the copyright unconditionally for the absurd sum of 500 francs, so the
novel hardly relieved his distress. But the bigger and better-paying re-
views suddenly started opening up for him. There were further *Contes
cruels;* and *Axël,* the drama on which he had been working for years,
began to appear in sections even as he revised it. A lecture tour in Bel-
gium was successful enough to raise him out of the pit of necessity. He
was just starting to see the first gleams of that general public recognition
in the coming of which he had never ceased to believe when his health,
undermined by malnutrition and pulmonary weakness, began to give
way. Once begun, his decline was rapid. Removed to the Hospital of John
of God, he was unmercifully badgered during his last weeks by Huysmans, who, with all the intemperate zeal of a new convert, threatened
him with hellfire and damnation unless he married the warm-hearted,
illiterate woman who had nursed him in the days of his deepest distress,
and by whom he had had an illegitimate child. Villiers held out as long
as he could, but in the end succumbed to a marriage which (whatever its
human rightness) mocked those dreams by which, more than most men,
he had lived. He died on August 19, 1889, in the fiftieth year of his age.
A few months later, *Axël* was published in its completed form; four years
after that, its first recitation in a Paris theater created a major sensation.
Villiers never became and probably never will become a broadly popular
author, but the kind of success to which he aspired, he finally got. That
it came too late for him to relish it is the kind of observation he would
have ascribed contemptuously to Tribulat Bonhomet.

Like many of the great modern writers, Villiers de l'Isle-Adam was a
man at profound odds with the way of the world into which he was born.
Thus, when he turned to the novel, he had to impose many strident, even
awkward, angularities on its traditional form. The nineteenth-century
novel in general is a structure of accommodation based upon the central
realities of human nature, that is (in the customary loose phrase), of flesh
and blood. Characters are supposed to possess a degree of verisimilitude.
They are portrayed within a social context. They are provided with motives, which animate a plot extended through linear time. More commonly than not, their problems involve love, money, and manners,
culminating in a reconciliation of which the common symbol is marriage. What obstacles are overcome on the way to that culmination, how
manners are reconciled to nature, passion to prudence, and energy to
status, are obviously matters of wide variation. But the novel of Villiers
de l'Isle-Adam stands so far apart from these various modes of sympathy-

manipulation as to put it on the very outside rim of fiction as the conventional norms define it.

A number of themes in *Tomorrow's Eve* were lifelong, deeply meditated elements of Villiers de l'Isle-Adam's existence. He loathed common sense, materialism, making money, getting ahead, the very idea of progress—a slothful doctrine, Baudelaire called it, fit only for Belgians. He therefore despised science (of which he knew practically nothing), viewing it as the collective blindness of a society of Tribulat Bonhomets. It comes as no surprise, therefore, that in the novel Edison, the arch-scientist and mage of scientists, is shown to be fundamentally contemptuous of his own craft. Like Tribulat Bonhomet before him, he pushes his materialism toward its own negation—toward a profoundly religious and mystical idealism, in light of which the mere armature of electro-mechanical Hadaly can serve far more subtly than her flesh-and-blood original as a core for the crystallization of Lord Ewald's fervent Byronic soul.

In Villiers' drama *Axël*, Master Janus teaches the hero, "You are nothing but what you think: think then the eternal." And again: "You possess the true being of all things in your will: you are the god that you can become." So it is, in the novel, with Lord Celian Ewald. Edison, his master, teaches him to clothe the bare bones of a scientific construct with the heavenly intimations and intuitions of his own mind. His given name speaks of his heavenly origin; heaven lay about him, as Hadaly knows instinctively, in his infancy. And how does the master mind of Edison intuit all this, if not by himself transcending his own scientific outlook— by looking, like Tribulat Bonhomet before him, through the keyhole of material reality into the world of the Infinite?

Villiers de l'Isle-Adam's readiness to recognize in his supreme antagonists aspects of himself no doubt stems from his long fascination with the Hegelian dialectic; it relates also to what could be called his polemical imagination. Most of his books take the form of arguments and draw their sense of dizzying uncertainty from our awareness that the debaters are wagering their entire existence on the outcome. Poe, with whom Villiers has sometimes been compared, is much more the Gothic spooker, drawing on the common properties of demonic possession, madness, and necrophilia to make our flesh crawl; Villiers is an inspired equilibrist of the dialectic. Nothing stirs him like the spirit of contradiction, of revulsion.[2] Conjuring up before his inner eye the reality he loathes, he launches into flights of visionary eloquence from which elements of ingenious sophistry and specious debating tricks are rarely absent, but which convince us sometimes that the spirit of illuminated prophecy is no stranger to his pen.

For a fact, he knew nothing of science and cared less; even in terms of the science of the 1880's, much technical jargon in the book is mere mumbo jumbo. Yet he knew or imagined things about the future of science and of scientific applications that have since come true. When he wrote, the telephone was limited in its range to a few hundred yards; he foresaw its power to traverse in an instant almost limitless distances. When the phonograph was a scratchy contrivance for recording "Mary Had a Little Lamb," Villiers saw that it could bring an entire opera into a closet. The developments of electric lighting and flash photography that he describes in *Tomorrow's Eve* are far in advance of what was possible when he wrote. The spark which races out into infinite space to recapture sights and sounds that long ago vanished from earth is still waiting to be developed, but to conceive of it in the 1880's was an act of imagination beyond Jules Verne. Our radio telescopes and planetary probes, though altogether different in principle, are not much less amazing than his imaginings—as the central Cylinder which controls Hadaly is simply an embryonic computer.

To be sure, in most instances Villiers simply extrapolated on developments that were, in some measure, already under way. Some of them were doubtless brought to his notice by the rhetoric accompanying the election of Edison, in 1878, to membership in the French Légion d'Honneur. More startling and original is Villiers' intuition of the uneasy symbiotic relation between man and his machines, his sense that as machines are becoming more human, humans are becoming, physically and spiritually, more mechanical.

There had, of course, been previous adumbrations of the theme. Folklore has its golems and artificial monsters, philosophy its enthusiasts for mechanical explanations of human behavior. Fantastic fiction has its odd, doll-like figures such as the mechanical lady of Hoffmann's tale "The Sandman," with whom a malignant hypnotist makes the hero Nathaniel fall fatally in love. One thinks automatically of ill-made monsters, such as that fabricated by Doctor Frankenstein or the cheap and handy humanoids manufactured under the trademark of Rossum's Universal Robots. But none of these fantasies invades the precincts of human nature as subtly and as insidiously as the android wrought by the mage of Menlo Park in Villiers' narrative. For the real roots of this creation I think we must look first at a character type very frequent in nineteenth-century life as well as in literature: that is, the moral idiot on principle, the man whose sense of human community has been seared as with a hot iron by the idea of self-interest. He is Gradgrind, he is Murdstone, he is Homais, he is Valenod; in his meek phase he is Joseph Prudhomme, in his aggressive cycle, Robert Macaire.[3] In England he is the vulgar utilitarian, in France the crass positivist. More than any individual he is the system of middle-class, cash-nexus, common-sense, self-interest values. At least in the mind of Villiers de l'Isle-Adam, it seems likely that the idea of a mechanical woman did not grow directly from previous instances of mechanisms resembling people, but indirectly, from people resembling mechanisms, and rather vulgar mechanisms at that. Life, as we know, *was* getting more mechanical, as mass production and mass populations reacted on one another all across the Western world.

In addition, a variety of intellectual strains made this fact appear par-

ticularly painful and oppressive to the author of *Tomorrow's Eve*. Most
agonizing of these strains was that generated by Catholicism in crisis.
The revolution of 1789 had completely shredded the French church, ex-
propriating its wealth, extirpating its priests, and destroying most of its
popular support among the laity. Restoring the church after the material
defeats which the Revolution had piled on top of its intellectual defeats
during the eighteenth century was a task calling for something more than
ideology. The cold and empty demonstrations of men like Bonald were
soon succeeded by a more militant approach, known as "ultramontan-
ism,"[4] which attracted such vehement exponents as de Maistre, Lamen-
nais in his early phase, Lacordaire, and Veuillot. Never a large party, the
ultras were vociferous and argumentative; their prose style was commonly sharper than that of milder Catholics. Faith and authority were at
the heart of their intellectual position—faith in the infallible church,
insistence on its authority. The chaos of individual judgments, made
evident during the Revolution, had led merely to anarchy and then to
tyranny. A solid rock on which all could stand was imperative; and that
could only be the Catholic church, founded by Peter, descending from
him by direct succession, claiming through the words of Christ himself.
From that charter followed dominion over secular rulers and private judgments throughout the world, and the total, unquestionable authority of
a single head, the pope.

Amid the turmoil of nineteenth-century nationalism, industrialism,
and exploding populations, this strain of conservative ecclesiasticism
steadily gained ground in the church, reaching something like a climax
in the late reign of Pope Pius IX. Enraged and terrified by events of 1848,
when only foreign armies could restore the pope to control of his temporal possessions, Pius became increasingly reactionary and authoritarian. In a famous encyclical of December 8, 1864, he claimed for the
church complete control of all culture, science, and education; he demanded dominion over secular governments and denounced a long list of
errors, starting with religious tolerance. In a final memorable sentence
he asserted that the pope and the church "neither can be nor ought to be
reconciled with progress, liberalism, and modern civilization."

Nothing in the record of Villiers de l'Isle-Adam's life and opinions
suggests that the pope's encyclical shocked or disturbed the train of his
thought, but it can hardly have failed to sharpen his basic hostility to
everything that was going on around him. Progress, liberalism, and modern civilization were represented at the moment by the regime of Louis
Napoleon, devoted to industry and technology, business and money, so-
cialism, imperialism, and religious indifference. This was, obviously, a
mixed bag of social values, but it left little room for the values of a
conservative Catholic aristocrat like Villiers. Even the enemies of the
Second Empire were alien to his concerns. The Prussian forces which
crushed and humiliated France in 1870 represented the same energies
more efficiently organized. In its collapse, the Second Empire gave rise to

the Paris Commune, led by red revolutionaries who showed their colors by executing dozens of priests, including the archbishop of Paris. Wherever one looked in Europe, the powers to which the pontiff had declared himself unalterably opposed raged uncontrollably; they were challenged only by movements more radical yet—progress by revolution, liberalism by terror, "modern" civilization by one claiming to be of the future. In 1870 the pope was pushed out of his own papal states, which in a plebiscite voted overwhelmingly to affiliate with the new secular state headed by King Victor Emmanuel.

Practically, the position of the church's conservative supporters was very difficult. As authoritarians, they upheld the absolute power of a church which had no independent power at all and existed only by permission of a secular monarch. Their claim that the church had power over all private judgments meant nothing when a man need only declare himself some sort of protestant to be exempt from its jurisdiction altogether. But symbolically, a supreme insult to the old church was the creation of a new one, deliberately based on the hateful principles of progress, liberalism, and modern civilization. Old believers like Villiers were bound to see it as a grotesque parody of their church, to think it an obscene buffoonery. It took itself with the utmost seriousness, however, and attracted many believers, some of considerable distinction. Positive philosophy grew out of four volumes published between 1830 and 1842 by Auguste Comte; as a rational, secular religion, it was consciously designed to replace the old superstitious, authoritarian faith. Humanity itself was the god of Comtist religion, utility the final test of every idea and institution. Great men like Gutenberg, Shakespeare, and Galileo were the saints of the new Positivist religion;[5] there would be, under its dispensation, absolute freedom of thought and speech, but an influential secular, unpaid priesthood presiding over an industrial society. Woman, while excluded from political action, would exercise extraordinary influence as moral guardian. Positivism, someone said, was Catholicism minus Christianity; like all capsule formulas, this one is crude and inexact, but the idea of an *ersatz* religion devoid of all sanctity, all sacrifice, and all supernatural sanctions accounts for the sheer rage with which Villiers and many of his fellow believers regarded rational Positivism and all its works. Hence, no doubt, the relish with which Villiers seized on the idea of a frankly mechanical human being as the fulfillment of a Positive world and, in a special dialectical sense, an antidote to it. The sacred horror with which he contemplates making love to a machine closely resembles that which penetrates the soul of Des Esseintes when (in Huysmans' 1884 novel, *A rebours*) he regards the universal corruption of a business civilization which has adulterated even the sacred bread and wine of the sacrament. The wafer is now made of potato meal mixed with potash and pipe clay, the wine is mixed with alum, elderberries, salicylate, and litharge. How could the Son of God be expected to enter into such a nauseous mixture? Much the same set of feelings among the beleaguered ultramontanists—fears that they were being robbed of their religion by the corruptions of a secular world—created widespread paranoid suspicions during the late reign of Leo XIII, pope from 1878 to 1903. Especially in France, ultra congregations were convinced that the pope had been kidnapped by freemasons and was being held prisoner in the vaults of the Vatican while an impostor paraded as pope. Part of the evidence supporting these wild fears was Leo's moderate and indeed amateurish interest in science. (He once wrote, for example, a little Latin versicle on photography.) But "normal" as such interests were, the very texture of normal life seemed to the ultras erosive of their faith. A puff of steam, shorthand for the industrial revolution, had blown away the universal church and the rock on which it stood. The normal and the sensible would henceforth be mere gauzy veils for the diabolic. As Edison remarks to Lord Ewald with—alas!—utter common sense, the original Miss Alicia Clary (that is, the flesh-and-blood dummy) would be the absolute feminine ideal for three-quarters of modern humanity. Only for the uncommon man, who looks for the living spirit behind the veil of flesh, is she a fatal torment.

Another strain of thought leading toward *Tomorrow's Eve* stems from a familiar crux in the philosophy of Descartes, the nexus between soul and body, where it should be sought and how it can be supposed to work. After considerable meditation, Descartes placed it in the pineal gland, but the second question he hardly tried to answer. Whatever the mechanism, it must clearly be of the utmost subtlety and complexity; perhaps for this reason, the philosopher denied utterly that mere animals could have such an apparatus—rather, he concluded, they were simply mechanisms. As a matter of fact, men are machines too, as Descartes sees them;[6] but they are machines connected to minds, as animals are not.

The mechanical bias of Descartes' thinking had a major influence on eighteenth-century philosophy. One of the boldest of his followers found the idea of a soul to be unnecessary to account for human any more than animal behavior. Doctor Jacques LaMettrie's *L'Homme machine* (1750), an instance of behaviorism before its time, seriously proposed the view of man as a collection of what we would call conditioned reflexes. Drawing the strongest possible conclusions from his premises, LaMettrie declared that the soul is just the thinking part of the body and dies with the body; as there is no afterlife of reward or punishment, sensual enjoyment is the only good to be pursued on earth. This frankly atheistic point of view caused great scandal at the time, and even tolerant Holland became too hot for the doctor. But the fuss was only indirectly over his mechanical concept of man; the real cause of the furore was his atheism, and that only because it was outspoken and categorical. In the tendency of his thinking LaMettrie was in sympathy not only with his own century, but with those to follow. He wanted to explain humanity as much as possible on mechanical principles, and if "as much as possible" turned out to be "entirely," so much the better. Such has been the movement of thought in modern times. The study of genes and genetic inheritance subtracted a sizable area of human behavior from the control of the conscious mind, not to speak of the immortal soul. We now know ourselves to be rather elaborately programmed, not only genetically but also chemically, through glandular balances or imbalances with which our conscious minds have nothing to do. We all understand what boisterous tricks unruly libido and tyrannical super-ego are capable of playing with what we now apologetically call our "selves." The more of us there are, and the more we are encouraged to suppose ourselves "individuals," the more social engineering is required to condition us into conformity or— just as convenient—into predictable modes of nonconformity. The mores of sex, class, nationality, language, work, order, and social discipline are drilled into us now, as they always were in the past. We are more conscious of them only because the illusion of being individuals is now more generally held out to us and now more completely betrayed in actuality. For though man is not a machine, he is forced to act like one by society, which is.

Thus most of the actual automata devised by mechanical ingenuity during the eighteenth and nineteenth centuries stirred two easily reconciled responses in their beholders. Imitating one or two human mannerisms, they amused by their verisimilitude; but, being jerky and clumsy in their operation, they produced complacency at their inadequacy.[7] About the middle of the eighteenth century Jacques Vaucanson exhibited a flute player, a tambourine player, and a duck. (The latter was the hit of the show because it could eat, drink, and quack.) Other robots and automata, such as those by Knauss, Maelzel, Kempelen, and Maskelyne, graced the music halls and amusement parks of Europe, Each could do one thing after a fashion—paint, write, draw, or play a musical instrument. As a class, they can be divided into those which were truly clockwork ingenuities, and those which concealed a human operator somewhere inside the simulacrum and were therefore instances of conjuring and legerdemain. Chapuis and Droz (*Automata*; Neuchatel, 1958) are the chroniclers of the first class; John Cohen (*Human Robots in Myth and Science*; London, 1966) takes a broader purview, which includes the second class. But these are all clumsy humanoid devices such as Villiers has Edison ridicule cruelly in the fourth chapter of his second book. Enhanced by trick camera work, but still representing the two basic types, they are still with us as R2D2 and C3PO of *Star Wars*. But the true genesis of Hadaly, the Ideal given material form, lies elsewhere than in these poor mechanical dummies—though perhaps she owes a distant debt to the spirit of Cartesian dualism.

Romantic irony is almost as old as romanticism and the philosophical movement, based on analysis of the powers and structures of the mind, out of which romanticism grew. In its simplest form, it is no more than a contrast between private imagination and publicly verifiable fact, but that simple formula can be given innumerable shadings. The contrast may be managed to the advantage of either element, playfully or bitterly, with wit or pathos. We in the English tradition think of romantic irony chiefly in connection with Byron and his jaunty way of evoking passionate sentiments, only to turn on them abruptly with the ridicule of social common sense. That mode of play had its followers on the continent, in Heine and Pushkin notably. In Germany a somewhat different mode of serious playfulness is associated with prose narratives by E. T. A. Hoffmann, Ludwig Tieck, and Jean-Paul Richter. (These perfunctory lists indicate merely a few authors in whom the quality of romantic irony is particularly striking; there is no major romantic author who does not make use, one way or another, of a literary effect inherent in his mode of vision.) But a strain of the process running very close to the art of Villiers de l'Isle-Adam can be traced through his contemporaries and intimates, Baudelaire and Mallarmé. It focuses on a pair of French conceptions for which English poets of the same period have no close equivalent, expressed in the words *idéal* and *azur*. Both are formulas to express an extreme, abstract, intense form of positive idealism which contrasts absolutely with the grubby colors, shapes, and smells—and much more painfully with the ignoble compromises—of this low world in the here and now. The scale of contrasts has been shifted, from our (Anglo-Saxon) point of view, sharply upward. Idealism is expressed not in seeking the best of the pragmatic values, but in rejecting them all for something more spiritual, less easily definable, closer to the absolute. Both *idéal* and *azur* imply, as much as aspiration upward, abhorrence of materiality.

In defending *Les Fleurs du mal* before a court of law, Baudelaire defined his theme, almost in a line of poetry, as "l'agitation de l'esprit dans le mal" (*Oeuvres*, Pléiade ed., p. 181). That the spirit is distressed amid the crudities and ugliness of the nineteenth century can only be due to its knowledge of an ideal reality, and Baudelaire repeatedly implies that the poet is in close touch with this finer element. Indeed, he is adapted to it so particularly that when placed on the gross earth he can only be clumsy or pathetic. Like the albatross, he is king of the *azur*, a region of freedom, purity, elevation. Ashore or on the boat's deck, his wings impede him, and he is the helpless butt of oafish sailors. Again, in a sonnet to Mme Sabatier, the poet contrasts the squalor of a debauched and blackened life with the unreachable azure of spiritual skies (XLVI, "L'Aube spirituelle"). Elsewhere, azure is the sphere of beauty, where she sits enthroned like a mysterious sphinx (XVII, "Beauté"); or it defines a realm of luxurious and noble preexistence where the poet's being, with its high aspiration and secret sorrow, was determined (XII, "La Vie antérieure").

A natural corollary to so low a view of the common life and so high an estimate of another sphere is to welcome death as a gateway out of misery and perhaps into something better. This most romantic of themes resounds through Baudelaire's work like a tonic chord. In CXXVI, "Le Voyage," death is the only captain who can carry us away from this cramped and monotonous world, where all the vulgarities are known long before

they happen. Death in CXXIV, "La Fin de la journée," is a voluptuous dark
into which the poet contemplates sinking with relief; in "Le Mort joy-
eux" (LXXII), he looks forward to the experience with joyous defiance.
His recurrent images of the abyss ("le gouffre") and his nostalgia for
"néant" (nothingness) speak the same language.

The example of Mallarmé reinforces the same constellation of values
noted in Baudelaire, the poet making use of many of the same words to
deepen without basically altering the diagram of energies being presented. Like Baudelaire, Mallarmé assumes that the poet naturally inhab-
its another sphere, that of the ideal or the dream. In rejecting Wagner's
reliance on legend, he speaks (oddly, to English ears, but with full Cartesian backing) of the French spirit as "strictly imaginative and abstract,
therefore poetic." Hence any actual poem, whether "successful" or not,
is in the nature of a descent, a falling from a higher antecedent sphere, a
shipwreck. *Azur,* used repeatedly, defines the limitless world of the Ideal,
from which we are separated only (but, in this life, irrevocably!) by windows—transparencies of space and thought dividing the world's smelly
hospital from the depths of pure spiritual existence. For Mallarmé as for
Baudelaire, the poet can feel only disgust and pain at the vulgarities of a
herd existence where "ici-bas est maître," where down-here is master.
And for him, as for Baudelaire, death was a constant, alluring attraction,
escape from a mode of existence by which he could not help feeling
degraded. Precisely because Villiers and Mallarmé were both absorbed in
their personal dreams—not merely *habitués* but lifelong *habitants* of a
supramundane vision, the worldly anteroom of which was literature—
they felt themselves to be kindred spirits. Mallarmé was more than a
little touched with the spirit of Buddhism which was so strong in his
intimate friend Cazalis. Villiers, on the other hand, was drawn by his
lineage and his stiff personal pride to a peculiarly militant if not dogmatic
Catholicism.[8] His pauper's arrogance gave edge to his disdain for the
complacent vulgarians around him; his wit was a blade readily drawn in
defense of an ideal that he saw dishonored and insulted—not even inten-
tionally!—every day of his life.

We should not overlook a tendency of extreme Catholicism, toward the
end of the nineteenth century, to develop a mystical streak and a fascination with the occult for which the last novels of Huysmans, the many
writings of the Abbé Alphonse Louis Constant (a.k.a. Eliphas Lévi), and
the careers of Sâr Péladan the magician and Stanislas de Guaïta the con-
jurer provide ample evidence. Villiers de l'Isle-Adam was involved in
these dark cross-currents, where faith *in extremis* flowered into superstition. His great closet drama *Axël* is built on Rosicrucian principles and
culminates in a suicidal erotic tryst between two maddeningly attractive,
utterly distinguished (and therefore doomed) aristocrat adepts. The underground chapel where they are finally joined in love and death lies far
beneath Count Axël's ancestral castle in the depths of a trackless forest;
it is remarkably similar to Edison's underground laboratory in *Tomor-*

*row's Eve*, as Axël's magic has about it a certain theatrical touch found also in Edison's scientific displays. For this entire development, mingling spiritualism with a kind of sympathetic magic, there was literary precedent in the semi-occult fictions of Balzac *(Séraphita, Louis Lambert)* and in the quasi-scientific religiosity of Victor Hugo. But the real force authenticating all nineteenth-century occultism was of course reactive; it was the response to those waves of mechanical materialism, philosophic as well as practical, in which Europe seemed to be sinking. Since the days of the gnostics, witchcraft and spiritualism have regularly been invoked as antidotes to a too-confident, too-deadening materialism.

Finally, behind all these literary and religious fashions we may discern a deepening philosophical strain probably not articulated in detail by more than a fraction of those who responded to it, but nonetheless influential. More here even than previously, we shall have to resort to capsule formulas and gross stereotypes to describe this tendency, but its importance must be acknowledged, however perfunctorily. To begin with Villiers' favorite philosopher, Hegel, he is typical of the romantic philosophers in proposing that all thought begins with a sundering, a declaration of division between subject and object, and ends with a reconciliation, a rediscovery of self, which is a completion and an annulling and a raising to a higher level of that original premise. It is self-recognition, it is self-annihilation; it is self-discovery, it is self-creation. *Aufheben* is the German verb that compresses these several contradictory-complementary meanings in its single nutshell. From the very begining this dialectical process had at least a latent application to the relation between the sexes. The dialectic of the sexes begins with a separation or distinction and negates that with their conjunction, which leads to a new dialectic cycle on a new plane—to the generation, perhaps, of a child, of a new historical epoch, or of a transcendent vision by the two people themselves redefining their own identities. Hegelianism was but one of many nineteenth-century philosophies of transcendence; it was one of the few that made transcendence part of a regular process. Much of its appeal lay in the ambiguity (amounting almost to complete openness) of that space which lies between the achievement of synthesis and the development of the next dialectical cycle. Thanks to that moment of openness, Hegelianism can represent itself as a key to the understanding of a world-historical necessity and an instrument of personal liberation and transcendence. The spectacular violence of a *Liebestod*, whereby a couple fulfill and die to their social rational appetitive selves, in order to live (if at all) in the cold flames of spiritual affinity, falls within the range of the Hegelian dialectic. And it fascinated Villiers, as it fascinated all those artists to whom the *Idéal* seemed a marvelous, endless promise hung just beyond the veil. From its imaginative enactment they drew a deep sense of exaltation and of triumph over the world; it was the ultimate, unanswerable hauteur, a negation which negated once and for all all the negatives of existence. Diminishing spirals are the pattern imposed by the *Liebestod:*

the ego finally fulfills itself by destroying itself. Maeterlinck, D'Annunzio, and Villiers are at one in this respect with their master Wagner. Deepening obsession is the theme, fixation the process, self-annihilation the end. Instead of displaying the successful working-out of a problem, the literary work ripens a fatal condition given from the beginning.

A parody *Tristan und Isolde* with the heroine personated by an assemblage of circuits and solenoids? That's one way to look at *L'Eve future.* Another way, less extreme, is to see it as a product of that imaginative, abstract, poetic *esprit français* of which Mallarmé spoke—an *esprit* which never, even in the thunderclaps of world-transcendence, forgets to leaven its theatricalities with a salting of ironic wit.[9]


NOTES

1. In view of his absurd anti-Semitism, it is an obvious irony that Villiers owed so much of his success to Jewish admirers and editors.

2. This spirit is out of control only in Book IV of *Tomorrow's Eve*, but it is seriously out of control there, and the frantic diatribe against promiscuity—more ridiculous than ever a hundred years after it was written—threatens to throw the entire novel out of balance. What experiences lay behind these Swiftian invectives against feminine arts (so at variance with the lighter ironies of Baudelaire and Wilde) we cannot know, but it is clear that Villiers, being like Swift a clean-minded man, was also like Swift a man of nasty ideas.

3. Gradgrind of *Hard Times*, Murdstone of *David Copperfield*, Homais of *Madame Bovary*, Valenod of *Red and Black*; Prudhomme the creation of Henri Monnier, Robert Macaire adapted by Daumier from an 1823 melodrama.

4. "Beyond the mountains": the phrase was originally geographical, designating people "the other side of the Alps" from the Italian point of view. Theologically, as used particularly in France in contrast with "Gallican," it denotes one who looks to Rome and the authority of the pope as the central principle of his religious life. To an outsider, it often looks like placing the church above religion.

5. Sections of Mexico City and some other South American cities are laid out on Comtist lines; the main avenues are named for major benefactors of humanity, lesser streets for figures lower in the hierarchy.

6. He is said to have constructed for himself a mechanical person, about which (or whom) we know disappointingly little. Whether it was male or female, had or lacked a pineal gland, would be matters of the greatest interest.

7. Modern jokes about how we can always pull the plugs on computers when they get smarter than we are betray this long-standing complacency on the defensive. Particularly upsetting has been the recent devel-

opment of computers which play chess not only well but at the grand-master level, and more consistently than most of the grand masters. Quite possibly within the lifetime of men now living, the world champion at this ancient game will be a black box.

8. What principle of chivalric rectitude kept Villiers from relishing degradation like a *poète maudit*, or from telling us of the worm in his own heart, we cannot know. Some puritanical streak there was, which now limits the measure of our intimate sympathy with his inflexible spirit.

9. In an appendix to the novel, I have tried to identify as many as possible of Villiers' epigraphs. The quality of his reading, and of his memory alike, is illustrated by his handling of these minor details.

A new biography by A. W. Raitt, *The Life of Villiers de l'Isle-Adam* (Oxford University Press, 1981), provides further information on Villiers and his work for the English-language reader.

# *Tomorrow's Eve*

# ❧ ADVICE TO THE READER ❧

It seems proper to forestall a possible confusion regarding the principal hero of this book.

Everyone knows nowadays that a most distinguished American inventor, Mr. Edison, has discovered over the last fifteen years a prodigious number of things, as strange as they are ingenious—among others, the Telephone, the Phonograph, the Microphone, and those admirable electric lightbulbs which have now spread across the earth's surface—not to speak of a hundred other marvels.

In America and in Europe a legend has thus sprung up in the popular mind regarding this great citizen of the United States. He has become the recipient of thousands of nicknames, such as "The Magician of the Century," "The Sorcerer of Menlo Park," the "Papa of the Phonograph," and so forth and so on. A perfectly natural enthusiasm in his own country and elsewhere has conferred on him a kind of mystique, or something like it, in many minds.

Henceforth, doesn't the personage of this legend—even while the man is still alive who inspired it—belong to the world of literature? For example, if Doctor Johann Faust had been living in the age of Goethe and had given rise to his symbolic legend at that time, wouldn't the writing of *Faust*, even then, have been a perfectly legitimate undertaking?

Thus, the Edison of the present work, his character, his dwelling, his language, and his theories, are and ought to be at least somewhat distinct from anything existing in reality.

Let it be understood, then, that I interpret a modern legend to the best advantage of the work of Art-metaphysics that I have conceived; and that, in a word, the hero of this book is above all "The Sorcerer of Menlo Park," and so forth—and not the engineer, Mr. Edison, our contemporary.

I have no other qualifications to note.

*To the Dreamers*
   *To the Deriders*

# BOOK I

# Mr. Edison

# MENLO PARK

The garden like a lady fair was cut,
That lay as if she slumbered in delight
And to the open skies her eyes did shut;
The azure fields of heaven were 'sembled right
In a large round, set with the flowers of light,
    The flowers de luce, and the round sparks of dew,
    That hung upon their azure leaves did show
Like twinkling stars, that sparkle in the evening blue.

                                                —Giles Fletcher

TWENTY-FIVE LEAGUES from New York, at the heart of a network of electric lines, is found a dwelling surrounded by deep and quite deserted gardens. The doorway looks out across a grassy lawn crossed by sanded paths and leading to a kind of large isolated pavilion. To the south and west two long avenues of ancient trees bend their shadows in the direction of this pavilion. This is Number One Menlo Park; and here dwells Thomas Alva Edison, the man who made a prisoner of the echo.

Edison is forty-two years old. A few years ago his features recalled in a striking manner those of a famous Frenchman, Gustave Doré. It was very nearly the face of an artist *translated* into the features of a scholar. The same natural talents, differently applied; mysterious twins. At what age did they completely resemble one another? Perhaps never. Their two photographs of that earlier time, blended in the stereoscope, would evoke an intellectual impression such as only certain figures of the superior races ever fully realize, and then only in a few occasional images, stamped as on coins and scattered through Humanity.

When one compares the features of Edison with those on ancient coins, they offer a speaking likeness to those medals of Syracuse which show the features of Archimedes.

One evening of a recent autumn, around five o'clock, the marvelous inventor of so many illusions, the magician of the ear (who, almost deaf himself, like a Beethoven of Science, has been able to create for himself this imperceptible instrument—thanks to which, when it's adjusted to the orifice of hearing, deafness not only dissolves, but yields to the sense of sound in its most delicate form), Edison, in brief, had retired to the darkest corner of his personal laboratory, that is, to the pavilion isolated from his main house.

On this particular evening, the engineer had dismissed his five acolytes, stewards of his shop—devoted workmen all, subtle and learned artisans, to whom he gave princely salaries, and whose lips were sealed in his interests. Seated in his American armchair, leaning on his elbow, alone, with a cigar at his lips—he, so little of an idle dreamer, the tobacco simply serving to dissipate in smoke his masculine projects—with a remote and vacant eye, his legs crossed, enveloped in his loose gown, already legendary, of black silk with a violet sash, seemed lost in a profound reverie.

To his right, a lofty window, open to the west, unfolded a vast panorama, within which every object was overcast with a golden reddish glow.

Here and there about the room one might glimpse, atop the cluttered tables, various precision instruments, intricate and obscure gear-boxes, electrical apparatus, telescopes, mirrors, enormous magnets, retorts amid a tangle of tubes, flasks full of mysterious fluids, and slates scrawled over with equations.

Outside, beyond the horizon, the setting sun shot glances and streaks of light through the distant curtains of foliage atop the New Jersey hills, covered as they were with maples and pines; occasionally it lit up the room with a touch of purple or a ray of gold. Then on every side a light red as blood flared from angles of polished metal, from prisms of crystal, from the swollen outline of batteries.

The wind quickened. Showers during the day had freshened the lawns of the park—and had revived as well the heavy, heady Asian flowers blossoming in their green boxes under the windows. Dried flowers, hanging from the roof of the room, swung loose, galvanized by the breeze as if it brought them a memory of their former fragrant life in the forests. Under the subtle influence of this atmosphere, the thought of the dreamer, generally quick and brisk, relaxed and submitted insensibly to the seductive attractions of dream and twilight.

# PHONOGRAPH'S PAPA

'Tis he! . . . Ah! said I, opening my eyes wide in the
dark, it is the Sand-Man!
—Hoffmann, *Night Tales*

ALTHOUGH HIS FACE, despite its graying temples, gives the impression of perpetual youth, Edison is a disciple of the skeptical school. He only invents, he says, in the same way that corn grows—by instinct.

Cool of manner and always conscious of his unhappy youth, he has the taut, dearly bought smile of a man whose mere presence declares to one who meets him: "Become something if you can; I am." Confident in his judgments, he has no use for even the most promising of theories until they are incarnated in facts. Profoundly "humanitarian," he takes more pride in his industry than in his genius. Though shrewd, yet when he assesses himself, he's in despair at being such a dupe. His favorite foible is to think himself IGNORANT, by a kind of legitimate naïveté.

Hence that simplicity of welcome and the mask of rough frankness— sometimes even the show of familiarity—with which he veils the icy realities of his thought. The man of proven genius, who has had the honor of being poor, can always value at a glance the passing figure who chats with him. He knows how to weigh to a scruple the secret motives of those who admire him, how to test a man's probity and real quality and determine the degree of his sincerity down to the finest scruple. And all this without the slightest suspicion on the part of his interlocutor.

Having given proof of the good sense and originality with which he is endowed, the great electrician supposes he's earned the right to trifle a bit with his own ideas in the course of his private meditations. There, as one sharpens a knife on a whetstone, he hones his scientific thought on various tough sarcasms, the sparks of which fall even on his own discoveries. In a word, he pretends to fire on his own troops, but mostly with blank cartridges, in order to harden them for battle.

Gladly falling victim, then, to the charms of this absorbing evening, Edison by way of recreation peacefully enjoyed the excellent flavor of his Havana and yielded to the poetry both of the hour and of solitude—that beloved solitude which it's in the very nature of fools to fear.

Like any simple mortal, he abandoned himself passively to all sorts of fantastic and bizarre reflections.

# THE LAMENTATIONS OF EDISON

All grief is but a diminution of self.
—Spinoza

H E WAS MURMURING to himself in an undertone:

—What a latecomer I am in the ranks of humanity! Why wasn't I one of the first-born of the species? . . . Plenty of great words would be recorded now, *ne varietur*—(*sic*)—word for word, that is, on the surface of my cylinders, since the prodigious development of the machine now allows us to receive, at the present moment, sound waves reaching us from a vast distance. And these words would be engraved on my cylinders, with the tone, the phrasing, the manner of delivery, and even the mannerisms of pronunciation that the speakers possessed.

We needn't pretend to that life-creating cliché, *Fiat lux!*, a phrase coined approximately seventy-two centuries ago (and which besides, according to immemorial tradition—perhaps invented, perhaps not—could never have been picked up by any recording machine). Still, I might have been able to record—for example, just a little after the death of Lilith, while Adam was still a widower and I would have been lurking behind some secret thicket in Eden—first of all that sublime soliloquy, "It is not good for man to live alone!," and then "Ye shall be as gods!," then "Increase and multiply!," and lastly the gloomy jest of the Almighty, "Here is Adam become as one of us!"—and all the rest. Later, when the secret of my vibrating diaphragm was well known, wouldn't it have been pleasant for my successors to record during the great days of paganism, for example, the famous "To the most beautiful!," the angry "Quos ego!," the oracles of Dodona, the chants of the Sybils—and all the rest? All the important speeches of men and gods, down through the ages, would have been indelibly engraved in the sonorous archives of copper, so that by now no doubt would have been in any way possible concerning their authenticity.

Even among the noises of the past, how many mysterious sounds were known to our predecessors, which for lack of a convenient machine to record them have now fallen forever into the abyss? . . . Who nowadays could form, for example, a proper notion of the sound of the trumpets of Jericho? Of the bellow of Phalaris' bull? Of the laughter of the augurs? Or of the morning melody of Memnon? And all the rest?

Dead voices, lost sounds, forgotten noises, vibrations lockstepping into the abyss, and now too distant ever to be recaptured! . . . What sort of arrows would be able to transfix such birds?

Edison touched with a casual finger a button of porcelain set in the wall beside his chair. A blinding blue jet leaped from an electric condenser just a few feet away—a jet capable of striking dead a certain number of elephants. It blazed like lightning through a block of crystal, then disappeared in the same hundred-thousandth of a second.

—Yes, said the great engineer, continuing his meditation, I have this little spark . . . which is to sound what the greyhound is to the tortoise. It could give the sounds a start of fifty centuries and yet chase them down in the gulfs of outer space, ancient refugees from the earth! But on what wire, along what trail, could I send it? How teach it to bring the sounds back, once it has tracked them down? How redirect them to the ear of the investigator? This time, at least, the problem seems insoluble.

Sadly, Edison tapped off the end of his cigar with a little finger. After a silence, he rose with a half-smile and began to walk up and down in his laboratory.

—And to think that after six thousand and some years of painfully doing without my phonograph, he murmured again, humans were so still so insensitive that all they could do was make jokes when my first venture came forth. "A childish toy!" most people grumbled. Of course, I understand that when people are taken by surprise, some stock phrases are necessary to ease the adjustment . . . Still, in that situation I would have tried to develop a few phrases superior to those crude jests that the public struggled to crack over my project.

For example, I would have complained that while the phonograph was reproducing sounds, it was unable to represent the sound, say, of the fall of the Roman Empire. It can't record an eloquent silence, or the sound of rumors. In fact, as far as voices go, it is helpless to represent the voice of conscience. Can it record the voice of the blood? Or all those splendid sayings that are attributed to great men? It's helpless before the swan song, before unspoken innuendos; can it record the song of the Milky Way? No? Ah, I go too far. —In any case, I see clearly that to satisfy my peers I must invent a machine that replies before one has even addressed it—or which, if the experimenter says to it, "Good morning, how are you?" will answer "Thank you, just fine, and youself?" Or, if someone in the audience sneezes, it will cry out, "Gesundheit!" or "God bless you!"—something of that sort.

—Men are amazing.

—I agree that the voice of my first phonograph sounded a bit like the voice of conscience talking with the crafty Pulcinello; but you might have expected that before men made merry with it, they might have waited till progress had improved it, as it did the first plates of Nicephore Niepce or Daguerre, ancestors of modern photography.

—Well, since there's no overcoming the craze for skepticism regarding my work, until things change I'll just have to keep secret the amazing, the ultimate development of my research . . . which I have, right here, underground. And Edison tapped lightly on the floor with his foot. —I'd hardly let it go for less than five or six million old phonographs; and since everyone wants a good laugh, well, I'll have the last one.

He paused a few seconds, then shrugged his shoulders:

—Bah, he concluded, there's always something good at the root of human folly. Let's dispense with the empty jokes from now on.

Suddenly a soft whisper, the voice of a young woman murmuring very gently, was heard close by:

—Edison?

# SOWANA

How to be astonished at something?
—The Stoics

Yet not a shadow was there.

He started.

—Is it you, Sowana? he asked aloud.

—Yes. This evening I yearned for fine dreams. I took the ring; I have it on my finger now. You needn't raise your voice; I'm close beside you, in fact I've been listening for some minutes now, while you were playing with words like a child.

—And, physically, where are you?

—Lying on the furs in the room downstairs, behind the aviary. I think Hadaly is asleep. I gave her her pills and her fresh water, so that now she is quite . . . revived.

The voice of the being called Sowana—laughing over its last word—seemed to come, always quietly and discreetly, from a pillar supporting the violet curtains. In fact it was a sounding box and reverberated in response to distant whispers carried by electricity—one of those new condensers, invented barely yesterday, by which the individual syllables and tone of the voice are distinctly transmitted.

—Tell me, Mistress Anderson, Edison resumed after a moment's thought, are you sure you could hear what another person might say to me here?

—Yes, if you repeated it yourself, very softly between your lips, as the other person spoke; the different tones of your answers would enable me to understand the dialogue. You see, I'm like one of the Genies of the Ring, in the *Arabian Nights.*

—And so if I asked you to attach the telephone wire on which we're talking now to the person of our young friend, the miracle of which we've often spoken would occur?

—No doubt about it. It's a marvel of thought and ingenuity, but perfectly natural now that it's been brought to reality.

Look: for me to hear you, in the mixed and marvelous state where I now am, all saturated in the living fluid accumulated in your ring, there's no need of a telephone. But for you to hear me, you or any one of your visitors, isn't it true that the telephone whose mouthpiece I'm now holding must be linked to a sounding-box, however concealed?

—Mistress Anderson, tell me . . .

—Give me my dream name. *Here* I am no longer just myself. *Here,* I forget . . . and no longer suffer. The other name calls me back to that horrible land to which I still belong.

—Sowana, you are absolutely sure of Hadaly, aren't you?

—Oh, you've taught me all about her, your beautiful Hadaly, and I've studied her so thoroughly that I'll answer for her . . . as for my reflection in a mirror. I'd rather be in that vibrant child than in my own self. What a marvelous creature! She exists in the wonderful state where I am at this moment; she is imbued with our two wills, united in her; she is a *single* duality. She is not a consciousness, she is a spirit! When she says to me, "I'm but a *shade,*" my thoughts are shaken: Ah, I've just had the presentiment—that she is going to incarnate!

The great inventor made a slight gesture of surprise and reflection.

—Ah, well. Go to sleep, Sowana! he replied softly. Alas! he continued, we need a third living soul to bring the Great Work to fruition; and who on earth would dare to think himself worthy of it?

—All right, but tonight I shall be ready, said the voice with a drowsy intonation. A single spark and Hadaly will appear! . . .

There was a moment of mysterious silence after this conversation, as strange as it was incomprehensible.

—In fact, Edison murmured as if to himself, the memory of a similar phenomenon doesn't save one from a certain dizziness. Rather than deepen the sensation, I much prefer to think again, of all those words—unheard and unheard-of words—whose tones are forever lost to Humanity because they did not think up the Phonograph before my time.

What lay behind that sudden frivolity of spirit with which the great engineer seemed now to treat the secret—the so extraordinary secret—of which he had just been thinking?

Ah, men of genius are made this way: often one suspects they are trying to blind themselves to their own true thoughts. It's only at the moment when that thought unveils itself, like a lightning flash, that one perceives what motives they had for *seeming* distracted, even while in solitude.

# A SUMMARY SOLILOQUY

You will fall silent, oh sinister voice of the living!
—Leconte de Lisle

—IT'S CHIEFLY IN the mystic world, he resumed after a bit, that the lost opportunities seem beyond retrieval. Oh, for the first vibrations of the good tidings brought to Mary! The resonance of the Archangel saying Hail! a sound that has reverberated through the ages in the angelus. The Sermon on the Mount! The "Hail, master!" (*Shalom, rabboni*, I believe) on the Mount of Olives, and the sound of the kiss of Iscariot. The "Ecce homo" of the tragic prefect! The interrogation in the house of the high priest! I'd want to hear that entire trial, the legal aspects of which have been so shrewdly reviewed in our times by that subtle Master Dupin, president of the French Legislative Assembly, in a book as learned as it is timely. How learnedly the erudite counselor distinguishes there, simply from the point of view of legal practice at the time, every different sort of procedural error, all the omissions, nonsequiturs, improper deals, and careless details of which Pontius Pilate, Caiaphas, and the violent Herod Antipas rendered themselves judicially guilty, in the course of this affair.

For a few moments, the engineer meditated in silence.

—It's apparent, he resumed, that the Word Made Flesh paid little attention to the exterior and sensible parts either of writing or of speech. He wrote on only one occasion, and then on the ground. No doubt He valued, in the speaking of a word, only the indefinable *beyondness* with which personal magnetism inspired by faith can fill a word the moment one pronounces it. Who knows if all the rest isn't trivial by comparison? . . . Still, the fact remains, He allowed men only to print his testament, not to put it on the phonograph. Otherwise, instead of saying, "Read the Holy Scriptures," we would be saying, "Listen to the Sacred Vibrations." But alas, it's too late now . . .

The footsteps of the scientist resounded on the floor. Around him, the shades of twilight deepened.

—What's left on earth for me to put on the phonograph? he murmured sarcastically. You'd really think that fate allowed my instrument to appear only at the moment when nothing that man says is worth preserving anymore . . .

After all, though, what's that to me? Invent! Invent! That's my job.

What matter the sound of the voice, the mouth which speaks, the age or the moment when a particular idea was revealed, since throughout the centuries every idea has existed *only in terms of the mind that reflected it?* Is there any reason to think that those who have never learned to read would ever have learned to listen? To hear the sound is nothing, but the inner essence, which creates these mere vibrations, these veils—that's the crucial thing.

# MYSTERIOUS SOUNDS

Let him who has ears to hear, hear!
—New Testament

So SAYING, EDISON placidly lit another cigar.

—No need to exaggerate the disaster, he said, resuming his stroll and puffing at his cigar in the gathering dusk.

—If the phonograph never had a chance to record the authentic, original sound of those famous words, well, that's too bad; but to worry about missing those enigmatic or mysterious sounds that I was thinking about just now, that would be ridiculous.

For they are not what has disappeared, but rather the awe-inspiring character with which they were invested in the hearing of the ancients— and which all by itself served to animate their basic insignificance. So that neither then nor nowadays could I possibly record exactly sounds whose significance and whose reality depends on the hearer.

Even my Megaphone, though it can increase the dimensions (so to speak) of the human ear—and, scientifically speaking, this in itself is a giant step forward—cannot, by itself, increase the value of what the ear hears.

Even if I could completely free the auditory senses of my contemporaries, now that the spirit of analysis has abolished in their minds the intimate sense of those sounds from the past, my efforts would be vain; for that intimate sense constituted, in effect, their true reality. If I could record them and transmit them to the present age, they would constitute nothing more, nowadays, than dead sounds. They would be, in a word, sounds completely different from what they actually were, and from what their phonographic labels pretended they were—*since it's in ourselves that the killing silence exists.*

It was while the sounds were still mysterious that it would have been really interesting to render the mystery palpable, and transferable, by catching it in some sort of machine and fixing it across the centuries . . .

—And yet, what am I saying? the electrician suddenly murmured: I was forgetting that reciprocity of action is the essential condition of all reality. So that, in the last analysis, one can say that *only the walls of the city of Jericho heard the trumpets of Joshua, since only they were fitted to do so.* Neither the army of Israel nor the besieged Canaanites recognized anything unusual in the sound: which comes down to saying that *nobody ever heard it.*

A comparison: suppose I place the *Mona Lisa* of Leonardo da Vinci in front of a Pawnee Indian or a Kaffir tribesman, or even certain bourgeois of any nationality you want. However powerful the glasses or lenses with which I improve the eyesight of these children of nature, can I ever make them really *see* what they're looking at?

So I conclude that it's the same story with noises as with voices, and with voices as with signs—no man has a right to regret their loss. And in any case, though there are no more supernatural noises nowadays, I can still register some fairly important ones, like the roar of the avalanche, of Niagara Falls, or of the stock market, the sound made by an eruption or by a cannon, a tempest, a mob scene, thunder, wind, oceans, battles, et cetera.

A sudden reaction gave Edison pause in the middle of his thought.

—So it's true that from now on my Aerophone is the master of all these hubbubs; and their occurrence from now on, being perfectly familiar, is deprived of all interest.

It was a melancholy conclusion.

—Decidedly, I repeat, the phonograph and I have arrived too late in the history of humanity. A consideration so discouraging that, if I weren't a man of special practical vigor—I'd probably go and lie down, like a new Tityrus, in the shade of some pastoral beech tree; and there, with my ear applied to the receiver of my Microphone, I would let the days slide past while for amusement I listened to the grass grow—and told myself that a God, most likely, was responsible for my free time.

At this point in his meditation, Edison was interrupted by the striking of a bell, clear and resonant, which resounded through the gathering darkness.

# A DISPATCH

—Take care: it is . . . —I don't see clearly.
—Let him come in!
—Lubner, *The Specter*

T HE ENGINEER PRESSED the spring of a hydrogen lamp which happened to be closer to hand than the electric light switch. As it touched the fragile strip of platinum, the gas jet burst into flame. A night light flared; the whole immense studio was suddenly illuminated.

Edison went over to a phonograph, and with a flick of the finger set the machine in motion (for he avoids talking in his own person as much as possible, except to himself).

—All right, what is it? What do you want? the phonograph called into the telephone; it spoke in the slightly impatient voice of Edison.

—Is that you, Martin?

A vigorous voice replied, as from the center of the room, though not a soul was to be seen.

—Yes, I'm here, Mr. Edison; I'm calling from New York, at your Broadway office. I'm forwarding a dispatch received here for you, just two minutes ago.

The voice came from a speaker, perfected but not yet made public—something like a small polyhedral ball suspended from the ceiling by an electric wire.

Edison turned his eyes toward a telegraphic receiver standing on its base beside the phonograph. A sheet of telegraphic paper was already in place.

An imperceptible shiver, a murmur as of spirits in the air, stirred the receiver into action. As the electrician reached forth his hand, the paper leaped from its receptacle, bearing the following swiftly printed message, which Edison carried under the lamp to read.

—NEW YORK, BROADWAY, FOR MENLO PARK NO. 1. —8.1.83.4:35 P.M. TO THOMAS ALVA EDISON, ENGINEER. *Arrived this morning: will visit you this evening. Affectionate greetings.*

—LORD EWALD

Seeing the signature, the engineer gave a cry of surprise and pleasure.

—Lord Ewald! he exclaimed. How can it be? He? Back in the United States? Ah, let him come, my dear, my distinguished friend!

And after a silent smile, in which one might have recognized the skeptic of a few moments ago, he went on:

—No, I've not forgotten that admirable young man who saved my life, all those years ago now, when I was dying of hunger and collapsed in the street up there near Boston.

Everyone else walked past me, saying, "Poor fellow!" But he, the best, the most gracious of Samaritans, without wasting any time on pity, found it in his heart to pick me up, and with a handful of gold to save my life, my work! —And so he remembered my name? I'll receive him with open arms! Don't I owe all my success to him—and the rest of my life?

Edison stepped quickly to a tapestry and laid his finger on an electric button behind it. In the distance, beyond the park and near the main house, a bell sounded.

Almost at once the voice of a merry infant rang out from the corner of an ivory desk by Edison's side.

—What is it, father? said the voice.

Edison seized the speaker of a machine hidden behind the drapes.

—Dash, he said, you will admit a visitor to the pavilion tonight, Lord Ewald. Greet him as you would me . . . He is at home here.

—Very well, father! said the same voice, which this time, thanks to a remote switching mechanism, seemed to arrive from the center of an enormous magnesium reflector.

—I expect that he'll dine with me tonight. Don't wait up for me. And be good children. Good night, now.

A charming burst of childish laughter rippled through the shadows on all sides. You would have thought an invisible elf, hidden in the atmosphere, was jesting with a magician.

With a smile Edison replaced the speaker of the telephone and resumed his stroll. As he passed by an ebony table, he absentmindedly tossed the dispatch among the apparatus littering its surface.

By accident, the paper dropped on an object of a striking and remarkable character—an object whose very presence in such a place was inexplicable. Accidental as it was, the juncture of these two objects seemed to attract Edison's attention; he paused, considering the event and reflecting on it.

# THE DREAMER TOUCHES
# A DREAM OBJECT

Why not?
—The slogan of the Modern Age

IT WAS A HUMAN ARM, lying on a cushion of violet silk. The blood seemed to have clotted at the shoulder joint; only a few purple blotches on a chiffon scarf nearby gave evidence of a recent operation.

It was the arm and right hand of a young woman.

The delicate wrist was encircled by a viper of enameled gold; on the ring finger of the pale hand glittered a circlet of sapphires. The slender fingers still held a pearl-colored glove, worn several times no doubt.

The flesh still retained an appearance so vital, the surface of the skin was so pure and satiny, that its appearance was as cruel as it was fantastic.

What unknown danger could have necessitated such a perilous amputation?—particularly since the most glowing health seemed still to flood through this soft and gracious fragment of a youthful body?

An icy thought would have frozen the mind of any stranger who had come on the sight.

In fact, the great cottage of Menlo Park, which with its surroundings looks like a castle lost in the woods, is a kingdom to itself. As everyone knows, Edison is a dauntless experimenter who is gentle only to his proven friends. As an engineer and an electrician, his discoveries of every different sort, of which only the least strange are known to the public, generally give nothing more than the impression of a mysterious positivism. He has compounded anesthetics so powerful that, if one takes the word of his flatterers, "one of the damned, swallowing them, would instantly become completely indifferent to the most exquisite tortures of Gehenna." When a new experiment was afoot, what would cause a physicist to draw back? The existence of others? His own?

Ah, when it's a question of a new discovery, what scholar worthy of the name could think even for a moment, without shame and dishonor, of considerations of this order? Edison, surely, less than any other man; and God be thanked for that fact!

The European press has occasionally cast some light on the character of his experiments. All he cares about is the main point; in his view, the details deserve nothing more than the passing glance with which a philosopher honors—and perhaps too much at that—mere contingencies.

Some years ago, according to the American newspapers, Edison had found the secret of stopping short, without the least inconvenience, two trains headed toward one another on a collision course under a full head of steam. He then persuaded the director of a branch line of the Western Railway to make an immediate trial of the system, in order to safeguard the patent.

One fine moonlit night, the switchmen therefore set two trains packed with passengers on the same line, heading for one another at thirty leagues per hour. But the engineers lost their nerve at the last minute, in the face of imminent danger, and went quite counter to the instructions of Edison, who was standing on a nearby hillside to watch the experiment and chewing on a cigar.

The two trains collided with a terrible crash. Within an instant, several hundred victims were scattered across the landscape, helter-skelter in every direction. People were crushed, burned, and ground to bits, men, women, and children, both the engineers, and the firemen, of whom it wasn't possible to discover even a trace.

The great experimenter murmured simply,—Clumsy idiots!

Any other funeral oration would, in fact, have been superfluous: apart from the fact that eloquence isn't his business.

Since then, Edison is astonished only that the Americans shrink from a second trial, or, as he sometimes says, "a third, if need be"—until, in fact, "the procedure is successful."

Any visitor who remembered such experiments from the past—experiments many times renewed—might have had reason to suspect a similar trial in pursuit of some new form of knowledge, at the sight of this radiant arm so rudely torn from its socket.

But as he stood by the ebony table, Edison noted the chit of telegraph paper where it had fallen between two fingers of the hand. He touched the arm and started, as if a new idea had crossed his imagination.

—Wait, he murmured, what if by some chance this visitor were the one who is to awaken Hadaly!

The word "awaken" was pronounced by the engineer with a sort of hesitation, a curious half-shudder. After a second he shrugged his shoulders and smiled.

—Splendid, now I'm getting superstitious, he concluded.

He passed by the table and resumed his stroll around the room. Evidently preferring the darkness, he turned out the light when he reached it.

Suddenly, outside, across the valleys, the moon passing a gap in the clouds shot a ray through the curtains and directed it, as if with malign intent, onto the table. The pale light caressed that inanimate hand, wandered across the arm, lit up the eyes of the golden viper, and caused the blue ring to sparkle. Then once more night covered all.

# RETROSPECTIVE

Glory is the sunshine of the dead.
—Honoré de Balzac

SINKING EVER DEEPER into the dark corners of his reverie, Edison, once more in a mocking mood, resumed his thought:

—What is most surprising in history, almost unimaginable, is that among all the great inventors across the centuries, not one thought of the Phonograph! And yet most of them invented machines a thousand times more complicated. The Phonograph is so simple that its construction owes nothing to materials of scientific composition. Abraham might have built it, and made a recording of his calling from on high. A steel stylus, a leaf of silver foil or something like it, a cylinder of copper, and one could fill a storehouse with all the voices and noises of Heaven and Earth.

So what was engineer Berossus thinking about, that priest of Bel in Babylon? If, four thousand and two hundred years ago, he had put aside his studies on the forms of the gnomon, with a little bit of observation and reflection he could certainly have discovered my apparatus. And how about the subtle Eratoshenes? Instead of spending half a century in his observatory at Alexandria nearly two thousand years ago, all of it devoted to measuring the arc of the meridian between the solstices (and I concede he did it very exactly), wouldn't he have been better advised to think first of recording a sonic vibration on a metal plaque? And the Chaldeans? Why they could have . . . But no! They lived with their heads in the clouds . . . The powerful Euclid? The logical Aristotle? And Pythagoras, the poetic mathematician? Or the great Archimedes, he who single-handedly defended Syracuse, inventing fearful grappling-hooks and burning mirrors to destroy the Roman fleets far out at sea—didn't he have the same faculties of observation as I do? If I discovered the Phonograph by noting that my voice caused the bottom of my hat to vibrate when I talked into it, didn't he discover his law of fluids by noting the water in his bath? Why didn't he note, long before me, that the vibrations of sound all about us make signatures that can be transcribed like writing?

Ah, if it hadn't been for the criminal act of that soldier in the army of Marcellus, who murdered Archimedes as he was working over a difficult equation, I feel sure he would have beaten me to my discovery. And how about the engineers who built the temple at Karnak, or those of Abu Simbel? Or what of the architects of the sacred citadel of Angkor Wat, those unknown Michelangelos of a temple into which one could fit a couple dozen Louvres, and which is half again as lofty, I think, as the pyramid of Cheops—what of them? Their temple is still to be seen in the northern part of Cambodia; every architrave, every courtyard, every immense column (and there are hundreds of them) is formed and chiseled to perfection, and the whole thing set on a mountain surrounded on every side by a hundred leagues of desert. The temple is so ancient that it's impossible to discover the god for whom it was built, or the source or even the name of the nation that built it; everything about the building of this gigantic miracle has been lost in the night of time! Was it not easier to imagine the Phonograph than a temple like that? —And think of the artisans of King Gudea, dead six thousand years ago, but who is said by the Akkadian inscriptions to have been proud of nothing *except that in his time such progress had been made in the arts and sciences!*

Not to mention the sages of Khorsabad, of Troy, of Baalbeck!

And the mages, who served the ancient satraps of Media! The Lydian craftsmen who in a single night altered the entire landscape around Croesus! There were men of art in Babylon whom Semiramis employed to turn aside the course of the Euphrates. And the architects of Memphis, Palmyra, Sicyon, Babel, Nineveh, and Carthage! The engineers responsible for Is, Tadmor, Ptolemaïs, Ancyra, Thebes, Ecbatana, Sardis, Sidon, Antioch, Corinth, Jerusalem? And the mathematicians of Saïs, of Tyre, of Persepolis long since burned down, of Byzantium, Eleusis, Rome, Caesarea, Benares, and Athens? And think of all the miracle workers who sprang up by the thousands amid immense ancient civilizations—civilizations of which not a name, not a stone, not a wisp of smoke remained even in the time of Herodotus—why did none of them have the wit to invent, before my time, the Phonograph? At least we would now be able to pronounce their languages correctly, as well as their names. So many other names, supposedly immortal, are nothing now but syllables bearing no relation whatever to the sounds by which the phantoms were called whom we want to invoke. How was the world able to do so long without the Phonograph? I simply don't understand. Can it be that the wise men of these forgotten peoples were like our own, most of whom are good for nothing but to verify, then classify and improve, what ignorant men invent and discover?

There were good men and serious craftsmen on earth five thousand years ago. For example, the engineers of Rhampsinitus of the eleventh dynasty tempered copper more skillfully in those days than Spanish armorers can temper steel today. They were so skillful that now their secret is lost; not even the most powerful of our factories, using the most modern processes, can forge the least of the implements that they made of this metal. It is amazing, then, that among men of this . . . stamp . . . not a single one appeared who was interested in reproducing the sound of his own voice in an indestructible manner! . . . But perhaps after all it was invented, rejected, and so forgotten. More than nine hundred years ago the telephone was put to the test and rejected in ancient China, that country of incalculable antiquity and endless cycles, a country long familiar with aerostats, printing, electricity, gunpowder, etc.—in addition to a whole range of things that we haven't discovered even yet. Who hasn't heard of the discovery in Karnak of railroad tracks dating back three thousand years?—back to the times when peoples lived only by invasion and conquest? Happily, the inventions of modern man seem likely to be of "permanent" duration. Doubtless they said the same thing in the days of Nabonassar, or even in the age of Prince Xisuthros (Ut-Napishtim), that is, some seven or eight thousand years ago, as I calculate it. Of course nowadays we're all very "serious" about our accomplishments. On what grounds? I can't imagine. The main thing is to be very confident of our own value, that's all. Without which, every last one of us, having once filled his pockets, would sit back and fold his arms. Myself first of all.

# SNAPSHOTS OF WORLD HISTORY

Instant Photography

A MAN ENTERS: Sir, I'd like to have my pict . . .
THE PHOTOGRAPHER, LEAPING FORWARD: Say no more! . . . here it is.
—Cham

A̲T THIS POINT the glance of the engineer fell on that huge magnesium reflector around which the child's voice had been playing a moment before.

—Photography too has come along very late, he continued. Isn't it exasperating to think of all the pictures, portraits, scenes, and landscapes that it could have recorded once, and which are now forever lost to us? Painters use their imaginations; but it's absolute reality that the camera would have brought us. What a difference! . . . Well, there's no help for it; we'll never see again, we'll never *recognize* in their true features the things and the men of former times. Of course it's possible that man will some day be able to recover, either by electricity or by some more subtle means, the undying interstellar reverberations of everything that has occurred on earth; but we'd better not count too much on this discovery, for it's more than probable that the entire solar system will have been vaporized by then in the blazing nebula of the *Zeta* of Hercules, which is drawing us into its orbit with every second that passes. Or at any rate, our planet will have been struck by its satellite, crushed and reduced (for all that its crust is from three to ten leagues thick) to a mere *sack of charcoal;* or else one of our many oscillations on the axis of the planet will have buried us under an enormous layer of ice, as happened in the past. Any one of these things may have happened before we are able to reach into outer space and recapture there the eternal interstellar refraction of things here in the past.

Too bad. For it would have been delightful to possess good photographic prints (taken on the spot) of *Joshua Bidding the Sun Stand Still,* for example. Or why not several different views of *The Earthly Paradise,* taken from the *Gateway of the Flaming Swords;* the *Tree of Knowledge;* the *Serpent;* and so forth? Perhaps a number of shots of *The Deluge, Taken from the Top of Mount Ararat?* (I'll bet that busy Japheth would have carried a camera with him into the Ark, if that marvelous instrument had been available to him.) Later, we would have had photos of *The Seven Plagues of Egypt,* of the *Burning Bush,* and the *Passage of the Red Sea* (with shots before, during, and after the event). There would have been the *Mene, Mene, Tekel, Upharsin* of Belshazzar's Feast, the *Funeral Pyre of Sardanapalus,* the *Standard of Constantinople,* the *Head of Medusa,* the *Minotaur,* etc.; and we would rejoice today in postcards of *Prometheus,* the *Stymphalides,* the *Sybils,* the *Danaids,* the *Furies,* etc., etc.

And all the episodes of the New Testament—what prints they would provide! All the anecdotes of eastern and western history—what a collection! The martyrs, and all the examples of torture, from that of the Seven Maccabees and their mother to those of John of Leyden and Damiens, not forgetting the chief episodes of Christians set against wild beasts in the arenas of Rome, Lyons, and other cities!

One would want, too, all the scenes of torture, from the very beginning of social life down to recent events in the prisons of the Holy Inquisition, when the *Monks of Redemption,* equipped with their instruments of iron, spent their leisure time over the years in massacring Moors, heretics, and Jews. And the cruel interrogations that have gone on in the prisons of Germany, Italy, France, the Orient, everywhere, why not those too? The camera, aided by the phonograph (they are near of kin), could reproduce both the sight and the different sounds made by the sufferers, giving a complete, an exact idea of the experience. What an admirable course of instruction for the grade schools, to render healthful the intelligence of modern young people—perhaps even public figures! A splendid magic lantern!

And the portraits of all the great founders of civilizations, from Nimrod to Napoleon, from Moses to Washington, from Confucius to Mohammed! Pictures of all the famous women, from Semiramis to Catherine the Great, from Thalestris to Joan of Arc, from Zenobia to Christina of Sweden!

And photographs of all the beautiful women, including Venus, Europa, Psyche, Delilah, Rachel, Judith, Cleopatra, Aspasia, Freya, Maneka, Thais, Akedysseril, Roxalana, the Queen of Sheba, Phryne, Circe, Dejanira, Helen, and so on down to the beautiful Pauline Bonaparte! to the Greek veiled by law! to Lady Emma Harte Hamilton!

And of course we'd have all the gods as well, and all the goddesses, down to and including the Goddess Reason, without neglecting Mr. Supreme Being! Life-size, of course!

Well now, isn't it a shame we don't have photographs of that entire crowd? What an album it would make!

Natural history would provide a great field, especially paleontology. There's no doubt in the world that we have a very imperfect notion of the megatherium, for example, that paradoxical pachyderm, and that our notions of the pterodactyl as a gigantic bat, or of the plesiosaurus, monstrous patriarch of the reptiles—are, practically speaking, infantile. These strange creatures fought or flew, as their skeletons still bear witness, in the very place where I now stand today, and no more than a few hundred centuries ago, less than no time; less than a quarter or a fifth of the age of this bit of chalk with which I write on the blackboard.

Nature was quick to pass the sponge of her deluges over these awkward sketches, these first nightmares of Life. And yet, what curious prints might have been made of all these creatures! Alas, the vision is lost forever!

The great experimenter heaved a sigh.

—Yes, yes, everything fades, it's true; even discolorations on collodion, even scratches on steel plates. Vanity of vanities, all is vanity, to be sure! One is tempted to smash the camera, blow up the phonograph, and raise one's eyes to the vaults of heaven (which, for that matter, are only a figure of speech) to ask if this gauzy screen of the universe comes to us for free, or who fuels its great luminary? Who, in a word, pays the rent on this room of ours, insubstantial as it appears, within which the old riddle is constantly being propounded? And where did they dig up these heavy, old-fashioned stage trappings of Time and Space, so trite and patched-up that nobody believes in them anymore?

As for the faithful, I can propose to them a thought which they may well consider naive, paradoxical, superficial—but which is odd. God, we know, is supreme, all powerful, perfectly good; and over the centuries, as everybody knows, He has appeared to numbers of people: to dispute it would be heresy. Yet while all sorts of bad painters and mediocre sculptors have struggled to popularize their notions of His features, to make them *chic*, isn't it painful to think that if He would just allow the slightest, most humble photograph of Himself—or just permit me, Thomas Alva Edison, American engineer, His creature, to make a simple phonographic record of His True Voice (for thunder has lost most of its prestige since Franklin), *the day after that event, there wouldn't be a single atheist left on the earth!*

Thus the great electrician, talking only to himself, toyed playfully with the vague idea—actually a matter of indifference to him—of the vital reflexive spirituality of God.

—But in him who reflects it, the living idea of God appears only to the extent that the faith of the viewer is able to evoke it. Like every other thought, God can exist in the individual only according to the capacity of the individual. No man knows where illusion begins or what reality consists of. Thus, God being the most sublime of conceptions, and all conceptions existing only according to the particular spirit and the *intellectual* eyes of the seer, it follows that the man who dismisses the idea of God from his thoughts does nothing but deliberately decapitate his own mind.

As he pronounced these last words, Edison stopped short in his meditative stroll and looked fixedly out through the great windows into the lunar shadows.

—All right, then, he said suddenly, one challenge for another! Since Life takes such a high hand with us, and answers our questions only with a deep and dubious silence, there's nothing for us to do but see if we can't bring her out of it! . . . In any case, we can already give her a demonstration . . . of what she amounts to in our eyes.

At these words, the eccentric inventor trembled: he had just noted in a ray of moonlight, the dark shadow of a human being, who had moved between him and the light, behind the glass door leading out into the park.

—Who's there? he cried aloud, staring into the dark—and fondling gently in the pocket of his loose dressing-gown of violet silk the butt of a small revolver.

# LORD EWALD

You would have said that this woman cast her shadow straight into the heart of the young man.
—Lord Byron, *The Dream*

—IT IS I, LORD EWALD, said a voice; and even as it spoke, the shadow moved to open the door.

—Ah! My dear lord, I beg your pardon! cried Edison, groping his way toward the electric light. The trains are so slow nowadays that I didn't expect you for another three-quarters of an hour.

—That's why I had a special train with a super-pressurized engine under a full head of steam, said the same voice. I must get back to New York tonight.

Suddenly three oxyhydric lamps under blue-tinted shades flared up under the ceiling; they created an area of electrical luminescence which lit the laboratory as brightly as the midday sun.

The person confronting Edison was a young man of twenty-seven or twenty-eight years, tall of stature, and extraordinarily handsome.

He was dressed with such impeccable elegance that it would have been impossible to say of what it consisted. The lines of his build indicated a frame of exceptional solidity, such as is molded by the rugby games and regattas of Oxford or Cambridge. His features were, perhaps, a little cold, but at the moment lit up by a gracious and sympathetic smile, tinged with that sort of lofty melancholy which reveals the aristocracy of a character. Though the lines of his face were perfectly regular, the quality of their chiseling suggested supreme energy of decision. Masses of fine hair and a light blond moustache shadowed the whiteness of his youthful complexion. His large eyes, pale blue under almost straight brows, and supremely calm, were fixed on his interlocutor. His hand, gloved in severe black, held an unlit cigar.

His appearance was such that one would expect most women to feel in his presence the breath of an enchanting divinity; he was so good looking that his very nature seemed to bestow a grace upon one with whom he conversed. At first glance one might have thought him a Don Juan with the cold carelessness of the type. But a second glance would reveal in the expression of his eyes that grave and lofty melancholy the shadow of which never fails to signal a despair.

—My dear rescuer, said Edison warmly, moving toward the stranger with hands extended in welcome. How many times I've thought of that providential young man on the road near Boston, without whom there would be for me neither glory nor fortune nor life itself!

—No, my dear Edison, Lord Ewald answered with a smile, it's the other way around. I'm in debt to you, since it's through your agency that I was of some use to the rest of humanity. The proof lies in what you have made of yourself. The bit of money to which I think you allude meant nothing to me: in your hands, especially then, when you were needy, wasn't it far more valuable than in mine? I mean of course in terms of the general interest, which we're obliged never to overlook completely. I owe destiny all manner of thanks for having arranged that particular occasion to use my fortune. And indeed, that's why, in the course of my American trip, I took such pains to come and see you. I came *to thank you for the fact that I found you on the road near Boston.*

And Lord Ewald bowed, even as he shook the hands of Edison.

A little surprised by this speech, delivered with that sort of phlegmatic smile which resembles a ray of sunshine falling on ice, the famous inventor greeted his young friend.

—But how you've changed, my dear lord! Edison said cheerily, inviting Lord Ewald to an armchair.

—And you as well, more than I have! the young man answered, sitting down.

As Edison looked on his visitor, whose face was now in full light, he took notice at a glance of the terrible cloud which seemed to be weighing on his mind.

—My lord, he said abruptly, has the speed of your trip to Menlo Park left you, perhaps, a little unsettled? . . . I have here a cordial . . .

—Not at all, answered the young man. Why do you ask?

After a silence, Edison said simply:

—An impression, I beg your pardon.

—Ah, said Lord Ewald, I know what gave you that impression. It's nothing physical, believe me. It is, if I may say so, a long-standing, unremitting sorrow which has finally rendered my expression a bit careworn.

Adjusting his monocle, he looked carefully around him.

—My congratulations on your arrangements here, my dear scholar, he went on. You're one of the chosen few, and here's a laboratory brimming with promise. Is this one of your inventions, this marvelous light? It's as bright as a summer noon.

—All thanks to you, my dear lord.

—Really, you must have pronounced your *Fiat lux* to achieve this!

—As a matter of fact, I've discovered two or three hundred little things like that, if I may say so; I even hope to keep on a little further along the same road. I work all the time, even while sleeping—even in my dreams I work! I'm a kind of awakened sleeper, as Scheherazade would say. But that's all there is to it.

—You must understand the pride I feel in our having met one another on this vast, mysterious pilgrimage. I'm bound to think it was inevitable. As Wieland says, in his tale of *Peregrinus Proteus,* "There is no such thing as luck: we were bound to meet one another . . . and so we did!"

Even as these affectionate words were being spoken, the secret preoccupation of the young man was apparent. There was a moment of silence.

—My lord, said Edison, breaking the silence, will you permit me, as an old friend, to take an interest in your state?

Lord Ewald looked directly at him.

—You have just spoken, the engineer continued, of a sorrow which shows plainly on your face. Well, I'm not in a position to tell you, on the spur of the moment, what I'd like to do about it; but, look: Don't you agree that the worst sorrows are lightened by being shared with a devoted friend? Who knows? I'm one of those eccentric doctors who persist in thinking that there's no evil without a remedy.

Lord Ewald could not repress a slight gesture of surprise at this abrupt advance.

—Oh, he replied, the trouble I spoke of rises from a very commonplace accident; in fact, from an unhappy passion, the gloomy effects of which are with me forever. You see, my secret is of the simplest sort imaginable, so let's say no more of it.

—You, cried Edison, you suffering from an unhappy passion? The exclamation slipped out in spite of him.

—Excuse me, my dear Edison, interrupted Lord Ewald, but I have no right to waste on my own private affairs time which should be devoted to the general interest. It seems to me our conversation would be much more interesting if we brought it back to *your* concerns.

—My time? Well, everyone owes *you* a little bit of it. And we all know that those people who admire me today, the people who've formed gigantic corporations on the strength of my inventive achievements past or to come, would have let me die like a dog if they had been in your place. I'm not altogether forgetful of that episode. Humanity can wait; I believe it's superior to its own interests, as a Frenchman said somewhere. Personal affection has rights just as great as those of humanity, my lord; my feelings entitle me to insist on that measure of confidence that I requested just now, since I feel that you are in pain.

The Englishman lit a cigar and considered.

—Well, Mr. Inventor, he said at last, you speak so generously that I don't see how I can hold out against your kindness. Let me say, however, that I never had the slightest expectation that before I was fairly seated in your house, I would be choosing you for a confidant. But since you ask, here it is: I have the misfortune of being in love, painfully so, and for the first time in my life (and in our family, the first love is almost always the last, that is, the only one). She is a very beautiful person—well, let me say this, *the most beautiful person in the world,* in my opinion. At the moment she is in New York, in our box at the opera, showing off her earrings, and pretending to listen to *Freischutz.*—There; I take it you're satisfied now, Mr. Curiosity?

As these words were being spoken, Edison was watching Lord Ewald with a particular measure of attention. At first he made no answer at all; but, his face growing suddenly darker, he seemed to be burying himself in a secret thought.

—Yes, he murmured coldly, that would be a disaster, a real disaster, what you've told me.

And he stared out the window with a distracted air.

—Oh, Lord Ewald murmured, you can't even begin to understand the extent of it.

—My lord, Edison said after a moment, that is why you must tell me a little more.

—Ah, indeed! And what good would that do?

—I have, now, another reason for inquiring.

—A reason?

—Yes; I think I have, perhaps, *a means to cure you*—or, at the least . . .

—Alas, it's impossible, said Lord Ewald with a bitter smile. Science has no power in these areas.

—Science? I am a man who knows nothing, guesses sometimes, finds frequently, and who's always amazed.

—Besides, the love from which I suffer is of a quality which is bound to seem strange and even unthinkable.

—So much the better! So much the better, said Edison, opening his eyes wider and wider. But just give me a few details.

—But, but . . . I have reason to think they may be unintelligible, even to you.

—*Unintelligible!?* Wasn't it Hegel who said, *We must understand the Unintelligible as such?* Let us make the attempt, my lord! cried the engineer; and you will see then what light we can shed on the dark focal point of your trouble.—If you refuse me now, well . . . wait and see . . . I'll pay you back with some secrecy of my own.

—Very well, here's the story, said Lord Ewald, warmed by the cordial informality of Edison.

# ALICIA

She walks in beauty, like the night
Of cloudless climes and starry skies.
—Lord Byron, *Hebrew Melodies*

LORD EWALD, CROSSING his legs and puffing gently on his cigar, began his story.

—For some years now, I've been living on one of the oldest estates of my family, Castle Athelwold in Staffordshire. It's a bleak and foggy district, and the castle, one of the last, is surrounded by lakes, pine forests, and craggy hills, some miles from Newcastle-under-Lyme. Since my return from Abyssinia, I've been living a solitary existence there, having no relatives living, and feeling quite content with the society of our old retainers, who've been in the family for years.

Once I had done my military service, I assumed the privilege of living in this way, according to my tastes. A number of different thoughts on the spirit of the age led me to renounce, very early, all thoughts of a political career; and a number of distant voyages developed my natural taste for solitude. So this isolated existence satisfied my instinct for meditation, and I thought myself the happiest of men.

One day, however, I had to leave my barony and my sport of hunting in order to go to London and attend with my fellow peers a celebration of the anniversary of our sovereign's coronation as Empress of the Indies. A foolish and commonplace accident on this trip joined me with another person who was also going to London for the celebration. How did it happen? This is the story. At Newcastle station, the railroad carriages proved to be full. On the platform was a young lady who seemed greatly distressed at being unable to board the train. At the last minute she approached me, a total stranger, hardly daring to ask for room in the compartment where I was traveling alone; and of course that was a favor I could hardly refuse her.

Here, my dear Edison, let me remark that until this point the occasions for what people call worldly intimacies had always presented themselves to me in vain.

A certain unsociability in my nature had always held me back from any sort of good fortune of that character. If I never had a fiancée, it was part of my inner nature not to want or desire, even for an instant, any other woman than the one special person, still unknown, but destined perhaps to become my wife.

In a most old-fashioned way, I took conjugal love very seriously indeed. Those of my friends who didn't share my peculiar point of view on this matter used to surprise me; and even today I really pity the young men who under various sleazy pretexts betray *in advance* the woman whom one day they will marry. Hence that reputation for coldness which my friends spread about me, even as far as the household of the queen, after they had tried vainly to excite my interest in Russian women, Italians, or creoles.

Well, in any case, this is what happened: within a few hours I became passionately attached to this young lady in the railway carriage, whom I was seeing for the first time. By the time of our arrival in London, without even being aware of it, I was caught up in that first and no doubt last love affair which is traditional in our family. Within a few days, to put it in a word, intimate bonds had been established between us. They have lasted to this day.

Since you choose to act at the moment as a mysterious doctor from whom nothing must be hidden, it becomes essential to my story to describe, physically, Miss Alicia Clary. I shall not try to avoid expressing myself as a lover, and even, if possible, as a poet, seeing that this woman, even in the eyes of the most disinterested artist, would appear to be beautiful beyond any question, and in the highest degree.

Miss Alicia is about twenty years old, and slim as a silver aspen. Her gestures are gently and deliciously harmonious; her body is molded in lines to delight and surprise the greatest sculptors. Her figure is full, but with the pale glow of lilies; she has indeed the splendor of a *Venus Victorious*, but humanized. Her masses of brown hair have the brilliance of a southern night. Often, as she leaves the bath, she treads on this glittering cascade of hair, which doesn't lose its curls even in the water, and throws its shadowy luxury about her shoulders like the mantle of a cloak. Her face forms the most seductive oval, within which her mouth flowers like a deep-dyed rosebud. Her lips glow with fresh color as they draw back in a laugh to display the gleaming teeth of a young animal. Her lashes are alive with shadows, the lobes of her charming ears are fresh as April roses. Her nose, exquisitely straight, with translucent wings, continues perfectly the line of her forehead. Her hands are more pagan than aristocratic; her feet have the same elegance as those of Greek statues. And her features are lit by a pair of lofty eyes, dark of hue, and mysteriously penetrating behind her lashes. From this human flower rises a warm perfume which surrounds one and pervades the air, burning, intoxicating, ravishing. When she speaks, the resonance of Miss Alicia's voice is so penetrating, the notes of her singing are so vibrant and so profound, that whether she is reciting a tragic passage in noble verses or singing some magnificent aria, I am always amazed to find myself trembling with an admiration the like of which, as you shall see, I've never known before.

# SHADOWS

A nothing . . .
—A common phrase

—WHILE WE WERE AT London and during the court celebrations, the most radiant young girls in our nest of English swans passed unperceived before me. Everything which was not the presence of Alicia became painful to me: I was overwhelmed.

And yet, even during those first days, I was struggling vainly against an overwhelming impression that the young lady made on me, and from which I could not escape. I tried to discredit the judgments that her words and acts forced upon me every instant we were together. I accused myself of stupidity rather than admit what they meant, and I had recourse to all the devices of rationalization in order to destroy the evidence of my own thought. A woman! Isn't she just a child, troubled by a thousand anxieties, subject to influence from every direction? Shouldn't we welcome with the most gentle and friendly of smiles any evidence of her fantastic imaginings, of her changing tastes in trifles, alterations as swift as the flutter of a feather? This constant variation is part of woman's charm. A natural instinct is bound to lead us gently to correct, to modify by a thousand slow transitions (for which she will love us all the more, sensing their operation), to guide, in a word, this frail, irresponsible, and delicate creature, who spontaneously and naturally demands our support.—Well, then, I asked myself, did it make sense to judge so swiftly and unreservedly a creature whose thoughts might soon be changed by love (and this depended on me) until they became the reflection of my own?

Certainly I said all that to myself! And yet I could not forget that in every living creature there is an unchanging, essential base which imprints on all the ideas, however subtle, on all the impressions, whether changing or stable, of such a being, a certain aspect, color, quality, or *character*, in a word. And whatever *exterior* modifications they may undergo, these are the fixed qualities of such a creature's experience and thought. Let us call this substratum the *soul*, if you will.

But between the body and the soul of Miss Alicia, it wasn't just a disproportion which distressed and upset my understanding; it was an absolute *disparity*.

At this word of Lord Ewald's one might have noted that Edison's features suddenly turned pale. He made a gesture and shot a glance of surprise, maybe even of stupefaction. But he ventured not a word of interruption.

—It amounted to this, the young lord continued. The traits of her divine beauty seemed to be foreign to her *self*; her words seemed constrained and out of place in her mouth. Her intimate being was in flat contradiction with the form it inhabited. You would have thought, not only that her personality was deprived of what I think philosophers call plastic mediation, but that she had been shut up, by a kind of magical punishment, in the perpetual contradiction of her beautiful body. From time to time the experience (which I'll try to convey to you in a moment by an account of specific facts) was so completely evident that I came to consider it, I'd almost say, unquestionable. Yes, on occasion I was tempted to think, *quite seriously*, that in the dark spaces of Becoming this woman had somehow strayed by accident into this body, which did not belong to her at all.

—It's an unnecessary hypothesis, Edison replied. Still, almost all women—while they are beautiful, which isn't for long—give one similar sensations, above all when one is in love for the first time.

—If you'll just be good enough to wait a moment, said Lord Ewald, you will see that the case was much more complicated than that, and that Miss Alicia Clary could properly assume in my eyes the strange proportions, if not of an absolute novelty in humankind, at least of one of the darker and more sinister human anomalies. As for the *duration* of beauty— let it be of the most radiant sort and pass in a flash, yet if I die in that instant, won't that instant have been eternal for me? No matter how long beauty lasts, provided it has really made an appearance! And for the rest, am I not obliged to take fairly seriously an event which, in spite of the cold and skeptical indifference of my reason, confounds all at once my understanding, my senses, and my heart? Believe me, my dear doctor, I haven't come to your consulting room in order to describe to you, under the simpleminded supposition that my affliction is unique, some trivial case of hysterical dementia, more or less banal, such as one can find written up in all the medical textbooks. The case is of a different and much more astonishing order of physiological difficulty; you may take my word for that.

—Excuse me; would your grief perhaps spring from the fact that this handsome young person hasn't remained faithful to you?

—Would to God she were capable of infidelity! cried Lord Ewald. For then, I'd have no trouble, *since she would be another person!* Besides, the man guilty of having been betrayed in love has no right to complain of a fate he has deserved. What logic is that, to complain of a woman whom one hasn't been able to captivate a bit? The truth of this thought, instinctively and generally recognized, is what always colors with a certain absurdity the complaints of unfortunate husbands. You must believe that if a shadowy imagination, a momentary caprice of desire, had ever turned Miss Alicia Clary away from our mutual fidelity, I would have encouraged that inconstancy by viewing it with the most lofty inattention. On the contrary, it is clear that she accords me the *only love of which she is capable,* and I believe it is all the more "sincere," alas, because she feels it IN SPITE OF HERSELF.

—Would you be good enough, my lord, said Edison, to take up the story of this adventure in logical order, starting at the point where I interrupted?

—After several evenings, I learned from this new friend of mine that she was from a fairly good Scottish family, which had even risen to the nobility in these latter days. Seduced by a fiancé, then cast aside in favor of a fortune, Alicia had just left her father's house; she proposed to lead the independent, nomadic existence of a singer—that was an idea which she would later give up. Her voice, her appearance, her dramatic talent, all assured her—or so several people had solemnly told her—that she could easily make enough to meet her modest needs. As for her encounter with me, in the first moments of her flight from home, she thought herself extremely lucky. Since she could no longer be married, but felt a certain sympathy for my person, she accepted without further demands the love I pressed on her, and declared herself hopeful of soon being able to share my inclination.

—All things considered, Edison remarked, these declarations indicate a certain dignity of the heart, I imagine? Yes? . . . Or no?

Lord Ewald gazed on him, impassive, expressionless.

You would have thought he was touching on the most painful point of his entire melancholy confession.

# HOW SUBSTANCE CHANGES WITH FORM

*The same idea . . . maybe:*
Those who are absent are always wrong.—Wisdom of the World.
You have devoted friends: still . . . if you turn your back?—Goethe

WITHOUT ALTERING HIS tone of voice, he continued impassively:

—Yes; but—what you've heard was my translation, not the precise words of Alicia.

Another style, a different set of sentiments; and I see clearly that I must set before you the *text* itself. Substituting one's own style for that of a person whose character one is explaining, on the pretext that it's *pretty well* expressed that way, is putting the listener in the position of a night wanderer on the highway, who thinks he's petting a dog when really he's enraging a wolf.

Here, then, are her *exact* words:

—The man who betrayed her was nothing but a petty manufacturer, who never had any attraction for her apart from his money.

She never loved him, no, certainly not. She yielded to his importunities, thinking thereby to hasten her marriage with him; it was only to escape from her existence as an unmarried daughter that she resigned herself to him; this husband would be no worse than another. Besides, he promised to cut a decent figure in the world. But girls are bad judges in these things. Next time she'd know better than to believe in fine phrases. For example, it was very lucky that she hadn't had a baby. If her first adventure had been kept secret, she might have undertaken to *establish herself* with another lover.

But in her home town, her own family had, by a stupid kind of idiocy, most likely, spread the word abroad. She had been so angry at that, she decided to run away. Not knowing what else to do, she set her eye on the stage. Hence her trip to London, where the little bit of money she had saved would enable her to look for a good engagement. In the end, no doubt, such a career was bad for a girl's reputation; but since she had already committed the most serious fault of all, why should she be careful any more, on that subject at least? Besides, she would assume a stage name, so she would. Some very competent people had told her that her voice was fine, her figure good, and that she *represented* well, so she expected to meet with "some success." Then, when one has some money, other things can be arranged. When she had enough put aside, she would leave "the boards," take up a trade no doubt, get married, and would live HONORABLY. Meanwhile, she felt a real liking for me:—what a difference! She saw now that she was dealing with a "great lord." Besides, I was a gentleman—that "said it all."

*Et cetera;* I'll spare you the rest for now.

What do you think of Miss Alicia after this version?

—The devil! said Edison. The two stories make such different impressions that her words and your translation of them seem to have said two entirely different things; it's hard to imagine even a connection between them.

There was a moment of silence.

# ANALYSIS

> Hercules entered the lair of the wild Erymanthean
> boar, seized the great beast by the neck, and, drag-
> ging him out of those shadows, brought forth by
> main force under the blinding rays of the sun, the
> muddy snout of the stunned monster.
> —Greek mythology

—WELL THEN, CONTINUED Lord Ewald impassively, this was the train
of my thought, when I had finished studying the fundamental import of
this collection of phrases.

—This seems to be it, I said to myself. A young woman as luminously
beautiful as this one seems to be wholly unaware of the mysterious extent to which her body fulfills the absolute ideal of human perfection.
It's simply as a matter of business, of *trade,* that her theatrical training
enables her to interpret the inspirations of genius into mimic gestures;
those inspirations themselves she finds *hollow.* These immense, these
unique spiritual realities, real at least for all sensitive souls—she calls
them, with a vague smile, mere "poetry," "airy nothings." It's with a
blush, it's by subduing her real self, that she's able to listen to them, and
to *lower herself* (as one does to children's games) to the point of inter-
preting them.

If she were rich, her talent would be nothing but a source of amusement for her—a little less interesting, you might guess, than a game of
cards. That voice, which lays its golden enchantment on every syllable,
is nothing but an empty instrument: she sees it as a way of making a
living *less* WORTHY *than any other.* She uses it for lack of any other talent,
and as if impatient to abandon it (after she's got an easy fortune out of it).
The divine illusion of glory, the enthusiasm, the noble excitement of the
audience, are nothing for her but an infatuation of people with nothing
else to do, people for whom she thinks the great artists serve simply as
amusements.

What this woman regrets in her fault, far from being honor itself (which
for her is simply a superannuated abstraction), is simply the profit that
can be made on this capital, if it's prudently preserved.

She goes so far as to calculate the profits to be made from her fraudulent virginity if the story of her double dealing had remained unknown
in her home. She has no sense at all that regrets of this nature constitute
the only real dishonor, far more serious than a mere external accident of
the flesh. For anyone who defines herself in such a way, that accident is
an inevitable fatality, written in her temperament from the moment she
lay in her cradle.

Her total ignorance of the real nature of what she pretends or supposes
she's lost renders absolutely INSIGNIFICANT, in a word, the meaning of
this physical circumstance, either one way or the other.

When, then, was this girl actually deflowered? Was it before or after the physical event? Isn't she in fact bragging even when she talks about her "fall," since her manner of deploring this supposed fall is more impure than the fault itself? And as for her virginity, I say she never had anything to lose in this respect except a kind of nothingness, since she doesn't even have the excuse of having been in love.

Not having the faintest perception of the enormous gap which separates an abused virgin from a cheated prostitute, she confuses a simple physiological event with dishonor. She takes this event in the purely exterior and secondary sense as one which all the proprieties and conventions of society have forever, and as it were mechanically, proscribed.

For after all, suppose a girl to be seduced. If, considering her honor lost, she regretted *nothing but Honor alone*, wouldn't she be infinitely more admirable, morally, than those millions of "pure" women *who remain so only* OUT OF SELF-INTEREST?

She thus places herself within the immense crowd of women whose careful calculations relate to honor as caricature does to a human face— women who would cheerfully define honor as "a sort of luxury that only the rich can afford, but that other people can always buy when they have the price." What this signifies is simply that their own honor was always up for bids, however loudly they protested to the contrary. Such ladies instantly recognize one another by their language, and will say to one another with a sigh when they hear of some unfortunate, "What a shame the poor child *turned out* so badly!" Alicia, you may be sure, would know how to attract this sort of monstrous compassion, and would even be secretly flattered by it—the reproach amounting, with a conscience of this sort, to nothing more than having been an inexperienced dupe, having made a bad bargain as a result of insufficient practice.

She lacks a sense of shame to the point where she made me listen to things like this. Not one last remnant of feminine tact warns her that, simply from the point of view of calculated self-interest, she is erasing from my soul all traces of sympathy, all admiration for her! Her moral clumsiness is like ice on my heart. How can it be? This stunning beauty is the habitation of such appalling moral misery! I cannot understand it. In a word, this woman is of such a cynical candor, and so unconscious of it, that I can express my disdain only by leaving her—since, as I've said, I'm not one of those who can submit to accepting a body while they reject the soul.

A natural response would thus have been to give her a thousand guineas, which would have rendered her quite indifferent to the eternal farewell that accompanied them.

# HYPOTHESIS

Oh thou! . . . etc. . . .
—The poets

—Accordingly, I was about to renounce Miss Alicia and give her up on the spot, Lord Ewald continued, when a sudden misgiving caused me to hesitate. When Alicia stopped talking, her face, no longer clouded by the shadow rising from her silly and dishonest words, her features, I say, like those of a marble divinity, remained a flat contradiction of her previous speech.

With a person who was very beautiful, but in the range of *ordinary* perfections, I might not have felt this inexplicable sensation that I experienced with Miss Alicia Clary. With some other person, a trifle, a mere glance—the expression of her features, the stiffness of her hair, the texture of her skin, the movement of her hands, anything of that sort might have reminded me of her hidden nature. A thousand imperceptible signs! And I would have . . . recognized her identity with her self!

But here, let me tell you again, the non-correspondence of the physical and the intellectual made itself felt constantly, and in the proportions of a paradox. Her beauty, I assure you, was beyond reproach, defying the subtlest analysis. From the outside, and from the brow to the feet, a sort of Venus Anadyomene; within, a personality absolutely FOREIGN to this body. Imagine, if you will, this abstraction brought to life: a bourgeois Goddess.

I came thus to believe that all the laws of physiology had been overturned in this living hybrid—or else, just possibly, that I was in the presence of a being whose grief and pride had overflowed all measure, and who deliberately denied her own nature in a spirit of ultimate bitterness, absolute disdain. In a word, it seemed to me impossible to understand this woman without attributing to her some sort of lyric sentimentalism like the following.

Lord Ewald, after collecting himself for a moment, continued:

—While still trembling from the terrible, frightful, irreparable wrong that had been done her—she hardened her soul to that mood of icy scorn which the first experience of betrayal engenders in noble minds. A mistrust so black that some people never recover from it led her to conceal a devastating irony behind that blank exterior on the assumption that no man could possibly conceive the depths of her despair.

She must have said to herself:—Since the appetite for mere sensations seems to have destroyed every noble sentiment among these new human beings (whose faces are all turned to the ground like beasts, but among whom I see I have to exist for a little while), this young man who talks to me of tenderness and divine passion must be exactly like the other ephemeral creatures of the age. He's bound to think on the same level as the others who've taken refuge in mere sensualism, and think they can measure every grief with an empty sarcasm—too concerned with trying to live even to imagine that there may be griefs which are literally inconsolable. He says he loves me! Is anybody capable of loving anymore? The fevers of youth burn within him; an instant's pleasure will dissipate them. If I listened to him tonight, he would leave me tomorrow, more desolate than ever . . . No, no! Before I listen again to hope, wrapped as I still am in my first grief, let me take a little counsel from that first bitter experience. First of all, I must make sure that he too isn't reciting a role for my benefit; since I don't expect to give anyone the right to smile at a grief from which I suffer through my entire being, and above all don't want my lover to suppose I've forgotten the past.

All I have left is my own integrity; let everything else perish rather than that. I must be unforgettable in the thought of that man who will be the chosen companion of my fallen grandeur. No, I will never deliver myself up, either in a kiss or by a word, to this new stranger until I am sure I can be received by him to whom I give myself. If his passionate words mask nothing but a trifling fancy—well, let him keep them along with those presents of his which I accept with careful indifference, only because I am wearied with his much too ingenious urgencies. I want to be loved as no one is loved these days! Not simply because of my beauty, but because I understand my own misfortune.

All the rest is vanity. Like the marble divinity I resemble, my only duty is to make those who approach me feel (and forever, forever) how exceptional I am. To the task, then! I must be exactly like their women, the gross average women who pass in the street. Let none of the light with which I was born ever gleam in my eyes! Let every word I speak be smeared over with mediocrity, with nullity! If you are an actress, let this be your first creation. Put on your mask; you play to an audience of yourself. If you are a superlative artist, here your triumph will be, not glory, but love. Assume that ignoble role in which most women of this century undertake to parody their own natures, under the pretext that FASHION constrains them to it.

This, then, will be the test. If he persists, in spite of that utter poverty of spirit which I will ruthlessly feign, if he still persists in his pretense of love, that will prove *he's no more worthy of me than of any other female*, and that I represent to his appetites nothing but a sum of pleasures, nothing but a momentary intoxication like that of wine—and, in short, that *if he really knew my essential nature, he would consider it ridiculous.*

Then I would say to him: Off with you, go to one of those other women, the only sort you can love, those who are dead to all feeling for another destiny. Be gone!

If, on the other hand, he were to leave me, without even trying to capture my real self—if he goes off in despair, he too, but without even having had the idea of profaning the dream that I will have inspired in him, that he will never lose—then, at that sign, I will recognize *that he is of my country!* I will sense that indefinite quality which is the only serious thing on earth, it will appear in his eyes, wet with sacred tears! I will know that he merits all my devotion, and a few moments then will suffice to raise us—ah, to the seventh heaven!

Meanwhile, if the test reveals in him the lie I suspect, if I see myself condemned to solitude, well, so be it, welcome solitude! And already I feel myself revived by voices more splendid than those of the senses and the heart. I shall be betrayed no more! Art alone erases the past and liberates me for the future. Dismissing, therefore, those *so-called real* attachments to the earth, I shall transcend myself without the least regret into those undying imaginary beings created by Genius, and bring them to life with my mysterious song. They will be my only companions, my only friends, my only sisters. And then perhaps some great poet will appear, as there was for Maria Malibran, who will immortalize my beauty, my voice, my soul, my ashes! Thus I shall bury my grief in the light, and disappear into those regions of the Ideal to which the insults of humanity can never attain.

—Deuce take it! said Edison.

—Yes, resumed Lord Ewald, such was the *impossible* inner life with which, in an effort to understand this woman, I tried to endow her. You see now that, to be worthy of such an inner life, she must have been prodigiously, amazingly beautiful, don't you?

—In fact, my friend, you make clear to me that a lord may well be called Byron! Edison replied with a smile. And you must take disillusion remarkably hard if you resorted to all this impractical poetry rather than admit the banal reality. Come now, isn't this bundle of sentiment the stuff of grand opera? What woman could ever think it all up, outside of a few creatures on the far limits of mysticism? One doesn't run a fever of this sort except for a deity.

—My dear and subtle confidant, I recognized, myself, though too late, that this was a sphinx without an enigma; I'm a dreamer who's already undergone his punishment.

—But, said Edison, why are you still in love with her, after analyzing her to this point?

—Ah, because waking up doesn't always bring with it forgetfulness of the dream, and man shackles himself with links of his own imaginings! Lord Ewald replied. This is what happened.

Lost in the fantasy with which I enwreathed my love, she and I soon belonged to one another. Then, what evidence was necessary to prove to me that the actress—*wasn't really acting!* The day when I finally recognized this fact irrevocably, I resolved at once to free myself of this phantom. But the bonds of beauty are strong and deep. I was ignorant of their intrinsic power, when, falling victim to my own fantasy, I ventured into this passion. They had already sunk deep into my flesh when, disillusioned forever, I tried to shake them off. I woke up, a little like Gulliver in Lilliput, held down by a million strings. Then I felt myself lost indeed.

Burned by the embraces of Alicia, my native energies had weakened. During my long sleep, Delilah had cut off my hair. Rather than abandon the body, like a man of courage, I shrouded my soul; I fell silent.

Never has she suspected the transports of hideous rage that have coursed through my veins on her account. How many times have I come close to destroying both her and myself! A forbidden indulgence, a mere mirage, has thus linked me helplessly to this marvelous dead shape! Alas! Miss Alicia now represents for me nothing but a habitual presence, and I swear to God that it would be impossible for me to possess her.

At this speech, at the light which gleamed in the young man's eyes as he pronounced the last phrase, Edison gave a mysterious start. But he remained silent.

—Thus it is, Lord Ewald concluded, that she and I exist together yet at the same time are separated.

# DISSECTION

> Fools are unpardonable for this, that they render men indulgent to evil.
>
> —Jean Marras

L ORD EWALD HAD fallen silent.

—Would you be good enough, my lord, to define a few points for me? Everything here bears on a few subtleties, which are in themselves of some interest. For example: Miss Alicia Clary wouldn't be a . . . a *stupid* woman, would she?

—Certainly not, Lord Ewald responded with a melancholy smile. There's not a trace in her of that almost sacred stupidity which, because it's an extreme, has become almost as rare as intelligence. A woman who's lost all her stupidity, can she be anything but a monster? What is more depressing, more debilitating, than that hateful creature they call a "clever woman"—unless, perhaps, it's her counterpart, the man who "talks well"? Cleverness, in the social sense, is always the enemy of intelligence. Wouldn't you agree that a collected, believing, modest, and slightly *stupid* woman, who with her marvelous instinct divines the sense of a phrase as if through a veil of light, is a supreme treasure and a true companion, to exactly the same extent that the other woman is an anti-social scourge?

Miss Alicia, now, like every other mediocre being, is far from being *stupid*. She's simply *foolish*. Her dream would be to appear before the world as a "clever woman," because of the "brilliant" reputation, the special advantages, that she thinks such a reputation would give her.

This rabid housewife would enjoy the mask of a clever woman like a new hairdo, as an agreeable way to pass the time, but she would think it not very *serious*. And thus she would find a way to remain mediocre, even in her pursuit of this flat and perverted ideal.

—What form does her foolishness take in everyday life? Edison asked.

—She is afflicted, replied Lord Ewald, with that form of pretended good sense which is negative and derisive, which cuts everything down as far as possible, which comments only on the most insignificant realities, those which the devotees of this manner call the concerns of common sense. As if real living people could possibly devote their entire lives to such boring and obvious considerations about which we can reach agreement with an absolute minimum of speech!

There's a deep but hidden correspondence between certain people and these non-topics, a kind of reciprocal attraction or instinctive magnetism that draws them together. One calls to the other, they are attracted, they draw together, and mingle. From this sort of commerce they get no sustenance; on the contrary, those who engage in it rot inwardly and perish of the natural vulgarity in which they smother. From the physiological point of view, these cases of inept positivism, which are becoming so common nowadays, are nothing but bizarre forms of hypochondria. It's a variety of mental disorder which leads the victims to repeat, even in their sleep, "important"-sounding words, which seem to give "weight" and substance to life *simply by being repeated.* For example, the words *"serious! positive! good sense!"* and so forth, when repeated *at random*, without any particular application. Our maniacs imagine, and sometimes rightly, that the simple articulation of these syllables confers on anyone who enunciates them a certificate of mental capacity. So that they soon acquire the lucrative and mechanical habit of continually pronouncing these vocables—and this practice before long steeps them thoroughly in the mindless hysteria with which the words are soaked. The most astonishing thing is that they then acquire dupes of their own, that they succeed in gaining official power in different states, when in fact their smug, smiling, silent nullity merits nothing but the asylum. Well then, the soul of this woman whom I love, alas! is twin sister to those I've described. In everyday life, Miss Alicia is the Goddess Reason.

—Good! said Edison. Next step. If I've understood you correctly, Miss Alicia is not a *pretty* woman?

—Certainly not! said Lord Ewald. Believe me, if she was nothing but the prettiest of women I wouldn't pay so much attention to her, not for a minute. You know the saying: Love of the beautiful is horror of the pretty. Just a moment ago I spontaneously tried to give you an idea of her by recalling the stunning form of *Venus Victorious*. Well, a simple question: any man who found the *Venus Victorious* to be "pretty" wouldn't be intelligible, would he? Any human creature capable of sustaining, even for an instant, the weight of serious comparison with such a statue couldn't possibly evoke in any healthy mind the sort of impression that's left by the sight of what we call a "pretty woman." In the qualities that are really at issue here, she's as much her contrary as the most hideous of the

Eumenides. You could arrange their three types at the apexes of an isosceles triangle.

The only misfortune that has befallen Miss Alicia is thought! . . . If she were deprived of all thought, I could understand her. The marble *Venus*, in fact, *has nothing to do with thinking*. The goddess is veiled in stone and silence. From her appearance comes this word: "I am Beauty, complete and alone. I speak only through the spirit of him who looks at me. In my absolute simplicity all thought defeats itself since it loses its limits. All thoughts sink together in me, confused, indistinct, identical, like the ripples on rivers as they enter the sea. For him who reflects me, I am the deeper character he assigns me."

This meaning of the statue, which *Venus Victorious* expresses with her contours, Miss Alicia Clary, standing on the sand beside the ocean, might inspire as her model—if she kept her mouth shut and closed her eyes. But how to understand a Venus Victorious who has found her arms again in the dark night of time, and reappears in the middle of the human race—only to bend on the devoted world that comes to pay her its passionate homage the dull, sly, crafty eye of a would-be matron, whose mind is nothing but the marketplace where all the ghosts of that false common sense we just denounced assemble solemnly to perform their boring chaffer?

—Good, said Edison. Next question. Miss Alicia is not an *artist*, is she?

—My God! cried Lord Ewald. I should say not. Didn't I tell you she was a performer, a virtuoso? And isn't a virtuoso the direct and mortal enemy of Genius, and so, by direct consequence, of Art itself?

Art, as you know, has no more connection with virtuosity than Genius has with Talent; the differences are in fact beyond all measurement.

The only living souls who deserve the name of Artists are the creators, those who awaken impressions that are immense, unknown, and sublime. The others? . . . who cares? The followers and imitators may pass; but these virtuosos who come to pretty up, but really to enfeeble, the divine work of Genius? There are wretches in the art of music, for example, whose whole talent is to "weave a thousand variations," a "set of brilliant fantasies" till the Last Judgment sounds. What a stench of monkeys! Haven't you sometimes seen one of these types after a long concert run two fingers through his long hair and gaze mournfully up at the ceiling as evidence of his inspiration? Such puppets make one feel ashamed; they seem to have souls only metaphorically, as we speak of the soul of a violin.—Well, that's the sort of soul Miss Alicia has! . . . But, being essentially mediocre, she lacks even that bastard instinct which makes the virtuosos think that music is beautiful—though they have less right to say so than the deafest of the deaf. But she, when she talks of her supernatural voice, of her delicate inflections, of the shadings and timbres of her song, she says she has "a gift for pleasing." She thinks people a little "crazy" to be interested in such things. Enthusiasm always stirs her to a bit of pity, because she thinks it inappropriate for *people of distinc-*

*tion.* And in this way, as you observe, she has found a way to refine on the foolishness and complacency even of the virtuosos. When she sings herself, thanks to various requests on my part (for singing bores her, being nothing but *drudgery at a trade for which she was never intended, alas!),*—she often stops suddenly, if admiration makes me close my eyes, to say "that she *really doesn't understand how a gentleman can get so excited over these airy nothings,* when he should be thinking of the *dignity befitting his station in life!"* You see: it's a simple case of mental rickets.

—She isn't a *good* woman? Edison asked.

—How could she be, since she's a fool? said Lord Ewald. One's only good when one's stupid. Oh, I could have understood a criminal, a vicious, a sinister person, with the depraved tastes of a Roman empress—yes, and preferred such a character a thousand times over. But, without being good, she has none of these wild appetites, born at least from a deep sense of pride. Good, you ask? No. Not the least trace in her of that sublime goodness which transfigures all ugliness and lays its blessed balm on every wound.

Mediocre above all, she's not even wicked; she's silly in her goodness, as she's niggardly rather than miserly; always foolishly, never stupidly. She has that instinctive hypocrisy of hearts which are weak and dry as punkwood, so that she's no more worthy of the kindnesses she renders than of those she receives. When a kindness is done out of foolish sentimentality, doesn't that double one's sense of its bitter irrelevance? Listen, my dear Edison: One evening at the theater I was watching Miss Alicia Clary while we were attending some melodrama or other, sprung from the pen of one of those phrase-forgers, one of those literary brigands who with their jargon-mongering and their banal fictions, their stale jests and grimaces, murder in their audiences all sense of moral elevation—much to their own self-satisfaction and profit! Well, I watched the admirable eyes of this woman fill with tears as a result of the abject dialogue on stage! And I watched her weep as one would watch rain fall. Morally speaking, I would have preferred raindrops; but physically—there's no denying it, even if one would—even such tears as those, on those cheeks, were splendid. Her tears bathed her diamonds in new splendor; they rolled down that sublime, pale face, behind which, nevertheless, there was nothing but emptyheaded foolishness in a slight state of agitation! So that in the end I could only admire gloomily this simpleminded exudation of animality.

—Excellent, said Edison. Miss Alicia, I take it, is not without some sort of religious affiliation?

—Not at all, said Lord Ewald. I rather indulged myself in analyzing the religiosity of this disturbing woman. She is a believer—not through the revivifying love of a Divine Redeemer, but because that's the conventional thing and it's very much "the thing to be." When she comes from church on Sunday morning, the way she holds her prayer book quite resembles on another level the way she tells me "that I'm a gentleman"; the implications of it make me blush. And so she believes in a God of enlightened and comprehensible sublimity. She populates her paradise with martyrs who never exaggerate anything, with the Respectable Elect, with saints on their best behavior, with well-trained virgins and sensible cherubim. She believes in heaven, but a heaven of rational dimensions!— Her ideal would be a completely *commonplace* heaven, for the sun itself seems to her too much "in the clouds," too airy and abstract.

She finds the phenomenon of death very shocking; it is an excess that she doesn't quite understand; "not quite the way we do things nowadays." That's about the sum of her religious ideas. To sum up, what's disconcerting in her is the fact of that almost superhuman beauty covering as with a sacred veil that character of dull moderation, that vulgarity of mind, that exclusive and almost feebleminded consideration for nothing but the *exterior* values attached to Wealth, Faith, Love, and Art—that is, for nothing but what is vain and illusory in them. It is this shrinking of the spirit, in a word, which recalls the results obtained by the natives who live by the banks of the Orinoco, when they bind the skulls of their children between boards to keep them from ever being able to think of things which are too lofty. Clothe this basic character in a measure of placid complacency, and you have more or less a just impression of the character of Miss Alicia Clary.

After a silence, Lord Ewald continued.—I say, then, that the simple spectacle of this woman has killed my joy. When I look at her and listen to her, she gives me the sensation of a temple profaned, not by rebellion, impiety, and barbarism with their bloody torches, but by greedy ostentation, timid hypocrisy, empty and mechanical fidelity, unconscious coldness of heart, a superstition of unbelief—and in addition by the renegade priestess of the temple itself. For her, the goddess of the temple is beneath blasphemy, hardly worth a smile; and yet she continues to recite the empty legend to me, interminably, and always in the same flat, complacent tone of voice.

—Before we conclude, said Edison, didn't you tell me that, in spite of her lack of vibrations, she was a girl of good family?

An imperceptible flush rose in the cheeks of Lord Ewald at these words.

—I? I don't recall saying any such thing, he replied.

—You said that Miss Alicia Clary belonged "to some good family of Scottish origin, recently ennobled."

—Ah, to be sure, said Lord Ewald. But that's another matter. It's not even a form of praise; on the contrary. In this century, one must *be*—or be *born*—noble; the days are long gone when one could *become* so. Nobility is conferred in our countries, nowadays, with a grimace. And we think it can only be harmful to certain bloodlines, strong though they may be to start with, if they are inoculated carelessly with this dubious and feeble vaccine, which has done nothing but poison so many confirmed and unshakable bourgeois.

And, as if sunk in secret reflections, he added very softly, with a grave smile:

—Perhaps that's even the *cause* of it, after all.

Edison, with the aristocracy of his genius (a kind of quite special nobility which will always humiliate the egalitarians), replied smilingly:

—The fact is, one doesn't become a racehorse simply by making an appearance at the track. Only, the most remarkable thing that results from all this analysis is that you don't perceive that this woman *would be the absolute feminine ideal for three-quarters of modern humanity!* Ah, what a pleasant existence any one of a million men would lead with such a mistress, given that he were rich, handsome, and young like you!

—It's killing me, said Lord Ewald as if to himself. And, on your analogy, perhaps that's what constitutes the difference between a thoroughbred and a plow-horse.

# CONFRONTATION

Under his heavy hood of lead, the sinner spoke but
this one word: "I can no more!"
—Dante, *Inferno*

ABRUPTLY LORD EWALD cried out, yielding to some youthful aggravation which he had hitherto repressed:

—Ah! Who will deliver this soul out of this body for me? You would think she was some dreadful mistake of the Creator's! I never supposed my heart would be locked in the pillory of this freak. Did I ever ask for so much beauty at the price of so much misery? Never. I'm entitled to complain. A girl with a simple, natural heart, with lively features, lit by warm and honest eyes—I would have accepted life with her; I wouldn't have wearied my spirit over her. I would have loved her in all simplicity and directness, as people do.—But this woman! . . . Ah, there's no cure for it. What right does anyone so beautiful have to be so devoid of spirit? By what right is this unparalleled form able to appeal at the deepest level of my spirit, to some sublime emotion—only to destroy my faith in it? My eyes are constantly imploring her, "Betray me if you will, but exist! Live up to the spirit of your own beauty!"—and she never understands me. It is as if a God were to appear in person before a worshipper in the act of invocation, his spirit full of adoration, fervor, and ecstasy; and the God, bending down to his worshipper, would say gently to him, "I do not exist." Such an event would be no more incomprehensible to me than is this woman.

I'm not a lover, I'm a prisoner; my despair is limitless. The pleasures that this living morbus has accorded me were more bitter than death itself. Her kiss rouses me to nothing but thoughts of suicide. Indeed, that is the only way out for me now.

Lord Ewald, relaxing from his paroxysm of grief, finally resumed his normal tone.

—We traveled. Thoughts and feelings change sometimes as one crosses the frontiers. I don't know exactly what I had hoped for; a surprise of some sort, a healthful diversion. Though she never knew it, I was treating her like an invalid.

Well, neither Germany nor Italy, neither the steppes of Russia nor the splendors of Spain nor the beauties of youthful America could stir or distract or interest this mysterious creature. She looked with a jealous eye on the masterpieces of art, which she thought deprived her for a moment of my total attention; she never understood that she herself constituted a part of the beauty of these masterpieces, and that they were so many mirrors that I was setting before her.

In Switzerland, watching the sun rise on Monte Rosa, she cried (and with a smile quite as enchanting as that sunrise on the snow), "Ah, I don't really like mountains, they're so oppressive."

In Florence, before the marvels of the age of Leo X, she yawned discreetly and murmured, "Yes, it's all quite interesting, isn't it?"

In Germany, when she heard some Wagner, she said, "But there's no tune you can follow in all that music! It's quite insane!"

One of her tricks is to call anything which isn't simply silly or base "the stars."

So at every moment I hear her murmuring, in her divine voice, "Anything you choose, but, please, not *the stars!* You see for yourself, my lord, it's not *serious.*"

That's her favorite formula, which she repeats mechanically, expressing in this simple refrain nothing but her native instinct to debase anything which rises above the humblest level of the earth.

"Love" is one of those words which have the power to make her smile, and I swear she would wink derisively at it if her sublime features answered to the grimace she makes in her soul—since she does apparently have a soul. And I have confirmed that she does have one, *in those rare and terrible instants when she seemed to have some dark instinctive fright of her own marvelous body.*

Once in Paris this extraordinary event took place. Questioning my own eyes, unsure of my reason, I got the idea—sacrilegious, even crazy, I agree—of confronting this living despondency with the great marble who is, as I told you, her image—the *Venus Victorious* herself. I simply wanted to see what this insufferable woman would say in such a presence. One day, then, I took her, half-playfully, to the Louvre, telling her, "My dear Alicia, I'm going to give you a little surprise." We passed through the corridors, and I put her without further preparation in the presence of the eternal statue.

This time Miss Alicia raised her veil. She looked at the statue with a certain surprise; then, amazed, she cried aloud childishly:

—Look, it's *me!*

The next moment, she added:

—Yes, but I have arms, and besides I'm more distinguished looking.

She shivered; her hand, which had dropped my arm to seek support from a railing, returned, and she said to me in an undertone:

—These stones . . . these walls . . . It's cold here; let's go away.

Once outdoors, as she still remained silent, I had some undefined expectation of an extraordinary word from her. And in fact I was not disappointed. Miss Alicia, still following out the train of her thought, drew me close and then said:

—*Well, if they spend all that money on this statue—then—I may do well too!*

I swear, her words made my head spin. Folly, inflated to celestial proportions, seemed to me like an eternal curse. Not knowing how to answer her, I bowed.

—I certainly hope so, I told her. And I took her home. That duty done, I returned to the Louvre.

I reentered the holy hall; and after a single glance at the goddess, whose form contains the starry night—ah, for the only time in my life, I felt my heart swell with one of the most mysterious sobs that ever stifled a mortal man.

So it is that this mistress, an animated dualism who repels and attracts me simultaneously, holds me to her by that very process, as the two poles of this magnet attract by their contradictory impulses a bit of steel.

Yet I am not capable by nature of submitting for long to the attractions (however powerful they may be) of one whom I half-despise. Love into which no sentiment enters, where no intelligence mingles with mere sensation, seems to me an insult to myself. My conscience cries out that such love is a prostitution of the heart. The bitter thoughts to which this *first love* has given rise have inspired me with a profound distaste for all women, and sunk me in the depths of an incurable melancholy.

My passion, which began as a craze for the figure, the voice, the perfume, and the EXTERIOR charm of this woman, has become absolutely platonic. To think of her as mistress would *revolt* me nowadays. I am attached to her by nothing more than a kind of painful admiration. What I really would like would be to see Miss Alicia dead, if death didn't result in the effacing of all human features. In a word, the presence of her form, even as an illusion, would satisfy my stunned indifference, since nothing can render this woman worthy of love.

In response to her pleas, I have decided to put her on the London stage—which means, in other words, *that I no longer care to live.*

For the moment, just to show myself that I wasn't completely useless on this earth, I have come to greet and shake your hand, before removing myself for good . . .

That is my story. You asked for it. You see there is no help for me. Your hand now, and farewell.

# REMONSTRATIONS

There's no way to *re-possess* oneself from this trouble.
—Montaigne

—MY DEAR COUNT EWALD, said Edison slowly, what's all this? Over a woman? Or not even that; over such a woman! You? I feel as if I were dreaming!

—So do I, replied Lord Ewald with a sad and wintry smile. But just imagine. This woman was for me like one of those clear springs which in sunny countries rise in the shadows of ancient forests, exquisite in their murmurings. If, some summer day, you are carried away by the beauty of their deadly ripples and drop into them a leaf, still green and young and vital, it will be turned to stone when you take it out.

—You're right, said Edison thoughtfully. And as he watched the young man, he distinctly saw the thought of suicide moving through the deep, withdrawn gaze of Lord Ewald.

—My lord, he said, you've fallen prey to a youthful ailment which cures itself. Have you forgotten that everything, sooner or later, is forgotten?

—Oh, said Lord Ewald, replacing his monocle, do you take me for just another fickle fellow? My character and my inner nature are so formed that even as I recognize the absurdity of this "passion," I still remain subject to its enchantment, its power, its grief. I know where I've been hit. The wound is mortal. And now, my friend, since I've made my confession, let's say no more of it.

Edison raised his head and studied for a few moments this pale and, alas, too noble young man, as a surgeon studies a patient who's been declared incurable.

He reflected; he hesitated. You would have said he was assembling his thoughts and his energies for some strange, unimaginable project.

—Come now, he said, let's take stock. You are one of the most brilliant lords in Britain. You know there are companions for you who could light up every pleasure in life, girls of radiant beauty whose love is given but once and forever; yes, consecrated hearts, creatures of the rising sun and of ideal perfection. And on your part, my lord, you who are possessed of such a subtle intelligence, who have nobility, energy, wealth, any sort of splendid future you choose to pursue—here you are, without help or recourse against this woman. At a word, at a sign, thousands of others, just as handsome as this one, will spring up before you! Among them, there will be let us say a hundred charming creatures, who will leave behind them nothing but happy thoughts and warm memories. And of that hundred, say, there will be ten with devoted hearts and flawless reputations; and among them, again, one woman to carry your name for life—for there is always one Hypermnestra among every fifty Danaids.

Thanks to this woman, if you look forward across thirty or forty years of expanding and exalted delight—the delights of every day—you can imagine yourself looking back over a really splendid life, leaving to England a sturdy stock of children, proud of your name and worthy of your blood. And you now, like a spoiled child, would reject this rich garner of delight that destiny offers you, and this future for which sons of Eve by the thousands would risk their lives or wear them out in endless struggles—you would throw away this heritage, abdicate your position, abandon existence, simply because of a passing female whom accident chose out of five million others exactly like her to destroy your future. You take this shadowy creature in all seriousness, though in a few years her memory will be for you like nothing so much as those black and stupefying smoke clouds that rise from the pipes of hashish smokers. Will you allow me to say it? If Miss Alicia Clary instinctively prefers the penny to the guinea, her influence seems to have been contagious for you—and that, let me say, is a real misfortune.

—My friend, replied Lord Ewald, don't be so hard on me, since I'm much harder on myself than you are, and to no avail.

—I'm speaking in the name of the young woman who will be your salvation, Edison persisted. To whom are you leaving her? One is responsible for the evil that flows from the good one has failed to do.

—I tell you again, I've thought of many others, Lord Ewald replied, but it's in my nature to love only once. In my family, if one is afflicted, one disappears, without condolences or discussions. That's it; we leave the "subtleties" and the "compromises" to other men.

Edison seemed to be measuring in his mind the extent of the disease.

—Yes, he murmured, as if to himself, it's a bad situation, it really is! The devil! What the devil!

Then, as if on a sudden impulse:

—My dear lord, he said, as I am perhaps the only doctor on earth who can do much for your cure, I demand, in the name of my gratitude to you, a positive, definitive answer to this question. Once and for all, do you tell me that you can never consider this affair of yours—which is uncommon only for you—as one of those worldly incidents, passionate if you will, maybe even intense in its feelings, but without the slightest vital significance for you?

—Miss Alicia Clary may become tomorrow, and for many other men, an evening's diversion; that's perfectly possible. But as for me, I shall never recover. At life's deepest level, I see nothing but her form.

—Despising her as you do, you persist in immolating yourself on her beauty—quite idealistically it appears, since you have told me your feeling for her has become remote and frigid?

—Remote and frigid; yes, that's how it is, replied Lord Ewald. I feel no more desire for her. She is the radiant obsession of my spirit, that is all. I feel myself possessed by her, as the sorcerers of the Middle Ages used to say.

—You deliberately refuse to reenter the life of society, then?

—I do indeed, said Lord Ewald, rising from his chair. And on that note, my dear Edison, let me urge you to flourish, to enjoy your fame, to be useful to the human race! I must leave you. Achilles, they say, died of a wound in the heel. And now, for the last time, farewell. I have no right to waste in idle and personal chatter any more of those hours which are so precious for humanity.

So saying, Lord Ewald, still cool and collected, took up his hat, which he had placed over the tube of a huge telescope by his side.

But Edison rose also.

—Come now, he cried, do you suppose I'm going to sit by and let you blow out your brains without trying to save your life, when I owe you my own life and everything that goes with it? Do you suppose I asked all those questions out of idle curiosity? My lord, you are one of those invalids who can only be cured with poison; I thought it my duty therefore to try all the arguments I could, before deciding to minister to you, if you agree, in a terrible and sinister manner; for your case is completely exceptional. The remedy consists of *fulfilling your wishes!* (Devil take me, the engineer murmured to himself, if I ever expected to make this first experiment with you as the subject!) Some characters and circumstances are bound to intersect; very likely I was actually expecting you this evening—without knowing it, of course. Well, now I see it all; I must try to save your existence. And as there are some wounds that one can heal only by deepening them and making them worse, *I want to fulfill your dream in its entirety!* My lord Ewald, didn't you cry out just now, when you were talking of her, "Who will deliver this soul out of this body for me?"

—I did, murmured Lord Ewald, somewhat taken aback.

—All right, then! I'LL DO IT.

—You . . . you . . . how?

—But you, my lord, Edison interrupted in a tone of sharp solemnity. Never forget that in accomplishing your dark desire, I yield . . . only to Necessity.

# BOOK II

# The Pact

# WHITE MAGIC

Beware! By playing the phantom you become one!
—Precept of the Kabbalah

THE TONE AND GLANCE with which the electrician accompanied these words made his listener tremble. He stared questioningly at the great man.

Was Edison in his right mind after all? What he had just suggested outstripped all understanding. The best thing would be to await further explanation.

Still, an irresistible magnetic force flowed from those last words of his. Lord Ewald felt it, despite himself, and sensed that some prodigious experience was about to be unveiled. Turning from Edison, he cast his eyes silently over the array of objects around him.

And under the eerie electric lights, which cast over everything a frightful pallor, these various objects, like monsters risen from a scientific underworld, assumed disturbing and startling aspects. The laboratory seemed, positively, a place of magic; within it, the natural could only be the extraordinary. Besides, Lord Ewald reflected, the greater part of his friend's discoveries were still unknown, and the paradoxical quality of those he had heard about surrounded Edison in his eyes with a kind of intellectual halo within which the man himself appeared as at a diminished center.

For him, Edison was like an inhabitant of the distant kingdom of Electricity.

After some time he felt himself overcome by a complex of feelings, within which he could strangely distinguish curiosity, stupefaction, and a mysterious hope of something *New*. The vitality of his entire being seemed raised to new powers.

—It's a simple question, said Edison, of . . . *transubstantiation*. But I have a number of steps to take at once.—On the main point . . . do you accept?

—What you said was serious?

—Of course. Do you accept my offer?

—I do indeed; and I give you a free hand, said Lord Ewald with a melancholy smile, already turning a little bitter.

—All right, said Edison, glancing at the electric clock over the doorway. I'll begin immediately, right? Time is precious, and I need three weeks.

—Is that all? I'll give you a month, said Lord Ewald.

—I don't need it; in matters of time I'm always on the dot. Let's say it's now eight twenty-five. At this very hour and this very place twenty-one days from today, Miss Alicia Clary will appear before you, not simply transfigured, not just made the most enchanting of companions, nor merely lifted to the most sublime level of spirituality, but actually endowed with a sort of immortality. In a word, the present gorgeous little fool will no longer be a woman, but an angel; no longer a mistress but a lover; no longer reality, but the IDEAL!

Lord Ewald look upon the inventor with an astonishment not untinged with fear.

—Oh, I will explain to you all my procedures! continued the latter. The result is so marvelous by itself that I have no fear of spoiling its deep splendors by submitting them to scientific analysis. You will never be disillusioned. Indeed, just to reassure you on the perfect lucidity of my mind, I'll put you in possession of my secret this very night. But, first of all, to work! The explanations will emerge, as the work progresses, of their own accord. But first, if I recall correctly, Miss Alicia Clary is now in New York, at the Opera, is that right?

—Yes.

—What's the number of her box?

—Number seven.

—You didn't explain to her where you were going or why you were leaving her alone?

—She wouldn't have been interested, so I said nothing.

—Has she ever heard my name?

—Perhaps . . . but she forgot it.

—Excellent! said Edison, meditatively; this was very important.

Going to the phonograph, he lifted the needle, examined the track till he found the passage he wanted, replaced the needle, set the machine in front of the telephone, and flicked a switch.

—Martin, are you there? the phonograph said to the telephone.

There was no answer.

—So that's it! The rascal is taking a nap; I bet he's snoring! Edison grumbled, with a smile.

He set to his ear the receiver of a supersensitive microphone.

—Exactly, he said, that's it. When he's had his grog, after dessert, he feels he deserves a siesta—and to keep from being interrupted, the rogue takes the receiver off the hook.

—How far away is this person you're calling? asked Lord Ewald.

—Oh, just in New York, at my Broadway office, Edison replied absentmindedly.

—What! you can hear a man snoring twenty-five leagues away?

—I could hear him from the North Pole! said Edison, especially the way he's snoring now. Do you think any character in your fairytales could venture to say as much without provoking the children to cry out, in disgust at the absurdity of the story, "Oh, no! not that! That's impossible!" But I can do it now, and tomorrow nobody will be surprised at it. Fortunately, I've foreseen the present incident; I have a shocking little arrangement over there . . . But, no, that's too much; I won't punish him with a spark.—Wait, there's an Aerophone by my bedside, connected with this telephone over here. That'll make a noise to rouse him, and the whole neighborhood as well.

So saying, he applied another apparatus to the phonograph.

—I just hope the horses in the street outside aren't making too much racket, he murmured.

The phonograph repeated its question.

Three seconds later, the deep voice of a man just roused abruptly from sleep seemed to come out of the hat which Lord Ewald was holding in his hand and which happened to be touching a speaker hanging near the young man.

—Huh? What? Where's the fire? cried the voice, in frightened tones.

—There, now, said Edison, with a chuckle, our man seems to be up.

He picked up the speaker of the first telephone, into which he now spoke himself.

—No, Martin, that's not it, my friend. The temperature on the automatic fire alarm is just sixty-seven degrees; you needn't worry on that score. I just want you to deliver, immediately and by hand, the message that I'll be sending you in a minute.

—I'm standing by for it, Mr. Edison, said the voice, more calmly now.

Already the electrician was tapping out, in quick bursts of code, a message on the Morse transmitter that stood on a pedestal by his side.

—Do you read me? he asked by way of the telephone.

—Right! I'll carry it myself, came the reply.

And, thanks to a gesture either accidental or joking, by the engineer who had his hand on the central control panel of the laboratory, this speech seemed to come from all the corners of the room at once, from a dozen different speakers. You would have thought twelve distinct individuals were reciting exactly the same words in perfect unison within the room. Lord Ewald looked around him, in search of them.

—Give me the answer right away! Edison added, in the tone of voice one uses to catch a man who's running away.

Then, turning toward the young lord:

—Everything's in order, he said.

He stopped, looked at him fixedly, then addressed him coldly, and in a manner rendered particularly emphatic by his sudden change of tone.

—My lord, said he, I should warn you that we are now going to depart together from the domains of everyday life—domains inadequately understood, no doubt, but too much frequented, as you'll no doubt agree. Indeed, we are going to leave the realm of Life properly so called, and penetrate another world of phenomena which will surprise and even astound you. I will give you a key to understanding their linkage. But to explain to you exactly the operation of the various parts—that, I must begin by saying is quite beyond me, as it is beyond human kind in general—at least for now, and I'm afraid forever.

We are going to observe, nothing more. The Being whose sight you are about to experience is of an indefinable mental condition. Its appearance, even when one is accustomed to it, always causes a certain shock. For us it presents no physical danger; still, I'm bound to warn you, that to see it for the first time without danger of mental collapse, you had best summon to your aid all your coolness . . . and even a bit of your courage.

After a pause Lord Ewald nodded assent.

—Good, he said. I will try to command all my emotions.

## SECURITY MEASURES

I'm not at home to anyone! Do you hear? Not to ANYONE!
—The Human Comedy

Edison stepped to the great window and closed it, pulled the inner shutters to, and fastened them. The heavy fringes of the curtains closed. Passing to the door of the laboratory, he bolted it shut. That done, he threw a switch which kindled a signal light of bright red flame which was installed above the pavilion, and which indicated to anyone in the neighborhood that a dangerous experiment was under way.

The flick of a switch on the central control panel rendered instantly deaf and dumb all the micro-telephonic communication channels, except for that from New York.

—Now we're separated a bit from the world of the living! said Edison, sitting down beside his telegraph. Even as he manipulated various wires with his left hand, he was scribbling with his right long strings of dots and dashes, moving his lips inaudibly.

—Don't you have on you a photograph of Miss Clary? he asked as he wrote.

—It's true. I had forgotten it, said Lord Ewald, drawing a card case from his pocket. Here she is, in her native purity of marble! Look at it, and see if in my words I've exaggerated beyond the reality.

Edison took the photo and glanced at it.

—Prodigious! he cried. It's nothing less than the famous VENUS of the unknown sculptor! It's more than prodigious, it's absolutely stunning! I concede the point.

Turning aside, he touched the switch of a nearby battery.

The spark appeared, as requested, between the double points of a platinum fork; it hesitated there for a couple of seconds, giving its shrill cry, as if trying to decide which way to flee.

A blue wire, seeming to be already saddled for Infinity, approached it. The other end of this wire was lost in the earth. No sooner had the hesitant spark recognized its metallic genie than it leaped aboard and disappeared.

An instant later, a heavy roar was heard under the feet of the two men.

It rolled toward them as if from the depths of the earth, as if from the bottom of an abyss; it was a heavy, grinding noise. One would have thought a coffin was being snatched from the darkness by genies, torn from the earth and raised to the surface.

Edison, still holding the photograph in his hand, kept his eyes riveted to a spot on the wall opposite him at the other end of the laboratory. He seemed anxious and attentive.

The noise ceased.

The electrician placed his hand on an object that Lord Ewald could not make out very well.

—Hadaly! he called aloud.

# APPARITION

Who lurks behind this veil?
—The shrouded image at Sais

A T THIS MYSTERIOUS NAME, a section of the wall at the south end of the laboratory turned silently on its secret hinges, revealing a small alcove previously hidden behind the masonry.

The full blaze of the electric lighting suddenly focused on the interior of this spot.

Hanging against the concave semicircle of the wall, curtains of black moire dropped elegantly from an arch of jade to trail on the white marble of the floor; their deep folds were decorated here and there with butterflies embroidered in gold.

Standing on this dais, a sort of BEING appeared, its form suggestive of nothing so much as the *unknown*.

The vision seemed to have features compounded of shadow; a string of pearls across her forehead supported a dark veil which obscured the entire lower part of her head.

A coat of armor, shaped as for a woman out of silver plates, glowed with a soft radiance. Closely molded to the figure, with a thousand perfect nuances, it suggested elegant and virginal forms.

The trailing ends of the veil twined around the neck over the metal gorget, then, tossed back over the shoulders, were knotted behind her back; thence they fell to the waist of the apparition like a flowing head of long hair, finally dropping to the ground, where they were lost in shadow.

A scarf of black batiste was knotted about her waist like a loincloth, and trailed across her legs a line of black fringe into which brilliants had been sewn.

Within the folds of this veil was visible the glittering blade of a drawn dagger. The vision rested her right hand on the handle of this poniard, while her left hand, hanging by her side, held a golden flower. On all the fingers of her hands glittered rings set with various stones; they seemed to be fastened to her fine gloves.

After an instant of immobility, this mysterious being descended the single step of her platform and advanced toward the two spectators in all her disquieting beauty. Though her step seemed light, her footfalls resounded through the room; under the strong lights, her armor glittered.

Three steps away from Edison and Lord Ewald, the apparition stopped. Then, in a voice deliciously grave:

—Well, my dear Edison, here I am! she said.

Lord Ewald, not knowing what to think, looked at her in silence.

—The time has come for you to live, if you wish, Miss Hadaly, Edison replied.

—Oh, I don't insist on living! the voice murmured gently from beneath its heavy veil.

—This young man has accepted in your behalf! said the engineer, tossing into an electrical apparatus the picture of Miss Alicia.

—As he desires it, so let it be! said Hadaly, after a pause, and with a slight bow toward Lord Ewald.

Edison also looked toward the young man; then, with a touch of his finger, he caused a powerful magnesium light at the other end of the laboratory to burst into flame. Directed by a precise reflector, an intense beam of light focused on a lens directly before the photograph of Miss Alicia Clary. Above it, another complex of lenses and mirrors multiplied the refraction of its penetrating rays.

A square of colored glass appeared almost instantly in the center of the objective; then, sliding out of its groove, it entered a sort of mechanical cell, perforated with two circular holes.

The incandescent ray passed through the imprinted glass by the first of these holes, emerged in full color from the second, which was capped by the inverted cone of a projector—and within a gigantic frame, on a screen of white silk high on the wall, appeared life size the luminous and transparent image of a young woman, a flesh-and-blood statue of the *Venus Victorious*, if such a thing ever lived and breathed in this land of illusions.

—Really, murmured Lord Ewald, I'm in a dream, I think!

—This, said Edison, turning toward Hadaly, this is the form in which you will be incarnated.

She took a step toward the radiant image, which she seemed to contemplate a moment from under her veil.

—Oh! . . . So lovely! . . . And you will force me to live! she said softly, as if to herself.

Then, lowering her head, and with a deep sigh:

—So be it! she said.

The magnesium flared out; the vision on the wall disappeared.

Edison held out his hand at the level of Hadaly's brow.

She trembled a bit, then held out wordlessly the symbolic golden flower to Lord Ewald. He accepted it, not without a vague shudder. She turned and, like a sleepwalker, returned to the strange place from which she had come.

Having reached the threshold, she turned and, raising her two hands to the dark veil over her face, she blew a distant kiss to those who had evoked her. The gesture was bathed in the fresh and warm grace of an adolescent.

She stepped back, pushed aside a section of the dark drapes, and disappeared.

The wall closed behind her.

The same dark noise was heard, but this time fading away and vanishing in the depths of the earth. It dwindled to nothing.

The two men were once more alone under the bright lamps.

—Who is this strange creature? asked Lord Ewald, fastening in his lapel the emblematic flower of Miss Hadaly.

—*It is not a living being,* Edison replied quietly, his eyes on the eyes of Lord Ewald.

# PRELIMINARIES TO A MIRACLE

Without phosphorus, no thought.
—Moleschott

$A$T THIS REVELATION, Lord Ewald, staring into the eyes of the terrifying scientist, seemed to be wondering if he could believe his ears.

—I tell you, Edison resumed, that this metal which walks, speaks, answers, and obeys is not the covering of any *person* in the ordinary sense of the word.

And as Lord Ewald continued to look at him in silence:

—No, *nobody,* he went on. So far Miss Hadaly is nothing at all *from the outside* but a magneto-electric entity. She is a Being in Limbo, a mere potentiality. In a little while, if you wish, I will open before you all the secrets of her magical nature. But here (he went on, gesturing to Lord Ewald to follow him), here is something which may be able to give you more insight into the words you have just heard.

And, guiding the young man through the labyrinth of apparatus, he led him toward the ebony table on which the moonlight had shone briefly before Lord Ewald's visit.

Amazed again, Lord Ewald stared at the unexpected human relic which now was lighted by an eerie electric brilliance.

—What is it? he asked.

—Look at it carefully.

The young man picked up the hand.

—How can that be? What's the meaning of it? This hand . . . but it's still warm!

—Don't you find anything more extraordinary than that about this arm?

After examining it another moment, Lord Ewald suddenly exclaimed under his breath.

—Oh! This, I swear, is a miracle as surprising as *the other*, enough to baffle the most skeptical. Without the wound, I would never have been aware of the masterpiece!

The Englishman seemed fascinated; he picked up the hand and compared it with his own.

—The weight! The modeling! The exact coloration! he went on, almost dumbfounded. Isn't it real flesh that I touch at this moment? My own shivered at it, upon my word!

—Oh, it's better than real! Edison said simply. Flesh fades and grows old. This is a combination of various exquisite substances, elaborated by chemistry; it's a direct rebuke to the complacency of "Nature." (And, by the way, I'd like to be introduced to that great lady "Nature" some day, because everybody talks about her and nobody has ever seen her.) This *copy*, let's say, of Nature—if I may use this empirical word—will bury the original without itself ceasing to appear alive and young. Before growing old, it will perish in a thunderclap. It is artificial flesh, and I can explain to you how it's produced; or else you can read Berthelot.

—How's that? You were saying . . .?

—I say: it is artificial flesh, the electrician repeated. And I think I'm the only one who can make it of this quality!

Lord Ewald, incapable of expressing the turmoil these words had created in his mind, inspected once more the unreal arm.

—But, he finally asked, this pearly fluid, this warm fleshy glow, this intense life . . . how were you able to create the miracle of this disturbing illusion?

—Oh, that aspect of the question is nothing! Edison replied with a smile. It was done quite simply with the aid of the sun.

—The sun! murmured Lord Ewald.

—Exactly. The sun allowed us to catch, in part, the secret of its vibrations, said Edison. Once the delicate tones of dermal whiteness are caught through a series of lenses, I had no trouble in reproducing them. This supple bit of solidified albumen, the elasticity of which is due simply to hydraulic pressure, I was able to reproduce by means of an extremely subtle photochromic operation. I had an admirable model to copy. As for the rest, the ivory humerus contains a magnetic marrow, in constant contact with a network of induction wires woven through the flesh after the fashion of nerves and veins, a network that controls the steady release of caloric heat, which just gave you the impression of warmth and malleability. If you want to know where the elements of this network are placed, how they nourish themselves (so to speak), and how the static fluid transforms its energy into something like animal heat, I can explain the whole thing to you: this is simply an obvious matter of workmanship. This is the arm of an Android of my making, animated for the first time by this vital, surprising agent that we call Electricity, which gives it, as you see, all the soft and melting qualities, all the *illusion* of life!

—An Android?

—An Imitation Human Being, if you prefer. The mistake to be avoided, now, is that the facsimile may surpass the original. Do you recall, my lord, those artisans of former days who tried to create artificial human beings? Ha, ha, ha, ha!

Edison laughed like one of the Cabiri in the forges of Eleusis.

—Poor fellows, for lack of the proper technical skills, they produced nothing but ridiculous monsters. Albertus Magnus, Vaucanson, Maelzel, Horner, and all that crowd were barely competent makers of scarecrows. Their automata deserve to be exhibited in the most hideous of wax museums; they are disgusting objects from which proceeds a rank smell of wood, rancid oil, and gutta-percha. Degraded works of that sort give man no sense of power; instead, they only force him to bow his head before the great god, Chaos. Just call to mind that succession of jerky, extravagant movements, reminiscent of Nuremberg dolls! The absurdity of their shapes and colors! Their animation, as of wigmakers' dummies! That noise of the key in the mechanism! The sensation of vacancy! In a word, everything in these abominable masquerades produces in us a sense of horror and shame. Contempt and disgust join together in a grotesque ceremony. They look like the idols of the Australian archipelago, fetishes from the jungles of equatorial Africa; these mannequins are nothing but an outrageous caricature of our species. Yes, such were the first sketches of Androids.

As he spoke, Edison's face sharpened and hardened. His eyes seemed to be probing imaginary shadows; his voice became curt, cold, didactic.

—But today, he resumed, that period is past. Science has multiplied her discoveries; metaphysical conceptions have been refined. The techniques of reproduction, of *identification* have been rendered more precise and perfect, so that the resources available to man for new ventures of this sort are now different—oh, completely different—than they used to be. Henceforth we shall be able to realize—that is, to MAKE REAL—potent phantoms, mysterious presences *of a mixed nature*, such as pioneers in the field could never have conceived, and at the thought of which they would have smiled sadly and cried, "Impossible!"—Think now, didn't you, just now, find it difficult to smile at the appearance of Hadaly? And yet I assure you, she is nothing but an uncut diamond so far. She is the *skeleton of a shade* waiting for the SHADE to exist! The sensation you just had from touching one of the arms of a female Android didn't seem to you remotely like what you would have had from touching the arm of an automaton—am I right? Try something else: would you like to shake this hand? Who knows? Perhaps it will respond.

Lord Ewald lifted the fingers and shook them gently.

Amazement! The hand replied to this pressure with a courtesy so sensitive and remote that the young man could only think it must be a part of some invisible body. Deeply distressed, he laid down the shadowy object.

—My word! he murmured.

—Well, Edison went on coolly, all this is still nothing! Nothing, I tell you, nothing at all! *(But the things that are called nothing! Ah, I could tell you!)* Nothing in comparison with the task that lies ahead. Ah, the task that lies ahead! If you could conceive! If you . . .

Abruptly he fell silent as if struck by a sudden idea, one so terrible that it cut short his speech.

—Really, cried Lord Ewald, looking once more around him, it seems to me that I've come into the world of Flamel, Paracelsus, or Raymond Lull, the magicians and alchemists of the Middle Ages. But where is all this leading, my dear Edison?

But the great inventor, suddenly become very thoughtful, sat down and considered his young friend with a new and worried expression.

After a short silence:

—My lord, he said, it's just struck me that for a man endowed with your imagination, the experiment could well lead to tragic consequences. Consider this: when you stand at the entry to a steel factory, you can make out through the smoke some men, some metal, the fires. The furnaces roar, the hammers crash; and the metalworkers who forge ingots, weapons, tools, and so on, are completely ignorant of the *real* uses to which their products will be put. The workers can only refer to their products by conventional names. Well, that's where we all stand, all of us! Nobody can see the real character of what he creates because every knife blade may become a dagger, and *the use to which an object is put changes both its name and its nature.* Only our ignorance shields us from terrible responsibilities.

Uncertainty is a quality to be cherished, therefore—if not for it, who would dare to undertake anything?

The worker who molds a bullet says to himself, secretly and silently: "This is work done at random: *and perhaps it will simply be lead thrown away.*" And so he completes his task, the end of which is hidden from him. But if he saw before his eyes the gaping, gory, mortal wound that this bullet, among others, is bound and indeed predestined to create (and which, as a consequence, is virtually a part of his work), the mold would fall from his hands, if he were an honest man; and perhaps he would deny his children their daily bread, if the price of that bread were the accomplishment of this murder—for he would shrink, by instinct, from making himself an accomplice of that future homicide.

—Well? interrupted Lord Ewald. What are you getting at, Edison?

—Just this. I am the man who holds the liquid lead over the fire; and just a moment ago, as I was thinking of your temperament and your mind forever ravaged by cynicism, it seemed to me that I saw the wound before my eyes. *The thing I want to tell you* may restore your health or prove *worse than fatal,* remember that. So I am the one who hesitates now. We both have parts to play in the experiment. And in reality I think it is much more dangerous, for you at least, than it appeared at first glance. The danger, which is of the most horrible sort you can conceive, is a danger for you alone. No doubt you're already in danger, since yours is one of those hearts that a fatal passion almost always leads to a miserable end; and no doubt, too, I run a risk in trying to save you. But if the outcome of the experiment is not that for which I hope, I believe, I really do believe, *that we would be better off to stop right here!*

—Since you assume such a particularly solemn tone, Lord Ewald replied with an effort, I might as well tell you, my dear Edison, that I expected to put an end to my miserable existence this very night.

Edison shuddered.

—So you needn't hesitate any further, the young man concluded icily.

—The die is cast! murmured the engineer: He is the one! Who would ever have supposed it?

—One last time, will you be good enough to answer me: What are you getting at?

In the instant of silence that followed, Lord Ewald felt pass across his forehead a chilly gust from the Infinite.

Ah, then! Edison cried in a voice of thunder, raising his glittering eyes, if that's the challenge I am sent by the Unknown, so be it! Listen now. I offer to accomplish for you, my lord, what no man has ever dared to attempt for another. I owe you a life, my own; the least I can do is to give you yours.

You say your being, your vital joy, have been taken from you by a human presence? By the light of a smile, the gaiety of an expression, the softness of a voice? A living woman leads you, by her attractiveness, to your death?

All right! Since this woman is precious to you—I AM GOING TO STEAL HER OWN EXISTENCE AWAY FROM HER!

I'm going to show you, with mathematical certainty and on this very spot (the demonstration may freeze your soul, but you cannot refute it), I'm going to show, I say, how, making use of modern science, I can capture the grace of her gesture, the fullness of her body, the fragrance of her flesh, the resonance of her voice, the turn of her waist, the light of her eyes, the quality of her movements and gestures, the individuality of her glance, all her traits and characteristics, down to the shadow she casts on the ground—her complete identity, in a word. I shall be the murderer of her foolishness, the assassin of her triumphant animal nature. In the first place I will reincarnate her entire external appearance, which to you is so deliciously mortal, in an Apparition whose HUMAN likeness and charm alone will surpass your wildest hopes, your most intimate dreams! And then, *in place of this soul which repels you in the living woman, I shall infuse another sort of soul,* less aware of itself perhaps (but about this sort of thing, who can tell? and what does it matter?), a soul capable of impressions a thousand times more lovely, more lofty, more noble—that is, they will be robed in that character of eternity without which our mortal life can be no more than a shabby comedy. I will reproduce this woman exactly, I will duplicate her, with the sublime assistance of Light! And then, projecting her through her RADIANT MATTER, I will fill with the visions of your melancholy the imaginary soul of this new creature, a creature capable of amazing the angels. I will cast Illusion to the ground and enclose it in a prison! In this vision, I will compel the Ideal itself to become apparent, for the first time, to your senses, PALPABLE, AUDIBLE, AND FULLY MATERIAL. I will recapture, even as it fleets away, the first moment of this enchanted mirage, which you pursue now so vainly through your memories. And then, fixing it, almost eternally, do you understand, in the single true aspect under which you first perceived it, *I will duplicate the living woman in a second copy, transfigured according to your deepest desires!* I shall endow this Shade with all the songs of that Antonia described by the tale-teller Hoffmann, with all the passionate mysticism of Edgar Poe's Ligeia, with all the burning seductions of that Venus conceived by the mighty musician Wagner! And finally, to restore you to life, I promise—and I can prove to you in advance, that I absolutely have this power—I promise to raise from the clay of Human Science as it now exists, a Being *made in our image,* and who, accordingly, will be to us WHAT WE ARE TO GOD.

And the engineer, raising his hand, made solemn oath.

# AMAZEMENT

I was MUMMIFIED with astonishment.
—Théophile Gautier

A̲T THESE WORDS Lord Ewald stared blankly at Edison; you would have thought he was *refusing to understand* what had been said to him. After a minute of stupefaction:

—But . . . such a creature could never be anything but a doll, without feeling or intelligence! he cried, for lack of anything else to say.

—My lord, said Edison solemnly, you may take this on my word of honor: you will have to be careful, when you compare the two and listen to them both, *that it isn't the living woman who seems to you the doll.*

Not yet having recovered his self-possession, the young man smiled bitterly, with a kind of constrained politeness.

—Let's not argue that point, he said. The conception is stunning; the finished project will always smack of machinery. Come now, don't ask me to think that you can create a woman! And as I listen to you, I ask myself if your genius . . .

—I swear to you, in the first place, *you will not be able to distinguish one from the other*, the engineer interrupted quietly. And for the second time I tell you, I am in a position to prove it in advance.

—IMPOSSIBLE, Edison.

—For the third time, I promise to furnish you *immediately*, however little you want it, proof positive, *point by point* and *in advance*, not that the thing is possible, but that it is mathematically *certain*.

—You can reproduce the IDENTITY of a woman? You, a man born of woman?

—She will be a thousand times more identical to herself . . . than she is in her own person! Yes, I assure you! since not a day passes without changing some outlines of the human body, and the science of physiology demonstrates to us that the body changes *completely* all of its atoms, every seven years approximately. Does anyone's body really exist at any given point? Does one ever resemble oneself? When this woman, and you, and I, were just an hour and twenty minutes old, did we resemble what we are tonight? The very idea of resembling oneself! What is this, a prejudice out of the ice age, or the time of the cavemen?

—You will reproduce her with her beauty, even that? Her flesh? Her voice? Her posture? Her very look?

—With electromagnetic power and Radiant Matter, I will deceive the heart of a mother, and much more easily the passion of a lover. Just listen! I will duplicate her so exactly that if in a dozen years or so she should happened to see her unchanged ideal double, she will be unable to look at it without tears of *envy*—and of terror!

After a moment's thought, Lord Ewald murmured under his breath:

—But to undertake the making of such a creature would be, I should think, like tempting . . . *God*.

—That's why I haven't told you to accept! Edison replied, speaking in a low voice and very simply.

—Will you infuse into it an intelligence?

—A particular intelligence? No. INTELLIGENCE, yes.

At this titanic phrase, Lord Ewald stood as if petrified before the inventor. Their gazes crossed in silence.

A game had been proposed. The stakes were, literally, nothing less than a soul.

# EXCELSIOR!

Under my care, patients may lose their lives;—but never hope!

—Doctor Ryllh

—I REPEAT, MY DEAR GENIUS, the young man replied, you undoubtedly mean well; but what you say is nothing but a dream, as terrifying as it is impractical. Still, I'm touched by the warmth of your sympathy, and I thank you for it.

—My lord . . . you know perfectly well that the idea is practical, since you hesitate before it.

Lord Ewald wiped his brow.

—Miss Alicia Clary would never agree to take part in this experiment, and besides, I must admit, I should be very reluctant to involve her in it.

—This is simply part of the problem, and concerns me alone. Besides, *the work would be incomplete, that is to say* ABSURD, if it were not accomplished completely without the knowledge of Miss Alicia, of whom you're so careful.

—But what about me? cried Lord Ewald. I count for something too in my own love affair, I suppose!

—You'll never understand how much you count, I assure you, said Edison.

—Well, then, what devious subtleties will you use to convince me, me myself, of the *reality* of this new Eve, even supposing you succeed in making her?

—Oh, that's a question of immediate sense impressions, into which reason enters only as a belated and unimportant assistant. Does one ever reason about an enchantment one is experiencing? Besides, the logic to which I will expose you will simply be the exact impression of what you are now trying to hide from yourself. I am human. *Homo sum.* The Work will answer your questions far better with its mere presence.

—I can raise objections, can't I—indeed, I insist on it—during the course of the explanations?

—If A SINGLE ONE of your objections persists, we will stop short and go no further.

Lord Ewald turned thoughtful again.

—Alas, my eyes are fearfully clearsighted; I should warn you of that.

—Your eyes! Tell me, don't you suppose you see quite distinctly this drop of water? Well, if I place it between these two crystal slides under the objective of this solar microscope and then project its exact image onto that white silk screen where your bewitching Alicia appeared just a minute ago, won't your eyes repudiate their original impressions in the face of the more intimate spectacle that the drop of water reveals of its own accord? And if we think of all the hidden realities that this drop of water still conceals, we will understand that even the power of our instrument, which is nothing but a kind of crutch to the eye, is utterly insignificant. The difference between what it shows us and what we can see without its help, by comparison with all the things it *might* show us, is, practically speaking, imperceptible. Never forget that the only things we see in objects are those which our eyes *suggest* to us. We only form our ideas of them from the few glimpses of their real being that they let us catch; we possess them only to the extent we are able to experience them, each one of us according to his own nature. And Man, like a solemn squirrel, scurries forever around the spinning wheel of his own EGO without being able to escape from the illusion in which he is caged by his ridiculous senses. Thus Hadaly, when she deceives your sight, will do nothing else in reality than what Miss Alicia does.

—Seriously speaking, Mr. Magician, Lord Ewald replied, do you actually think I'm capable of "falling in love" with Miss Hadaly?

—That, in fact, is exactly what I would have to fear if you were a man of the common sort, Edison declared. But your confession has relieved my mind on that score. Didn't you swear before God, just a moment ago, that every idea of possessing your beautiful mistress was forever ruined within you? I tell you, then, you will love Hadaly as she deserves to be loved, for herself alone; which is a much finer thing than simply being in love with her.

—I'll *love* her?

—Why not? Won't she be incarnate forever in the only form under which you can conceive of love? And, matter for matter (since we've just reminded ourselves that flesh, being never the same, exists almost exclusively in the imagination), flesh for flesh, that created by Science is more . . . serious . . . than the other.

—One can only love an animate being! said Lord Ewald.

—Well, then? asked Edison.

—The soul is the unknown; are you going to animate your Hadaly?

—One animates a bullet, say, by giving it a speed of X. Well, X is the unknown, too.

—Will she know who she is? Or rather what she is, I should say?

—Do we know so well ourselves who we are and what we are? Will you demand more of the copy than God has seen fit to grant to the original?

—I meant to ask if your creature will be capable of self-awareness?

—No doubt about it! said Edison, as if surprised by the very question.

—What! Do you mean to say . . .? cried Lord Ewald in amazement.

—I say: No doubt! Since this depends on you. And in fact it's on you alone that I depend for this part of the miracle to be accomplished.

—On me?

—On whom else? Is there anyone else I could depend on to be as interested in the problem as you are?

—Well, then, said Lord Ewald gloomily, will you kindly tell me, my dear Edison, where I ought to go in order to catch a spark of that sacred fire with which the World Spirit infuses us? My name is not Prometheus, merely Lord Celian Ewald, and I'm nothing but a mortal man.

—Bah! cried Edison. Every man bears the name of Prometheus without knowing it—and none escapes the beak of the vulture. My lord, I tell you the simple truth: a single one of those still-divine sparks, drawn from your own soul, with which you have tried so often (but always vainly) to inspire the blank mind of your present mistress, will serve to give life to the shadow.

—Prove this to me, cried Lord Ewald, and then, perhaps . . .

—So be it; and right away.

You have declared, Edison continued, that the creature whom you love, and who for you is the sole REALITY, is by no means the one who is momentarily embodied in this transient human figure, but a creature of your desire.

That is what does not exist in her; much more, *you know it doesn't exist there.* For you're not a dupe—neither of the woman nor of yourself.

You deliberately close your eyes, those of your understanding, you deliberately stifle the voice of your conscience, in order to be able to find in this mistress of yours only the phantom you desire. For you at least, her *true* personality is nothing but the Illusion planted in your entire being by the power of her beauty. This Illusion is the one thing that you struggle against all odds to REVIVE in the presence of your beloved, in spite of the frightful, deadly, withering nullity of the real Alicia.

What you love is this *shadow* alone; it's for the shadow that you want to die. That and that alone is what you recognize as unconditionally REAL. In short, it's this objectified projection of your own soul that you call on, you perceive, that you CREATE in your living woman, and *which is nothing but your own soul reduplicated in her.* Yes, that is your love; and, as you see, it is nothing but a continual and ever-fruitless attempt at redemption.

There was another moment of profound silence between the two men.

—Well, then, Edison concluded, since it's established that you are living now and have lived in the past with nothing but a Shade, onto which you project from your own fervid soul a fictive existence, I offer you a chance to project the same feelings on a shadow of your spirit realized from without—that's the only difference. Illusion for illusion, the Being of this mixed presence called Hadaly depends on the free will of him who will DARE to conceive it. *Suggest it to her from the depths of your self!* Affirm her being with a little of your vital faith, as you affirm the being (no more than relative at best) of all the illusions that surround you. Blow the breath of life on those ideal features! You will see then how the Alicia of your desires will become tangible, concentrated, animated in this Shade. Give it a try, then, if some last hope still stirs within you. And then you will judge in your own intimate conscience whether this auxiliary Creature-Phantom which leads you back to the love of life doesn't really merit the name of HUMAN more than that living specter whose sorry so-called "reality" was never able to inspire you with anything but the desire for death.

Lord Ewald reflected a moment in silence.

—The deduction is in fact both specious and profound, he murmured with a faint smile. But I suspect I should find myself rather too *alone* in the company of your unaware Eve.

—Less alone than with her original; that's already been shown. Besides, my lord, that would be your fault, not hers. What the devil! One has to feel oneself a deity in fact, when one ventures to make such wishes as we're talking of here.

Edison paused.

—Besides, he added in an odd tone of voice, I don't think you're taking into account the *novelty* of the impressions you'll receive when for the first time you stroll across the lawn in full sunshine, with the Android-Alicia at your side, turning her parasol to shade her face from the sun with all the natural grace of the original. You smile? You think that, especially when they've been warned in advance, your senses will quickly discover the differences between my work and that of "Nature"? Well, listen here now. Miss Alicia perhaps has some dog, a greyhound or a Newfoundland that knows her? Do you have a special favorite among your hunting hounds?

—I have my dog Dark, a black greyhound, and very devoted to us, whom we've taken on our trip.

—Good. This animal, said Edison, is endowed with a sense of smell so powerful that living beings with their different odors actually paint their portraits on the central nervous system through the seven or eight different receptors making up the dog's nasal apparatus.

—I will bet you that this dog—one who would pick out his mistress from among a thousand others in the dark—if we take him away from your presences for a week or so, and then bring him back into the presence of Hadaly as she will be transfigured, will come running at the voice of the Illusion, will recognize her without hesitation, simply from the fragrance of her dress. Better still, put in the presence simultaneously of the Shadow and the Reality, I tell you it is the Reality that he will bark at, in his confusion, and the Shadow—only the Shadow—whom he will obey!

—Aren't you promising a good deal, here? murmured Lord Ewald, disconcerted.

—I promise nothing but what I can fulfill. The experiment is already completely successful; it's an established fact within the discipline of physiology. And besides, if I can completely deceive the senses (they are far sharper than our own) of a simple animal, why should I hesitate before the test of imposing on human senses?

Lord Ewald could hardly restrain a smile at the bizarre ingenuity of the electrician.

—And then, Edison concluded, even though Hadaly is a very mysterious creature, you must look at her without any exaggeration. Consider it this way: *her operation will be a little more dependent on electricity than that of her model;* but that's all.

—How do you mean, than her model? Lord Ewald demanded.

—Of course! said Edison. Haven't you ever admired, on a stormy day, a beautiful young brunette combing her hair before a great mirror, in a slightly darkened room, or one where the curtains have been drawn? The sparks crackle in her hair, and glitter like magic fires on the teeth of her tortoise-shell comb; they are like thousands of diamonds streaming off a black wave on the open ocean at night. Hadaly will provide you with such a spectacle if Miss Alicia has not already done so. Brunettes are full of electricity.

After an instant:

—Well, Edison asked, are you willing to attempt this INCARNATION, my lord? Hadaly, through this flower of grief which is of virgin gold, pure without the slightest alloy, offers you a chance to save from the catastrophe of your love a little melancholy.

Lord Ewald and his interlocutor stared at one another, silent and solemn.

—I must say, the young man murmured under his breath, speaking as if only to himself, this is the most terrible dilemma ever placed before a desperate man. And in spite of myself, I still have all the trouble in the world to take it seriously.

—That will come, said Edison; leave it up to Hadaly.

—Another man, if only out of curiosity, would waste no time in accepting the opportunity you offer me.

—That's why I wouldn't make the offer to just anyone, Edison replied with a smile. If I should bequeath the formula to humanity, I pity the reprobates who try to misuse the help she can bring; that's all.

—See here now, said Lord Ewald, the word in these surroundings may well sound like a sacrilege: but will there always be time to . . . suspend . . . the operation?

—Oh, even after the whole thing is done, since you will always be able to destroy her—drown her if you like—*without upsetting the Deluge in the least.*

—No doubt, said Lord Ewald, sunk deep in his own thoughts. But it seems to me that *then* it won't be the same thing.

—Then I advise you to have nothing to do with it. You're suffering; I talk to you of a remedy. Only the remedy is just as effective as it is dangerous. I tell you a thousand times over, you are always free to refuse.

Lord Ewald seemed perplexed, and all the more so because he would have found it impossible to say precisely why.

—Oh, as for the danger! . . . he said.

—If it was nothing but physical danger, I would tell you directly: Accept!

—You think, then, it's my reason that would be threatened?

A moment of silence:

—My lord Ewald, Edison resumed, you are beyond doubt the most noble nature that I have encountered on this earth. A malignant star has cast its ray on you, and led you into the world of Love; there your dream has fallen to earth, its wings shattered, at the breath of a deceptive woman whose constant dissonance rouses in you at every moment that corrosive grief which is eating you away, and will necessarily lead you to your grave. Yes, you are one of those least splendid melancholics who scorn to survive this sort of test, despite the common example all around them of people who struggle against illness, misery, and love. The grief of this first disappointment was such, in you, that now you think yourself quits with your fellow men—despising them because they submit to live under the whips and scorns of such a destiny. The spleen has cast her winding sheet over your thoughts, and now that clammy figure which counsels suicide has spoken in your ear the word that will persuade you. You are deathly ill. For you it's simply a question of hours, you just told me so clearly yourself; the outcome of the crisis is not even in doubt any longer. If you walk out of this room, it's to your death; death shows through your entire presence, oppressive, imminent.

Lord Ewald, without replying, tapped off the ash of his cigar with the tip of his little finger.

—Here I offer you your life again—but at what price, perhaps! Who can calculate the price at this time? The Ideal has lied to you! "Truth" has destroyed your every desire? A woman has frozen your senses?

Well, then, farewell to that so-called Reality, slut that she was from the start!

I offer you, myself, a venture into the ARTIFICIAL and its untasted delights! But . . . if you are not going to be able to retain control of it! . . . Come, my lord, between the two of us, we form an eternal symbol: I represent Science and the omnipotence of its delusions; you are Humanity with its paradise lost.

—Then make the choice for me, said Lord Ewald quietly.

Edison shuddered.

—That is impossible, my lord, he replied.

—In a word . . . *putting yourself in my place* . . . would you risk your life in this absurd, unheard of, yet somehow challenging adventure?

Before this challenge, Edison paused, looking on the young man with his customary fixity, now deepened by a secret mental reservation that he did not want to express.

—I should have, he said at last, rather different reasons than most men in making my personal option. I don't believe that anybody else should base himself on my example.

—What would you decide?

—If I were placed in your dilemma, I should make the choice that seemed to me the least dangerous . . . *for me personally.*

—Well, what would that choice be?

—My lord, you don't doubt my attachment to you, the deep and tender affection that I feel for you? . . . Well, on my inmost conscience, then . . .

—What would be your choice, Edison?

—Between death and the alternative I have offered you?

—Yes!

Terrible, the great electrician bowed before Lord Ewald:

—I should blow out my brains, he said.

# OF THE SWIFTNESS OF SCHOLARS

Who wants to change old lamps for new?
—Aladdin, in the *Thousand and One Nights*

After a moment's thought, Lord Ewald glanced at his watch. His forehead had darkened.

—Thank you, he said with a wintry smile. And now, farewell.

In the shadows, a bell sounded.

—I'm afraid I must tell you it's a little late, said Edison. After your first words, *I set things in motion.*

He rapped on the phonograph crouched at his feet like a dog.

—Well, what is it? the phonograph asked, barking into its own telephone.

The deep voice of the invisible messenger rang out in the middle of the laboratory, sounding like the speech of a man out of breath from running:

—Miss Alicia Clary, in Box Number 7 of the Grand Theater, is leaving the hall, and will take the twelve-thirty express for Menlo Park!

Lord Ewald, hearing the name cried aloud in this manner, and struck by the unexpected news, made a gesture.

The two men stared at one another in silence: between them trembled an unspoken challenge.

—The thing is, said Lord Ewald, I haven't taken any quarters for the night in Menlo Park.

Even as he spoke, Edison was operating the transmitter of his telegraph; the wires trembled.

—Just a minute, he said, and slid a sheet of paper into the receiver, which ten seconds later dropped it on the table.

—You spoke of quarters? It's all taken care of; here is something I hope will suit, he said coolly, reading what had just been printed on the paper. I've just rented for you a perfectly charming villa, with private grounds of its own, about twenty minutes from here. The staff will be expecting you there anytime in the course of the night. You will dine with me here, I hope, along with Miss Alicia Clary? That's settled, then. When the train pulls in, my servant, furnished with this new photograph, which reproduces simply the face of Miss Venus Victorious, will offer her my carriage on your behalf and bring her here. There's no chance of a mistake or a misunderstanding; hardly anybody arrives here at such a late hour. So there's no reason for you to be disturbed about anything.

Even as he talked, he withdrew the miniature portrait from an automatic camera, penciled a couple of hasty lines on it, and tossed it into a receptacle fixed on the wall.

The receptacle was part of a network of pneumatic tubes; a tiny bell, beside it, acknowledged receipt of the message and conveyed the assurance it would be carried out.

Turning back to the telegraph, he continued to send out what were, no doubt, other orders.

—That takes care of it, he said abruptly. Then, turning to Lord Ewald:

—My lord, he added, it goes without saying that if this is your desire, we'll say not another word regarding the project we were discussing just now.

Lord Ewald raised his head; his blue eyes glittered.

—Really, now, it would be too much to hesitate any longer, he said simply. This time I accept, my dear Edison, once and for all.

Gravely, Edison bowed.

—Very well, he said. *I expect, my lord, that you will do me the honor to live for twenty-one days more; for I too have given my word.*

—*Agreed: but not one day more!* said the young man, with the quiet, icy intonation of an Englishman whose mind is settled, and who will not go back on his pledge.

Edison glanced at the second hand of the electric clock.

—I will hand you the pistol myself at nine o'clock of the day we have agreed on, he said, if I haven't restored in you the will to live. Unless perhaps, in order to destroy yourself, you prefer to make use of our recent prisoner, the power of lightning; there are no mistakes with that.

He turned to the telephone.

—And now, added the engineer, as we are about to undertake a fairly dangerous trip this very instant, will you pardon me while I say good-bye to my children; for one's children are really something.

At this last expression, master of himself though the young lord was, he shuddered.

Edison had already grasped a telephone hidden in the draperies and called two names into the apparatus.

Far out in the night winds at the foot of the park, the ringing of a bell, muffled here by the tapestries, replied to him.

—*Many thousand kisses!* Edison called paternally into the mouthpiece of the instrument, and blew several kisses with his words.

Then something strange occurred.

Around the two searchers into the unknown, the two travelers into the shades, there burst from every side (thanks to some twist that Edison had given to a commutator) a joyous rain of charming childish kisses, as of infants crying in their silvery voices:

—Wait, papa! Wait, papa! Again! Again!

Edison pressed to his cheek the receiver of the telephone which was bringing him these baby kisses.

—Now, my lord, I am ready, he said.

—No; you must stay behind, Edison, said Lord Ewald forlornly. I am useless; it's better that I confront, alone if that is possible . . .

—Let's go, said the engineer, the glitter of confident genius in his eyes.

# TIME AT A STOP

But the other thought! the thought in the BACK OF
THE HEAD!
                                                        —Pascal

THE PACT WAS SEALED.

Taking up two great bearskin coats from a hanger on the wall, the engineer, suddenly grim of expression, offered one to Lord Ewald.

—Our journey will be cold, he said; better wear this.

Lord Ewald accepted silently; then, not without a slight smile:

—Would it be indiscreet to ask where we are going?

—Why, to see Hadaly, of course. To the land of thunder and lightning, where the flashes of electricity measure three meters seventy, Edison replied absently as he struggled into his Eskimo costume.

—Let's hurry then, Lord Ewald murmured, in a tone that was almost joyful.

—By the way, you don't have any last communication for me, do you? Edison asked.

—No, none, replied the young lord. I'm eager to talk a bit more, I admit, with that pretty veiled creature whose nothingness was very agreeable to me. As for the trifling observations that come to mind, we'll have time to consider them later.

At these last words Edison lifted his head under the radiant lamps and pulled off his bearskin coat.

—Here now, he cried, have you forgotten, my lord, that my name is Electricity, and that it's your thinking I must struggle against? *Right now* is the time to talk. Come out with all your trifling worries and objections, or I won't know what I have to oppose! At best, it's no trifling task to pit oneself against an Ideal such as yours. I tell you truly, Jacob himself would think twice before wrestling with such a shadow. Come now, tell the whole story to the doctor who says he's going to cure your sickness.

—Oh, my thoughts so far . . . concern mere *nothings*, said the young man.

—Plague take it! cried the engineer, now you're talking plain nonsense! *Mere* NOTHINGS? But if just one of these nothings is overlooked, the Ideal is lost! Do you recall that Frenchman's joke: "If Cleopatra's nose had been a bit shorter, the whole face of the globe would have altered." A *nothing?* But even in our own time what determines the most serious things in the world? Yesterday a kingdom collapsed because someone was tapped with a fan; today, an empire fell because someone didn't tip his hat. You must allow me to judge the nothings—the vacant voids—at their proper value. Nothing! it's a thing so useful that God himself didn't hesitate to draw the world out of it; and the same thing happens every day. Without Nothing, God declares implicitly, it would have been practically impossible for him to create the Becomingness of things. We are no more than a perpetual state of *being no more*. The Void is negative matter, essential yet conditional, without which we would not be sitting here and talking tonight. It's precisely in connection with our present project that I have to be careful of the Nothings. Tell me all about these little *nothings* that disturb you; we can take our trip later.—Devil take it, he added, we have plenty of time before your living lady arrives and I pluck her of her peacock feathers. Three hours and a half, at least.

So saying, he dropped the fur coat beside his chair and sat down, leaning on an old Volta battery; then, crossing his legs and fixing his eyes on those of the young man, he waited.

Lord Ewald, having also sat down, began:

—I was asking myself, in the first place, why you questioned me so particularly on the intellectual character of our female *subject?*

—Because I had to know in what way you yourself conceive of intelligence, Edison replied. You have to understand that the least troublesome of my jobs is mere physical reproduction. If the first preliminary is simply to give Hadaly the paradoxical beauty of your living lady, the really serious task is creating the Android in such a way that, far from disenchanting you like her model, she will be worthy in your eyes of the sublime body in which she will be incorporated. Unless I do that, there's no advantage in changing one for the other.

—How will you prevail on Alicia to lend herself to this experiment?

—It'll take no more than a few seconds during our supper tonight; you will see, I'll persuade her. If I used *Suggestion* to decide her . . . but, no, persuasion will be enough. After that, it will be a matter of a dozen sittings, in the presence of a terra-cotta model, which will disarm her suspicions. She will never even see Hadaly, and will never conceivably suspect what we're about.

Now, we want Hadaly to take on a human appearance, and to leave this almost supernatural atmosphere within which the fiction of her being is taking shape. Accordingly, it's essential, don't you agree, that this Valkyrie of Science must take on a contemporary shape in order to live among us. She has to assume the customs, habits, and the appearance of a woman, and the conventional contemporary dress.

That's why, during these various sittings, dressmakers, glovemakers, corsetiers, milliners, and bootmakers will exactly duplicate the entire wardrobe of Miss Alicia Clary, who, without even noticing what is happening, will yield all of her secrets to her beautiful shadow, as soon as the latter comes forth into the world. Once all the measurements have been taken for a complete wardrobe, you can have a thousand others made, of every sort, without her even having to try them on.

It goes without saying that the Android will use the same perfumes as her model, and will have, as I explained to you, exactly the same natural odors.

—And how does she travel?

—But just like anyone else! Edison replied. Plenty of travelers are
stranger than she will be! Miss Hadaly, once *warned* that she's going on
a trip, will behave irreproachably. A bit sleepy and silent perhaps, not
talking in fact to anyone but you, very softly and at rare intervals; but
even if she's seated right next to a stranger, there is no reason for her to
lower her veil. No, neither by day nor at night. And besides, you will
travel alone, I suppose, my lord? Well, what problem do you foresee? She
can challenge the keenest human sight.

—An occasion might arise when some words could legitimately be
addressed to her, couldn't it?

—In that case you would simply remark that the lady is a foreigner and
"doesn't know the language," which would close the incident. When
you're on board a ship, where, for example, the simple problem of equilibrium is very considerable *even for us*, I can assure you that Miss Hadaly won't subject you to any of those difficult crossings during which
living ladies take to their hammocks anytime the sea is rough, or undergo
sudden drastic fits of seasickness, painful to the point of being ridiculous.
Hadaly knows nothing of these ailments; and in order not to humiliate,
by her calm, fellow travelers whose organisms are more defective than
hers, she can make her sea voyages after the fashion of the dead.

—You mean, in one of our coffins!? Lord Ewald asked in surprise.

Gravely Edison bowed his head in sign of affirmation.

—But . . . not sewed up in a gravecloth, I imagine? the young man
murmured.

—Oh, as a living work of art who has never known swaddling clothes,
she has nothing to do with shrouds, either. See here: among her other
treasures, the Android possesses a heavy coffin of ebony lined with black
satin. The interior of this symbolic jewel-case will be molded precisely
to the feminine form it is to contain. That is her dowry. The panels of the
top open at the touch of a small golden key shaped like a star; the lock,
when it's open, is kept under the pillow of the sleeper.

Hadaly knows how to enter her coffin by herself, either clothed or
unclothed; she can lie down there, and fasten herself in, using strips of
batiste solidly fastened to the interior walls, so that the lining of the
casket does not even touch her shoulders. Her face is veiled; her head,
with its crown of hair, rests on a cushion against which it is held by a
jewelled band which keeps it motionless. If it were not for her constant
gentle breathing, you would think she was Miss Alicia Clary, who had
died just that very morning.

On the closed panels of this prison is fastened a silver plaque, bearing
the name HADALY in the identical letters which in Iranian signify the
IDEAL. Above it will be your ancient coat of arms, which will sanctify
this captivity.

This handsome coffin should be placed in a cedar chest carefully lined
inside; its simple rectangular shape will provoke no comment. This precious jail of your dream will be ready in three weeks. Then, when you go

back to London, a word to the customs office on the Thames will suffice to get your mysterious parcel into the country.

When Miss Alicia Clary receives your farewell note, you will be in your castle of Athelwold, where you can resurrect her shadow . . . the celestial one.

—In my country house? . . . Yes, in fact, there it would be possible! Lord Ewald murmured, as if to himself, as if lost in a terrible melancholy.

—There and only there, in that cloudy countryside, surrounded by pine forests, bleak lakes, and enormous rocks, there you will be able to open, in perfect security, the prison of Hadaly. I suppose you have in that castle of yours some spacious, splendid apartment furnished after the fashion of Queen Elizabeth's days?

—I do, said Lord Ewald with a bitter smile. And in happier days I took the pains to decorate it myself with all sorts of marvelous artworks and precious decorations. The old room addresses the spirit only in the voice of the past. The single enormous stained-glass window, hung in ancient drapes embroidered with lilies in gold thread, opens onto an iron balcony whose railing, still impeccable, was forged under the reign of Richard III. A stairway buried in moss leads down into our ancient park, through which shaggy, overgrown pathways reach away ever further under the shadow of giant oaks.

I had intended this royal room for the fiancée of my life, if ever I had discovered her.

Lord Ewald, after a mournful shudder, continued.

—Well, so be it! I shall be trying to achieve the impossible; yes, that is where I will bring this delusive apparition, this galvanized phantom of hope! And since I can no longer love or desire or possess *the other* . . . the other phantom . . . I can hope that this vacant form may become the abysm on whose gloomy edge as I sit watching them, my final hopes will fade from view.

—Indeed: this house is the very place best suited to the Android, I agree, said Edison solemnly. You see how it is; though I'm not much of a dreamer myself, I readily associate myself with the vision of your soul, which is dear to me on other scores. Only there in your house will Hadaly be like a mysterious sleepwalker, wandering about the lakes or across forbidden heaths. In this solitary castle, where your old servants, your books, your huntsmen, and your musical instruments all await you, both persons and objects will quickly become accustomed to the new arrival.

She will walk surrounded by a halo of reverence and silence, since your servants will have been told never to address a word to her. You can say, for example, if you have to justify that order, that in consequence of a great danger from which you rescued her, this solitary companion of yours has made a vow never to speak to anyone but you.

There her angelic singing, in that voice which is dear to you, accompanied by the organ or whenever you choose by a splendid American piano, will spread through the majestic autumn evenings, rising above

the whispering of the breeze. Her accents will deepen the charm of summer evenings and explode across the beauty of the dawn, mingled with
the songs of the birds. A legend will cluster about the folds of her long
dress, when people will have seen her pass, alone, across the lawns of
your park, wandering through the afternoon sunshine or straying under
the brilliance of a starry night. An unforgettable spectacle, of which nobody will know the incredible secret, except you. Perhaps one day I shall
come to visit you in this half-solitude where you have undertaken to defy
two constant dangers: madness and the Deity.

—You will be the only guest I shall receive, replied Lord Ewald. But
since the *conceivability* of this adventure is now established, let us see
if the miracle itself is possible, and what unheard-of means you will use
to bring it about.

—Agreed, said Edison. But I should warn you that knowing the mechanism of the puppet will never explain to you how it becomes the phantom—any more than the skeleton which lies beneath the surface of Miss
Alicia Clary can possibly explain to you how *her* mechanism, integrated
with the beauty of her flesh, idealizes itself to the point of developing
those contours on which your entire love is founded.

# AMBIGUOUS PLEASANTRIES

Guess, or I devour you.
—The Sphinx

—EVERY TORCH NEEDS a match, the electrician continued. However
clumsy it may be in itself, this method of striking a light, don't we finally
admire it when the light comes forth? Someone skeptical in advance
about this method of making light, someone who was so shocked at it
that he wouldn't even try to put it in practice, wouldn't even deserve to
seek the light, would he? I'm right, am I not? Well, what we're going to
talk about is nothing but the *human machine* of Hadaly; that's what our
doctors call it. If you're already familiar with the charm of the Android
when she's *fully completed*, as you already know the charm of her model,
no explanation can keep you from feeling that charm—any more than
seeing the flayed skin of your living beauty would prevent you from
loving her still, if afterwards she appeared before your eyes *as she is
today.*

The electrical apparatus of Hadaly is no more her *self* than the skeleton
of your friend is her personality. In a word, when one loves a woman it
isn't for one particular joint, nerve, bone, or muscle; rather, I think, it's
for the unique ensemble of her being, penetrated as it is with her organic
fluids—because, with a simple glance of her eyes, she transfigures this

whole concatenation of minerals, metals, and vegetable matter which have been fused and purified into the stuff of her body.

The unity generated by these various radiant techniques is the only mysterious thing about them. Let us not forget, my lord, that we are about to talk of a vital process which is just as ridiculous as our own, and which can shock us only by its . . . novelty.

—Good, said Lord Ewald, with a grave smile. Let me begin then. A first question: why the armor?

—The armor? said Edison. I explained that before. It is the plastic scaffolding on which will be overlaid, penetrating it and penetrated itself by the unity of the electric fluid, the fleshly incarnation of your ideal friend. It contains within itself the interior organism common to all women. In just a moment we shall be studying it on Hadaly herself, who will be amused and delighted, no doubt, at the prospect of displaying the mysteries of her luminous being.

—Does the Android always talk with the voice I heard? asked Lord Ewald.

—Can you seriously ask such a question, my lord? cried Edison. No, a thousand times no! Didn't Miss Alicia's voice once undergo changes? The voice you have heard in Hadaly is her childhood voice, wholly spiritual, like the voice of a sleepwalker, not yet feminine! She will have the voice of Miss Alicia Clary, as she will have all the rest of her properties. The songs and words of the Android will forever be those that your lovely friend will have dictated to her—unknowingly, without ever laying eyes on her. Her accent, her diction, her intonations, down to the last millionth of a vibration, will be inscribed on the discs of two golden phonographs . . . perfected miraculously by me to the point where now they are of a tonal fidelity . . . practically . . . *intellectual!* These are the lungs of Hadaly. An electric spark sets them in motion, as the spark of life sets ours in motion. I should warn you that these fabulous songs, these extraordinary dramatic scenes and unsounded words, spoken first by the living artiste, captured on records, and then given new *seriousness* by her Android phantom, are precisely what constitute the miracle, and also the hidden peril of which I warned you.

Lord Ewald was shaken by these words. He had not dreamed of this explanation of *the Voice*, that virginal voice of the lovely phantom. He had simply wondered. Now the simplicity of the solution erased his smile. The dark possibility—still much disturbed, no doubt, but still a *possibility*—of the total miracle, appeared before him distinctly.

More resolved than ever to learn where the extraordinary inventor could be leading, he renewed his questioning:

—Two phonographs of *gold?* Was that what you said? No doubt they are a good deal more handsome than ordinary lungs. But why gold?

—In fact, they are of virgin gold, said Edison, laughing.

—Why?

—Because, in addition to the fact that it yields a more feminine resonance, more sensitive and more exquisite, especially when it's treated in a certain way, gold has the marvelous quality of not oxidizing. You might take notice that in order to create a woman I had to have recourse to the rarest and most precious of substances. It's a circumstance very flattering to the fair sex, the electrician added gallantly.—Still, he added, I had to use iron for the joints.

—Ah? said Lord Ewald, lost in a dream; you had to use iron for the joints?

—No doubt about it, said Edison: of course it's one of the important elements making up our own blood, our own bodies. Under many circumstances, doctors prescribe it. It's only natural to include a component without which Hadaly would not have been altogether . . . human.

—Why particularly in the joints? asked Lord Ewald.

—A joint consists of a socket and a head that fits into it. In Hadaly's structure, the socket is a magnet powered by electricity; and as the metal on which magnetism works best (better by far than nickel or cobalt), iron in the form of steel is what I have had to use for the heads of her bones.

—Really? said Lord Ewald placidly. But iron and steel oxidize; your joints will rust.

—*Ours* do, indeed, said Edison. But here on my shelf is a bottle of oil of roses, heavily perfumed, tightly stoppered, which will lubricate the joint as well as any synovial membrane.

—Oil of *roses?* queried Lord Ewald.

—Yes; it's the only one which, when it's prepared in this fashion, does not evaporate. Besides, perfumes are appropriately feminine. Once a month, you'll slip about a teaspoonful through Hadaly's lips while she seems to be napping; it's a bit like dealing with a woman when she's pregnant. You see, she's Humanity incarnate. As for the subtle essence, it will spread throughout the magneto-metallic systems of Hadaly. This bottle is more than enough for a century of use; I don't think, my lord, there will be occasion to renew the supply.

There was a touch of sinister levity in the engineer's last word.

—You say she breathes?

—Always; exactly like us, said Edison. But without consuming oxygen! We burn the stuff up, you and I, rather like steam engines: but Hadaly takes air in and out by the automatic, unvarying movement of her breast, which rises and falls like that of an ideal woman who's always in good health. The air, as it passes through her lips and delicate nostrils, will be gently warmed by electricity and perfumed with the soft scent of ambergris and roses, the lingering recollection of her oriental elixir.

The normal posture of the future Alicia (I'm talking of the *real*, not of the living woman) will be to sit or lean with her cheek in her hand . . . or else to stretch out on a sofa . . . or on a bed, just like a woman.

She will remain there without any movement other than her breathing.

To rouse her to her mysterious existence, all you need do is take her by the hand, setting in motion the fluid in one of her rings.

—One of her rings? demanded Lord Ewald.
—Yes, Edison replied, that on her index finger; it's her wedding band.
He gestured at the ebony table.
—Do you understand why that surprising hand and arm responded to the pressure of your hand, just a moment ago?
—Certainly not, replied Lord Ewald.
—It was because when you grasped it, you put a bit of pressure on the ring, said Edison. Now Hadaly, if you noticed, has rings on all her fingers, and the various stones set into them are all *sensitive*. Outside of those long, otherworldly scenes of intimacy (scenes during which you will have no reason to be concerned with her, since she will carry those hours completely inscribed in her person, so that they will constitute in effect her personality), there may be moments when, without wanting to call anything so sublime from her, you will simply want to ask her one thing or another. Well, on such an occasion, whether she's seated or lying down, she will gently rise up, if you simply take her right hand, rub softly the amethyst on the ring of her index finger, and say to her: "Come, Hadaly." She will come to you, better than the living woman. Your pressure on the ring should be light and *natural*—as when you press softly and with a bit of tender feeling the hand of the model. But such nuances are necessary only in the interests of the illusion.
Hadaly will walk straight ahead and quite unaided if you touch the ruby placed on the middle finger of her right hand; or, taking an arm, and supporting herself languidly on it, she will follow the movements of a friend, not just like a woman, but in *exactly* the same way that Miss Alicia Clary does. That's a concession you must make to her *human machine* by manipulating those rings: but it shouldn't scandalize you. Think of the various other prayers and invocations, much more humiliating than these, to which lovers sometimes resort in order to obtain a pale moment of affection. Think of all the hypocrisies to which Don Juan himself must condescend in order to bring some willful little baggage to a semblance of obedience . . . Living women too have rings one must press.
Touch ever so gently the turquoise on her ring finger, and she will sit down. Besides all these rings, she has a necklace, every pearl of which has a specific correspondence. A completely explicit Manuscript (a magician's formula book in which you can't go astray!)—something absolutely unique under the heavens, of which she will make you a gift—will provide a guide for you through the subtleties of her character. With a little experience (ah, you realize! a woman takes some knowing!)—everything will become *natural* for you.
Throughout this speech the gravity of Edison's expression was absolute.
—As for her diet . . . he resumed.
—What's that? interrupted Lord Ewald, gazing fixedly into the steady eyes of Edison.
—You seem surprised, my lord? Edison said equably. Perhaps you were

expecting to let this admirable creature die of hunger? It would be worse than murder.

—What do you mean by her diet, my dear magician? cried Lord Ewald. This time, I declare, the thing surpasses my wildest dreams.

—This is the nourishment that Hadaly takes, once or twice a week, Edison continued. I have in this old trunk various boxes of lozenges and pills which she takes of her own accord, strange little girl that she is. It's quite enough to place a container of them on a table at some fixed distance from her bedside, and point it out to her by touching lightly one of the pearls in her necklace.

She's a mere child in everything that pertains to this world; she simply doesn't know. You must teach her. We all start in her condition, yes, you and I as well. Indeed, she seems to have trouble remembering; but we, too, often forget, sometimes for our own good.

She drinks from a dainty cup of jasper, made specially for her, and her manner of drinking is exactly like that of her model. Her cup should be full of fresh water, filtered ahead of time through charcoal, that is to say, very pure, and then mixed with various salts for which you will find a formula in the Manuscript. As for the lozenges and pills, they are lozenges of zinc and pills of potassium dichromate, sometimes peroxide of lead. Today we humans take a whole mass of medications borrowed from chemistry: she is no different. You see for yourself, she is very temperate, and takes only what she needs. Happy the humans who can follow her example! I should say that when she doesn't find to hand the nourishment she wants when she wants it, she faints—or, more precisely, she dies.

—She dies? murmured the young lord with a smile.

—Yes, so as to give her chosen lover the really divine pleasure of reviving her.

—A delicate attention! Lord Ewald replied almost gaily.

—When she remains motionless and closes her eyes, a glass of very fresh water and a few lozenges and pills will bring her back to herself. However, as she may not have the strength to take them herself, it may be necessary to bring the tourmaline of her middle finger in contact with an electric battery. That's all she will need. Her first word after waking up will be to ask for some fresh water. At this point, because of the harsh metallic odor that will remain in her from the stale water of an interior crystal goblet, you must not forget to infuse the first cupful with various reactive agents, for which you will find the formulas and the dosage in the Manuscript. Their effect on this discolored water is instantaneous. Next you place the induction wire on the black diamond of her little finger, which connects with an alternator capable of heating a strip of platinum white-hot in a second. Then you drop into *your* personal battery the element of carbon which was withheld perforce while you were connecting the wire. During this process you won't forget to make use of the appropriate energizing instruments.

I'm sure you're well aware that glass which has been tempered, even by ordinary processes, can withstand a temperature equivalent to that of molten lead. Well, mine would withstand the temperature of melting platinum, and that even when it is less than half the thickness of that crystal goblet which is located within the Android, between her two lungs. Thus the heat created within this crystal by the current transmitted through the diamond is of a quality which instantly raises the temperature there to around four hundred degrees. Meanwhile the reactive agents of which I spoke to you, working on the atomic structure of the metallic substances tainting the water, draw them out and reduce them in a few seconds to a sort of dust, very white and very light. A moment later our lovely Hadaly will give forth from her half-closed lips little puffs of pale smoke, colored with this dust, which has no odor other than that of boiling water, mildly perfumed, to be sure, by contact with the distilled oil of roses of which I told you. In a matter of six seconds the inner crystal will be clear and pure again. Then Hadaly takes a glass of pure water and a couple of her lozenges; and there she is again, as alive as you or me, ready to obey all her rings and all her pearls, just as we obey all of our impulses.

—You mean it? She emits puffs of smoke from between her lips? Lord Ewald demanded.

—Just as we do ourselves all the time, Edison replied, indicating the cigars they were both holding. Only she doesn't keep in her mouth the slightest trace of metallic dust or of smoke. The fluid consumes and dissipates everything in an instant. If you want to justify it, you can just think she's fond of smoking her hookah . . .

—I noted a dagger at her belt?

—It's a weapon that no man could possibly parry, and every blow it deals is mortal. Hadaly makes use of it to defend herself in the event that, during her lord's absence, some visitor might try to take advantage of her apparent slumber. She does not forgive the slightest offense; she recognizes only her one chosen man.

—She can't see, however? asked Lord Ewald.

—Bah! Who knows? replied Edison. We don't see all that well ourselves, for that matter. In any case, she intuits or knows by experience where her heart lies. Hadaly is, let me remind you again, a slightly somber child, who knows nothing of death herself and inflicts it readily.

—So the first comer would be unable to disarm her?

—As for that, Edison declared with a laugh, I'll challenge any Hercules on earth to try it, or for that matter any creature on earth, in the sky, or under the ocean.

—How so?

—Because whenever she chooses to exercise it, the arm holding this weapon wields the power of a thunderbolt, said the inventor.

A tiny opal on the little finger of the left hand is the secret switch that connects the apparatus of the blade with an extremely powerful current.

The noise of the spark, which is about a foot long, is muffled within her body; apart from that, it's like a miniature lightning bolt. The gay trifler, the merry rake who tries, for example, to "snatch a kiss" from this sleeping beauty will find himself rolling on the floor, his face blackening, his limbs broken, struck down by a silent stroke of thunder beneath the feet of Hadaly before his finger even grazed her dress. She is a faithful friend.

—Ah, that's right! So it would be! murmured Lord Ewald. The kiss of this gallant would close a circuit.

—This is the special wand with which one touches the beryl finger in order to neutralize the current of the opal; the dagger now drops harmlessly to her side. I made the wand of specially tempered glass, tough as any metal; the formula was lost in the days of the emperor Nero, but I rediscovered it.

And seizing a long glittering wand that lay beside him, Edison swung it violently against the ebony table. The glittering star at its tip resounded; the stem bent but did not break.

There was a moment of silence. Then, as if in jest, Lord Ewald asked:

—Does she take baths?

—But every day, *naturally!* replied the engineer, as if astonished at the question.

—Ah! said the Englishman, drily. And how is that managed?

—You know very well that all photographic prints should stay at least several hours in a special solution which reinforces them. Well, here the photographic action of which I've already spoken is indelible, since the epidermis on which it's printed has been impregnated with a fluoride solution which renders it permanent and waterproof. A little rosy pearl on the left side of her necklace just above the breasts controls an inner arrangement of ports which hermetically seal the bath water away from the inner workings of the bather. You will find in the Manuscript a list of the various perfumes of which this semi-vital darling makes use, after her baths. I will also record on the Cylinder of Gestures that magnificent toss of the hair that you mentioned to me as typical of your beloved when she leaves her bath. Hadaly, with her customary gift for creating a perfect illusion, will reproduce it precisely.

—The Cylinder of Gestures? queried Lord Ewald.

—Ah, that! I'll show it to you down there, said Edison, smiling. You must have it before your eyes if I'm to explain it. But for the moment you see, if I may summarize, that Hadaly is in the first place a superlative machine for creating visions, almost a creature in her own right, a stunning likeness. The faults that I've left in her, out of politeness to Humanity, are simply a consequence of the fact that there are women of several sorts in her, as there are in every living woman. (But in her you can erase them.) She is many featured, in other words, like the world of dreams. But the supreme type who dominates these visions, HADALY herself, is, if I may use the word, perfection. As for the other characters, she *plays* them; she's a marvelous actress, endowed, if you'll take my word, with a talent far more concentrated, more sure of itself, and certainly much more *serious* than that of Miss Alicia Clary.

—After all, though, she isn't a *being!* said Lord Ewald gloomily.

—Oh! As for that, the world's most powerful minds have always been asking themselves what is this notion of Being, considered in itself. Hegel, through the prodigious process of his dialectic, has demonstrated that when you consider the pure idea of Being, the difference between that and Nothing is simply a matter of opinion. Hadaly, all by herself, will resolve every question you have about her BEING, and without any help from me, I promise you that.

—By words?

—By words.

—But *without soul,* will she have any consciousness?

Edison stared at Lord Ewald in amazement.

—I beg your pardon. *Isn't that exactly what you asked for when you cried out,* WHO WILL TAKE AWAY THIS SOUL FROM THIS BODY FOR ME? You called for a phantom, identical with your young friend, *but without the consciousness with which she seemed to be afflicted.* Hadaly has come in answer to your call; that's all there is to it.

Lord Ewald remained thoughtful and grave.

# COSI FAN TUTTE

A woman never separates her likings from her taste.
—La Bruyere

—Besides, EDISON RESUMED jovially, do you suppose it's any great loss for Miss Hadaly to be deprived of a consciousness like that of her model? Isn't she, to the contrary, much better off without it? At least you must think so, since the "consciousness" of Miss Alicia Clary seems to you a deplorable superfluity, an original sin against the masterpiece of her body. And then, the "consciousness" of a woman! I mean, a *woman of the world!* . . . Oh! Oh! What a notion! It's an idea that once baffled a council of the church. A woman only sees things according to her personal inclinations, and twists all her "judgments" to conform with the opinions of the man she's attracted to. A woman may be married ten times over, be sincere every time, and yet be ten different persons. Her consciousness, you say? But this gift of the Holy Spirit, consciousness, takes the primary form of an aptitude for intellectual friendship. In the days of the ancient republics, any young man who couldn't by the age of twenty years prove that he had a friend, a kind of second self, was declared a reprobate, an *infamous person,* in short. History knows a thousand examples of admirable friends—*all male:* Damon and Pythias, Pylades and Orestes, Achilles and Patroclus, and many more. Name me two women who were friends, in all the course of human history. The thing is impossible. Why? Because each woman knows her own mental emptiness too well ever to be the dupe of another. Just notice the expression with which one modern woman looks at the dress of another, turning as she passes to look her over, and you will be forever persuaded of it. From the aspect of her emotional life one vanity of vanities dominates or vitiates all her best intentions; to be loved is for her (and in spite of all her protestations) almost always a secondary consideration. All she really wants is to be *preferred*. That's the single word demanded by this sphinx. That's the reason why each of our lovely flowers of civilization (it's a rule to which there are very few exceptions) always despises a little the man who loves her, because by that very circumstance he becomes guilty of the awful crime *of being unable to compare her with the others.*

At bottom, modern love (if it is not, as contemporary physiology would have it, simply a matter of mucous membranes) looks to a physical scientist like a mere matter of equilibrium between a magnet and the object it attracts. Thus consciousness, without being wholly alien to the phenomenon, is perhaps indispensable only in one of the two poles. It's an axiom confirmed by a thousand experiments every day, notably those involving suggestion. And this is why you suffer.—But I'd better stop here, said Edison, with a laugh. What I'm saying seems to me to bear on a larger number of living women. Fortunately, we're by ourselves here.

—Unhappy as a woman has made me, murmured Lord Ewald, I still think you talk of women with a great deal of severity.

# CHIVALRIC DISCOURSE

Consolatrix of the afflicted.
—Christian litanies

THE ELECTRICIAN RAISED his gaze.
—Just a moment, my lord! he said.
Will you be good enough to note that in these remarks I place myself not at all in the sphere of Love, but simply on the level of so-called lovers. If we change the basis of the question and depart from the sphere of carnal desire, oh, then I'll express myself in an entirely different manner. If among the women of our own race—the only ones who matter to us, since we cannot take seriously, that is, *choose for our own* a Kaffir, a Polynesian, a Turk, a Chinese, a Red Indian, and so on—if, I say, among those of our race who no longer have in their blood a trace of the cattle or the slave, we consider those purified, elevated spirits, consecrated by prolonged dedication to duty, by self-abnegation and free devotion—surely I should think myself strange indeed if I didn't bow my spirit before those women who freely and gladly allow their wombs to be torn apart repeat-

edly, so that we may be allowed to think! How can one forget that on this stellar speck, lost in a corner of the boundless abyss, on this invisible half-cooled atom, there live so many chosen spirits from the upper atmosphere of Love, so many wonderful life-companions! I won't even try to recall all those thousands of virgins who in olden days smiled amid the flames and in the butchery of the torture chamber, on behalf of some faith which by a sublime process transfigured their instinct into pure soul; and I pass by, as well, all those mysterious heroines, among whom glitter particularly the liberators of their countries, and those who, while being dragged off under the chains and into the slavery of defeat, affirmed to their husbands even as they expired in a lingering, blood stained kiss, that steel has no power over the living spirit! And I omit also all account of those numberless women of spirit who endured unknown humiliations, endlessly devoted to the destitute, the suffering, the outcast and abandoned, asking nothing more in recompense than the hard, mocking smile of those other women who did not imitate them. For there are, and there always will be, women who will be fully inspired by some principle more lofty than that of Pleasure. *Such women have nothing to do, don't you agree, either with this laboratory or with the question that lies between us!* We make a categorical exception of these noble flowers of Humanity, radiant arrivals from the *real, true* world of Love; and then, considering only the women that one can buy or conquer, I will uphold the thesis I just expressed as absolute and unbreakable. A point which allows us to conclude once more with a word from Hegel: "It amounts to the same thing, whether you say a word once or repeat it for eternity."

# TRAVELERS INTO THE IDEAL: THE TRAIL DIVIDES!

> They reached the Sea of Shadows, in order to discover what it contained.
> —The Nubian geographer Ptolemy Hephaestion

LORD EWALD ROSE WITHOUT replying to these last words, slipped into his enormous fur coat, put on his hat, buttoned his gloves, adjusted his monocle, and lit a new cigar.

—You have an answer for everything, my dear Edison, said he. We can leave whenever you're ready.

—Right away, then, said Edison, following suit; we've lost half an hour already. The train from New York to Menlo Park will arrive in a hundred fifty-six minutes, that's a bit more than two hours and a half—and we'll need just under an hour and three-quarters to run through the outlines of the experiment.

The room where Hadaly lives is under ground, and at some distance from here. As you can well understand, I couldn't leave the Ideal around where every Tom, Dick, and Harry could get at her. Despite the long nights and years of work that this Android has cost me, in the midst of my other work, she has remained my secret.

See here now. I've discovered under this house of mine, at a depth of several hundred feet, two enormous underground caves, formerly the burial grounds of the aboriginal Algonquin tribes who in ancient ages used to inhabit this area. These grave-mounds are by no means rare in the States, particularly in New Jersey. I've brought in a heavy layer of basalt from the volcanoes of the Andes in order to reinforce the earthen walls of the main cave. In the second I have stored, with all reverence, the mummified bodies and powdery bones of our sachems, and then closed up the entrance to this underground cemetery, no doubt forever.

The first room is therefore that of Hadaly and her birds (for I had a lingering superstitious feeling that I shouldn't leave all alone this daughter of my mind). It's a little like fairyland, this kingdom of hers. Everything works by means of electricity. Or rather, it's like lightning-land, I'd say, full of high-tension currents deriving from my most powerful generators. And that's the habitat of our taciturn Hadaly. She, another person, and myself are the only ones who know the road. Although the journey there offers, as you'll see, certain difficulties for an outsider who undertakes it, I should be surprised if anything untoward happened to us this evening. Apart from that, our furs will protect us from pneumonia which the long underground tunnel might otherwise bring down on us. We will go like an arrow.

—It's completely fantastic! said Lord Ewald with a smile.

—My lord, said Edison, glancing shrewdly at his interlocutor, here's a bit of humor that you've recovered already! It's a good sign.

They stood together a moment, muffled and motionless, lighted cigars at their lips, their long fur coats drawn tightly around them, the collars pushed up under their hats.

The electrician led the way; both walked toward the shadowy end of the laboratory and toward the wall, now massive and impenetrable, from behind which Hadaly had appeared.

—I must confess, Edison continued, that when I'm in need of solitude, I go to visit this sorceress who dispels all cares. Above all, when the fire dragon of a discovery is beating his invisible wings within my head, I come here where I can only be overheard by her if I talk to myself. After a while I return to the surface of the earth, my problem solved. She is my own private nymph, my Egeria.

Even as he spoke these joking words, the engineer touched the controls of a small switch; the current flowed, the panels of the wall opened as if by magic.

—Let's go down! said Edison, since it seems that in order to discover the Ideal, we must first pass through the kingdom of the moles.

Then he gestured to the mass of solid draperies:

—After you, my lord, he murmured, with a grave and stately bow.

# BOOK III

# An Underground Eden

# EASY IS THE DESCENT INTO AVERNUS

Mephistopheles: Up or down, it's all the same.
—Goethe, *Faust*, Part II

Both stepped across the luminous threshold.

—Hold onto this support, said Edison, indicating to Lord Ewald a ring of metal. He seized it. The Engineer grasped a handle hidden behind the dark curtains and pulled it vigorously.

A square of white pavement shifted gently under their feet; it dropped straight down, guided by four steel rails at the corners. This, then, was the artificial tombstone that had raised Hadaly before them previously.

For several minutes Edison and Lord Ewald continued to descend after this fashion; the light above them receded in the distance. The pit was evidently very deep.

—An odd way to go looking for the Ideal! thought Lord Ewald, standing silently by his silent companion.

Their platform continued to sink into the earth.

Shortly both were enveloped in absolute darkness. The atmosphere was damp and smelled of the earth; their breath condensed in it.

The moving marble never paused or hesitated; the light above looked no bigger than a star; they must have been far indeed from that last glimmer of humanity.

It disappeared completely. Lord Ewald felt himself in a bottomless pit. But he said nothing to break the silence of the electrician by his side.

Now the swiftness of their descent increased to the point that their support seemed to fall away beneath them. The platform whirred through the darkness, making a monotonous noise.

Suddenly Lord Ewald pricked up his ears; he seemed to hear somewhere near him a melodious voice, mingled with bursts of laughter and other cries.

The speed diminished gradually, there was a light jolt.

A luminous porch turned silently to face the two travelers, as if some "Open, Sesame!" had made it swing on enchanted hinges. An odor of roses and musk, a sense of absolute languor, filled the air.

The young man found himself in a spacious underground chamber, like those which in former days, under the palaces of Baghdad, served to fulfill the fantasies of the caliphs.

—Enter, my lord, you've already been introduced, said Edison, who was swiftly fastening the rings of the vehicle to two heavy cast-iron grills built into the rock alongside it.

# ENCHANTMENTS

The air is so soft there, it keeps one from dying.
—Flaubert, *Salammbô*

LORD EWALD STEPPED FORWARD over the pelts of wild beasts covering the floor and surveyed this new scene.

A powerful pale blue light flooded the entire immense area. At intervals, enormous pillars supported the basalt dome, forming galleries to the right and left of the entry as far as the center of the hall. Their decoration, modifying the ancient Syrian style, converted them from base to capital into giant sheaves of wheat, with silver morning glories intertwined against a bluish background. At the center of the vault, dangling from a long golden wire, hung a giant lamp, blazing like a star, but with its electric rays softened by a blue shade. The vault itself, jet-black and of enormous height, loomed with the solidity of the tomb over the brilliance of this fixed star: it was the very image of Heaven as it appears, black and threatening, from far outside the atmosphere of our planet.

The half-circle which formed the rear of the room opposite the entry rose on either side in elegant slopes like gardens; and there, under the caress of an imaginary breeze, swayed thousands of tropical vines and Oriental roses, Polynesian flowers with their petals drenched in perfume, their pistils luminous, their leaves gleaming like green jewels. The allure of this Niagara of flowers was overwhelming. A flock of birds from Florida and the southern states of the Union chattered away throughout this artificial garden; a rainbow of bright colors seemed to rise over this part of the hall, and to radiate beams of light through prisms, from the height of the circular walls to the base of a great alabaster fountain at the center, within which an elegant plume of snowy water rose and fell in glittering drops.

From the entryway to the gardens on both sides, from the main circle of the vault to the furred rugs of the floor, the lower walls were hung with curtains of heavy cordovan leather, stamped with designs in gold.

Beside a pillar Hadaly, still heavily veiled, was standing erect, resting one hand on the case of a grand piano; lighted candles were reflected from its polished surface.

With youthful grace, she curtsied a quiet welcome to Lord Ewald.

On her shoulder a bird of paradise, superbly imitated, balanced daintily his crest of precious stones: With the voice of a youthful page, this bird seemed to be chatting with Hadaly in an unknown tongue.

A long table of cut porphyry, placed beneath a great silver-gilt lamp, reflected the light from its flawless surface; at one end of it was placed a silken cushion, like that which in the laboratory supported the radiant arm. A surgeon's case, complete with glittering instruments, stood open on a little ivory shelf nearby.

In a corner at some distance a brasier of artificial flames which reflected off silver mirrors served to warm the splendid hall.

There were no furnishings apart from a couch of black satin, a small
round table between two chairs, and on one of the walls, about the height
of the lamp, a great ebony frame enclosing a white screen and crowned
with a rose of gold.

# BIRDSONGS

Neither the song of the morning birds nor the night
and its solemn owl . . .
                                    —Milton, *Paradise Lost*

ON THE RISING GARDEN PLOT of the flowery banks, a flock of birds,
balanced atop the flowering plants, parodied Life to the extent that, while
some of them were whetting their beaks and pluming their feathers,
others had replaced the warble of birds with the sound of human laughter.
Lord Ewald had scarcely taken a step or two when the whole flock of
birds turned their heads toward him, stared at him at first in silence, and
then burst all at once into a cackle of laughter, within which both male
and female voices were heard. For a moment, the young man felt he was
facing an assemblage of human beings. He stopped short, trying to come
to some understanding of the situation.

—I suppose this is some pack of demons that this sorcerer Edison has
shut up inside these birds of his, he thought, staring at the cacklers
through his monocle.

The electrician, left behind in the darkness of the tunnel, was no doubt
just finishing the job of tying up his fantastic elevator.

—My lord, he cried, I had forgotten. Our feathered friends are welcom-
ing you with a song. If I'd been warned in advance of what was going to
befall us this evening, I could have spared you this chorus of derision,
simply by cutting off the current from the battery that animates these
featherheads. Hadaly's birds are nothing but winged condensers. I thought
fit to give them human voices and human laughter instead of the old-
fashioned, meaningless song of the normal bird—it seemed to me more
in harmony with the Spirit of Progress. Real birds are so bad at repeating
the words one teaches them! I thought it might be fun to catch on the
phonograph a few admiring or curious phrases spoken by my occasional
visitors, and then to install them in these birds by means of electricity—
thanks to one of my still-undisclosed discoveries. But now Hadaly will
make them stop. You needn't give them more than a moment of your
attention, while I finish tying up the elevator. You understand, we don't
want it playing any nasty tricks on us, like going back to the surface of
the earth and leaving us down here.

Lord Ewald looked once more on the Android. Under the peaceful breathing of Hadaly the pale silver of her breast rose and fell. Suddenly the piano began to play the rich harmonies of a prelude, the keys moving by themselves as if under pressure from invisible fingers. And the gentle voice of the Android began to sing to this accompaniment, her voice coming from beneath the veil with intonations of supernatural voluptuousness:

> All hail to you, young man without a grief!
> Love cries her curses on me through the skies,
> And woeful Hope berates me for a thief.
> Flee me, then! Get you gone! Shut tight your eyes,
> And spurn me as you would a withered leaf!

Listening to this unanticipated song, Lord Ewald felt himself overwhelmed by a kind of fearful amazement.

Then, on the flower-crowded slopes there began a kind of witch's sabbath, absurd enough to make one dizzy, and yet with a kind of ugly, infernal overtone. Frightful squawking noises, as of random visitors, poured from the throats of the birds; they were cries of admiration, questions either banal or preposterous, canned laughter and applause, occasional deafening snorts as of noses being blown, offers of money.

At a gesture from Hadaly, this parody of Glory was instantly cut off.

Lord Ewald turned his eyes once again to the Android, in silence.

Suddenly the pure voice of a nightingale rang through the shadows. All the other birds fell silent, as they do in a forest when the voice is heard of the prince of the night. This seemed an enchantment. Was the foolish bird actually singing underground? No doubt the dark black veil of Hadaly suggested to him the night, and he mistook the lamp for moonlight.

The flow of delicious melody terminated in a ripple of melancholy notes. This voice, coming straight from Nature and recalling the forests, the skies, and the immensity of space, seemed strange indeed in this place.

# GOD

> God is the place of spirits, as space is the place of bodies.
>
> —Malebranche

LORD EWALD LISTENED.

—It is a lovely voice, is it not, my lord Celian? said Hadaly.

—Yes, replied Lord Ewald, eyeing curiously the dark, indiscernible figure of the Android. Yes, it is the work of God.

—Then, she said, you must admire it; but don't try to understand how it is produced.

—What would be the danger if I tried? Lord Ewald asked, with a smile.

—God would withdraw from the song! Hadaly murmured placidly.

Edison entered.

—We can take off our fur coats now, he said briskly, for the temperature is controlled here and always balmy. This is our lost Eden, rediscovered.

The two travelers slipped out of their heavy bearskin coats.

—But, the engineer continued (in the suspicious manner of a Bartholo, who sees his young mistress in conversation with an Almaviva), you were already having a chat, I believe? Don't let me interrupt you; go on, go on!

—What a strange idea you had there, my dear Edison, to give a real nightingale to an Android!

—Ah, the nightingale, said Edison with a chuckle. Well, the fact is, I'm a lover of Nature, so I am. I really was fond of the song of that bird, and his death a couple of months ago caused me, I assure you, genuine sadness.

—How's that? said Lord Ewald. The nightingale that was singing here died two months ago?

—Yes, said Edison; I recorded his final song. The phonograph which plays it here is actually twenty-five leagues away. It stands in a room of my New York house, on Broadway. I've connected it to a telephone, the wire of which reaches into my laboratory up above; an extension brings it into the cave, down to this group of blossoms, and culminates in this particular flower.

—You see, this is what sings; you can touch it, the stalk insulates it. It's a tube of tempered glass; the calix, where you see the light glowing, is the actual speaker. It's an imitation-orchid, quite well made . . . more brilliant in color than those which perfume the brilliant clouds of dawn on the plateaus of Brazil and upper Peru.

As he explained this, Edison lit his cigar at the fiery heart of a rose camelia.

—You don't say! That nightingale who was singing his heart out is really dead? murmured Lord Ewald.

— Dead, you say? Not altogether, since I've recorded here his song and his spirit. I evoke it by means of electricity; that's spiritualism put in really practical terms, right? And since the form taken by electricity here is nothing but heat, you can light your cigar at that harmless little glow, in the very same artificially perfumed flower where the bird's soul sings like a melodious light. You can light your cigar at the soul of that nightingale.

And the electrician stepped aside to manipulate various numbered switches in a small box set on the wall beside the door.

Lord Ewald, disturbed by the explanation, stood gloomily by. A chill lay on his heart.

Then he felt that someone was touching his shoulder; he turned about; it was Hadaly.

—Ah, she said softly, in a voice so melancholy that it made him shiver. That's how it is, you see! . . . God *has withdrawn from the song!*

# ELECTRICITY

Hail, holy Light, offspring of Heaven first-born!
—Milton, *Paradise Lost*

—Miss Hadaly, said Edison, with a slight bow, we've just arrived from the Earth, and the trip has left us a bit thirsty.

Hadaly approached Lord Ewald.

—My lord, she said, would you prefer ale, or some sherry?

Lord Ewald hesitated a moment:

—Some sherry, if you please, he said.

The Android turned away to take from a shelf a salver on which glittered three Venetian glasses of opalescent hue, alongside a bottle of wine, still in its straw, and a fragrant box of heavy Havana cigars.

She placed the salver on a sideboard, poured the old Spanish wine, and then, taking two glasses in her glittering hands, presented them to her visitors.

Then, returning to fill the last glass, she turned about with a charming gesture, leaned against one of the columns of the cave, and, raising her glass almost to eye level, said in her melancholy voice:

—My lord, to your loves!

It was impossible for Lord Ewald to frown at this perhaps too free expression—so grave was the intonation of the toast, in the general silence of the room, so exquisite and graceful beyond all mere convention was the comportment of the speaker. The gentlemen were struck mute in admiration.

Hadaly gently tossed aside the wine of her glass. The fine sherry glittered in brilliant droplets as it fell to the floor like a fine dew of liquid gold.

—Thus, Hadaly said, in a slightly playful tone, I drink in spirit by means of Light.

—But come now, my dear enchanter, Lord Ewald said softly to Edison, how can Miss Hadaly reply *to the things I say to her?* To me it seems completely impossible that anyone could have foreseen my questions— above all to the extent of having engraved replies to them on discs of gold. This behavior, it seems to me, is enough to astound the most "realistic" man in the world—to use an expression belonging to that person we were discussing earlier.

Edison looked at the young Englishman without at first answering.

—Allow me to keep the secret of Hadaly to myself, at least for a while, he replied.

In response, Lord Ewald bowed slightly: then like a man who, finding himself surrounded by marvels, resolves henceforth not to be astonished by anything, he sipped his sherry, placed the empty glass on a side table, tossed away his old cigar and took a new one from the box on Hadaly's salver, lit it as calmly as Edison had done at a luminous flower nearby— and then seated himself on an ivory stool, to wait until one or the other of his hosts should see fit to vouchsafe him some explanation.

But Hadaly had returned to her post by the piano.

—Do you see this swan? Edison resumed. It contains within it the voice of Alboni. With my new machine I made a record, in the course of a European concert and without the singer's knowledge, of Norma's prayer, "Casta diva," when that great artist was singing it. Ah, how deeply I regret that I wasn't on earth in the days of the famous Malibran!

The loudspeakers of all these so-called birds are tuned as precisely as Swiss chronometers. They operate by means of a current which reaches them through the stems of the flowers.

Though they are so small, they are capable of an enormous resonance, especially if we amplify it by means of my Microphone. This bird of Paradise could give you, all by himself and with just as much intelligence as the united brains of all the singers whose voices are contained in him, a complete rendition of Berlioz's *Faust* (orchestra, chorus, quartets, solo-ists, encores, applause from the audience, renewed applause, down to the vague, indistinct comments made by the listeners). To increase the vol-ume, all we need do is multiply it by using the Microphone. As a result, if you were seated in a hotel room, placed this bird on the table, and adjusted the tiny speaker to your ear, you could have an entire concert to yourself without waking your neighbors. An immense volume of sound, worthy of an opera hall, would pour forth for you from this tiny rosy beak—so true it is that human hearing is an illusion like all the rest.

This hummingbird could recite for you Shakespeare's *Hamlet* from the beginning to end, without a prompter, and with all the expression of the very best tragic actors on our stage today.

These birds are the everyday musicians and actors of Hadaly; in their throats I have left untouched only the song of the nightingale—he is the only one in Nature who seems to me to have the right to sing. You understand that since Hadaly lives here, almost always alone, and several hundred feet underground, I felt bound to provide her with some distrac-tions. What do you think of my aviary?

—You have here a sort of scientific materialism that puts to shame the imaginary world of the Arabian Nights! cried Lord Ewald.

—But you must also realize, Edison replied, what a marvelous Sche-herazade I have here in Electricity! ELECTRICITY, my lord! People don't realize, in the world of high society, what minute but all-important steps it takes every day. But just think! Thanks to Electricity, the day is coming when there will be no more autocrats, no more cannon, no more battleships, no more dynamite or armies!

—That, I fear, is a mere dream, sighed Lord Ewald.

—My lord, there are no more dreams, the great engineer replied in an undertone.

He remained for a moment sunk in thought.

—Now, he resumed, since this is your desire, we are about to examine seriously the organ of this new electro-human creature, Tomorrow's Eve, if you will, who with the aid of Artificial Generation (already very much in vogue during recent years) seems destined within a century to fulfill the secret purpose of our species, at least among the advanced peoples. Let us forget, then, all questions which are foreign to this one. I think digressions—and don't you agree?—ought to be like those flying saucers, which children seem to throw at random to a great distance but which, thanks to an essential instinct of return built into the object itself, always return to the hand that threw them.

—But, Edison, said Lord Ewald, before we begin, would you be good enough to let me ask one last question; for it seems to me more interesting even than the examination you propose to make.

—What! Even here? Even before the experiment on which we agreed? said Edison, in surprise.

—Yes.

—What's your question? We're short of time; let's get on with it.

Lord Ewald raised his eyes to look directly into those of his friend.

—What seems to me the most mysterious thing of all, he said slowly, even more than this amazing creature, is *the reason which led you to create her.* Above all else, I should like to know how you first conceived this unheard-of notion.

To this very simple request Edison, after pondering a long time, replied slowly:

—Ah, that's my secret, my lord, and now you ask for it?

—I revealed my own to you, at your urgent request! Lord Ewald replied.

—Well, then, so be it! Edison cried. Besides, it's logical. Hadaly on the outside is nothing but a consequence of the inner Hadaly who took shape within my brain. Knowing the full complex of reflections from which she derives, you will understand her all the better when she allows us, very shortly, to study her interior.

—My dear miss, he added brusquely, turning toward the motionless Android, would you be kind enough to leave us alone for a while, Lord Ewald and myself. The things I am going to tell him ought not to be heard by a young lady.

Without replying, Hadaly retired slowly toward the dark back of the cave, bearing aloft on her silver fingertips her bird of paradise.

—Now have a seat on this sofa, my lord, the engineer began. My story will take about twenty minutes to tell, but I think it has some points of interest.

And when the young man was seated, leaning on an elbow on the porphyry table:

—These are the reasons why I created Hadaly! said Edison.

# BOOK IV

# The Secret

# MISS EVELYN HABAL

If the devil holds you by a hair, pray! Or you may
lose your head.
—Proverbs

HE PAUSED A MOMENT, to collect his thoughts.

—In Louisiana some years ago, he began, I had a friend named Edward
Anderson; he had been my friend since boyhood. He was a young man of
great good sense, physically attractive, and a devoted companion. In just
six years he had been able to liberate himself, honorably, from the clutches
of poverty. I was present at his wedding, which was a joyful occasion, for
he was marrying a woman whom he had loved for a long time.

Two years passed, during which his situation in life continually improved. In the world of commerce people considered him a judicious,
substantial person, and a man of unusual energy. He was an inventor as
well. His trade being in cotton, he discovered a method of sizing and
watering the cloth which was more economical by sixteen and a half
percent than any previously used; as a result, he made a fortune.

A secure situation in life, two children, and a true helpmeet for life, an
intelligent and contented wife, that amounted, for this fine young man,
to a sufficient sum of happiness, wouldn't you say? One night in New
York, however, at the conclusion of a banquet at which the end of the
Civil War had been celebrated with rousing cheers, two of his dinner
companions suggested that they all go off, to end the festive evening at
the theater.

Anderson, as an exemplary husband and an early riser, rarely stayed
out late, and he always felt uneasy away from home. But that very morning a little domestic quarrel had taken place, a completely futile argument with his wife, who had asked him *not to attend* that banquet,
without being able to explain why she felt that way. Thus, sensing that
his "character" was at stake, and not caring too much what he did, Anderson agreed to accompany his two friends. It's my own opinion that
when a women who loves us asks us *without any precise motive* not to
do something, a man with real character will take her request into consideration. However . . .

At the opera, they were giving Gounod's *Faust*. Anderson was a bit
dazzled by the theater lights and lulled by the music; before long, he was
overcome by the sort of torpid, sluggish good fellowship that's the general
consequence of such occasions.

Because of some remarks being made in the box next to his, his vague
and wandering glance fell upon a very pretty little golden blonde among
the performers of the ballet. He glanced at her for a second, then turned
his attention to the opera.

Between the acts, he could hardly avoid going to the bar with his two friends; and, once there, the fumes of the sherry prevented him from being fully aware that they were all going backstage.

He had never seen a theater from that vantage point; it was a curiosity, and he was much astonished by it.

Along came Miss Evelyn, the pretty blonde. The gentlemen spoke to her, and before long there were exchanging the banalities appropriate to the occasion, all more or less jokingly. She was indeed a very attractive child. Anderson, distracted by the busy scene around him, paid not the slightest attention to the dancer.

A minute or two later, his friends, who had been married for some time and maintained the usual modish double menage, were talking quite naturally of oysters and of a particular brand of champagne.

This time Anderson declined, as he certainly should have done, and in spite of the voluble insistence of his friends he was about to take his leave when the absurd memory of that little spat in the morning returned to his thoughts, exaggerated by his present circumstances.

In fact, his wife must certainly be asleep by this time, wasn't it so?

Wouldn't it actually be better to come home a little later? Shouldn't we try it? It was only a matter of passing an hour or two! As for the doubtful part being played by Miss Evelyn, that concerned his friends, not him. He *didn't even know why* this girl was slightly displeasing to him, physically speaking.

And after all, it was a day of national rejoicing that provided an excuse for any sort of difficulty to which a junket of this sort might possibly lead. And so forth, and so on.

He hesitated, nevertheless, for a few seconds. The very respectable air of Miss Evelyn decided him. So they would all go to supper together.

Once at table, it happened that Miss Evelyn, who had noted Anderson's somewhat withdrawn manner, set herself with the most carefully veiled deliberation to exercise her seductive arts. Her modest manners gave her presence such intoxicating charm that, at the sixth glass of champagne, the notion—oh, it was nothing but the merest spark of an idea! but in short, the vague possibility of an escapade brushed across the mind of my friend Edward. It was simply (so he told me later) because of the *effort* involved, when he tried, by rousing his sensual imagination, to overcome an initial aversion to the general appearance of Miss Evelyn, by setting before himself the possible pleasure of possessing her—he was seduced, in short *by the aversion itself.*

And yet he was an honorable man: he adored his charming wife, and he rejected these impulses as being simply the products of carbonic acid fizzing in his brain.

The idea returned; temptation, redoubled by the circumstances and the hour, glittered before him and glanced invitingly at him!

He thought of going home; but already his desire had been roused in this futile struggle staged by conscience, and his mind seemed afire.

A trifling joke on the austerity of his behavior was reason enough to remain.

Knowing little about nightlife, he only became aware somewhat later that one of his two friends had slipped under the table (apparently he found the carpet there more convenient than his distant bed), while the other, who had suddenly turned pale (as Miss Evelyn explained to him with a laugh), had deserted the party without explanation.

When the black doorman came to say that Anderson's cab was waiting, Miss Evelyn gently invited herself along, asking, as was perfectly proper, if he would be kind enough to take her back to her house.

It's bound to seem harsh—unless one is an out-and-out blackguard—to behave severely toward a pretty girl, particularly when one has been joking with her for a couple of hours and she's played her role of congenial companion all that time.

Besides, it didn't mean a thing, he would leave her at her door, and that would be the end of it.

So they went together to her house.

The chilly air, the darkness, the silence of the streets all increased the whirl in Anderson's head; he felt a little sick and very sleepy. In short, he found himself (was it in a dream?) accepting a hot cup of tea from the white hands of Miss Evelyn Habal—now wearing a robe of pink satin, seated before a crackling fire in a warm room, perfumed and alluring.

How had all that come about? As soon as he became aware of himself, he seized his hat hastily and rose without asking any more questions. Seeing which, Miss Evelyn declared that, thinking him more indisposed than he really was, she had sent away the cab.

He said he would find another.

At these words Miss Evelyn lowered her head and turned pale; two discreet tears glistened on her lashes. Flattered in spite of himself, Anderson tried to soften the abruptness of his departure by "a few reasonable words."

That seemed to him more "gentlemanly."

After all, Miss Evelyn had taken care of him.

It grew later still; he took a banknote and placed it, as a farewell gesture, on the tea table. Miss Evelyn picked it up, not too ostentatiously, as if thinking of something else, then, with a shrug and a half-smile threw it in the fire.

It was a gesture that disturbed the excellent manufacturer. By now he hardly knew where he was. The idea of not having behaved like a "gentleman" made him blush. He was distressed to think that he had grossly wounded his gracious hostess. Judge, if you will, his mental state from that thought. He remained indecisively by the door, hanging his head.

Then Miss Evelyn, still sullen, seized the key to the door, turned the lock with it, and flung it out the window.

At this point the serious, practical man was roused in Anderson; he grew angry.

But a sob, stifled in a little lacy handkerchief, mollified his anger.

What should he do? Break down the door? No, it would have been absurd. Any hubbub at this hour of the night was to be avoided. Wasn't it better after all to take heart and submit gracefully to one's *good* fortune?

Already his thoughts had taken an abnormal and quite extraordinary turn.

After all, when you thought about it, the infidelity of the adventure would be only very indefinite.

Besides, his retreat was cut off.

And then, WHO WOULD KNOW IT? No consequences were to be feared. And then, what a trifle! He would give her a diamond, and never see her again.

The big banquet earlier in the evening would explain many things . . . even supposing, even admitting that . . . Ah, no doubt he would have to make up some little lie, purely formal and venial, to satisfy Mrs. Anderson! (This necessity, as a matter of fact, rather annoyed him; this . . . But enough! He would think of it tomorrow.) Besides, tonight, it was already too late. And in any case, he swore on his honor that never again would the dawn find him in this room . . . and so on, and so forth.

He was at that point in his soliloquy when Miss Evelyn, coming toward him on tiptoe, threw her arms around his neck with delicious recklessness and remained hanging there, her eyelids shut, her lips seeking his. That sealed his doom.

We may hope, I daresay, that Anderson as a gallant and ardent cavalier knew how to enjoy to the full these hours of delight that Destiny had just imposed on him with such delicate violence.

Moral: A decent man without worldly wisdom makes a wretched husband.—A glass of sherry, if you please, Miss Hadaly?

# SERIOUS SIDES OF LIGHT ADVENTURES

At the word "money" she gave a glance which passed like the flash of a cannon in the midst of its smoke.
—H. de Balzac, *Cousine Bette*

LORD EWALD EXPRESSED AGREEMENT with this last judgment and asked his friend to continue the story.

—Here is my opinion of escapades and follies of this nature, Edison declared. As he spoke, Hadaly silently poured new sherry into the glasses of her two guests, then once more withdrew.

—I really believe it's a rare occurrence when at least one of these frivolous adventures (to which one expects to devote no more than a couple of hours, a bit of remorse, and a hundred dollars or so) does not exercise a baneful influence on the rest of one's entire existence. But poor Anderson had fallen directly upon a woman who was deadly to him, though she must have seemed nothing but the most banal and insignificant of them all.

Anderson was wholly incapable of dissimulation. Everything was visible in his face, his expression, his attitude.

Mrs. Anderson, a courageous young person who had waited up for him all night (as wives traditionally do), simply looked at him when he came in for breakfast next morning; and that look told her everything. Her heart sank; her instinct had been confirmed. It was a cold and gloomy moment.

Having told the servants to withdraw, she asked him how he had been since the night before. Anderson told her with an uneasy smile that, having found himself a bit under the weather at the end of the banquet, he had gone to a friend's house where the celebration continued a while longer. To which Mrs. Anderson replied, pale as marble: "My friend, I don't intend to give your infidelity any more importance than its object deserves; I will only say your first lie had better be your last. You are better than your behavior, or so at least I hope; and your face at this moment is pretty good proof of the fact. Your children are quite well; they are sleeping in their room upstairs. To let them see and hear you this morning would be to humiliate you even further. All I ask of you, in exchange for my pardon, is that you don't ask me to extend it again."

So saying, Mrs. Anderson retired to her bedchamber, holding back her tears till she had closed the door behind her.

The truth, the insight, and the dignity of this reproach had as their chief effect the inflicting of a frightful wound on my friend Edward's self-esteem—a wound all the more dangerous because it struck at the sentiments of genuine love that he had for his noble wife. From that day forward, his hearth grew ever more chill. After several days, after a constrained and glacial reconciliation—he felt that he could see in his wife nothing more than "the mother of his children." Having nothing easier to hand, he returned to Miss Evelyn. Before long his domestic situation, for no better reason than that he felt himself guilty, became irksome . . . then disagreeable . . . and finally hateful and unbearable; that's the customary path by which these things develop. Then, in less than three years, Anderson managed to ruin, by a series of careless and irresponsible deficits, first his own fortune, then that of his family, and finally that of various third parties who had seen fit to invest their money with him, till finally he stood on the verge of a scandalous and shameful bankruptcy.

At that point Miss Evelyn Habal abandoned him. Isn't it inconceivable? I still ask myself why, to tell you the truth. Up to that point, she had given every sign of really being in love with him.

Anderson had changed; he was no longer the man he had been, either physically or morally. His original weakness had spread across his nature like an oily streak. Even his courage seemed to have deserted him, along with his fortune, in the course of this affair—so that he was crushed by a desertion that, as he said, "nothing seemed to justify," especially during "the financial difficulties that he was experiencing." By a kind of misplaced shame, he ceased to keep up our old friendship; for I would certainly have made every effort to pull him out of this frightful quagmire into which he was slipping. He developed an extreme nervous irritability; he saw himself aging, disorganized, failing, and alone. At the last minute, the miserable man seemed to awake from his dream and—would you believe it?—in an access of frenzy and despair, put an end to his own life.

Here you must allow me to remind you, my lord, that before he encountered this deadly female, Anderson was of a nature as straightforward and finely tempered as the very best. I state the facts without passing judgment. I recall that during his lifetime, a trader who was his friend blamed him ironically for the probity of his conduct, called it incomprehensible, suggested that he was crazy—and then, in secret, went off to imitate him. Well, on with the story. What happens to us we often draw on ourselves, that's all.

Statistics in Europe and America will furnish us with a growing number of similar cases, rising into the tens of thousands every year—identical, or all but identical, with this one. In every city there are examples of young men, either students or workers, members of the idle rich, or excellent fathers of families as people say, who have been given a little moral twist by a weakness of this sort, and who finish their careers in the same way, blindly and irrationally—for this sort of twist enslaves a man in the same way exactly as opium does.

Farewell family, children, wife; farewell dignity, duty, fortune, honor, country, and God! It is the effect of this corrosive contagion called passion to attack the meaning of these words within the brains of anyone who has been inoculated with it; and for such deserters to the cause of gallantry, life shortly reduces itself to a mere spasm. You observe, I take it, that our statistics concern only the men who actually *die* of this disease; that we take account only of those who committed suicide, were murdered, or were executed.

The rest swarm in the galleys or choke up the prisons; that's the common trash. The figure of which we speak (and it amounts to fifty-two or -three thousand over the last few years alone) is growing so fast that we may expect it to double within the next few years—all the faster as provincial theaters open up in the smaller towns, in order to raise the artistic standards of the growing populace.

The outcome of my friend Anderson's interest in choreography affected me, in any case, so deeply—struck me so much to the quick—that I became obsessed with the idea of analyzing precisely and in detail the nature of those seductions which had been able to disturb such a heart, such senses as his, such a conscience, and bring the man to such a wretched ending.

Never having had the pleasure of seeing with my own two eyes the dancer of my friend Edward, I undertook to guess in advance, and simply from the effect she had produced—by figuring the probabilities, by sheer guesswork, if you will—what she must have been, physically speaking. Of course my predictions might result in an aberration, as I think they say in astronomy. But I was curious to know if I could reckon right, departing as I thought from a half-certainty. In a word, I proposed a work of pure calculation—out of motives similar to those of Leverrier, who always declined to set his eye to a telescope, yet who predicted almost to the minute the appearance of Neptune, and the exact spot in space where that planet would be found. His predictions were far more certain than all the telescopes in the world.

To me Miss Evelyn represented the X of an equation which could, after all, hardly have been more simple since I knew both terms of it: Anderson, and his death.

Certain elegants among her friends had told me (and on their honor!) that this creature was unquestionably the prettiest and most voluptuous little kitten for whom they had ever nourished a secret itch on the face of this earth. Unfortunately (for you see how I am) I didn't recognize in them any authority to express, even in the most tentative form, the opinions that they put before me so positively. Having observed myself the destruction that knowledge of this girl had wrought in Anderson, I frankly mistrusted the round-eyed gaze of these enthusiasts. And so with the aid of a bit of dialectical analysis (that is, not forgetting the sort of man I had known Anderson to be before his disaster, and recalling the strange impressions he had left with me when he talked of his love), I began, let's say, to feel such a remarkable difference between what everyone told me of Miss Evelyn Habal and WHAT SHE MUST HAVE BEEN IN REALITY, that the crowd of her admirers and enthusiasts began to seem like a melancholy collection of hysterical ninnies. And this is why.

Unable to forget that Anderson's first impressions were of an "insignificant" woman, and that only intoxication had led him, for a few moments, to overcome an initial and instinctive aversion for her—and besides, that the imaginary personal charms that his fellow debauchees attributed *generally* to the chorus line (grace, charm, and irresistible and indescribable art of pleasing—all that sort of stuff), could only be such in terms of their own individual senses and tastes—I was led to think very doubtfully of her personal attractions. For though there's no absolute criterion of taste in the matter of sensuality, I couldn't in all logic fail to suspect the reality of charms capable of appealing IMMEDIATELY to the leprous tastes and debauched senses of these sordid and cold-hearted revelers. Thus the account they made of her seductive qualities, speaking to me *in confidence and* ON FIRST ACQUAINTANCE, simply indicated that her nature must be as sordid as theirs—in other words, that Miss Evelyn Habal must be, both physically and morally, of a particularly perverse *banality*. Besides, the minor question of her age (concerning which Anderson had always been evasive) seemed to be of a certain value in the matter; I made inquiries. The voluptuous little kitten was in fact only thirty-four.

As for the "beauty" of which she might boast—supposing always that the aesthetic plays any part at all in affairs at this level—I repeat, what sort of beauty could I expect to find in this woman, given the frightful degradation that prolonged possession of her had produced in a nature like that of Anderson?

# THE SHADOW OF THE UPAS TREE

By their fruits ye shall know them.
—The Evangelist

—LET US, I SAID TO MYSELF, light up the interior of this passion by directing onto it the luminous principle of the attraction of opposites; I'll bet the judgment of an official moralist against a penny that our estimate will be right.

The tastes and senses of my friend, as a single look at his face and well established standards would prove, could only be of the most simple, most natural, most primitive; I presumed therefore that they could only have been sterilized and corroded to the point of disaster through being *strangled by their opposites.* Such an entity could have been utterly abolished only by the power of nothingness. Only the absolute void could have imposed on him this particular *manner* of vertigo.

However little rigor my method may have seemed to possess, therefore, it was absolutely *necessary* that in spite of all the adoration with which she was surrounded, Miss Evelyn Habal should really be a person whose actual appearance would make people run away, howling with laughter or terror—even (if they had had eyes in their heads to look at her clearly and realistically just one time) those people who sang her praises so lavishly and loudly.

It simply *had to be* that they were all dupes of an illusion, pushed to extraordinary lengths, no doubt, but a simple illusion after all. In a word, all the various attractions of this curious creature had been *patched onto* the intrinsic paltriness of her individuality. That, then, was the ravishing deceit, beneath which this absolute nullity of any quality whatever was dissimulated, and this was the fraud that could deceive the first superficial glance of a passer-by. As for the more lasting illusion of Anderson, not only was it nothing unusual, it was actually inevitable.

Some of these females, in fact—I mean those who are degrading and fatal *only* for men of a special and particularly honorable nature—know instinctively how to accustom such a lover gradually to the various vacuities of their character, and how to do so with the utmost ingenuity.

Naturally, casual acquaintances never have a chance to become aware of these flaws. But the serious and upright man they insidiously accustom, by a series of gradual and imperceptible blurrings of the vision, to a kind of sweetish half-light that gradually depraves his moral and physical retina. They have this secret talent for revealing each of their ugly failings with so much discretion that it passes for an advantage. And in the end they are slowly, insensibly, able to convert their reality (often frightful) into the original vision (often charming) that they first presented. Custom prevails, lowering curtains over the sight; haze and darkness settle in; the illusion deepens—and the capture of the personality can no longer be prevented.

Such an operation seems to be evidence of a keen mind, a clever intelligence, does it not? But that's an illusion as great as the other.

These creatures understand nothing but this trick of theirs, they can do nothing else, they understand nothing else. They are strangers to everything else in the world: it doesn't interest them. Animals are exact in the same way, they are programmed at birth and for life. No mathematician could introduce a single extra cell into the hive of a swarm of bees, and the form of the hive is precisely that which contains the greatest number of cells in the smallest possible space. We could find many such examples. The animal is never deceived, never fumbles at his task. Man, on the other hand (and this is what constitutes his mysterious nobility, the hand of divinity upon him), is subject to development and to error. He is interested in all things and loses himself in them. He aims higher. He feels that he alone, in the entire universe, is not a finished product. He has the aspect of a forgotten god. By an impulse both natural and sublime, he asks himself *where he is;* he tries to reconstruct his own starting point. He examines his own intelligence, testing it against his doubts, as if after some immemorial fall which no one recalls exactly. Such is man in his reality. But the quality of beings who, though we list them among humanity, still cling to the instinctive world, is to be perfect on a single point, but *completely* limited to that one action.

Such are these "women," modern Furies of a sort, for whom the man they select is simply a victim to be weakened and degraded. By a kind of fatality, they obey blindly the obscure urgings of their malignant essence.

These creatures of man's second fall, these inciters of evil desires, these dispensers of forbidden pleasures, may pass unperceived through the arms of a thousand carefree lovers who take a passing fancy for them—pass, and even leave an agreeable memory behind. *They are fatal only to the man who lingers over them to the exclusion of all others till his heart is contaminated with an abject need of their embraces.*

Wretched the man who accustoms himself to the lulling of these sirens who destroy all sense of remorse! Their malice makes use of the most insidious, most paradoxical, most anti-intellectual devices of seduction in order to stupefy, little by little, a heart which had been pure and unstained till their evil power took command of it.

No doubt in every man there slumber ugly desires, rising from the fumes of flesh and blood, and terrible when unleashed. Certainly, since my friend Edward Anderson succumbed, the germs must have been in his heart, as in limbo; him I neither excuse nor judge! But I declare her guilty, above all, of a capital crime, that pestilent creature whose function it was to unleash knowingly, deliberately, the hundred-headed hydra within him! She was in no way comparable, I think to Eve, simple-minded Eve, whose love—it was fatal, no doubt, but still love—dragged her toward the Temptation that she thought would raise her companion in Paradise to the station of a god. This was a deliberate assailant, avid with a secret and instinctive lust to drag down—almost in spite of herself—into the most sordid spheres of instinct, into the most abject darkness of the spirit, the soul of a man from whom she wanted nothing except one day to be able to contemplate with idiot satisfaction his destruction, his despair, his death.

Yes, that's what these women are: trifling playthings for the passing playboy, but deadly to men of more depth, whom they blind, befoul, and bind into slavery through the slow hysteria which distills from them. Thus, to accomplish their dark mission, which they can hardly avoid performing, *even in spite of themselves,* they lead their deluded lovers through ever-deepening clouds of folly, to a state of cerebral anemia and shameful ruin, or to the blockish suicide of Anderson.

All by themselves, they conceive of their project in its totality. At first they offer, like an insignificant apple, the taste of an *unknown* pleasure— already degrading, however! which a man agrees to accept only with a weak, uneasy smile, and, *even before the deed,* with a sense of remorse. How to steer clear of these alluring but detestable acquaintances who are, in case after case, *exactly the women that one shouldn't encounter!* Their pleas and feignings, so subtle and artificial that one senses the craftsman's instinct behind them, *almost* (Ah, I say *almost!* The whole thing is in that word for me!) oblige a man to sit down with them at this table where before long the demon of their evil nature constrains them, yes, them too, to furnish the man with nothing but poison. At that point, it's all over; the work is begun, and the malady will follow its course. Only a god can save him; and only by a miracle.

From such facts, duly analyzed, we may draw our conclusion in the following draconian edict:

These "neutral" women whose thought begins and finishes at the loins— and whose nature is therefore to focus ALL the thoughts of every man they meet on that spot, even though their bodies shelter nothing in the way of spirit but a mean and selfish calculation—these women, I say, are less remote in REALITY from the animal species than from our own. Hence the man worthy of his name has the rights of high and low justice over this species of deadly female, by the same title that he claims these rights over other members of the animal kingdom.

If, then, one of these women, by fraudulent means and by taking advantage of one of those unlucky moments in which every living being finds itself defenseless, has been able to ensnare a worthy man (handsome, young, brave, devoted to duty, industrious, intelligent, and hitherto irreproachable in his life)—yes, I think this woman should not have the RIGHT to mislead such a man, willy-nilly, to the pit where that hellcat was able to lead my friend Anderson.

But as it is in the nature of these neutral yet negative beings to abuse men, since their very existence is degrading and, worse, contagious, I conclude that it's the right of the man as against the woman (if, by some miracle, he is enabled to see what has been victimizing him) to inflict a summary execution on her, in the most secret and certain manner that he can, without the least scruple or form of legality, any more than one would hesitate about killing a vampire or a viper.

Consider the facts again; they are important. As a result of momentary mental confusion, due to the intoxication of that supper (a unique event, perhaps, in the life of this man), this vigilant vampire recognizes her possible prey, intuits his hidden, still-unawakened sensuality, weaves her web, catches him in it, leaps on him, ties him hand and foot, lies to him and poisons him as her trade teaches; and at the same time also strikes at his wife, unblemished, responsible, and chaste, with her lovely children, waiting anxiously for her husband, now for the first time inexplicably late—you see, I repeat, that in a single night she corrodes with her potent poison the moral and physical health of this man and his family.

Suppose her to be questioned next day by a judge; she would reply blithely, "That at least, once he was awake, this man was perfectly free to protect himself by not coming to see me anymore." But she knows perfectly well—since as a result of her fearful instincts this is the only thing she does know—that *this* man *of all others* can escape her only by an effort far more violent than he anticipates, an effort which every relapse (and she will try to provoke them constantly) can only render more difficult.

And the judge will not know what to reply or what decision to render. Will this woman then have the *right* to press on her odious work, to drive her blind victim *helplessly* toward his destined precipice?

So be it, then. But just reflect how many thousands of women have been executed for less subtle assassinations. That is why, man having a duty to his fellow man, if my friend could not himself bring down justice on this "irresistible" purveyor of poison, I saw exactly what I had to do.

So-called modern spirits, that is to say tainted with the most skeptical of egoisms, will cry out when they hear me: "Oh, come now! What's the matter with him? Such fits of highflown morality—aren't they, to say the least, out of date? After all, these women are handsome, they're good looking; everybody knows they use these qualities to make their fortunes, which is nowadays the main aim in life—especially nowadays when our 'social organizations' don't permit them many other ways to get ahead. And afterward? Well, why not? It's the great struggle for existence, the great *Kill or be killed* of modern times. Every man for himself! Your friend was nothing but a simpleton after all, guilty on any accounting of a *shameful* weakness and of sensuality amounting almost to madness; no doubt, he was also a boring and tiresome 'protector' as well. My word, let him rest in peace!"

Well and good. It goes without saying that these statements seem rational only because they consist of vague, imprecise clichés; indeed, they aren't much different, in my judgment, so far as their bearing on our question is concerned, from these: "Is it raining?" or "What time is it?" And though they don't realize it, such statements reveal in the speakers a condition of moral servitude very much like that of Anderson.

"These women are *handsome, beautiful!*" they say?

Come, now! Beauty is a matter that concerns art and the human soul. Those loose women of our time who do in fact have a certain superficial beauty do not, it will be noted, produce their malign effects *on men of the sort I've described;* they have no reason to stoop to temptations which in the first place they would consider unattractive. They never inflict so much pain, and they are infinitely less dangerous, because their lie is never complete. The greater number are even possessed of a certain simplicity which makes them capable of a few elevated sensations, even of an occasional devotion! *But those who can degrade a man like Anderson to such vileness and such a death* cannot be *beautiful* in any *acceptable* sense of the word.

If there are some who *seem* beautiful at first glance, I declare that their faces or bodies must, inevitably, contain some traces of abject infamy which deny the rest and affirm their real nature. And in fact, *given the kind of passion they arouse, and the consequences to which it leads,* it's plain their power over the lover comes in no way from their illusory beauty, *but rather directly from those hateful traits* which make the lover merely *tolerate* the bit of conventional beauty they do possess, and disgrace. A casual passer-by may desire these women for their bit of beauty: the lover, never! And yet our idle commentators say, "These women *are pretty!*"

Even granting that the word means different things to different people, nobody knows at what price these women are pretty, after they have made their first three steps in life past childhood. And I maintain the price has some bearing on the matter, this time.

For the *prettiness* of their persons is quick to become *artificial* and in time VERY ARTIFICIAL. No doubt it's difficult to recognize at a glance; but *the fact remains.* "What matter (our philosophers will cry out) if the whole thing makes an agreeable impression? Are they anything, for us, but fleeting moments of pleasure? If the enjoyment of their persons is not disagreeable to us when spiced up with artificial aids and supplements, what matter how they prepare the synthetic diet on which they feed us?"

I think I can show you shortly that it matters a good deal more than these careless amateurs suppose. In any case, if we look these dubious adolescents in the eye (ah yes, *pretty* they are, no doubt), we'll surely see in those eyes the glare of the obscene cat who sleeps within them, and that sight will spoil on the spot whatever charm they may have *borrowed* from their contrived and artificial youth.

If, begging pardon for the sacrilege, we place alongside them one of those simple young girls who still blush rosy red at the first sacred words of young love, we'll see at once that the word "pretty" is a little generous when applied to that banal assemblage of powder, rouge, false teeth, false complexions, false hair whether red, blonde, or brunette—not to speak of the false smiles, false glances, and false pretenses of "love."

So it's not right to say of these women that they're pretty or ugly, beautiful or young or blonde or old or brunette or fat or thin—since even if it was possible to know it, and affirm it before they had suddenly changed to some other appearance, even so, *the secret of their malignant charm is not there.* Quite the contrary!

Though it baffles the mind to conceive it, the axiom which summarizes these female *witches* in their relation to man is that *their morbid and fatal influence on their victim is in direct ratio to the quantity of moral and physical artifice with which they reinforce—or, rather, overwhelm— the very few natural seductive powers they seem to possess.*

In a word, whether they are pretty, or beautiful, or ugly, or anything else, it *isn't for that reason* that *their* lover (the one who is going to succumb before them) grows attached to them and blinds himself! *These personal characteristics have nothing whatever to do with it.* This is the single point I wanted to make, because it's the most important.

I pass, among the people of this world, for an inventive and imaginative fellow; but, let me assure you, my imagination, even heightened by my avowed hatred for Miss Evelyn Habal, could never—no, never, never— have conceived to what a fantastic and unthinkable degree this axiom would be confirmed by . . . what we are about to see, hear, and touch, this very minute.

Now a concluding comparison, before we come to the demonstration.

All beings have their *correspondences* in the lower orders of nature. Such a correspondence, which is as it were the figure of the superior being, clarifies its nature in the eyes of the metaphysician. To recognize it, one need only consider the results produced by these creatures on those who come near them. Well, in the world of vegetables (where we must look to find a correspondent being, since these deadly Circes, in spite of their human forms, are essentially creatures of the animal world), their correspondent form is the upas tree, of which they are, by analogy, simply so many poisonous leaves.

One sees it first, gilded by the sun and glittering. Its shade, as you know, benumbs the senses, fills the mind with feverish hallucinations, and, if one lingers under its influence, becomes fatal.

Thus the beauty of the tree must be *borrowed* and *adventitious* to its real nature.

And in fact if you strip the upas of its millions of caterpillars, which are brilliant and poisonous, it will be nothing but a dead tree with dirty pinkish flowers, from which the sun can no longer strike a glint. Its very power to harm disappears if one transplants it away from its native habitat—when it promptly perishes, disdained by one and all.

The caterpillars are necessary to it; it *appropriates* them to itself. They attract one another, the tree and its innumerable caterpillars, because of the deadly action they can accomplish together, which *calls them forth* to a synthetic unity. Such is the upas tree, the manchineel tree if you will; certain varieties of love cast the same sort of shade.

And when one strips from these women whose allure is so deadly their corrupting artificial attractions—like so many caterpillars—there remains of most of them what remains of the upas tree under the same circumstances.

Replace the sun by the imagination of the man who looks on them, and the illusion, precisely because of the secret effort it requires, appears all the more sparkling and attractive. Look at these women with a cold eye for *what produces* the illusion, and it will dissipate in thin air, leaving a sense of invincible disgust, deadly to the slightest stirring of desire.

Miss Evelyn Habal thus became for me the subject of a curious experiment. I determined to discover her, not to prove my theory, which has been true for all eternity, but in order to state it under conditions as *complete* and *beautiful* as they could possible be.

—Miss Evelyn Habal! I said to myself. *I wonder what that could possibly be!*

I set out to track her down.

The delicious child was at Philadelphia, where the ruin and death of Anderson had made for her a splendid reputation; she was much sought after. I went there and made her acquaintance in a few hours. She was quite ill; consumption was preying upon her—upon her physical constitution, of course. So that in fact she only survived for a short time after her dear Edward.

Yes, death took her from us several years ago.

Still, I had enough time before she died to verify in her my presentiments and theories. After all, you understand, her death mattered very little; I can make her come into our presence as if nothing had ever happened to her.

The enticing little ballerina is going to favor us with a dance, accompanying herself with a song, a performance on the tambourine and castanets.

With these last words, Edison rose and pulled at a cord which hung from the ceiling beside a tapestry.

# DANSE MACABRE

And it's hard work being a beautiful woman!
—Charles Baudelaire

A LONG STRIP OF transparent plastic encrusted with bits of tinted glass moved laterally along two steel tracks before the luminous cone of the astral lamp. Drawn by a clockwork mechanism at one of its ends, this strip began to glide swiftly between the lens and the disk of a powerful reflector. Suddenly on the wide white screen within its fame of ebony flashed the life-size figure of a very pretty and quite youthful blonde girl.

The transparent vision, miraculously caught in color photography, wore a spangled costume as she danced a popular Mexican dance. Her movements were as lively as those of life itself, thanks to the procedures of successive photography, which can record on its microscopic glasses ten minutes of action to be projected on the screen by a powerful lampascope, using no more than a few feet of film.

Edison touched a groove in the black frame and lit a little electric light in the center of the gold rose.

Suddenly a voice, rather flat and stiff, a hard, dull voice, was heard; the dancer was singing the *alza* and *ole* of her fandango. The tambourine began to rattle and the castanets to click.

The gestures, glances, and lip movements were reproduced; so were the wrigglings of the hips, the winking of the eyes, the thin suggestion of a smile.

Lord Ewald stared on this vision in silent surprise.

—Well now, my lord, cried Edison, isn't this a ravishing little girl? Just look at that! All things considered, the passion of my friend Edward Anderson was not inconceivable. What hips! What beautiful blonde hair; really, it's like burnt gold! And that complexion, so pale and yet so warm! Note the curious long eyes! And those little rosy fingernails where the dawn seems to have wept tears of dew, they glitter so brilliantly. And those delicate blue veins, do you see how they glow in the excitement of the dance? The youthful freshness of arms and neck, do you see it? Her pearly smile, her rich red mouth? Those elegant brows of arched gold? Her finely etched nostrils, nervous as the wings of a butterfly? That breast, so firm and full, which seems to be straining under its satin? Those delicate legs, so beautifully modeled? Those delicate feet, so finely arched?—Ah, Edison concluded with a long sigh, Nature is very beautiful after all! And this particular creature is certainly a morsel fit for a king, as the poets say.

The electrician seemed lost in a romantic reverie. You would have thought he was waxing sentimental over the girl himself.

—You're quite right, said Lord Ewald; make fun of Nature if you choose, but even though it's true that this pretty young creature dances better than she sings, still, I suppose, if sensual pleasure was what attracted your friend, this young lady must have appeared to him extremely desirable.

—Ah? said Edison, still dreamy, but with a strange accent. He looked at Lord Ewald.

He turned to the tapestry and adjusted a collar on the cord controlling the lamp. The first filmstrip leaped from its track; the image disappeared from the screen. A second heliochromic band quickly replaced the first and began running as quick as light before the reflector. On the screen appeared a little bloodless creature, vaguely female of gender, with dwarfish limbs, hollow cheeks, toothless jaws with practically no lips, and almost bald skull, with dim and squinting eyes, flabby lids, and wrinkled features, all dark and skinny.

And the whining voice continued to sing an obscene song, and the whole creature continued to dance just like the previous image, with the same tambourine and the same castanets.

—Well, said Edison, smiling, what do you think?

—Who or what is that little witch? Lord Ewald asked.

—Why, Edison replied placidly, it's the same person; simply, this is the true one. It is the person who was hiding beneath the appearance of the other. I see you've never really taken a serious accounting of the improvements in the art of make-up during these modern times, my lord!

Then, resuming his enthusiastic tone, he cried aloud:

—*Ecce puella!* Here is the radiant Evelyn Habal, stripped like a tree of its caterpillars, of all her alluring devices! Isn't she enough to make one die of desire? Ah, the poor lovelorn child! How lively she is in our picture! The dream of love fulfilled! What profound passions, what ardent love she could inspire! Isn't it beautiful when we can gaze on Nature pure and simple? Can we ever hope to rival this Nature? I'm bound to give up and hang my head—don't you agree? Or do you think it was just by the power of Suggestion that I obtained these last poses? Ridiculous! Don't you think that if Anderson had seen her this way at first, he would still be by his fireside with his wife and his children—and that this would have been better for him in the end? What is this craft called "make-up"? Women have fairy fingers, it's clear! And once the original impression is produced, I tell you the illusion clings forever, and even feeds on the most odious of faults. And finally, it fastens itself with fingernails like those of a demented chimera, even on the most hideous of all women.

A really sly puss need only know the art of confessing her faults to make of them an effective screen, and use it to inspire passion in the unpracticed men whom she has imperceptibly blinded. It's no other than a matter of vocabulary: the skinny girl becomes delicate, the ugly one is lively, the dirty one casual, the liar is clever, and so forth and so on. And, a single imperceptible step at a time, one reaches the stage where this little girl's lover arrived at a shameful death. Read the thousands of newspapers which every day and in every land repeat the same story and you will see that, far from inflating my figures, I am understating them.

—Do I have it on your word, my dear Edison, asked Lord Ewald in an undertone, that these two visions are of one and the same woman?

At this question, Edison once more looked into the face of his young friend, but this time with an expression of grave melancholy.

—Ah, you really have rooted the Ideal deep in your heart! he cried at least. Well, since that's how it is, I must really convince you this time! And in fact you force me to it. Look, my lord; here is the real reason why that poor Edward Anderson destroyed his dignity, his body, his honor, his fortune, and his life.

And he drew from the wall, under the luminous image which continued its sinister dance, a deep drawer:

—Here, he went one, here are the spoils of this charmer, here are the devices of this seductive creature! Will you be kind enough to provide us with a bit of light, Miss Hadaly?

The Android rose, picked up a perfumed torch, and, after lighting it at the blossom of a flower, took Lord Ewald by the hand and drew him gently toward Edison.

—Indeed, the engineer continued, if you thought at your first view of Miss Evelyn Habal that her charms were *natural,* I fear you are going to have to revise that impression. For as a person whose appearance was defective she was, I might say, a paragon, a model, a prodigy, a nonpareil, the supreme type of which other women, God be thanked, can only be pallid copies! See here now.

At this word, Hadaly raised her torch over her veiled head to illuminate the dark drawer, standing beside it like a statue at the side of a tomb.

# EXHUMATION

Weep, o ye Venuses and Cupids!
—Catullus

—Now see here, Edison blared through his nose with the accents of an auctioneer. Here we have the girdle of Venus, the scarf of the Graces, the very arrows of Cupid himself.

First of all, the tresses of Salome, the glittering fluid of the stars, the brilliance of sunlight on autumn foliage, the magic of forest noontides, a vision of Eve the blonde, our youthful ancestress, forever radiant! Ah! To revel in these tresses! What a delight, eh?

And he shook in the air a horrible mare's nest of matted hair and faded ribbons, streaked here and there where the coloring had worn away, mottled and tangled, a dirty rainbow of wig work, corroded and yellowed by the action of various acids.

—Here now is the lily complexion, the rosy modesty of the virgin; here is the seductive power of passionate lips, moist and warm with desire, all eager with love!

And he set forth a make-up box filled with half-empty jars of rouge, pots of greasepaint, creams and pastes of every sort, patches, mascara, and so forth.

—Here we have the calm magnificence of the expression, the pure arc of the brows, the deep shadows of passion, eloquent of sleepless nights! We have also here the delicate veins of the temples and the rose colors of the features, suffused with sudden joy at the sound of the young lover's footsteps!

And he pulled forth various hairpins blackened with rust, blue pencils, lipstick brushes, lacquers of China white, eyebrow pencils, boxes of Smyrna kohl, and so forth.

—Here are the gleaming white teeth, so girlish, so glittering and fresh! Ah, the first kiss on those provocative lips, which displayed them behind a dazzling smile!

And he played, like a pair of castanets, with the upper and lower dentures of a set such as one sees on display outside a dentist's office.

—Here is the glitter, the sheen, the pearly glow of the neck, the youthful softness of shoulders and arms; here is the alabaster gleam of the lovely undulant throat!

And he held up, one after another, the different implements of complexion-creation—lotions, powders, creams, and so forth.

—Here now are the lovely breasts of our siren, from the salt sea waves of morning! From the foam of ocean and the rays of the sun, here are the ethereal contours of the heavenly court of Venus!

And he waved aloft some scraps of gray wadding, bulging, grubby, and giving off a particularly rancid odor.

—Here are the thighs of the wood nymph, the delirious bacchante, the modern girl of perfect beauty, more lovely than the statues of Athens, and who dances with such divine madness!

And he brandished aloft various old girdles, falsies, and apparatus of steel and whalebone, busks of orthopedic function, and the remains of two or three ancient corsets so complicated, what with their laces and buttons, that they looked like old dismantled mandolins, with their strings whipping at random about them.

—Here are the dainty, the exquisitely formed legs of the ballerina!

And he waved aloft, while holding them as far from himself as possible, two heavy, smelly stockings, once of a rosy color, but now most notable for the wads of stuffing they contained.

—Here is all the brilliance of the nails, both toe and finger, the glitter of those delicate little hands! Ah, the Orient! surely that must be the source of these luminous colors!

And he showed them the little bottles of polish and their brushes still stiff and dirty with different shades of coagulated lacquer.

—Here is the elegant step, the arch, the dainty poise of a feminine foot, where nothing betrays the presence of a servile, a base, or a greedy race.

And he knocked against one another a pair of high-heeled shoes, with soles constructed to conceal the real dimensions of the foot, and bits of cork built in to give the appearance of an arch.

—Here is the BASIS of the smile, whether naive, mischievous, cajoling, lofty, or sad, the real machinery of those enchanting expressions and "irresistible" glances for which the lady was famous.

And he displayed an enlarging mirror in which the dancer had studied, down to the last line, the "values" of her physiognomy.

—Here now we have the healthful aroma of youth and life, the personal savor of this animated flower!

And he brought forth vials of synthetic perfumes, products of the chemical industry, devised to counter the regrettable emanations of nature; and he placed them among the rouge pots and eyebrow pencils as carefully as if they were exotic specimens.

—Here now are some more serious perfumes, though produced by the same factory; their scent, their color of iodide, and their mutilated labels give us reason to suspect what sort of *forget-me-not* the poor child could offer to her chosen admirers.

Here are some other ingredients and objects, oddly shaped to say the least; out of deference to our dear Hadaly, we had better say nothing of their possible use, don't you agree? They suggest, however, that this naive creature had a certain skill in the craft of rousing men to innocent transports of excitement.

And, to conclude, said Edison, here are certain herbs and specimens from the shops of the chemist and the herb-seller; their special virtues are well known, and they indicate that Miss Evelyn Habal, in her modesty, did not feel herself destined for the joys of family life.

Having thus terminated his catalogue, the sinister engineer threw everything back in the drawer pell-mell, and then, having reburied what he had exhumed, he dropped the lid on it like a tombstone, and shoved the drawer back into the wall.

—I trust, my lord, he concluded, that you are now edified. I do not believe, I refuse to believe, that there ever existed among the most bedaubed and bepraised of our light ladies, any one more . . . recommended . . . than Miss Evelyn; but what I swear, what I can witness, is that *all are, or will be tomorrow (with the help of a little artifice), more or less of her family.*

And he turned to a pitcher nearby to wash and then dry his fingers.

Lord Ewald remained silent, deeply surprised, profoundly depressed, and lost in thought.

He watched Hadaly as she silently extinguished her torch in the earth of a tub holding an artificial orange tree.

Edison returned.

—I understand, he said, how under certain circumstances one might kneel before a grave or a tomb; but before this drawer, before these relics! . . . It's hard to conceive of, isn't it? And yet aren't these in fact *her true remains?*

He pulled once more at the cord controlling the projector. The vision disappeared, the singer fell silent; the funeral oration had concluded.

—We're far removed here from Daphnis and Chloe, said he.

And then, as if providing a tranquil summary:

—Well, he said, was it really worthwhile to become a crook, to deprive one's family of everything, to forget all one's hopes and dreams, and to fling oneself blindly into the pit of a disgraceful suicide, for no better reason than this, *the contents of this drawer?*

Ah! people who are too confident of their facts! What poets they are, when they themselves begin to think about taking a flight in the clouds! And to think that fifty-two or -three thousand such cases (many perhaps less monstrous than this one, but just about identical in kind if they were investigated thoroughly) occur every year in England and America. And most of those who fall victim to the moral horror of these "irresistible" executioners are people endowed with the strongest instincts of practical common sense; they are the most "realistic" of men, and the most disdainful of those unworldly dreamers who, from the far reach of their chosen solitude, look sorrowfully on.

# HONI SOIT QUI MAL Y PENSE

Thus, darting afar their glances of rage,
Each sex will decline on its separate stage.
—Alfred de Vigny, *Destinies*

—WELL THEN, EDISON continued, when I had assembled these proofs that my unhappy friend had never held in his arms anything but a sad phantom, and that underneath all her paraphernalia the hybrid creature of his passion was as false as his love itself—to the point, in fact, of being nothing but *the Artificial giving an illusion of life*—I drew, as I was bound to, just one conclusion:

Since in Europe and America thousands of reasonable men every year leave their wives and allow themselves to be destroyed in thousands of episodes *almost* identical with this one . . .

—Oh, come now! interrupted Lord Ewald, you must admit that your friend encountered the most unbelievable exception in the world, and that the wretched outcome of his love affair can be excused or understood only as the effect of clinical madness calling for medical treatment. So many other female vampires are truly seductive in their charms, that trying to make a general rule on the basis of this single incident would be a gross paradox.

—I said something like that myself, replied Edison. Still, perhaps you forget that you yourself found perfectly natural the first appearance of Evelyn Habal; and without insisting further on the way our elegant ladies have brought chemical laboratories into their boudoirs (where a proverb tells us that neither husband or lover should ever venture), I will tell you that the moral idiocy of women who produce such disasters more than compensates for the little they have which is physically not repulsive. Stripped as they are even of the feelings that animals possess, and courageous as they are only to destroy or bestialize, I prefer not to say what I think of the malady they spread and which some people choose to call love. Indeed, part of the whole evil comes from the fact that some mealy-mouthed people make use of this word "love" in place of a *real* one.

Well then, I thought, if the Artificial, when assimilated to or even amalgamated with human nature, can produce such catastrophes; and since, consequently, any woman of the destructive sort is more or less an Android, either morally or physically—in that case, one artifice for another, why not have the Android herself? In this sort of passion it's always impossible to escape from a strictly personal illusion, and since all these women are more or less artificial, since they themselves suggest the notion of replacing natural with artificial, let's spare them the trouble, if that may be. These women want us to weep salt tears if their whims or their crimes decree that we must be separated from their rouge pots? Let's try to change their lie for another. That way will be easier for them and for us. In a word, if the creation of an electro-human being, capable of working a change for the better in the spirit of mortal man, can be reduced to a formula, let us try to obtain from Science an equation for Love. To say no more, *it will not have the evil effects which we've shown to be inevitable in the human race as it now exists;* essentially, it's a matter of fighting fire with fire.

Once the formula is found and diffused throughout the world, it may well save within a few years thousands and thousands of lives.

And nobody will be able to raise impudent objections against me, *since it's the normal action of the Android to neutralize within a few hours any low and degrading desires for the original model that may exist in the most inflamed of hearts; and this is accomplished by saturating it with a profound awe hitherto unknown, the irresistible effect of which I do not think anyone can possibly imagine who has not experienced it.*

Accordingly, I went to work; I struggled with the problem, one concept at a time. In the end—aided by a sort of prophetess named Sowana, about whom I'll tell you later—I discovered the formula of which I had dreamed; and out of it, in a single creative burst, I raised from a shadow, Hadaly.

# DAZZLEMENT

Rational philosophy weighs the possibilities and declares:
"There's no way to disintegrate light."
Experimental philosophy listens and remains silent through the
centuries; then suddenly she displays the prism and says:
"Light is disintegrated."

—Diderot

—SINCE SHE HAS BEEN standing alone in these hidden caverns, I have
been looking for a man sure enough of his own intelligence, and desperate
enough, to undertake the first experiment; and it is you who are going to
complete this work, you who have come—you who, possessing perhaps
the most beautiful woman on earth, are sickened by her to the point of
wanting to die.

Having thus brought his fantastic tale to a close, the electrician turned
toward Lord Ewald and indicated the silent Android who stood beside
them, holding her two hands against her veil as if to conceal her still
invisible features.

—Now, said Edison, do you still want to know *how* this vision of the
future is going to be realized? Are you certain that your deliberate illusion will be strong enough to withstand this explanation?

After a silence, Lord Ewald said simply: Yes.

Then, with a glance at Hadaly:

—One would think she was suffering, he said, as if considering with a
kind of grave curiosity this fantastic and yet somehow very real anomaly
that stood before him.

—Not a bit of it, said Edison. She has taken the attitude of a child about
to be born—she is hiding her face before life.

There was a moment of silence.

Come, Hadaly, he cried abruptly.

At these words, the Android stepped forward, veiled and shadowy, toward
the porphyry table.

The young man looked at the electrician: already bent over his glittering surgeon's case, Edison was choosing from among his crystal scalpels.

Having reached the edge of the table, Hadaly turned about and spoke
graciously, locking her hands behind her head:

—My lord, she said, preserve, if you will, a little indulgence for my
humble unreality, and before you despise the thought of it, recall for a
moment the human society which obliges you to have recourse to a mere
phantom in order to recapture Love.

As she finished speaking, a sort of electric shock ran across the flexible
armor of Hadaly; Edison captured it with the aid of a wire held between
two long pincers of crystal and made it disappear.

It was as if the soul of this human form had been carried off.

The table tilted up; the Android now stood with her back to it, her head resting against the cushion.

The electrician stooped and loosened two steel clamps riveted to the floor, slid them beneath the feet of Hadaly, and then moved the table back to its horizontal position, with the Android now lying on it like a corpse on the dissecting table in an amphitheater.

—Think of the picture of Andreas Vesalius, said Edison with a smile. Though we're alone down here, we're imitating the general idea of it at this moment.

He touched one of the rings of Hadaly. The outer integument slowly drew open.

Lord Ewald shuddered and grew very pale.

Until that point doubts had still lingered in his mind.

In spite of everything his learned guide had said, he had found it impossible to admit that the Being which had given him, up to now, the illusion of a living woman enclosed in a suit of armor was in fact a fictive being created by Science, patience, and genius.

Now he found himself face to face with a marvel the obvious possibilities of which, as they transcended even the imaginary, dazzled his understanding and made him suddenly feel to what lengths a man who wishes can extend the courage of his desires.

❧ BOOK V ❧

# Hadaly

# FIRST APPEARANCE OF THE MACHINE IN HUMANITY

When one solitary meets another in a remote spot,
they won't be thought to recite the Lord's Prayer.
—Tertullian

EDISON UNTIED THE BLACK VEIL at the beltline.

—The Android, he said inexpressively, is divided into four major parts:

1. The living system of the interior, consisting of equilibrium, walking, talking, gestures, senses, the expressions of the face which is still to come, and the inward regulator of movements, or, to put it more simply, "the soul."

2. The plastic mediator, that is to say the metallic envelope which isolates the inner spaces from the epidermis and the flesh; this is a sort of armor with flexible articulations, within which the interior system is solidly fastened.

3. The flesh (or artificial flesh, to call it by its proper name), placed over the plastic mediator and adhering to it. When penetrated by the animating fluid, it forms the traits and contours of the imitated body, with the particular and personal emanation of the body to be reproduced, the hollows and swellings of the bony structure and the musculature, the system of veins and arteries, the sexuality of the model, all the proportions of the body, and so forth.

4. The epidermis or human skin, which includes and consists of the coloring, the porosity, the features, the special glitter of the smile, the delicate marks of expression, the exact lip movements of speech, the hair and the entire system of down, the eye assembly, with the associated individuality of the glance, not to speak of the teeth and mouth systems and those of the nails.

Edison delivered this lecture in the monotonous tone of one setting forth a geometrical theory the QED of which is practically contained in the first proposition. From his tone of voice Lord Ewald gathered not only that the engineer was going to resolve all the problems raised by this monstrous set of affirmations, but that he had already resolved them, and was simply concerned to set forth the proof of established facts.

That was why the English lord, stirred beyond expression by the terrible assurance of the scientist, felt the icy chill of Science at his heart during this extraordinary explanation. Nevertheless, playing the man of the world, he spoke not a word of interruption.

Edison's voice had become singularly grave and melancholic.

—My lord, he said, at least I have no surprises to set before you. What would be the point? Reality, as you are about to see, is surprising enough in itself without any special tricks of mine. You are about to witness the birth of an ideal being, since you will be present at an illustrated explanation of the inner workings of Hadaly. Can you imagine a Juliet submitting to such an examination without causing Romeo to faint?

Actually, if one could form a sort of retrospective moving picture of the woman one loves in her very first physical manifestations, and *what she was like when she made her very first movements*, I imagine most lovers would feel their passion melt away into a sentiment where the Lugubrious would fight it out with the Absurd and the Inconceivable.

But the Android, even in her first beginnings, offers none of the disagreeable impressions that one gets from watching the *vital processes* of our own organism. In her, everything is rich, ingenious, mysterious. Look here.

And he applied his scalpel to the central apparatus fastened at the level of the cervical vertebrae of the Android.

—This is the point at which the life of man has its focus, he said, continuing his lecture. It's the place in the spinal column from which springs the marvelous tree of the nervous system. Touch this point with a needle, and (as you realize) our life will be snuffed out on the spot. This is the root of our entire sympathetic nervous system, on which, for example, our continued breathing depends; so that, if one touches it ever so delicately, we die of suffocation. You see that in this matter I have respected the example set by Nature; these two inductors, isolated at this very point, control the activity of the golden lungs of the Android.

Let us first take, as it were, a bird's eye view of the organism in its entirety; I'll explain its detailed workings a little later.

It is by means of an intricate code recorded on these metal discs and automatically read off them, that warmth, motion, and energy are diffused through the body of Hadaly, through an interlaced network of complex wires, exact imitations of our nerves, arteries, and veins. It is by means of these little discs of hardened glass (their operation is quite simple, and I'll explain it to you in a moment) that the current distributed through the electrical network is modulated, so that motion can be communicated or inhibited in any one of the limbs or in the entire person. This is the basic electro-magnetic motor, which I have miniaturized while at the same time multiplying its power; *all* the various inductors of the mechanisms are connected with it.

This particular electric spark (it's on loan from Prometheus) has been trained to circle this magic ring, and thereby to produce respiration, by acting on this magnet, placed vertically between the two lungs where it can influence this nickel strip leading to a stainless steel sponge, which moves and then returns to its original position under the regular influence of the isolator here. I have even thought of those profound sighs that sorrow draws from the depths of the heart; Hadaly, being of a gentle and taciturn disposition, is no stranger to them or to their special charm. There is no woman who does not know how easy it is to imitate these melancholy sighs. Actresses can produce them by the dozen—each warranted of the highest possible quality—to produce their proper illusion in us.

Here are the two golden phonographs, placed at an angle toward the center of the breast; they are the two lungs of Hadaly. They exchange between one another tapes of those harmonious—or I should say, *celestial*—conversations: the process is rather like that by which printing presses pass from one roller to another the sheets to be printed. A single tape may contain up to seven hours of language. The words are those invented by the greatest poets, the most subtle metaphysicians, the most profound novelists of this century—geniuses to whom I applied, and who granted me, at extravagant cost, these hitherto unpublished marvels of their thought.

This is why I say that Hadaly replaces *an* intelligence with Intelligence itself.

You see, here are the two almost imperceptible needles of pure steel, trembling within their grooves, which turn perpetually beneath them, thanks to the subtle, unceasing energy of that mysterious electric current: they wait for nothing but the actual voice of Miss Alicia Clary, I assure you. They will capture that voice from a distance without her knowing what is happening; she will be repeating, like a dutiful actress, scenes which she herself cannot possibly understand—the marvelous and unknown roles in which Hadaly will become incarnate forever.

Below the lungs, you see here the Cylinder on which will be coded the gestures, the bearing, the facial expressions, and the attitudes of the adored being. It is the exact analogy of those so-called barrel organs, on the cylinders of which are encrusted, as there are on this, a thousand little metallic points. Each of these points plucks a particular tone at a particular time and thus the cylinder plays exactly all the notes of a dozen different dance airs or operatic operas. So here; the cylinder, operating on a complex of electrical contacts leading to the central inductors of the Android, *plays* (and I can tell you exactly how) *all the gestures, the bearing, the facial expressions, and the attitudes of the woman that one incarnates in the Android.* The inductors of this Cylinder are, so to speak, the great sympathetic nervous center of our marvelous phantom.

To be more precise, this Cylinder is programmed to make possible some seventy different movements of a general character. It is approximately the same number that any well-bred woman can and should command. Our movements, apart from those of a few spastics and convulsionaries, are almost always the same: the different situations of life give them different overtones and make them seem different entirely. But I've calculated, by breaking them down into their fundamental components, that twenty-seven or twenty-eight different movements at the most suffice to compound an unusually rich personality. Besides, what is a woman who gesticulates too much? An unbearable creature. Accordingly, you will find here none but harmonious and graceful movements, the others being either shocking or useless.

Now the two lungs and the sympathetic nervous center of Hadaly are linked together by a single unique movement of which the fluid is the origin. Some twenty hours of recorded conversation, complex and captivating, are inscribed on her central tapes; thanks to the technique of galvanoplastics, they cannot be erased. Their *expressive correspondences* are likewise inscribed on the points of her Cylinder, micrometrically exact. It follows accordingly (does it not?) that the action of the two phonographs, combined with that of the cylinder, must produce a perfect synchronizing of words and gestures as well as of the movement of the lips. And so it is also with the glances of the eyes and the most subtle expressions of the features.

You understand that the ensemble of these different programs is regulated in every scene with split-second precision. No question but that it's much harder, mechanically speaking, than to record a melody with its accompaniments and complex harmonies on a single cylinder; but our instruments, as I've told you, have become so subtle and exact nowadays (especially with the help of our fixed lenses) that with a little bit of patience and some use of the differential calculus one can work out the whole procedure pretty exactly.

By now I can *read* the gestures recorded on this Cylinder as fluently as a printer's devil can read off, in reverse, a page of type in a forme; it's simply a question of habit. And so I will correct this first proof of mine to accord with the various physical habits of Miss Alicia Clary; capturing them is by no means difficult, as a result of the process of moving-picture photography of which you've just had a demonstration.

—But, Lord Ewald interrupted, a scene such as you describe supposes an interlocutor, doesn't it?

—Well, then, said Edison, won't you always be available to take that part?

—How will it be possible to foresee what I will ask the Android, or say in answer to her?

—Oh, that! said Edison. A short process of reasoning will convince you that the problem is very simple—though I don't think, in fact, that you've stated it quite accurately.

—Just a moment: whatever the problem may be, it's my personal freedom, in my thought as in my affections, that it will take away from me, if I submit my spirit to its domination!

Lord Ewald's voice verged on the shrill.

—What matter, if it ensures the REALITY of your dream? said Edison, calmly. And who is really free in any case? The angels of the old legend, perhaps! Perhaps, indeed, they are the only ones who can be said to have earned the title of Free! For they are delivered from Temptation . . . having seen the abyss into which those angels fell who undertook to think for themselves.

The two speakers stared silently at one another after this dictum.

—If I understand you correctly, Lord Ewald resumed in amazement, you are saying that *I myself* must learn *by rote* my various questions and answers!

—Don't doubt that you'll be able to modify them, *as you do in every-*

*day life*, and just as ingeniously as you please—in such a manner that the anticipated response will in every case fit exactly with what you say. *In fact, let me assure you that every part of the scene will correspond with every other part, absolutely.* What we are given is the great kaleidoscope of human words. Once the spirit is imbued with the tone and color of a subject, any vocable whatever can always be adapted to suit it, in the *perpetually approximate* world of human existence and human conversation. There are so many vague, suggestive words, which have such extraordinary intellectual elasticity! Their charm and profundity depend simply on the nature of that *to which they represent an answer!*

An example: let us suppose that a single word, the word *already!* is what the Android is going to say in a few moments. I take this particular word as an example, in lieu of many other possible phrases. You are expecting this word, which will be spoken in the grave and gentle voice of Miss Alicia Clary, and accompanied by a melting gaze of her lovely eyes pouring themselves into yours.

Now, just imagine how many questions or thoughts there are to which this one word can respond magnificently. It will be up to you to create the depth and beauty of her response *in your own question.*

This is what you are always trying to do, in life, with your living lady; the trouble is simply that when it's this special word for which you're waiting, when you are expecting it so desperately because it would form such a noble harmony with your soul that you would like to be able to *inspire* this woman with it, *never,* NEVER does she pronounce it. It will FOREVER be a sour dissonant note, *another word in short,* that her native judgment suggests to her—and it will wring your heart.

Well, now, with the future Alicia, the real one, the Alicia of your soul, you will no longer have to endure these sterile and bitter frustrations. The word that comes will always be the *expected* word; and its beauty will depend entirely on your own suggestive powers! Her "consciousness" will no longer be the negation of yours, but rather will become whatever spiritual affinity your own melancholy suggests to you. You will be able to evoke in her the radiant presence of *your own, your individual passion,* without having to worry, this time, that she gives the lie to your dream! Her words will never deceive your delicately nurtured hope! They will always be just as sublime . . . as your own inspiration knows how to make them. At the very least, you will never experience here that fear of being misunderstood which haunts you with the living woman; you will simply have to pay attention to the intervals between the words she speaks. In time, it may even become superfluous for you to articulate anything! Her words will reply to your thoughts, to your silences.

—Ah! Lord Ewald replied. If that's the extent of the comedy in which you are asking me to take part forever, it's an offer that I can only refuse— and I should tell you so at once.

# NOTHING NEW UNDER THE SUN

This is also vanity.
—Ecclesiastes

Edison at this speech laid down on the table beside the Android the glittering instrument with which he was performing the autopsy of his own creation, and raised his own sharp eyes:

—A comedy, my lord? said he. But don't you agree to perform a comedy all the time with the original? Since, by your own confession, you can do nothing but disguise or conceal from her your own sincere thoughts—and must do forever, out of mere politeness?

Oh, who under the sun could be so strange as to imagine that he doesn't enact a comedy every day of his life until his death? The only people who pretend to the contrary are those who don't realize what role they are playing. Everybody plays in the comedy! And must, perforce! And every man with himself! Being sincere—that is the only dream that is absolutely beyond all hope of realization. Sincerity! How would it be possible in any case, since nobody knows anything? Since nobody is really persuaded of anything? Since nobody even knows who he really is? A man tries to convince his neighbor that he is, himself, convinced on some point, despite the fact that in his poorly stifled conscience he understands, he sees, he feels how doubtful the whole thing is. And why does he do this? In order to drape himself in a completely imaginary faith, which deceives nobody for a single instant and which the neighbor pretends to believe only in the hope that someone will return the same favor to him sometime soon. Comedy, I tell you! Actually, if people *could* be sincere, no society would last for an hour—since all men pass their lives concealing their thoughts, as you very well know! I challenge the most outspoken man in the world to be sincere for a single minute without getting his face smashed, or finding himself obliged to smash someone else's. Again, what do we really know on any subject whatever that is not subject to a thousand different influences, from the age, from our social circumstances, from the temporary state of our spirits, and so on? As for love! Well, if two lovers could ever see each other *plainly, as they really are,* and know, really know, what they think, *and the way each one thinks of the other,* their passion would evaporate in an instant! Happily for them, they always manage to forget this inescapable law of physics, that "two atoms can never make real contact with one another." And they never reach into one another's minds except in that infinite illusion of the dream which is innate within every child, and by which the human race perpetuates itself.

Without illusion, all things perish; there's no escaping it. Illusion is light itself! Look at the heavens from above the lower levels of the atmosphere, at an elevation of only four or five leagues: you see an abysm the color of ink, across which are scattered red sparks without any glitter. Evidently, it's the mists and clouds, symbols of illusion which create light for us! Without them, nothing but perpetual shades. Our sky itself plays the comedy of light for us—and we should guide ourselves by its holy example.

As for lovers, as soon as they've *persuaded themselves* that they know one another, their attachment consists primarily of habit. They cling to a fantasy of their beings and their imaginations with which each has imbued the other; they hold to a phantom which each has conceived at the instigation of the other—eternal strangers that they are! But they are no longer devoted to one another *as they have recognized themselves to be.* An inescapable comedy, I tell you! As for the particular person you love, since she's nothing but an actress herself, and you think her most worthy of admiration when she's "acting a part," and she only charms you completely at such moments—well, what better can you ask for than her Android, which will be nothing but these special moments, selected and fixed for you, as if by enchantment?

—It's all very persuasive, said the young man, sadly. But . . . to hear exactly the same words for ever and ever? To see them always accompanied by the same expression, even though it's an admirable one? I'm afraid this comedy will very quickly come to seem . . . monotonous to me.

—I affirm, Edison replied, that when two persons love one another, every alteration of appearance can only involve loss of devotion; it can only alter the flow of passion and dissipate the dream. Hence these rapid revulsions of lovers when they see or think they finally see their true natures emerging from behind these artificial veils in which each of them has draped himself in order to please the other. They experience here nothing but a *difference* from their original dream, yet it suffices very often to make them hate or despise one another.

Why?

Because if one has discovered joy in a single special manner of thinking, what one wants at the bottom of one's heart is to preserve it without shadow or blemish, just as it is, without augment or diminution: for the best is the enemy of the good—*and novelty is the one thing that disenchants us.*

—Yes, it's true, murmured Lord Ewald, with a pensive smile.

—Well, then! The Android, as we've said, is nothing but the first hours of love, immobilized, the hour of the Ideal made eternal prisoner. And already now you are complaining that this hour will not spread its inconstant wings to leave you! Oh, human nature!

—You must also think, Lord Ewald replied with a thin smile, that this aggregate of marvels stretched out on the table before us is nothing but a dead and empty group of substances without any awareness of their cohesion or of the future prodigy which will rise out of them.

You may be able to deceive my eyes, my senses, and my intelligence by this magical vision: but can I ever forget, within me, that she is only an impersonal object? My own self-consciousness cries out to me coldly: How are you going to love zero?

Edison looked the Englishman up and down.

—I've already demonstrated to you, he said, that in passionate love there is nothing but vanity piled on lies, illusions on unconsciousness, maladies heaped atop mirages. —Love zero, you say? Once again I ask you, what difference does it make if you are the unity placed before this zero, as you are now and always were previously before all the zeros of life—and if this is in fact the only such zero which will never disillusion or deceive you?

Didn't you say that every idea of possession was dead and extinct in your heart? I offer you nothing, as I've very clearly stated, but a transfiguration of your living lovely—that is to say, the very thing you begged of me when you cried: "Who will deliver this soul from this body for me!" And now already you are frightened in advance at the monotony of having your own wish realized. You want, now, to have the Shadow as changeable as the Reality! Well, I must prove to you now, as I will, that *you are trying here to impose an illusion on yourself,* since you cannot be ignorant, my lord, that *Reality* herself is not so rich in alterations, variations, or novelties as you are trying to make yourself believe. Let me remind you that neither the language of happy love nor the range of expression in the human face is as various as *your secret wish to retain a melancholy that you're already beginning to question* leads you to suppose.

The electrician reflected a moment. Then:

—To make eternal a single hour of love, the most beautiful of all—that moment, for example, when the mutual avowal flowers into the explosion of the first kiss—oh, to stop time at that moment, fix it, define it, make that spirit fresh and that first vow eternal! Would not that be the dream of every human being? It is only as a way of trying to recapture that ideal instant that people continue to love, in spite of all the differences and diminutions brought by subsequent hours. Oh, to have that moment, all by itself! Everything else is sweet only as it augments and recalls that supreme instant. How ever to weary of experiencing and reexperiencing that unique joy; the great, monotonous moment! The loved one represents nothing but this work of recapture forever before one, forever to be reattempted—one drives oneself mad in the attempt to recapture it. All the other hours of one's life do nothing but recoin in small change this hour of gold! If one could reinforce it by a few of the better instants, culled from subsequent nights, it would appear to be the ideal made palpable of all human felicity.

Having said so much in general, I should like to ask you this. If your beloved could be incarnated for you as she was in the hour when she seemed most beautiful, the hour when some god inspired in her words that she did not in the least understand—but on the condition that you too would *repeat to her those words of yours which also made up a unique part of that moment, would you think you were "acting in a comedy" if you accepted this divine bargain?* Wouldn't you despise all the rest of the human vocabulary? And would this woman seem monotonous to you? And would you really grieve for all the subsequent hours when she seemed so different that you felt ready to die of it?

Wouldn't it be enough for you to have her soft glance, her gentle smile, her voice, her entire personality, as it was at that moment? Wouldn't you in fact think of reclaiming from Destiny all those other casual words, most of them either unfortunate or insignificant—of snatching them away from the treacherous moments which followed the flight of your first illusion? No, perfect repetition is no flaw in love. The man who loves, doesn't he repeat at every instant to his beloved the three little words, so exquisite and so holy, that he has already said a thousand times over? And what does he ask for, if not the repetition of those three words, or some moment of grave and joyous silence?

And in fact it's apparent that the best thing is to *re-hear* the only words that can raise us to ecstasy, precisely because they have raised us to ecstasy before. It's precisely the same here as it is with a beautiful picture or a noble statue in which one discovers every day new beauties, new depths of meaning. A lovely piece of music is more delightful to hear the second time over than it is the first; one reads over a fine book without tiring of it, in preference to a thousand others through which one doesn't even want to skim. For one single beautiful thing contains the essential soul of all the others. A single woman contains, for the man who loves her, the souls of all other women. And when one of these absolutely perfect moments brushes us with its wing, we are so constructed *that we want no others,* and we will spend the rest of our lives trying, in vain, to call this one back—as if the prey of the Past could ever be snatched from its jaws.

—Very well, so be it! said Lord Ewald bitterly. However, never to be able to *improvise* a single simple, natural word . . . that's bound to freeze up the springs of good will, even the most resolved.

—Improvise! cried Edison. Do you still believe that anybody improvises anything of any nature whatever? You don't believe that people are constantly *reciting?* Well, when you pray to God, isn't that all laid out for you in the prayerbooks that you learned by heart as a boy? Don't you read or recite, morning and night, the identical prayers, which were composed, *once and for all and all the better for that,* by men who had a gift for prayer, who knew how to go about it? Didn't God himself give you the formula for it, by saying: "When ye pray, let it be after this manner, etc." And isn't it true that for the last two thousand years other prayers have been nothing but pale dilutions of this one that he gave us?

Even in everyday life, isn't it true that most conversations have the formulaic sound of letter endings?

In actual truth, there's not a single word that isn't a repetition: and you don't need Hadaly to find yourself, every so often, in close conversation with a phantom.

Every human occupation has its repertoire of stock phrases—within which every man twists and turns till his death. His vocabulary, which seems to him so lavish, reduces itself to a hundred routine formulas at most, which he repeats over and over.

Probably you have never taken the pains or the pleasure to calculate the number of hours that a hairdresser who started in the trade at eighteen and is now sixty has spent saying to every chin he shaves: "Nice weather (or, rotten weather) we're having today." It's his way of starting a conversation, and if he gets an answer, it flows along for five minutes on this topic, to be *automatically* picked up by the next chin in his chair, and so on through the day, to be resumed again tomorrow. That makes a little more than *fourteen* solid years of the man's life, which is to say a quarter of his days on earth, more or less; the rest he employs in getting born, whining, growing up, drinking, eating, sleeping, and voting in an enlightened manner.

What do you expect anyone to improvise, alas! which hasn't already passed through a million mumbling mouths? We mutilate, we adjust, we reduce to commonplaces, we babble, and that's all. Is all that noise worth regretting? Was it worth saying in the first place, or worth being listened to? Isn't it plain that Death with his handful of mud will be along tomorrow to shut off all this insignificant blabber, all this hackneyed chatter in which we indulge when we think we're "improvising"?

And how can you hesitate to prefer, simply in terms of saving time, the wonderful verbal condensations composed by those who make a trade of words and a habit of thought—who could express by themselves alone the sensations of all Humanity? These global men have analyzed the subtlest shadings of the passions. What they have kept is the pure essence, which they express by condensing thousands of volumes into a single profound page. They are, in fact, us, whoever we may be. They are the incarnations of the god Proteus who lives in all our hearts. All our ideas, our words, our sentiments weighed to the last scruple are filed away in their minds, with their most remote ramifications, those which we have never dared or ventured to reach. They know before we do and better than we can everything that our passions can suggest to us of the intense, the magical, the ideal. We can do no better, I assure you; and I see no reason why we should take special pains to talk worse than they do, or to glory in our clumsiness on the score that at least it is our own, *personal* to us—since even this, as I've shown you, is nothing but an illusion.

—Go on then, with the anatomy of your inanimate lovely! said Lord Ewald after a pause for thought. I'm at the service of your discourse.

# WALKING

Known by her gait, the goddess' self appeared.
—Virgil

Responding to his friend, the engineer picked up his glittering glass tweezers and resumed his lecture:

—Time is short, he said, and I'll have barely time to give you a general idea of the possibility of Hadaly; but this will be perfectly adequate, the details being simply a matter of craftsmanship. What I must make clear to you above all is the really fabulous simplicity of the techniques used in my experiment.

In a word, I made it a point of pride to *demonstrate*, in this work, my ignorance before all the admirable pedants who are the glory of our kind.

Look here now: the Idol has silver feet, velvety as a tropical night. Finishing them off requires nothing but the addition of a snowy skin, the contouring of the ankes, the rosy nails and veins of your lovely singer, if I imagine her correctly. Though these feet seem light in their step, they are less so in reality, because their hollow interior is filled with quicksilver. This impermeable container of platinum which extends them is filled with liquid metal and rises, as it narrows, to the top of the calf in such a manner that the entire weight bears on the foot itself. In a word, we have here a pair of little buskins weighing fifty pounds each, and yet almost as skittish as those of a child. They seem as light as the feet of a bird, so powerful is the electro-magnet which controls them and operates the femoral joint in what will be a perfect imitation of human motion.

The metallic envelope is separated at the waist, where this black veil was knotted a moment ago, by this supple zone, consisting of many short, delicate steel wires which reach below the thighs to bind the entire structure of the hips to the waist itself and to the lower part of the abdomen. This band, as you notice, is not circular; it is oval, with a slight forward inclination, like the lower line of a corset prolonged toward a point.

This gives to the waist of the Android (once it is covered with flesh, both resistant and flexible) that graceful yielding quality, that firm undulation, that elegant elasticity which is so seductive in a mere woman. Note carefully that the wires are convex at the waist and concave at the forward part of the body, a circumstance which, thanks to the tension generated, allows the body to be held as erect as a delicate poplar tree, and also permits all the lateral movements available to the original. All the interactions of these steel wires are controlled; each one of them is under the direction of the central electric current which prescribes their individual flexions according to the pattern printed on the central Cylinder.

You will be surprised at the *identity* of the charm which these programs can diffuse through the various attitudes of the body. If you cannot believe that female "grace" amounts to so little, take occasion sometime to examine the corset of Miss Alicia Clary, and calculate the difference in her movement, in the very lines of her body, without this artificial guide! You see, there are some of these unequal and interlacing flexibilities in all our articulations, especially in those of the arms, whose infinite, languorous variations have cost me some long, sleepless nights.

Note also the turnings of the neck: joined with the movements transmitted by the wires of the waist, they are, I believe, of a delicacy and subtlety that cannot be faulted. It is the swan as woman; the degree of curvature and coordination is precise.

All this ivory bonework is superbly finished, don't you agree? This elegant skeleton is fastened to the plastic mediator by these crystal rings within which every bone is free to move according to the precise kind of motion that is desired.

Before I tell you how the Android gets up, let us supposed that she is standing still. You want her to walk a particular distance, which she translates automatically into a certain number of steps. I've already explained that all you need do is issue your command through the right ring, the amethyst, for the inner current to carry out the movements.

Here now is an explanation, much abbreviated and without commentary, of the physical theory involved in these charts of the Android; these are the technical *means* by which she walks, the *possibility* will come out in the course of the demonstration, which will follow at once.

At the end of the neck of each femur, you observe here a small golden shield, slightly concave, rather like the crystal of a watch and about the size of a silver dollar.

Both are slightly tilted toward one another and each is mounted on a long moving shaft built into the femoral bone itself.

In a state of rest, the upper part of these two shafts surmounts the height of the femur by about two millimeters, which produces a separation of the two little golden discs from the necks of their respective femurs.

The dimension of their diameters marked B—which corresponds to dimension A of the Android's inner hip joint—is joined by a concave track of stainless steel, along which moves freely a crystal spheroid which is chiefly responsible for the action of walking. This globe weighs about eight pounds, because its center is filled with quicksilver. At the least motion made by the Android it slides along the track from one to the other of these two golden discs.

Consider now, at the top of each leg, this little steel rod, hinged at the center; its two halves, opening below, play freely about a steel axle or hub. One end is solidly fastened to the dorsal interior of the plastic mediator—that is, *above* the zone of flexibility—the other to the anterior limit of each leg.

When the Android is lying flat, the two rods will be observed to fold at their centers, to form acute angles—and that in the anatomical area once immortalized under the name of Callipygian Venus. Note, please, that the steel hub which forms the apex of the angle is *lower* than the two ends of the rods.

You note these two solid interlocked arches which support the plastic mediator from within to about the height of the lungs, and which extend, each of them, to the point where the anterior portion of the rods is fastened to each leg.

There, these arches twine together and slip, like a running knot, over the *anterior* part of the rods.

When the inner cavity is closed, these steel pectoral bars, convex in form, adapt themselves in the manner of ribs to support and protect the internal mechanisms; they sustain and reinforce the two arches, and isolate them from all the other apparatus through which they pass beneath the phonographs.

At bottom, it's *more or less* the same physiological process by which humans walk, and though our machinery is a little better concealed, these means of locomotion differ from ours *only in their appearance to our eyes. What does that matter, as long as the Android can walk?*

The interaction of these steel wires serves to draw forward the weight of the torso, already somewhat inclined when the order to walk is given.

Above the angle of the rods, here are the magnets, each in communication with its wire, and here now is the master cable of the walking process. It is in direct contact with the electro-dynamic apparatus, from which it is separated by no more than three centimeters, just the thickness of the interruptor when this comes between the current and the wire.

This inductor reaches up into the thoracic cavity. There the two wires which correspond with the magnets of each leg come to receive their charge of dynamic current; each receives it in its turn, since one can get its charge only by interrupting the current leading to the other.

Except when the Android is lying down or when the interruptor is placed between the master cable and the magnets, the crystal spheroid is in constant motion from one golden disc to the other; it's held in that grooved track which moves in accordance with the movement of the legs. The first leg which receives the crystal ball in its golden cup will be the first to move.

So much for theory; here now is the demonstration necessary to understand this rough outline.

We will suppose that, thanks to the slight but decisive inner impulse imparted by the electric impulse of the amethyst ring, the spheroid of crystal moves to its place on the disc atop the right leg, drawn by the mysterious impulse which impels it there.

The disc, raised above the end of the bone, sinks beneath the weight of the ball; its long shaft sinks into the femoral bone, causing contact to be made between the disc and the neck of the femur. The lower end of the shaft, as it gives way, makes contact with the inductive wire for that leg, which consequently receives energy from the generator.

Electric current reaches the magnet of the upper hip articulation and instantly multiplies its power. This magnet strongly attracts the inner part of the connecting rod, the hub of iron; the acute angle widens on the spot to a straight line, and with considerable force, leading thus to the extension of the leg with which it is connected. This leg moves forward in its joint, but would remain suspended in air, if the weight of the body, communicated through the interlocked arches and the running knot to the anterior portion of the rods, were not carried forward toward the leg that has moved. Meanwhile that leg, under its own weight and that of the body combined, places its foot on the ground, having taken a step of about forty centimeters. I'll explain to you in a moment why the Android doesn't reel to one side or the other.

At the very instant when the foot touches the ground, a dynamic current reaches the magnets of the knee joint; and the knee, in its turn, flexes.

There's no abruptness in the *entirety* of this double tension, because each part *is integrated with the other.* Once the leg is covered with its artificial flesh, *which has all the elasticity of the real thing, it is human movement to the life.* There's some abruptness in the movement of our femur, but it is softened by the action of the knee which always flexes later, as in the Android. Animate the joints of a skeleton; they will always seem jerky and *automatic* to you. It is the flesh, once again, and the effects of clothing, which soften all that.

The Android, once having placed her foot on the ground, would stand still in that position if the flexing of the knee did not automatically push up, about three centimeters above the femoral bone, the shaft of that golden cup which cradles the crystal ball. The cup, raised up in this fashion and no longer held absolutely straight by the neck of the femur, inclines slightly, because of its original positioning, in the direction of the left cup. The crystal globe falls into its metal track, rolls toward the other cup, and its weight, impetus, and inclination cause it to gain the golden cup of the left femur and nestle into it.

No sooner has this cup dropped in its turn under the weight of the spheroid than the interruptor of the right leg moves into place; the magnets there cease to be under the influence of a current, the hub of the right-hand connecting rod, *because it is heavier than the two ends,* drops down and reverts to its original acute angle, while the left connecting rod, stretching itself out and gently bringing the weight of the torso to bear on its leg, *repeats the step of the Android—and so it proceeds indefinitely until the steps inscribed on the Cylinder have been taken, or until the ring is once again touched.*

I must point out that the current is turned off in one knee only after it is turned on in the opposite knee, without which arrangement the second knee *would flex too soon.* But this never happens when, for example, the Android goes to her knees, lost in a mystical ecstasy like those sleepwalkers who can be made to pose by their hypnotists as if in a cataleptic trance, or like the pose of hysterics, who can be made to freeze by simply placing close to their backs a flask of cherry water hermetically sealed.

It is the intimate integration of these various flexions and tensions that gives the Android her gait of absolute human simplicity.

As for the very slight noise made by the crystal ball on its track and in its golden cups, it is completely muffled by the layer of flesh. Even under the plastic mediator alone, one could barely hear it with a microphone.

# THE ETERNAL FEMALE

CAIN: Are you happy?
SATAN: We are powerful.
—Lord Byron, *Cain*

DROPS OF SWEAT STOOD like tears on the brow of Lord Ewald; he looked upon the features, now glacial in their austerity, of Edison. He felt that beneath this strident, scientific demonstration two things were hidden in the lecturer's infinite range of severely controlled secret thoughts.

The first was love of Humanity.

The second was one of the most violent shrieks of despair—the coldest, the most intense, the most far-reaching, even to the Heavens, perhaps!— that was ever emitted by a living being.

In fact, what these two men were really saying, one with his literal interpretations of mathematical calculations, the other with his silent consent, signified nothing other than what is contained in the following words, addressed unconsciously to the unknown X of all first causes:

"The young person whom you deigned to give me long ago, during the world's first nights, seems to me, nowadays, to have become the mere facsimile of the sister you promised, and I no longer recognize enough of your imprint in the spirit moving her desolate form to treat her as a companion.—Ah, my exile becomes a weary one, if I must regard simply as the plaything of my earthly senses the woman whose sacred and con- soling charms ought to raise before my eyes, so weary of the sight of the vacant heavens, at least the memory of what we have lost. After all these centuries and all these griefs, the permanent falsehood of this shadow by my side wearies me! It wearies me, and that's all it does; and I no longer care to grovel in those Instincts to which she tempts and attracts me, in an effort to believe, forever unsuccessfully, that she is my love.

"This is why, though but the creature of an instant, and knowing not whence I come, I stand here tonight in a grave, struggling—with a mock- ing laugh that contains all human sorrows, and with the help, such as I can obtain, of the old forbidden Knowledge—to capture at least the mi- rage (nothing, alas, but the mirage!) of her whom your mysterious Clem- ency still allows me to desire."

Such were, approximately, the thoughts lurking in reality behind the cold analysis of the somber genius.

Meanwhile, the electrician had touched a small enclosed transparent vessel full of distilled water located within the chest cavity of the Android. The concentrated carbon grid inside it slipped, at the almost imperceptible turn of a screw, into the water, and the current began to hum.

Suddenly the interior of the mechanism lit up like a human organism, flashing here and misty there, spangled with golden gleams and glittering lights.

Edison continued his talk.

—This lightly scented and pearl-colored smoke which seems to flower under the black veil of Hadaly is simply vapor from the water absorbed by the battery; heat is generated in the process, and escapes in the form of this moist cloud which you see coursing like the current of Life itself through our new friend. This vapor which circulates through her is always under control, and does no harm of any sort. Look, now!

And so saying, Edison grasped the hand of the Android, while the electric current diffusing itself through the thousands of electric nerve-ends in Hadaly hummed even more loudly.

—You see, *she is an angel!* he continued, speaking as solemnly as ever— if indeed it's true, as the theologians teach us, *that angels are simply fire and light!* Wasn't it Baron Swedenborg who went so far as to add that they are "hermaphrodite and sterile"?

After a moment of silence:

—We turn now to the question of equilibrium. It has two aspects; lateral and circular equilibrium. You've doubtless heard of the three sorts of equilibrium in physics: stable, unstable, and indifferent. It is a combination of them which sustains the movements of the Android. You will see that, to make Hadaly fall down, a stronger push is necessary than to make us fall—unless, indeed, it's your *desire* that she fall!

# EQUILIBRIUM

Stand up straight, my girl.
—Advice from a mother

—Equilibrium is achieved in the following manner, continued the *deus ex machina.* I will show you as a sample the lateral equilibrium; the rest, included within the dorsal structure itself, is of the same sort.

In the first place, given electric current and magnets, equilibrium is necessarily within our reach. It follows that:

1. Whatever the position of the Android, a perpendicular line can be drawn from between the two shoulder blades, down the spinal column, as far as the inside of the ankle, just as for us.

2. Whatever the position of these two "adorable" feet, they always constitute the limits of a horizontal line, from the middle of which springs a vertical, marking the real center of gravity of the Android. Let me explain why.

The two thighs of Hadaly are those of Diana the huntress! but their silvery interiors contain these two platinum cells, the function of which I will explain in a moment. Their surfaces, though polished, are held in place by the walls of the iliac cavities because of their irregular shape.

These cells, shaped above to conform to the iliac walls, are shaped below into rectangular cones inclined toward one another to form an angle of forty-five degrees to the vertical. The two points of these cells, if they were extended further, would meet at a point between the legs, just about the level of the Android's knees.

These two lines form, accordingly, the imaginary inverted apex of a triangle, the hypotenuse of which would be an imaginary horizontal cutting the torso in two.

The line of the terrestrial equator doesn't exist, but it's nonetheless a reality. Always in the mind, never anything but an intellectual construct, it is still just as *real* as if it were tangible, don't you agree? Well, such are the lines of which I'm going to tell you now, and whose reality underlies, at every moment of our being, our own equilibrium.

Having exactly calculated the various weights of the mechanisms fixed above this imaginary horizontal, and placed them at the desired angles, I suppose that the direction of these various weights could be schematized in a second triangle, placed like the first upside down, with its apex at the imaginary center of the hypotenuse of the first triangle. The base of this upper triangle would be formed by a second horizontal connecting the two shoulders. The apexes of both my triangles would thus fall on the same vertical axis.

Under the conditions so far considered, the entire weight of the body, standing erect and motionless, would necessarily fall along that imaginary vertical drawn from the middle of the Android's brow and ending at the center of a line drawn between her two feet.

But as every motion risks a fall in one direction or another, the two large and deep platinum cells are filled exactly half full of quicksilver. Just halfway below the surface of this metal they are connected to one another by these two flexible tubes of steel lined with platinum which you see in position here directly beneath the controlling Cylinder.

At the center of the upper disc which hermetically seals each of the cells is fastened the end of a sort of arc, forged of very pure, very sensitive, and very powerful steel. The other end is attached very solidly to the upper part of that silver cavity within the thigh which is the holder of the two cells, though they are by no means solidly attached to it. This arc not only is held down by the weight of the quicksilver, which is twenty-five pounds, but is forced into place by the weight of a single extra centimeter of mercury above the inner level of each cell. The arc would try to raise them by this extra centimeter toward the upper part of the iliac cavity if it were not held down to the exact level of the mercury by this little steel loop which the cell encounters at just this level on the wall of the cavity.

Thus the light tension of the arc remains constant because of this obstacle. The upper disc sealing each cell is therefore always in contact with the steel loop when the level of quicksilver is the same in both cells.

But whenever the Android moves, this level alters, because this particularly fluid metal is constantly flowing from one to the other of the two cells, by means of the two tubes. At the slightest inclination to one side or the other, they send an excess of quicksilver into the cell on the lower side of the body.

The slippery platinum cell, then, sliding down under this extra weight within its containing walls, increases the tension of the arc. Naturally, this flow of quicksilver in the direction toward which the Android is already leaning would lead her to fall even quicker, if the conical point of the metallic cell, as soon as the first centimeter of its incumbent quicksilver flowed away, did not, in the act of rising, release a current of electricity from the dynamo. Working through a system of magnets fixed to the wall of each cell, this reverses the flow of quicksilver and forces into the opposite cell just the quantity of quicksilver necessary to reestablish balance. This is the constant flux and reflux which, except when she is resting, corrects the basic tendency of the body to instability. Considering the angle at which the cones of the cells are set, we see that the Android's fixed center of gravity is only apparent, that the fluctuating level of the mercury controls the real one. Without that, the Android might fall, however prompt the transfer. But the actual center of gravity, thanks to this arrangement of the cones (and that's an extremely simple calculation, altogether elementary), is quite outside the Android, in the interior of a vertical which drops from the upper point of the cone's widening—from the point, I say, farthest from the apparent visual center of the Android—alongside her person, next to the unmoving leg, and so to the ground; and this balances laterally the weight of the leg that has been moved.

This oscillation, involving counterflow of the metal and displacement of the center of gravity, continues as long as the current which controls it is flowing. The tensions of the arc are continually in action at the slightest movement of the Android, and the level of the quicksilver in the two cells is constantly changing. The two steel tubes are thus equivalent to the balancing rod of an acrobat. But, from the outside, not a quiver is seen to betray this inner balancing of tensions from which the first equilibrium arises; nothing, any more than such quivering is sensed in us.

As for equilibrium as a whole, you see from the shoulder blades down to the lower lumbar vertebrae these intricate interwoven passages through which the quicksilver circulates constantly, counterbalancing its own weight by instant translations of its inertia into electro-magnetic systems. This is the apparatus which allows the Android to get up, lie down, bend over, stand, and walk as we do. Thanks to their delicate operations, you can see Hadaly stoop to pick up a flower without the slightest fear of falling.

# SOMETHING STRIKING

The wise man laughs only in fear and trembling.
—Proverbs

—I'VE DONE NO MORE than sketch for you in broad outlines the possibility of the phenomenon; the few minutes I have left (here it is, midnight already) will allow me only to indicate a few additional details.

Only the first Android was difficult. Once the general formula was written, as I've said before, all that remained was a kind of handicraft work. There's no doubt that within a few years substrata like this one will be fabricated by the thousands; the first manufacturer who picks up the idea will be able to establish a factory for the production of Ideals!

At this touch of wit, Lord Ewald, whose nerves were already on edge, began to laugh, lightly enough at first; then, seeing that Edison was laughing too, a strange sort of hysterical hilarity gained upon him. The place, the hour, the character of the experiment, the very idea that they shared—for a long moment everything seemed to him as terrifying as it was absurd, so that, probably for the first time in his life, he was overcome by a fit of convulsive laughter, the echoes of which resounded through this underground Eden.

—You are a terrible mocker, he said.

—We have no time to lose, replied the electrician. I'm now going to explain what procedures I will use to confer on this moving possibility the entire exterior appearance of your favored lady.

At the touch of his finger, the exterior covering closed slowly; the porphyry table tilted till its end touched the ground.

Hadaly was standing erect between her two creators.

Motionless, veiled, silent, you would have said she was looking out on them from behind the shadows that veiled her features.

Edison touched one of the rings on Hadaly's silver-gloved hand.

The Android quivered from head to foot; she became once more an apparition, an animate phantom.

The sense of bitter disillusion left in Lord Ewald's soul by the recent anatomy lesson faded somewhat at her new appearance.

Shortly the young man, having regained control of himself, looked at her anew, even though his reason still revolted at some of the things he had been told, with that indefinable sentiment which she had aroused in him before.

The dream began anew, picking up where it had left off only a short while previously.

—Are you quite recovered now? Edison asked the Android coldly.

—*Perhaps!* Hadaly replied, her marvelous dreamlike voice seeming to come from a far distance behind her black veil.

—What an expression! murmured the young lord.

Already the movement of respiration was stirring the breast of the Android.

Suddenly, crossing her hands and bowing gently toward Lord Ewald, she said to him in laughing tones:

—And, in return for my trouble, will you allow me to beg a favor of you, my lord?

—Gladly, Miss Hadaly, said he.

And while Edison was collecting his scalpels, she turned away toward the banks of subterranean flowers; then, having picked up a big black purse of silk and velvet, similar to that used by mendicant friars, she returned to the stupefied Englishman.

—My lord, she said, I believe that in the world no evening of pleasure is quite complete unless it includes some redeeming work of charity amid its other attractions. Will you therefore allow me to ask your charity in behalf of a most respectable young woman—a young widow—and her two children!

—What does this mean? Lord Ewald asked Edison.

—Well, in fact, I hardly know myself, the inventor replied. Let's listen to her, my lord; she often has little surprises of this sort for me.

—Indeed, continued the Android, I beg your charity in behalf of this poor woman—whom only the need to care for her children keeps alive: if she did not have to provide for them, I doubt if she would survive a single day. For undeserved misfortune has exalted her soul to the point where it thirsts for death. A kind of perpetual ecstasy has raised her out of this world, and renders her indifferent to all deprivation, and incapable of any effort to support herself—except for her children. Her present state of mind has numbed her to all worldly considerations, to the point that she has exchanged her name on earth for another, so she says, a name by which voices, strange voices, have called her in her dreams. —Will you then, you who come from the world of the living, answer this my first prayer by *joining your charity to mine!*

So saying, she took from a nearby table several gold pieces which she dropped into the purse.

—Whom do you have in mind, Miss Hadaly? asked Lord Ewald, coming closer.

—It is Mrs. Anderson, my lord Celian, the wife of that wretched man *who killed himself for love—as I'm sure you recall—for love of those miserable objects you saw over there, just a moment ago.*

And she pointed at the drawer in the wall, where the relics were kept.

Despite all his self-control, Lord Ewald recoiled before the sight of Hadaly, bowing to him and holding in her hand this purse for religious offerings.

Of all the images he had seen, this one appeared the most sinister, and something in this particular act of charity seemed to indict, through him, Humanity at large.

Wordlessly, he dropped several bank notes into the black purse.

—Thank you, in the name of the two orphans, my lord Celian! said Hadaly, disappearing amid the pillars of the cavern.

# I AM BLACK BUT COMELY

There are some secrets better not told.
—Edgar Allan Poe

L ORD EWALD WATCHED her disappear.

—What astonishes me most, my dear Edison, he said at last, what is most incomprehensible of all to me, is that your Android can converse with me, call me by name, answer my questions, and direct herself unfalteringly through the various obstacles of this room and the one upstairs. I say these facts are positively inconceivable in that they suppose some sort of discerning intelligence in her. You cannot explain to me by means of talking phonographs how she offers such precise replies to questions before a human voice has had time to record them, or how a moving cylinder can dictate to a metallic phantom gestures, motions, and steps, which I suppose could be calculated, but only after a very long, very complicated process. The thing is possible, I concede it; but it must demand enormous preparations and the most scrupulous exactitude.

—Well, I will simply say that the details you mention are, *of all others, the very easiest to create.* I'll prove it, you have my word. You would be even more surprised by the simplicity of the explanation, if I gave it to you here and now, than you are by the apparent mystery. But, as I've already said, in the interests of the necessary illusion, I think it best to put off revealing this secret. But, something else! Hasn't it struck your notice, my lord, that in all this time you haven't asked me a single question about *the present facial expressions of the Android?*

Lord Ewald faltered.

—Since her face is veiled, he said, I thought it would not be very discreet for me to ask about it.

Edison stroked his chin and looked at Lord Ewald with a grave smile.

—*I* supposed, he said, that you were not eager to create a memory in your mind which might rise up and disturb the vision I have promised you. The face that I could show you this evening would remain fixed in your thoughts, and would forever suffuse those future features in which your hopes are eternally embodied. The memory would impede your illusion, by constantly raising unconscious thoughts of duality. That is why, even if this veil concealed the face of an ideal Beatrice, *you don't want to see it*—and you are right. And it is for an analogous reason that I cannot reveal to you, today, the secret of which you just spoke.

—So be it! said Lord Ewald.

Then, as if trying to dissipate the mist of uncertainty that had just risen, he asked:

—Are you, then, going to cover Hadaly with a fleshy garment identical to that of my beloved?

—Yes, said Edison. I take it that you understand, my lord, we are not yet dealing with the Epidermis, but simply with the flesh, and that alone.

# FLESH

A woman's body! Sacred clay! Oh, marvelous!
—Victor Hugo

—YOU RECALL THE ARM and hand in my laboratory, which surprised you so much when you felt them up there? That's the identical substance I will use.

The body of Miss Alicia Clary is composed of graphite in certain proportions, of nitric acid, water, and various other simple chemical substances which can be identified through subcutaneous examination. That of course doesn't explain why you love the lady. Similarly, detailed chemical reconstruction of the elements making up the Android's flesh would serve no purpose here. The hydraulic press as it coagulates them into a homogeneous mass (just as life incorporates various chemicals to make our bodies) literally transfigures their various individualities into a synthesis which cannot be analyzed but can certainly be experienced.

For example, you couldn't possibly imagine the extent to which iron dust, reduced to an almost impalpable powder, magnetized, whitened, and distributed through the flesh, renders it susceptible to the action of electricity. The extremely fine nerve ends of those electric wires which pass through imperceptible openings in the plastic mediator reach far into the fibrous applications of this pseudo-flesh—over which the diaphanous membrane of the Epidermis is spread, and to which it is marvelously obedient. Carefully modulated electric currents animate these tiny particles of metal, and these impulses are translated into almost imperceptible movements according to the micrometric instructions of the central Cylinder. Some movements are interwoven with others, or overlaid upon them; this intergrafting of successive motions can be so subtly compounded as to give rise to what we can only call *instantaneous delays*. The steady continuity of the electric current eliminates any possi-

bility of jerkiness, and thanks to it, one can achieve smiles of infinite
subtlety, the expression of the Gioconda, tenderness, intimacy, and absolute identities which are really terrifying.

This flesh, which easily absorbs the gentle warmth created by my elements, responds to our touch with the magic illusion, the resilience, the
fresh firmness of living tissue; it creates that indefinable sentiment of
*affinity with human life.*

As it should half-appear to the sight, its outlines softened by the Epidermis, its tone is that of snow tinged with the smoke of amber and pale
roses; it also has a slight sparkle imparted to it by a very light dusting of
pulverized amianthus. Photochromic action makes the color permanent;
hence, the Illusion.

I have accordingly undertaken to make Miss Alicia Clary agree, this
very night, to take part in our experiment; she will not know what she is
doing, and will agree as eagerly as you can imagine. Let me assure you
that, given the single fact of feminine vanity, the task will be incredibly
easy—you'll appreciate it yourself.

Since we observe all the conventions here, my first assistant is also a
woman, a great unknown sculptress, who will begin work on a statue of
Miss Clary tomorrow morning in my studio. It's indispensable for this
work that your beloved be nude, and she will have no other witness than
this great artist, who never idealizes but copies exactly. In order to grasp
the precise mathematical form of our living lady, she will begin by taking,
very quickly, in response to my detailed instructions, and with instruments of the most absolute precision, measurements of the waist, height,
bust, feet, hands, legs, arms, and face with all its features, as well as the
weight of your young friend. It will be a matter of no more than half an
hour.

Hadaly, unseen, erect, but concealed behind the four large cameras,
will be waiting for her incarnation.

And then it will come to pass that this carnal substance, glittering and
human at the same time, will unite, by subtle and complex procedures,
with the plastic mediator of the Android, according to the natural proportions of the living beauty's body. As this substance can be worked to
great precision by very delicate tools, the vagueness of a preliminary
sketch disappears quickly; the original declares itself and the features
appear, but without color or great detail; it is the statue waiting for Pyg-
malion its creator. The head alone demands as much sustained work and
care as the rest of the body; this is because of the movement of the
eyelids, the delicacy of the earlobes, the slight motion of the nostrils
while drawing breath. Besides, there are some special transparencies to
come, like the veining of the temples and the folds of the lips, which are
made of material more finely formed by the hydraulic press than any
other part of the body. Imagine if you will the fine magnetic tolerances
(the magnets themselves are indicated by these thousands of luminous
points in this photographic enlargement of a smile) to which one must

work; a whole network of invisible inductors must be employed, each insulated from the others. Oh, in a general way I have all the materials and formulas to hand—but a *perfect* resemblance, which is indispensable, requires long and meticulous labor: seven days at least, which is what it took to create the World. Remember, if you will, that mighty Nature herself, with all her resources, still puts some sixteen years and nine months into creating a pretty girl! And all those rough sketches she has to go through! All of them modified every few days, leading to an end product that lasts all too short a time, and that a single illness can snuff out overnight!

Well, having made our first sculpture, we attack the problem of ABSO-LUTE resemblance of features and of the general lineaments.

You know the fabulous results obtained by photo sculpture. One can achieve an absolute transposition of the subject's appearance. I have new instruments, perfected to a miracle, which were designed years ago under my supervision. With their help we will be able to transfer the identical outlines, down to the very slightest and most gradual contours, down to a tenth of a millimeter! Miss Alicia Clary will thus be photosculpted directly onto Hadaly, that is, onto the first sketch, sensitized for that purpose, in which Hadaly will already have begun to take silent form.

At this point all imprecision disappears; the slightest touch of excess leaps to the eye! Besides, the microscope is available to us. For we *must* create this refraction with the total fidelity of a mirror. A great artist, whom I've inspired with enthusiasm for the special art of revising my phantoms, will come to provide the finishing touches.

The pattern of the flesh tones must be made perfect; for the Epidermis, which is still to come, is delicate as a flower petal, satiny and translucent, and colors fade so easily that we must forestall that process and fix them in advance—quite apart from the solar resources of which we shall be making use in just a little while.

At this stage we find ourselves in the presence of an Alicia Clary as she might be seen in the fog of a London evening.

This, however, is the moment—that is, before we even raise the question of the Epidermis and all the problems that implies—when we must concern ourselves with the intimate, indefinite, personal emanation which mingles with the fragrances she customarily uses, to float like a cloud around the woman you have loved.

It is, so to speak, the atmosphere of her presence, the "feminine fragrance" of Italian poetry. As we know, every feminine flower has a scent that is characteristic of her.

You spoke before of a sultry perfume whose charm still disturbed you and harrowed your heart even today. At bottom, it is the attraction, quite special for you, involved in the beauty of this young woman, which filled this sensual odor with idealized charm. A man basically indifferent to the lady would have remained indifferent to the perfume as well.

The first question, then, is simply to obtain mastery over the complex reality of the sensual perfume *in its chemical components*; the rest of the process is taken care of by your feelings. We proceed by perfectly simple techniques, as the perfume manufacturer fills his scents with the odors of particular fruits and flowers. The result is identity. The whole thing will be made clear in a moment.

## ROSY MOUTH, PEARLY TEETH

The beautiful Madame X . . ., for whose favors the cream of our noble youth were in fierce competition, owed in large part the charm of her dainty, pouting mouth to the daily use of Botot's patented antiseptic.
—Yesterday's commercial

—Bᴜᴛ ꜰɪʀsᴛ, ᴍʏ ʟᴏʀᴅ, a question, a rather odd question, if you will allow it. Does Miss Alicia Clary still make use of all her own teeth?

Lord Ewald, after a gesture of surprise, nodded in affirmation.

—I approve of the decision, Edison went on, though it's by no means in accord with American fashion. Here you must understand, all our fine misses who aspire to real elegance, even though they have in their mouths all the pearls of the Pacific, are starting to have them replaced by dentures which are far more compact, exact, and light than their own natural teeth. There are few exceptions to this rule.

However it may be with Miss Alicia Clary in this regard (and things, after all, can change very fast), her present set of teeth will be reproduced with a dazzling fidelity.

I have arranged for the excellent doctor Samuelson, accompanied by the dentist W. Pejor, to be in my laboratory on the day of the sixth sitting.

With the help of an anesthetic devised by me, and almost odorless, so Miss Alicia Clary will not even notice that she is breathing it, we will render her quite unconscious; during this lapse, we will take an exact print of her teeth, as well as of her tongue, with an eye to transferring exact duplicates of both into the mouth of Hadaly.

You have talked of the effects of light on the teeth when a person is smiling. Once the adaptation is completed, you will not be able to tell one set from the other.

## AROMATIC

Though roses fallen in the wind
Have blown away and out to sea,
You yet may breathe at every turn
Their fragrant memory in me.
—Marceline Desbordes-Valmore

—Wʜᴇɴ ʏᴏᴜʀ ᴘʀᴇᴛᴛʏ ꜰʀɪᴇɴᴅ wakes up, we will tell her that she has fainted, no more than that: every lady of "distinction" does so now and again, but to prevent any such incidents in the future, Samuelson will write a long and learned prescription advising her to take certain warm-air baths which are to be had only in an establishment of his founding.

Miss Alicia Clary will go there next day.

Once he has obtained a sample of the various transpirations of the young lady, from her head to her feet, he will subject them to precise analysis in an extremely sensitive array of machines. The process is very similar to that by which one identifies various acids by the use of litmus paper.

Of course this analysis will be done in his own private laboratory, with all the time in the world at his disposal. Once he has identified the different chemical components, he can easily reduce to formula the various perfumes of this attractive creature. No doubt he will achieve, with only infinitesimal variations, an exact correspondence.

Once this result is obtained, one dissolves the chemical compound in a liquid base, and saturates the flesh with it by a process of volatilization, proceeding through the body limb by limb and conforming in every way with the nuances of Nature, just as I previously said a clever perfumer can saturate an artificial flower with the appropriate odor. That is why the sample arm up above is imbued with the warm personal perfume of its model.

When the flesh is thus saturated with perfumes and covered by the Epidermis, the perfumes remain as permanently as in a sachet. The idealization, the associations, you will supply yourself. And let me tell you, that devil Samuelson on a couple of occasions has tricked the senses of an animal, by the exactness of his imitations. I have seen him drive a basset hound into a frenzy, barking and snapping at a piece of artificial flesh, because he had rubbed it with some simple chemical equivalents to the scent of a fox!

A fresh attack of hilarity in Lord Ewald interrupted the inventor.

—Don't mind me, my dear Edison, he cried. Go on! Go on! It's marvelous! I'm dreaming! I can't stop—and yet I don't really want to laugh.

—Ah! I understand your feelings, Edison said sadly. I understand them and I share them. But just think how many little *nothings* like this, added one to the other, produce sometimes an irresistible impression! Think of all the *nothings* on which Love itself depends!

Nature changes; the Android, never. We others, we live, we die—what do I know? The Android knows neither life nor illness nor death. She is above all the imperfections and all the humiliations. She preserves the beauty of the dream. She is an *inspiration*. She speaks and sings like a genius—better, even, for in her magnificent words are contained the thoughts of several geniuses. Her heart never changes; she hasn't got one. Your duty will be, therefore, to destroy her in the hour of your death. A fairly good charge of nitroglycerine, or of panclastite if you prefer, will be quite adequate to reduce her to dust and hurl her form to the outer limits of ancient space.

# URANIA

This star which gleams like a tear.
—George Sand

Hadaly APPEARED TOWARD the rear of the chamber; she wandered toward them through the flowering bushes of that perpetual summertime.

Draped in an ample robe of long black satin, and still carrying her bird of paradise on her shoulder, she approached her visitors from earth.

Once near the sideboard, she refilled two glasses of sherry and came in silence to present them.

Her guests having thanked her with a gesture, she carried off the empty glasses to replace them where they had stood.

—Twelve thirty-two, said Edison, glancing at his watch. Quick now, let's consider the matter of the eyes. By the way, speaking of your future eyes, Hadaly, tell me—can you see Miss Alicia Clary from here *with the eyes you now have?*

Hadaly seemed to draw back into herself for a moment before answering the question.

—Yes, she said.

—Well, then, tell us what she's wearing, what she's doing, where she is.

—She is alone, in a railway carriage that's moving quite fast; she has your message in her hand, and is trying to read it over. Here she lifts it in order to bring it closer to the light; but the train is going so fast, she can't hold it steady. She sits down; she cannot stand up anymore!

And at these last words, Hadaly laughed gaily; her laugh was echoed, more loudly, and in a strong tenor voice, by the bird of paradise.

Lord Ewald understood that the Android was making the point that she too could laugh, and at living beings.

—Since you have the gift of second sight, Miss Hadaly, said he, would you be kind enough to describe for us the costume she is wearing?

—She is wearing a dress of so light a blue that by lamplight it seems almost green, said Hadaly. She is fanning herself now with a fan of ebony, its ribs decorated with black flowers. On the material of the fan is represented a statue . . .

—This is beyond all belief! murmured Lord Ewald. She's right on every single point. Your telegrams must be amazingly swift!

—My lord, said the inventor, you may ask Miss Alicia Clary herself if three minutes after the train left New York for Menlo Park the incident that Hadaly has described for us didn't actually happen. But would you be good enough to chat with her for a moment while I go off to select some specimens of our incomparable eyes?

And he stepped off toward the rear of the cavern, tapped a stone in the last pillar, and seemed to lose himself in studying some small objects hidden in that spot.

—Would you be kind enough to explain to me, Miss Hadaly, Lord Ewald asked her, what can be the function of that complicated machine sitting on the table over there?

—Gladly, my lord Celian, replied Hadaly, turning aside to look from under her veil at the mechanism in question. It's another invention of our friend. It serves to measure the heat of starlight.

—Ah, yes! I recall there was some talk of it in the newspapers, Lord Ewald replied with fantastic equanimity.

—That's right, Hadaly went on. Before, long before the earth was even part of a nebula, stars were shining, as they had shone for a sort of eternity; but alas! so far from the earth that their light, though it travels at more than a hundred eighty six thousand miles a second, is only now arriving at the place in the cosmos occupied by earth. Indeed, it may be that numbers of these stars have been extinguished by the time earthly mortals were able to see their light; yet the ray emitted from these stars when they were alive continues to survive them, passing irrevocably into space, and perhaps arriving at our planet. So that the man who looks up and admires the stars is often looking at suns that no longer exist, which he nonetheless perceives as a result of that phantom ray, darting endlessly through the illusion of the universe.

Well, my lord Celian, this mechanism is so sensitive that it can record the energy, almost nonexistent, almost imaginary, of a beam from one of these stars. There are even some stars so remote that their light will reach the earth only when earth itself is a dead planet, as they themselves are dead, so that the living earth will never be visited by that forlorn ray of light, without a living source, without a living destination.

Often on fine nights when the park of this establishment is vacant, I amuse myself with this marvelous instrument. I go upstairs, walk across the grass, sit on a bench in the Avenue of Oaks—and there, in my solitude, I enjoy the pleasure of weighing the rays of dead stars.

Hadaly fell silent.

Lord Ewald felt his head spin; he fell back on the notion that what he was seeing and hearing, because it was impossible, could only be completely natural.

—Here are the Eyes! cried Edison, returing to Lord Ewald with a jewel case in his hand.

At his words the Android turned away and stretched out on the black couch, as if deliberately withdrawing from the conversation.

# THE EYES OF THE SPIRIT

My child has somber eyes, profound and vast,
Like you, oh Night immense, and lit like yours!
—Charles Baudelaire

L ORD EWALD'S DIRECT GLANCE challenged Edison:

—You told me that the problems of creating an electro-magnetic being were easy to solve, *the result alone was mysterious.* Indeed, you have kept your word; for already, this result seems to me almost completely foreign to the means used to obtain it.

—Note if you will, my lord, Edison answered, that hitherto I've only given you explanations, more or less conclusive, for certain preliminary *physical* problems presented by Hadaly. But I warned you that various other phenomena of an altogether different and superior order would manifest themselves in her—and it was there and only there that she became EXTRAORDINARY! Now among these phenomena there is one, of which I can observe the various evidences and consequences without being in any way able to account for what produces them.

—You're not speaking of electric current, are you?

—No, my lord; it is another sort of current which is now acting on the Android at this very moment. One experiences its action without being able to analyze it.

—Then it wasn't some clever trick with telegrams that enabled Hadaly just now to describe for me the costume of Miss Alicia Clary?

—If that had been the case, my lord, I would have begun by explaining it to you. I withhold from my explanations only that part of the Illusion which is strictly necessary in order to preserve the possibility of your dream.

—Still, I can scarcely believe that invisible spirits will taken on themselves the function of conveying to human beings information on random travelers.

—Neither do I believe any such thing, said Edison. Still, Doctor William Crookes, who has discovered a fourth state of *matter,* the radiant state (in addition to the three we knew before, the solid, liquid, and gaseous), gives us many accounts of spiritualist experiences; they are supported by serious scholars in England, America, and Germany who have seen, touched, and heard the same things that he has seen, touched and heard: I find his stories worthy of serious consideration.

—But you cannot really maintain that, here or elsewhere, this unconscious creature has actually seen the woman of whom we are talking. And yet the details she specified concerning the costume of Miss Clary are absolutely exact. However wonderful the eyes you have in this box, I don't suppose they have any such power as that.

—All I can tell you on this point *(for the present, at any rate)* is this:

*the power behind Hadaly's veil* which sees at a distance and through all obstacles sees without the aid of electricity.

—I hope you'll tell me more than that someday; will you?

—You have my promise; and she too will explain her own mystery on some evening of stars and silence.

—Good; but what she says is like those shadowy thoughts that the spirit encounters in its dreams; they dissipate the instant one awakens. Thus when Miss Hadaly was talking to me just now about those burnt-out stars she studies, she expressed herself, not altogether inexactly, but as if her "reason" were guided by a *sort of logic quite different from our own.* Will I be able to understand her?

—Better than I do! said Edison, you may be sure of it, my lord. As for her way of grasping the concepts of astronomy—Good Lord, her logic is as good as anyone else's. Ask some erudite cosmographer, if you choose, well, for example, *why a single solar system contains heavenly bodies rotating on different axes? Or, if you prefer, what are the rings of Saturn?* You'll soon see if he knows much more about these matters than she does.

—To hear you talk, Lord Ewald murmured with a smile, one would think this Android has a notion of the Infinite!

—Not much more than a notion of it, the engineer replied gravely; but that she has, and to establish the fact, you must question her according to the strangeness of her nature. That is to say, you must use no solemn, pompous language, but talk to her in an almost playful fashion. Her answers then will give an imaginative impression much more striking than ideas of a conventionally serious or even sublime character.

—Give me an example of the right sort of question, Lord Ewald demanded. Prove to me that somewhere within her lies concealed—in whatever shape or form—the notion of the Infinite.

—Gladly, said Edison.

He stepped over to the reclining Android:

—Hadaly, he said, let's suppose that by some impossibility a god, of the sort that used to exist, should rise up invisible and unlimited through the ether of the universe, and suddenly unleash alongside our world a flash of electricity of the same sort as that which animates you, but infinitely more powerful, and capable of neutralizing gravity itself—so that the whole solar system would be hurled into the abyss like a sack of apples being emptied out.

—Well? said Hadaly.

—Well, what would you think of such an event, if you were in a position to cast your eyes over the whole terrifying scene?

—Oh, said the Android, speaking in her grave, low voice, and lifting the bird of paradise to a perch on her silvery fingers, I suspect this episode would pass, in the infinite reaches of space, without attracting much more attention than you bestow on the thousands of sparks which flare up and die down in the fireplace of an ordinary family.

Lord Ewald stared at the Android without saying a single word.

—So now you see, Edison said casually, turning toward him, Hadaly seems to understand certain notions just as well as you or I. But she translates them only through a somewhat individualistic system of imagery, by her own personal metaphors, so to speak.

Lord Ewald stood still for a while, musing.

—My dear sorcerer, he said at least, I'm quite incapable of understanding these things that are going on around me; I put myself entirely in your hands.

—Here, then, are the Eyes! said the inventor, opening the jewel case before him.

# PHYSICAL EYES

Your sapphire eyes, like split almonds.
—The poets

THE INTERIOR OF THE strange box seemed to cast a thousand different glances at the young Englishman.

—Here now, are some eyes that would put to shame the gazelles of the vale of Nourmahal; they are jewels, gifted with a white so pure, a pupil so deep, that they are really upsetting—don't you find them so? The art of the great oculists has gone far beyond Nature in our time.

The solemnity of these eyes gives one, actually, the sense of a soul behind them.

The addition of color photography gives them, besides, a personal touch; the iris is the special point to which one is bound to transfer individuality of expression. A single question here: have you seen many fine eyes in the world, my lord?

—Yes indeed, said Lord Ewald; particularly in Abyssinia.

—You distinguish the flashing of the eyes from the beauty of the glance, do you not? Edison pursued.

—Of course, Lord Ewald replied. The woman you will be seeing before long has eyes of the most striking beauty when she looks off in the distance at nothing in particular—but when she looks at something specific and nearby, the expression of her look is enough, alas! to make one forget her eyes entirely.

—Now that's what simplifies many difficulties! cried Edison. Generally the expression of the human face is augmented by a thousand exterior influences, such as the imperceptible flutter of the lids, the immobility of the brows, the length of the lashes, and above all by what one is saying, the circumstances, the surroundings, the whole ambience which reflects itself in a glance. All that reinforces the natural expressiveness of the eye. In our days, well-bred women have all acquired one particular ex-

pressive glance, worldly, conventional, and simply charming (that's the
word for it); every man finds in it whatever he wants, and the woman is
free to pursue her personal thoughts while seeming to pay profound attention to something else.

One could easily copy this expression, since in itself it's nothing but a
copy—am I right?

—It's true, said the young man, smiling.

—But, the engineer went on, in the particular experiment we are making, the important thing is to catch, not the attentive glance, but rather
the vague one. And you've told me that Miss Alicia Clary commonly
looks out from behind her lashes. Well, here's how I will go about it. I
was talking to you just now about the radiant state of matter. Given the
most complete and perfect vacuum that can be produced (as in a hollow
sphere containing air which has been subjected to an extremely high
temperature, and then sealed), it's said that one can find in this void, as
complete as it can possibly be made, motions due to the presence of an
unidentifiable form of matter. Various induction wires having been fastened to the inner walls of this sphere, vibratory motions are felt within
the void; one can very well suppose that the beginnings of physical motion are there.

Here now are a number of artificial eyes, perfectly shaped and as pure
in color as fresh spring water. Among them I'll certainly find a pair corresponding with your friend's.

Once having established in the pupil what painters call a point of vision, and having created within the eyeball itself that necessary void, I
will insert within the pupil, by means of an extremely delicate inductor,
a tiny point of light—vague, almost invisible—created by electricity. The
marvelous work of the iris will then confer on this living point within
the eye itself a sense of vital personality. As for the motions of the eyeball, they are the work of invisible and extremely fragile steel springs on
which it quivers, turns, or rests immobile, according to the instructions
of the Android's central apparatus. Everything is inscribed there, in a
single coordinated program, as I told you—the glance, the eyelids, the
words, the gestures, the whole action. You can no more see these operations from the outside than you can guess the *real* motives of a woman's
sentimental glance from the impression it makes on you. Her skin, her
beauty, her exterior charms soften the mechanisms and blend it into an
idealized impression. Once the work of revision and correction has been
checked out microscopically, well, upon my word, I challenge you, my
lord, *to find a scruple more of that vital vacancy or void in the glance of
Miss Alicia Clary than in that of her phantom!* And, what's more, the
striking beauty of their eyes will be identical.

# HAIR

A ribbon held her hair yet left it free.
—Ovid

—As for hair, he went on, you understand that a practically perfect imitation is so easy, that we needn't dwell long on it.

We simply pick the counterpart hair carefully, perfume it with the various aromatic oils used by the lady, add a bit of her personal perfume, and you'll never know the difference.

Still, in this matter I advise the use of artificial materials only with some restrictions. For the lashes, eyebrows, and so forth, it would be very convenient if Miss Clary would be good enough to present you with one of her own tresses, preferably of a darkish color. Nature has her rights, and on occasion, as you see, I am glad to respect them.

Thus, with the aid of a painstaking but essentially simple work of preparation, everything will be made ready. The lashes will be counted and measured by a jeweler's loupe, in order to give special impact to the glance. This soft down, these ephemeral shadows about the snowy neck, like the finest shadings of Chinese ink on an ivory palette, those careless tendrils and the entire range of tints and shadings, in a word, will be reproduced with enchanting fidelity.

A few more details.

As for the nails, both of fingers and toes, upon my soul, no daughter of Eve will ever have possessed such dainty ones! Though exactly like those of your beautiful friend, they will have the glitter, the rosy glow of the living person—and they will be cut exactly like hers. You see already, I'm sure, that the difficulties here are too trifling for me even to bother explaining to you how I will overcome them.

Let's get on to the Epidermis, and be quick about it; we have barely twenty minutes to cover that topic.

—Do you realize, Edison, Lord Ewald said after a moment's silence, that it's really an infernal experience to see the details of Love in such a light?

—Not the details of Love, my lord, not at all, said Edison, looking solemnly on his friend. Only the details of "lovers," so called. And, let me say it again: *since that's all they are*—why hesitate before them? Is a doctor upset by what lies on a dissecting table when he's giving an anatomy lesson?

Lord Ewald remained pensive.

# EPIDERMIS

I would love to drink from the cup of your hands
If the water would not melt the snow.
—Tristan L'Hermite, *The Lovers' Walk*

—THERE IT IS! SAID Edison, pointing to a long cedar chest placed along
the wall next to the flaming brazier. That's where I keep the perfect
representation of human skin. You felt it when you picked up that separate human hand which is upstairs on the table. I've told you about the
extraordinary recent advances in color photography. Well, if the touch of
this skin disturbs every living being, the texture of its invisible, opaline
weaving is particularly receptive to impressions from sunlight; subjected
to light, it sometimes becomes radiant, like the complexion of a young
girl.

Notice also that here the difficulties of getting lifelike color are much
less than when we deal with a landscape, for example. In fact the complexion of our Caucasian race makes use of only two subtly graduated
colors, of which we have fairly good technical command; they are pale
white and rose.

Our colored projectors, then, imprint on this mock skin (once it has
been securely fastened to the fully formed flesh) the exact tints of the
nudity being reproduced. At that point it is the satiny quality of this
yielding substance, elastic and subtle as it is, which serves to give vitality, after a manner of speaking, to the results already obtained. The result
is to confuse completely the senses of human beings, to render the copy
and the original indistinguishable. What we have is Nature *and nothing
else;* neither more nor less, better nor worse, but Identity. Having taken
in the image of the living woman member by member, angle by angle,
through every slightest profile front and back, the new structure retains
everything so well that, if not destroyed by violence, it will outlast anyone who has seen it.

And now, my lord, said Edison with a glance at Lord Ewald, would you
like me to show you a fabric woven of this ideal skin? Shall I explain to
you the various ingredients of which it's compounded?

# THE HOUR STRIKES

MEPHISTOPHELES: The hands are on the very stroke!
It's just about to sound! The hour sounds!
—Goethe, *Faust*

—WHAT'S THE POINT? SAID Lord Ewald, rising. No, I don't want to see
this final gesture of the promised vision without seeing the vision itself.

There's no way to isolate any particular element in such a work; and I don't like to be in the position of smiling at a notion when I don't know what the total conception or the final result will be.

Everything I've seen is at the same time too remarkable and too simple to discourage me from taking such part as I can in the unknown adventure which, you say, is to develop from it all. You have proven yourself sure of your Android, to the point of daring to face that laughter which is sure to greet explanations so detailed and so hostile to every illusion. Well, now it's my turn to declare myself satisfied, and to wait the prescribed time before passing judgment on your work. But I'm also bound to say that, as of today, the venture in question *doesn't seem to me* as absurd as it did at the first moment; that's all I can say at this time, and all I ought to say.

The engineer's reply was calm.

—I would expect nothing less of the high intelligence you have displayed this evening, my lord. No doubt I could spring a surprise or two on some of those modern wits who divert themselves by denying my work before having seen it, and by accusing me of cynicism without having understood me. Indeed I could! Might I not address something like these words to them—without much fear of refutation?

"You pretend that it is impossible to prefer before a living woman the Android of this woman? That no man would undertake to sacrifice himself or his beliefs or his human loves for an inanimate object? You think there's no way a man could mistake for a soul the vapor that rises from a battery?

"But—these are words that you have lost the right to speak. Because of the steam generated in a boiler, you have repudiated all the beliefs which thousands of heroes, thinkers, and martyrs bequeathed you over more than six thousand years—you who have no sense of time beyond an eternal *Tomorrow* on which the sun very likely will never rise. What is this thing to which, since yesterday, you have chosen to sacrifice all the once immutable principles of those who preceded you on the planet, kings, gods, families, countries? It is this bit of steam, which whistles as it carries them off and dissipates them, at the wind's whim, among all the furrows of the earth, among all the waves of the sea! In twenty-five years, twenty-five million locomotive puffs have been able to plunge your 'enlightened souls' into utter disbelief of everything which was the true faith of humanity for more than six thousand years.

"You must allow me to feel some mistrust of all this sudden insight claimed by a group of people who have a pretty long record of being deceived in the past. If a little puff of steam, which began in the famous boiler of Papin, has been able to darken and disturb your love, and even your idea, of God—has served to destroy so many immortal expectations, sublime and innate though they were—why should I take with the slightest seriousness your pretended protestations, your smiles as of uneasy renegades, your pious moral pretenses, to which your everyday life gives the lie every day of the year?

"I have come with this message: Since our gods and our aspirations are no longer anything but *scientific*, why shouldn't our loves be so, too? In place of that Eve of the forgotten legend, the legend despised and discredited by Science, I offer you a scientific Eve—the only one, I think, now worthy of those blighted visceral organs which you still—by a kind of sentimentality that you're the first to mock—still call 'your hearts.' Far from being hostile to the love of men for their wives—who are so necessary to perpetuate the race (at least till a new order of things comes in), I propose to reinforce, ensure, and guarantee that love. I will do so with the aid of thousands and thousands of marvelous and completely innocent facsimiles, who will render wholly superfluous all those beautiful but deceptive mistresses, ineffective henceforth forever. These new beings will function in a second nature, rendered more perfect by Science, and at the very least their healthful assistance will render less painful the miseries that—say what you will—always attend sooner or later your hypocritical marital lapses. In a word, I have come, I, the 'Sorcerer of Menlo Park,' as they call me here, to offer the human beings of these new and up-to-date times, to my scientific contemporaries as a matter of fact, something better than a false, mediocre, and ever-changing Reality; what I bring is a positive, enchanting, ever-faithful Illusion. If it's just one chimera for another, one sin against another sin, one phantasm against all the rest, *why not, then?* My lord, I swear to you that within one and twenty days, Hadaly will be in a position to challenge all Humanity to give a direct answer to that question. For if a society has elected to pursue some sort of hazy general welfare which lies forever in the future, a make-believe Justice which never takes form, and a version of self-satisfaction which always remains miserable and childish; and if to achieve these values it denies what always before was called Penitence, Humility, Love, Faith, Prayer, the Ideal, and Hope for a condition beyond our lives of a single day—then I really must confess I don't see on what other principles modern man can oppose to my invention a logical objection which is defensible or even serious."

Lord Ewald remained silent, gazing thoughtfully at this remarkable man whose bitter genius, alternately dark and sparkling, concealed beneath so many impenetrable veils *the real motive inspiring him.*

Abruptly a bell rang within a pillar; it was a signal from the earth's surface.

Hadaly rose slowly, like someone still a little drowsy.

—Here is the living lady, my lord Celian, she said. At this moment she is entering Menlo Park.

Edison looked at Lord Ewald with a fixed, inquiring expression.

—Farewell, Hadaly! the young man said gravely.

The inventor came over to shake hands with his disturbing creature.

—Until tomorrow and a new life! he said.

At these words all the fantastic birds of the underground groves and brightly lit gardens, hummingbirds, parrots, turtle doves, blue kingfishers, nightingales, and birds of paradise—even the solitary swan in the fountain where the snowy spray continued to fall—seemed to emerge from their hitherto silent spell.

—Good-bye, passing friend! Good-bye! they chorused in a medley of voices, some male, some female.

—Back to earth now, said Edison, putting on his fur coat.

Lord Ewald put on his own.

—I had arranged to have our visiting lady guided to the laboratory, said the electrician. We will be there to greet her.

Once on the elevator, he undid the heavy anchor cables; the doors of the magic tomb closed behind them.

Lord Ewald felt that he was returning, with his spiritual guide, to the land of the living.

# BOOK VI

# . . . *And There Was* Shadow!

# DINNER WITH THE MAGICIAN

Now for the drinking, now for the light foot
Tripping fantastically!
—Horace

A FEW MOMENTS LATER Edison and Lord Ewald were back in the laboratory under the glare of the arc lamps, tossing their furs onto an armchair.

—Here is Miss Alicia Clary! said the inventor, looking into a darkened corner of the long room beside the draperies of the window.

—Where do you see her? asked Lord Ewald.

—There, in that mirror, said the engineer in an undertone, pointing to a vast looking-glass, dark as a stagnant lake by moonlight.

—I see nothing, said the other.

—It's a particular variety of looking-glass, said Edison. And in a way it's not surprising that your fine lady appears to me in her reflection, since that's what I'm going to take from her.—Just a minute, he added, turning a screw which released the bolt of the door; Miss Clary is looking for the keyhole; she has found the crystal latch . . . and here she is.

The laboratory door opened; on the threshold appeared a tall and remarkably attractive young woman.

Miss Alicia Clary was dressed in a glittering silk dress of pale blue which seemed sea-green under the electric lights; she was wearing a red rose in her dark hair, and diamonds sparkled at her ears as well as amid the flowers of her corsage. A sable wrap was thrown over her shoulders, and a veil of English lace cast an exquisite shadow over her face.

The woman was stunning; a living evocation of the presence of the *Venus Victorious*. Even at first glance, her resemblance to the divine statue appeared so striking, so incontestable, as to give one an indefinable shock. Here was certainly the human original of that amazing photograph which four hours earlier had been projected on the wall screen.

She remained motionless as if surprised at the appearance of the room, strange and even more than strange, that now confronted her.

—Please come in, Miss Clary! My friend Lord Ewald has been expecting you with the most eager anticipation; and, if you'll allow me to say so, now that you are here, I see exactly why.

The young lady replied, after the fashion of a saleswoman in a department store, but in a voice of perfect clarity, a voice to make one think of golden hailstones ringing against a sonorous crystal globe.

—Sir, she said, I've come without any special preparations, just like an artist, you understand. As for you, my lord, your message really amazed me. I thought . . . I didn't know what to think, really I didn't!

She stepped forward.

—In whose house have I the honor of being? she asked, with a smile that was intended to be slightly sarcastic, but which nonetheless seemed like a gleam of starlight across a frozen steppe.

—In mine, said Edison briskly; I am Master Thomas.

At these words the smile of Miss Alicia grew even colder.

—Yes, Edison continued with an obsequious expression, Master Thomas. Surely you must have heard of me? Master Thomas, general impresario for all the great theaters of England and America!

She stirred with excitement, and the smile reappeared, much more radiant now, and this time tinged with the notion of self-interest.

—Oh, but . . . I'm delighted to meet you, sir! she stammered.

Then, turning to whisper to Lord Ewald, she hissed at him:

—What's this? Why didn't you warn me? I do thank you for the introduction, since I want to be famous, and that is the thing nowadays. But this meeting isn't regular or reasonable, it seems to me. I can't be looking like a bourgeoise in the presence of people like this. But you, you've always got your head in the stars, my lord.

—Always, I'm afraid, said Lord Ewald, bowing stiffly as the young lady took off her hat and veil.

Edison had tugged at a metal ring hidden in the drapes; from the floor there suddenly rose up a magnificent candle-lit table on which had been arranged a splendid evening supper.

It was like a stage setting, a supper prepared by the fairies.

Three places were set in porcelain of Saxony; dishes of game and baskets of rare fruit stood beside them. Alongside the table was a serving cart holding half a dozen dusty wine bottles and various decanters of liqueur.

—My dear Master Thomas, said Lord Ewald, allow me to present Miss Alicia Clary, whose talents, both as a singer and as an actress, I have described to you.

Edison bowed respectfully.

—Ah, indeed! he said offhandedly. Well, I hope to be able to hasten your debut, one of these days, in some of our principal theaters, Miss Clary. But we can talk of all that as we eat, don't you agree? I find travel is always good for the appetite, and the air at Menlo Park is a bit sharp at this season.

—It's true! I'm hungry! said the young lady, so simply and naturally that Edison, duped by the magical smile that she had forgotten to wipe from her face, was taken aback and looked at Lord Ewald in amazement. He had, in fact, taken this charming and unaffected expression as an access of pure girlish enthusiasm. What could it possibly mean? If this sublime incarnation of beauty could say *in that way* just that she was hungry, Lord Ewald must have been mistaken, since this single lively, unforced note proved that she had a heart and a soul.

But the young lord, like a man who knows the precise value of everything that is said around him, never changed his expression. And in a moment Miss Alicia, feeling that she had said something too trivial before these "artist types," hastened to add with a simper, intended to be

witty and subtle, but which gave somehow an expression of comic sacrilege to her magnificent features:

—*Well, it's not very* POETIC, gentlemen; but we have to keep our *feet
on the ground, sometimes.*

At this word, which fell with the weight of a tombstone on the adorable
creature who, without knowing what she was doing, had thus so totally
and hopelessly betrayed herself—at this fatal word, which only a God can
forgive and wash in the blood of His redemption, Edison's brow cleared.
Lord Ewald's analysis had been exact.

—Charming! he cried, with an air of cordial good fellowship. You're
absolutely right, my dear lady!

And so saying, he led his guests to table with a gracious gesture of
invitation.

The blue dress of Miss Alicia, as it brushed over some batteries standing by, drew from them several sparks which were lost in the upper
lighting of the room.

They took their seats. A bunch of tea-rose buds, placed as if by elves,
indicated the young lady's place.

—I can't say how much I should be in your debt, sir, said she, once
seated and taking off her gloves, if through your agency a serious debut
at London, for example . . .

—Oh! replied Edison, but isn't it a pleasure almost divine, to launch a
star on her career?

—I should tell you, my dear sir, the young lady interrupted, that I've
already sung before some of the crowned heads . . .

— . . . a diva! cried Edison, enthusiastically, pouring out a bit of fine
burgundy for his guests.

—Well, now, sir, said Miss Alicia, in a manner at once peevish and
ingratiating, everybody knows that *divas* tend to be rather less than respectable in their habits; I shouldn't want to be thought like them in that
respect. Actually, I would have preferred a more honorable existence, and
my present career is one to which I have had to resign myself, because I
see that it's essential to be of one's age. And besides, when one can take
advantage of what one's got to make a good round fortune—however
bizarre one's talents—well, I find that all trades are about the same
nowadays.

The champagne flowed, frothing over the tops of the glasses.

—Life makes its demands on us! said Edison. I myself have little natural taste for haggling with temperamental artists and placating them all
day. Bah! The big organizations can adapt to all circumstances and make
themselves masters of everything. You must resign yourself, therefore,
to your glorious destiny, Miss Clary, as so many others have done—who
perhaps expected it as little as you! To your triumphs!

And he raised his glass.

Charmed by the unpretentious palaver of Edison (whose face, as Lord

Ewald observed it, seemed hidden under a black velvet mask), Miss Clary touched her glass to Edison's with a gesture so lofty and reserved that within her miraculous hands the glass took on the appearance of a goblet.

They drank together, all three; with that gesture, the ice seemed definitely to be broken.

And all around them, glancing off the cylinders, the angles of the reflectors, and the great glass discs, the lamplight trembled. An impression of solemnity, secret and almost occult, rose above the interweaving glances of the three diners. All three were pale; the great wing of Silence passed for a moment over them.

# SUGGESTION

> The questions and answers passing between operator and subject are nothing but a verbal veil, without significance, beneath which—direct, fixed, undistracted—the will of the suggester should remain fixed like a sword directly on the eyes of the patient.
>
> —Modern physiology

AND YET MISS ALICIA CLARY still smiled, and the diamonds on her fingers glittered every time she raised her golden fork to her lips.

Edison watched this woman with the keen glance of the entomologist who has discovered, after long searching, the fabulous night-moth which is destined, tomorrow, to form the jewel of a museum collection with a silver pin in its back.

—By the way, Miss Clary, said he, tell me now: what do you think of our theater in this country, eh? The stage sets, the singers; they are pretty good, don't you think?

—One or two of them are fairly attractive, yes, if that's what you like— but most of them . . . what frights!

—Perfect! You're absolutely right! said Edison with a laugh. Those old-fashioned costumes were so ugly! And how did you like the *Freischutz?*

—The tenor, you mean? she replied. His voice was a bit pale; he was a distinguished man, but cold, very cold.

—Always beware of the men a woman calls cold! said Edison under his breath to Lord Ewald.

—What did you say? asked Miss Alicia.

—I was saying that distinction is everything, absolutely everything in life.

—Yes, of course, distinction, said the young lady, raising her eyes, deep as oriental dawns, to the roof of the laboratory. I feel I could never possibly love anyone who wasn't distinguished.

Edison humored her bent.

—True, all the great men of history, Attila, Charlemagne, Napoleon, Dante, Moses, Homer, Mohammed, Cromwell, and so on, were gifted with the most exquisite distinction, or so history tells us. Such manners they had . . . such delicate charm . . . which they sometimes pushed to the point of coyness! And that of course is why they were so successful.— But, in fact, I was talking about the opera.

—Oh, the opera! Miss Clary said, with a pout as delicately disdainful as that of Venus glancing at Juno and Diana. Well, just between us, it seemed to me just a little . . .

—It is, isn't it? said Edison, arching his brows and speaking without the slightest inflection—it is just a little . . .

—Just so, said the actress, holding in both hands her tea roses and breathing them in.

—Well, in a word, it's not really up to date! said Edison in a dry and peremptory tone.

—Besides, Miss Alicia added, I don't like their shooting off guns on the stage. It startles the audience. And this opera starts with three gunshots. It's noise, not art!

—And then the action starts right away! said Edison, lending her support. The whole piece would be improved by cutting out those gunshots.

—Actually that whole opera, Miss Alicia Clary murmured, is nothing but a piece of *fantasy*, and all that sort of thing.

—And fantasy has had its day! You're absolutely right! We live in an age when only the *factual* has a claim on our attention. The fantastic doesn't exist for us! As for the music, didn't you think it rather . . . well, sort of blah, right?

And he twisted his lips in a derogatory leer.

—Well, of course I left before the waltz! said the young lady, as if that circumstance left her in no position to judge.

And her voice pronounced this sentence in contralto tones so rich and pure, so celestial even, that in the hearing of a foreigner who did not speak English Miss Alicia Clary, with her Greek features, would have seemed some sublime phantom of Hypatia, wandering by night across the Holy Land and reading by moonlight on the ruins of Sion some forgotten passage of the Song of Songs.

—That's different, of course, said Edison, without emotion. I understand, naturally, that you couldn't form an opinion on fragments—like the Forest Scenes, for example, or the Melting of the Bullets, or even on a *little bit*, like the Calm of the Night . . .

—That is part of my repertoire, sighed Miss Clary; but that soprano in New York was wasted on the part. I could sing it ten times over without putting as much effort into it as she did. You recall, don't you (the young singer added, turning to Lord Ewald), that night when I sang *Casta Diva* for you? I really don't understand how people can listen seriously to singers who "get all wrapped up" in the part, as we say. I think I'm in the middle of a crowd of madmen when I see absurdities like that being applauded.

—Ah, how well I understand you, Miss Alicia! cried the inventor.

Abruptly he paused.

He had just noted a glance that Lord Ewald, in a moment of gloomy distraction, cast on the rings worn by the young lady; and he understood instantly that his friend was thinking of Hadaly.

—But now, Edison resumed, raising his head, it seems to me that we are omitting a rather important topic.

—What's that? asked Miss Clary.

And she turning smilingly toward Lord Ewald, as if surprised by the silence he was preserving.

—It's the matter of the basic salary and special bonuses that you'll be wanting.

—Oh, she said, hastily turning her attention from the young lord; that's something I hadn't considered. I'm not a woman who thinks much of money.

—Like all hearts of gold! Edison replied gallantly, making a slight bow.

—Still, one needs the stuff, murmured the incomparable creature, with a sigh that a poet would not have hesitated to give to Desdemona.

—What a shame! cried Edison. Oh, bah! one needs so little *when one is a true artist.*

This time the compliment seemed to make little impression on Miss Clary.

—On the other hand, she said, a great artist is judged by the money she can command. I'm far richer now than my natural inclinations call for; but I really would like to owe my fortune to my own efforts—to my art, I should say.

—It's an admirable delicacy of sentiment, Edison replied.

—Yes, she replied, and if I could earn, for example . . . (she hesitated and looked at the engineer) . . . twelve thousand . . .

Edison frowned slightly.

—Or six? Miss Clary hastily added.

Edison's face cleared up a bit.

—Well, anywhere from five to twenty thousand dollars a year, Miss Clary finished, feeling bolder. And, with the smile of the divine Anadyomene lighting up her face, she seemed to suggest the goddess herself rising from the waves.—Well, with a sum like that, I really could feel quite content . . . because of the *glory,* you understand.

Edison's face also lit up.

—What modest ambitions! he cried. I imagined that you were anticipating that many guineas!

A shadow, as of disappointment, fleeted across the sublime brow of the young lady.

—Well, you understand, at the beginning, she said. One shouldn't be greedy, then.

Edison's face darkened once more.

—But you understand, my motto is "Everything for Art!" Miss Clary hastened to conclude.

Edison extended both hands.

—I recognize in you the disinterested devotion of a great soul! he said. But I shall not pursue the point; no premature flatteries. What could be a worse insult than excessive adulation? We shall wait a bit. Meanwhile, would you like a sip of this Canary wine?

Suddenly, as if just awakening, the young woman began to look about her.

—But . . . where am I? What is this place? she asked.

—This is the studio, said Edison solemnly, of the most original, most distinguished sculptor in the United States. She is a lady: no doubt that alone will recall to you her illustrious name. She is Miss Anny Sowana. I have rented to her this part of my estate, for use as her studio.

—Remarkable! . . . I saw in Italy the workshops of several sculptors, and their instruments weren't anything like these.

—Ah, well, I shouldn't be surprised, said Edison; these are the new techniques. Everything is done much more quickly these days; it's a matter of simplifying the old processes . . . But haven't you ever heard of Miss Anny Sowana, the great artist who works here?

—Yes, I think so, I must have . . . said Miss Alicia uncertainly.

—I was sure you would have, Edison continued; her reputation has crossed the oceans. She is not only a supreme artist in marble and alabaster, but the speed of her execution is literally prodigious! She makes use of hitherto unknown techniques, of all the most recent discoveries. In three weeks she can reproduce magnificently, and with an exactness that's positively uncanny, any sort of figure, animal or human. And, by the way, Miss Clary, you must be aware that nowadays, among all the best people, portraits are being replaced by statues. Marble is in fashion. The most distinguished ladies in society and in the arts have sensed, by way of their feminine tact, that the dignity and beauty of their physical presences could never be *shocking*. Miss Sowana is not here tonight because she is in New York, putting the finishing touches on a statue of the Queen of Otaheite, who happened to be in town.

—Is that so? said Miss Clary, much astonished. Then this has become respectable in good society?

—And of course in the world of the arts as well! said Edison. Do you mean to say you haven't seen the statues of Rachel, of Jenny Lind, of Lola Montes?

Miss Clary seemed to be searching the recesses of her memory.

—I really must have seen them . . . she said.

—And that of Princess Borghese?

—Ah, of course! That I remember well, I saw it in Spain, I think; yes, it was in Florence, the lady said thoughtfully.

Edison was all airy indifference.

—Ah, well, with a princess setting the example, he said, you understand that the thing has become completely a matter of course. Not even queens object any longer. When a great artist is endowed with extraordinary beauty, she owes it to herself to have a statue made . . . even before the public insists on putting it up! Your own, Miss Alicia, must often have graced the yearly exhibitions in London? How is it possible that I don't recall seeing it there? I should certainly recall seeing anything so strikingly attractive—but, I'm sorry to say, I don't.

Miss Clary looked downcast.

—No, she said, I have nothing but my bust in white marble and various photographs. I didn't realize that . . .

—Oh! cried Edison, but it's a crime against humanity! And worse still, from the publicity point of view, which true artists always consider the primary one, it's a serious omission. I'm not at all surprised that your career has been held back, and that you're not already listed among the superstars whose name alone is worth a fortune to a theater.

As he spoke these ridiculous words Edison discharged (as it were) a blaze of light from his own calm, clear eyes, deep into the wide eyes of the young lady.

—It seems to me you should have told me about all this, my lord, said Alicia, turning to Lord Ewald.

—I did in fact take you to the Louvre, if you recall, Alicia, said Lord Ewald.

—Ah, yes! To see that statue which resembles me, and which has lost its arms! But if nobody knows that it's me, much good that does!

—A word of advice: seize the opportunity that presents itself! Edison cried; and the full power of his magnetic gaze never left the two eyes of the beautiful young singer.

—Well . . . if it's the style nowadays, I'd really like to, said Alicia.

—Done. And since time is golden, you can rehearse for me various scenes from a number of new dramatic productions that I have on foot, even as Miss Anny Sowana (beg pardon: would you like a bit of this roast plover? white meat or dark?), aided by my advice, sets to work on a statue of you. She works so swiftly that in three weeks—well, you will see for yourself.

—Can we start tomorrow? cried the young lady. And how shall I pose? she asked, dipping her lovely lips in the champagne glass.

—We have here a woman of spirit, said Edison; no silly quibblings and hesitations here! What we do must cast all our rivals in the shade, and make such an impression on the public that the echoes of it are heard on both continents! It's a bold stroke we must think of.

—I ask nothing better, declared Miss Alicia. The main thing is success.

—From the publicity point of view, a full-sized marble statue of you is indispensable in the lobbies of Covent Garden and Drury Lane. Indispensable, I say! Because, as you understand, a magnificently beautiful statue of the singer predisposes the audience in your favor, sets the crowd to talking, attracts the interest of the directors. So you must pose as Eve; it's the most distinguished pose of all. No other artist, I dare say, will dare to take the role or sing the part, after you've made it yours, of *Tomorrow's Eve.*

—Dear Master Thomas, Eve let it be then. It's a role, I take it, in the new repertoire I shall be practicing?

—Naturally, said Edison. Perhaps, he added, smiling, the role will be brief, but it will be grand, and that's the main thing. And for a beauty as amazing as yours, it's really the only suitable role from every aspect.

—It's true, I'm very beautiful; and that's a fact! murmured Miss Clary, with a strange sort of melancholy.

Then she raised her head.

—What does Lord Ewald think of it? she asked.

—My friend Master Thomas has just given you some excellent advice, said Lord Ewald carelessly.

—I have indeed, said Edison quickly. And in any case, the greatness of your art justifies the statue, while the beauty of your figure will disarm all criticism. Aren't the Three Graces to be found in the Vatican? Didn't Phryne overwhelm with her beauty the Areopagus? Surely if success in your profession demands it, Lord Ewald will not be so cruel as to stand in your way.

—So we're all agreed, said Alicia.

—We are indeed; we'll start tomorrow! When she gets back around noon, I'll tell our immortal Sowana, so that she can come and get started with you. When would that be convenient for you, Miss Alicia?

—About two o'clock, if that . . .

—Two o'clock! Excellent. And meanwhile, not a word of this whole enterprise! If it got out that I'm taking a hand in your debut, I should be in the position of Orpheus among the Bacchantes; my other clients would tear me limb from limb.

—You needn't worry about that! cried Alicia.

Then she turned toward Lord Ewald.

—He's a very *serious* man, Master Thomas, she said to him in an undertone.

—Very serious indeed, said Lord Ewald; that is why my telegram was so urgent.

They had come to the dessert.

He glanced at Edison and noted that the inventor was scribbling a few calculations on the tablecloth.

—You're writing something? said Lord Ewald with a smile.

—Nothing, nothing, murmured the engineer. A notion that just came to me, which I want to be sure not to forget.

Just at that moment the glance of the young woman fell on the little artificial flower bestowed on Lord Ewald by Hadaly and which, no doubt by inadvertance, he still wore in his buttonhole.

—What's that? she said, laying down her liqueur glass and stretching out her hand.

Even as she spoke, Edison rose from the table and strolled over to open the great window looking out over the park. The moonlight was superb. He leaned against the railing, smoking, his back turned to the stars.

—It's a beautiful make-believe flower, she said with a smile; isn't it for me?

—No, my dear; you are too true for it, the young man replied simply.

Suddenly, in spite of himself, he closed his eyes.

There, on the steps of her magic alcove, Hadaly had just appeared. She pushed aside with her glittering arm the draperies of deep red plush.

Motionless in her armor and under her black veil, she stood there like a vision.

Miss Alicia Clary, having her back turned in that direction, could not see the Android.

Hadaly had no doubt been present, and had overheard the last few phrases of the conversation. From her fingertips she blew a silent kiss to Lord Ewald, who abruptly rose to his feet.

—What is it? What's the matter? cried the young woman. You frighten me!

She turned to look, but the draperies had closed, the apparition had disappeared.

Meanwhile, profiting by this momentary distraction of Miss Alicia's, Edison had stretched forth his hand before the face of the frightened woman.

Softly, gradually, her lids closed over her lustrous eyes; her arms, as if petrified into Paros marble, remained motionless, one resting on the table, the other, still holding its bouquet of pale roses, resting on a cushion.

Like a statue of the Olympian Venus rigged out in modern dress, she seemed fixed in this attitude; and the beauty of her features, in this posture, seemed almost superhuman.

Lord Ewald, who had seen the hypnotic gestures and the effect of instant torpor, took Alicia's hand, now suddenly cold.

—I've seen similar experiments many times, he said, but never one quite like this. You must have great powers of nervous energy and an amazing will . . .

—Nothing special, said Edison. We're all born with this vibrant faculty, though in different degrees; I've simply trained mine over the years, that's all. I will add that tomorrow, precisely at two o'clock, no human being will be able to prevent this woman (at least not without putting her in danger of death) from coming here to this stage and cooperating as best she can in the experiment on which we agreed. However, if you say just a single word now, there's still time: our entire project that we discussed this evening will be forgotten. You can talk as if we were alone; she will never hear us now.

During the moment of silence that followed this final challenge, the pale Android reappeared, pushing aside the heavy draperies, and remaining silent, motionless, and attentive behind her dark veil, her silver arms crossed over her breast.

Then the young lord, indicating the sleeping bourgeois beauty, replied:

—My dear Edison, you have my word already; and I assure you that when I make a commitment, I'm absolutely inflexible about keeping it.

Of course we both know only too well that within our species the extraordinary beings are few and far between; and when you subtract her personal beauty from this person beside us, she is exactly like millions and millions of others who share the same basic nature. And as between them and their male counterparts, as far as mental imperception goes, there's practically nothing to choose.

As a matter of fact, I'm far from being excessive in my demands on the intellectual attainments of a woman, even a "superior woman." If this creature were simply gifted with the minimum traces of tenderness, sheer animal tenderness for any creature whatever, perhaps just a child, I should consider the plan devised between us a sacrilege.

But you've just been able to observe the endemic, incurable egotistic aridity which, along with her wearisome complacency, animates this supernatural shape. And it's become standard for us that her pitiful *ego* can't animate anything, because within its absurd, mulish entity there's no faculty for forming the only sentiment that can complete a real human being.

Her heart, so called, can only grow steadily more sour in the atmosphere of dull boredom that her ideas, so called, diffuse around her. In addition, they have the horrible property of infecting with their miasma everything she approaches, including her own beauty—at least in my eyes. You could destroy her life without stripping her of that deaf, opaque, tricky, blinkered, pitiful mediocrity. She is that way made; and I don't know anyone except a God who at the solicitation of Faith might conceivably alter the inner nature of such a creature.

Why, then, do I choose to deliver myself, in fatal fashion if need be, from the love that her body has inspired in me? Why not simply content myself (as I'm sure the vast majority of my kind would do) with the exclusive enjoyment of her physical beauty, and pay no attention *to the spirit inhabiting it?*

Because I cannot by any process of reasoning erase from my conscience a secret inner certainty which is indelible and which harrows my whole being with unbearable remorse.

I feel, in heart, in body, in mind, that in every act of love one doesn't choose merely *the part that one desires;* that one betrays oneself by pretending to be able to exclude some part of the experience—just arbitrarily, and usually out of sensual cowardice. One cannot possibly exclude from the form with which one proposes to mingle one's own the very first principle which animates it and which, alone, *is capable of producing that form and the desires surrounding it:* one MARRIES the entire creature. I say that every lover who tries to stifle this thought, which is an absolute part of his own self, and penetrates his being like a shadow, must be a liar; willy-nilly, he possesses the soul with the body, and cannot simply exclude it from the act of possession whenever the idea of it threatens to disturb his pleasure.

But I cannot, I tell you, banish this inner evidence that obsesses me, every instant of my daily life, this thought that my *self*, my inner being, has been contaminated with this clammy spirit, moved only by muddy instincts, incapable of eliciting beauty from anything. Since things are only as they are conceived, and we are, ourselves, only what we can admire in things (that is, recognize of ourselves in them)—I swear to you in all sincerity that I feel myself degraded, almost forever, by the mere act of having possessed this woman. Not knowing how to *redeem* myself from this deed, I want at least to punish my momentary weakness by a kind of expiatory death. In a word, even though the whole human race should mock me for it, I insist on the peculiar privilege of TAKING MYSELF SERIOUSLY. My family motto is, after all, *Etiamsi omnes, ego non;* though everyone else conforms, I don't.

Once more let me remind you, my dear enchanter, that if it were not for this abrupt, strange, and almost fantastic proposal that you have made me, I would not be here to listen, across the breezes of this pale morning, to the chime of that distant bell.

No, I was disgusted with Time and all its trappings, as you know.

Now that I have the right to view the ideal mortal veil of this woman as a kind of spoils gained in a combat I have won too late, and from which I emerge mortally wounded, I presume to sum up this evening, and dispose of this veil, in the following words. "Since the power of your prodigious mind may perhaps allow you to do so, I entrust to you the task of converting this pale human phantom into a mirage capable of working a wondrous change in me. And if in this work you deliver, for my sake, the sacred form of this body from the malady of this soul, I swear on my part to attempt—through the breath of a hope still strange to my heart—the completion of this life-giving, redemptive illusion."

—Very well, said Edison thoughtfully.

—It is sworn! added Hadaly, in her melodious, melancholy voice.

The draperies closed. Behind them a spark glittered momentarily; the dull rumble of the marble platform, sliding as if precipitously into the earth, was heard for a few seconds, then disappeared.

With two or three quick movements of his hand around the head of the sleeper, Edison restored her to her senses, while Lord Ewald put on his gloves as if nothing but the most commonplace events had occurred.

Awakening, Miss Alicia Clary resumed the conversation at the very

point where hypnotic sleep had overtaken her, without the least recollection of the interval.

— . . . and why don't you answer me, if you please, My Lord *Count*
Ewald?

Hearing his title thus foolishly unfolded, Lord Ewald did not even condescend to that thin, bitter smile with which gentlemen of real nobility
sometimes greet the pretentious patents assumed by common riffraff.

—You must excuse me, my dear Alicia, he said. I'm feeling a bit tired.

The window had remained open to the starry night which was already
growing pale in the east; an approaching carriage rattled over the gravel
of the park walkways.

—I think this fellow has come to take you to your quarters, said Edison.

—It's really quite late, said Lord Ewald; and you must be sleepy, Alicia.

—It's true, I would like to *rest* for a while, said she.

—Here is the address of the house where you will spend the night, said
Edison. The driver knows the way, and I've seen the apartment myself;
it's quite satisfactory for travelers. I'll see you tomorrow, then, and meanwhile, good night.

And shortly the carriage was taking the two lovers through Menlo Park
to their improvised quarters.

Alone, Edison meditated a moment, and then closed the window.

—What an evening! he murmured. And what a strange girl! For all his
intelligence, that nice young lord simply doesn't see that her resemblance to the statue (and one can practically see the imprint of the stone
in her flesh) that this resemblance, yes, is nothing but a *sickness*, that
must be the result of some envious strain injected long ago in her bizarre
family. She was born that way, as some children are born speckled or with
web feet; in a word, she is an anomaly as odd as a giant! Her resemblance
to the *Venus Victorious* is nothing for her but a kind of elephantiasis of
which she will die. A pathological deformity, with which her wretched
little nature is afflicted. No matter, what is strange is that this sublime
monstrosity arrived in the world just in time to provide a proof of my
first Android. Come on, then; it's an elegant experiment, and there's
work to be done! Let there be *Shadow!* And now I suspect I, too, have
earned the right to a few hours' sleep.

Then, moving to the middle of the laboratory, he called aloud, speaking
softly but with a peculiar intonation:

—Sowana!

In response the pure, grave, feminine voice that he had heard earlier,
just as dusk was falling, replied from some invisible source in the middle
of the room:

—Here I am, my dear Edison. Well! What did you think of her?

—Several times the results were enough to disturb even me, Sowana!
Edison replied. Really and truly, she surpassed all our hopes. She is a
magician!

—Oh, it's really nothing yet! said the voice. *After the incarnation,* the effect will be supernatural.

—Go to bed now, and get some rest! Edison murmured after a moment's silence.

He touched a button, and the three radiant lamps went out instantly.

Only the night light still burned on the ebony table, lighting up on the cushion beside it the mysterious arm with its bracelet entwined with the golden viper; in the dark those blue reptilian eyes seemed fixed on the great electrician.

# THE PRICE OF FAME

The man who isn't ready to work twenty-four hours
a day has no place in my shop.
                                                —Edison

FOR SEVERAL WEEKS after that evening, the sun continued to shine cheerily on this favored district of New Jersey. Autumn advanced toward winter; the leaves of the great maple trees around Menlo Park turned red and gold, and each successive dawn found them a little drier, a little fewer in number.

Already Edison's house and gardens sank in darker and earlier shadows. The birds of the area, though still flitting through the bare branches and sparse foliage, fluffed up their plumage against the cold, began to tune their winter songs, and thought of migrating.

Throughout this Indian summer, the United States in general, and Boston, New York, and Philadelphia in particular, were disturbed by rumors that Edison had cancelled all his appointments since the visit of Lord Ewald.

Locked in his laboratory with his mechanics and assistants, he no longer appeared in public. The reporters, sent out on urgent assignment, found the doors closed in their faces; they tried to pump Mr. Martin, but he smiled and said absolutely nothing—which was frustrating. The newspapers and magazines were full of questions. "What was the Sorceror of Menlo Park up to now? What surprise could be expected from the Papa of the Phonograph?" A number of rumors began to circulate that the cash register (!) had at last been successfully adapted to work by electricity.

Some smart snoopers tried to rent rooms with windows overlooking the laboratory, in the hope of catching a glimpse of an experiment. Dollars squandered in vain! Nothing whatever to be seen out of those cursed windows! The Gas Company, much distressed by the news, sent out spies who were posted on the nearby hillsides, from which, with enormous telescopes, they inspected and reinspected every inch of the gardens till their eyes ached.

But in the direction of the laboratory a thick grove of trees obstructed their vision. They were able to see (and this was all they could see) a very handsome young lady dressed in blue silk, strolling across the lawn and pausing occasionally to pluck a flower from the gardens. This report from their agents terrified the Gas Company.

"—The engineer was trying to steal a march on them!—It was perfectly clear.—A young lady picking flowers? . . . That was the limit!—Dressed in blue silk? . . . No doubt about it! . . . He was making fun of them! He had discovered a way to split the atom, the demon!—But they wouldn't let him pull the wool over their eyes.—A man like that was a danger to society.—They would talk with their lawyers!—There was no need for him to think!" Etc.

The excitement was mounting to its height when word began to circulate that Edison had sent in haste for the excellent Doctor Samuelson, D.D.S., and the famous W. Pejor, the preferred dentist of American high society, a practitioner famous alike for the delicacy and solidity of his bridgework, and for an innocent tendency to rape his patients.

Immediately the rumor began to spread—a thousand lightning flashes could not have carried it faster—that Edison was sick, he was moaning with pain day and night, he was suffering from frightful inflammations and shooting pains, so that his entire head, swollen by a hideous attack of meningitis, had become as big as the capitol building in Washington.

A paroxysm of the cerebellum was certainly to be feared. In any case, it was all up with him; he had had it! The stockholders in the Gas Company, whose shares had recently lost a good deal of their value, were overwhelmed with joy at this good news. They flung themselves into one another's arms, wept with delighted relief, and babbled absolute nonsense to one another.

Their first plan was to have a communal celebration which would be climaxed by a community sing in which the demise of Edison would be celebrated in terms of the highest conceivable enthusiasm. But this plan was ditched by common accord, when they were all struck with the same luminous idea and rushed off in haste to buy, at newly reduced rates, shares in the Society to Exploit the Intellectual Capital of Edison.

But then Doctor Samuelson and his colleague the illustrious W. Pejor returned to New York and affirmed on their honor that the health of the miraculous sorcerer had never been better, and that during their visit at Menlo Park they had simply been working with the young lady in the blue dress who was helping Edison in some of his experiments with anesthetics. At once the stock market plunged, several million dollars changed hands; some speculators were in ecstasy, others in abject despair. At a stockholders' meeting of the Gas Company, three official groans were voted against the engineer—and carried out on the spot! In a country where everyone's attention is riveted on industrial activity and the exploitation of inventions, nothing is more natural than incidents like these.

Still, when the panic had partially subsided and the alerts had been called off, most people felt a little reassured, and the quantity of espionage diminished a trifle.

However, one fine night it became known that a good-sized chest had been shipped to Edison from New York; and then, as the wagon arrived in Menlo Park, some informal guards who had been posted by the roadside gave evidence of unanticipated moderation. Indeed, the techniques they employed on this occasion to find out what was going on were widely condemned as being far too half-hearted and indecisive.

In fact, they limited themselves to falling on the driver and the black workmen who were escorting the chest; without any idle preliminaries they beat them insensible with clubs and left them for dead by the highway. Then by the light of their torches they put themselves to open, with all the subtlety and delicacy of thought available to them, the mysterious chest. That is, they used cold chisels and sledge hammers to smash the hinges.

At last it was open, and they were free to examine the electric components of the intricate new computer evidently ordered by Edison.

The leader of the expedition, having made a minute inventory of the contents of the chest, found in it nothing but a new dress of blue silk, yes, absolutely new; a pair of lady's shoes, of the same shade; some stockings, extremely sheer, a box of perfumed gloves, an ebony fan with some intricate carvings, various pieces of black lace, a light girdle with pink ribbons, a couple of gauzy nightgowns, a box of jewels containing various diamond rings, pendants, and a bracelet, sundry vials of perfume, numerous handkerchiefs embroidered with the initial H, and various other objects of this general nature. It was a complete feminine wardrobe.

At this discouraging sight our agents, feeling distinctly stunned, formed a circle around the chest, but as a result of a warning glance from their leader they left every object in its place. After duly placing their chins in their hands for purposes of meditation, our gentlemen indulged in several grimaces expressive of discomfiture, not to say discomfort. At a complete loss, they crossed their arms, or slapped their big hands against their thighs, or raised their glances to the heavens, looking uneasily at one another out of the corners of their eyes. Then, half-stifled by the smoke from their torches, they began asking one another in mumbled undertones, and with a variety of choice expressions from the swill pail of their language, if in fact "the Papa of the Phonograph wasn't having a bloody jape with them."

Still, as their little prank might have dangerous consequences, the leader took a deep breath, gulped down his saliva, and issued his orders, helping them along with several of those choice imprecations which are so effective in conveying to a gang of barbarians an instant sense of reality. What he told them was to convey the *corpus delicti* with the well-known speed of light straight to its destination if they didn't want to be lynched on the spot.

The horde promptly set forth, stretching their legs to make good time. Having reached the gate of Edison, they were welcomed by Mr. Martin and his four merry men, who with glad smiles on their faces and revolvers in their hands thanked them warmly for all the trouble they had been good enough to take, assumed possession of the chest, and closed the gate on the noses of these gentlemen. As they stood gaping, they were blinded by a tremendous flash of magnesium, set off by the inventor who, in its light, photographed all their hirsute, hispid, hyrcanian mugs.

Some compensation for their troubles was due them, so next morning a highly circumstantial telegram was dispatched by Edison, accompanied by a group portrait of the entire gang (flash photo taken in front of his gate). Duly summoned by the constable, whom they made haste to obey, the worthy group was rewarded with a couple of months in a cool, shady place. In fact their employers, who had assigned them to the task, made haste to charge them most grievously before the constable, so deep was their solicitude for the disturbances caused to Edison. All these doings aroused more and more the excitement of public curiosity.

What was Edison doing? What could he have dreamed up this time? Some impatient souls dreamed of picking the lock on the gate and sneaking in. But the engineer had long ago issued a warning, by way of a public notice in the papers, that after dark various parts of his establishment, properly insulated from the ground, would be charged with a strong electric current. Anyone closing such a circuit would get his own personal KEEP OUT message inscribed unforgettably on his nervous system. What watchmen, what guards, what lookouts can compare with electricity? Imagine a thief trying to bribe it—above all, when he doesn't even know where it is! Unless one armed oneself with lightning rods, or wore thick porcelain clothing, any attempt at evasion would lead to unfortunate (not to say, clinical) consequences.

The gossip continued to spill forth. "—What do you suppose he's doing? What new combinations is he trying to make?—Shall we try asking Mrs. Edison?—You'd get a lot out of her!—Well, perhaps we could go at it indirectly. Maybe she knows something else.—How about the children? Not a chance there; trained from earliest youth to answer nosy questions by pretending to be deaf, they'd be a waste of time." And so finally it all came down to this conclusion: they would just have to wait.

Just about this time Sitting Bull, sachem of the last major tribe of American Indians, created a major disturbance by winning an unexpected and bloody victory over the army troops sent against him. As everyone has heard, he killed and scalped a great many young men from the eastern part of the country, and this event, widely reported throughout the nation, focused public attention for a while on the Indians, so that Edison was left for a few days in peace.

The engineer profited by this respite to send one of his technicians to Washington, where the most distinguished hairdresser and wigmaker in the country was to be found. With this messenger Edison forwarded a lock of long, wavy brown hair, with a note indicating to the last milligram and millimeter the weight and length of the tresses he wanted to duplicate as exactly as possible. The whole parcel was accompanied by four life-size photographs of a masked head, whose hair and hair styling were to be reproduced.

As the orders came from Edison, in less than two hours the hair had been arranged, weighed, measured, and fully prepared.

The messenger then handed to the artist a delicate layer of tissue, a piece of skin tissue so living in its appearance that for some time the hairdresser turned and returned it in his hands before crying:

—But this is a scalp! It's the top of someone's head, newly removed, cured by some process I've never seen before! It's staggering! Unless, perhaps, it's some new substance which . . . In fact, all the *hardness* of the wig is removed by this process!

—Now listen here, replied the messenger, this is made to fit precisely on the head, forehead, and temples of a lady in the very highest ranks of society. As a result of a bad fever, she has lost most of her hair, and she wants to replace it for a while with this. These are the perfumes and oils that she uses. What we want you to create is a masterpiece—never mind about the price. Get together, then, with three or four of your best workmen, night and day if you must, until you've fastened this hair into this tissue in an absolute imitation of nature. One thing to be careful of— don't try to OUTDO Nature!!! That would be quite beside the point! We want *Identity*, nothing else. You will have to use magnifying glasses, and compare your work constantly with the photographs, in order to reproduce the soft shadings of down, the little rebellious curls, the exact pattern of light and shade. Mr. Edison expects to receive your work in just three days; and I shan't leave here without it.

The hairdresser naturally received the announcement of this deadline with cries of protest; but on the evening of the fourth day the messenger, holding the box in his hand, passed through the gates of Menlo Park.

Now those in the neighborhood who were well informed began to whisper to one another about a certain mysterious carriage which arrived every morning at a secret gate newly cut in the wall surrounding Edison's estate. A young lady, almost always dressed in blue, and extremely handsome, of most distinguished appearance, was always the only passenger. She alighted and passed the day with Edison and his helpers in the laboratory; occasionally she wandered in the gardens. Every evening the same carriage arrived to pick her up and took her off to a luxurious cottage recently rented by a young English lord—superbly handsome, as everyone agreed.—"What was the point of all this secrecy surrounding such trivial events?—Why this sudden withdrawal from the world? . . . Why all these *romantic* episodes (there was no other name for them) in the world of Science?—At bottom, it wasn't, it couldn't be, serious!—Ah, what a strange man he was, that Edison! Eccentric, yes, that's what he was! Eccentric was exactly the right word for him!"

And from sheer weariness, people settled back to wait till the great engineer had recovered from his "frenzy."

# A NIGHT OF ECLIPSE

But one autumnal evening, when the winds lay
still in heaven, my beloved called me to her bedside. There was a dim mist over all the earth, and
a warm glow upon the waters, and amid the rich
October leaves of the forest, a rainbow from the
firmament had surely fallen.
"It is a day of days," she said, as I approached; "a
day of all days either to live or to die. It is a fair
day for the sons of earth and life—ah, more fair for
the daughters of heaven and death."
—Edgar Allan Poe, *Morella*

O N ONE OF THE LAST evenings of the third week, as dusk was falling, Lord Ewald dismounted from his horse before Edison's gate, had himself announced, and walked down the long gravel pathway leading to the laboratory.

Ten minutes previously, as he was reading the newspaper and awaiting the return home of Miss Alicia Clary, the young man had received the following telegram:

"Menlo Park: Lord Ewald 7–8–5: 22 p.m.: My lord, can you spare me a few moments?—Hadaly."

Instantly Lord Ewald gave orders to have his gelding saddled.

The sun was setting in flames after a somewhat stormy day; one might have thought that Nature was in sympathy with the expected event. Edison had chosen his time well.

It was the dusk of a dark day. To the west the rays of an aurora borealis spread across the gigantic sky the ribs of their sinister fan. The horizon looked like a stage setting; the air moved heavily beneath the gusts of a warm breeze which tossed the fallen leaves into heaps. From the south far into the northwest stretched long lines of heavy clouds like so many bundles of violet wadding edged in gold. The sky itself seemed artificial; above the hills to the north long, low streaks of light from the dying sun stretched out across the sky like livid sword slashes; behind them, the piled-up clouds cast dark and threatening shadows across the earth.

As the young man cast his eyes up to the heavens, they seemed to him at that moment the exact reflection of his thoughts. At the end of the walkway and on the threshold of the laboratory, he hesitated a moment; then, through the window, he saw Miss Alicia Clary. It was her last sitting; no doubt she was reciting one of her parts for Master Thomas. He entered.

Edison was seated quietly in his armchair, wearing a smoking gown, and holding some manuscripts on his knee.

At the sound of the opening door, Miss Clary turned sharply.

—My goodness, she cried, it's Lord Ewald!

As a matter of fact, since the terrible evening, the young man had made a point of not visiting the laboratory.

Edison rose to greet the elegant young man, who advanced toward him with a cool but sympathetic expression on his face. They shook hands.

—The telegram I received just now was so eloquent in its concision, that for the first time in my life I put on my gloves while already on horseback, said Lord Ewald.

Then, turning toward Alicia:

—Your hand, my dear! he added. You were rehearsing, I believe?

—Yes, she replied, but we're just about finished now. We were just working over a last passage or two.

Edison and Lord Ewald stepped aside several paces and conversed in undertones.

—Well, said the young man, your great work, your electric Ideal—our marvel, or rather yours—has it entered the world?

—Yes, Edison replied bluntly, she has. You will see her after Miss Alicia leaves. Take her away, my lord; arrange for us to be alone together.

—Already! said Lord Ewald thoughtfully.

—I kept my word, that's all, said Edison casually.

—And Alicia has no suspicions?

—A simple terra-cotta model has kept her on the wrong track, just as I said it would. Hadaly was hidden behind the impenetrable screen of my cameras, and Miss Anny Sowana showed herself an artist of genius.

—How about your assistants?

—They saw nothing in the whole operation but an experiment in photosculpture; I kept everything else secret from them. Besides, I only set the inner mechanism in motion and started the breathing process this morning. The sun was just rising (Edison added), and it promptly went into eclipse, out of astonishment.

—I must say that I feel some eagerness to see Hadaly, now that she's *become herself!* Lord Ewald murmured after a moment.

—Oh, you will see her tonight. But you won't recognize her, said Edison. And, by the way, I should warn you, the actuality is more terrifying than I thought it would be.

—Come now, gentlemen, cried Miss Clary, what's the conspiracy that you're whispering about over in that corner?

—My dear lady, said Edison, returning to her, I was just telling Lord Ewald of my absolute delight with your training, your talent, and the magnificent voice you've been granted; and I added that I had the very highest hopes as to the future which awaits you very soon indeed.

—Very well! But you might easily have said all that out loud, Master Thomas, was Miss Alicia's response. There's nothing in *that* to offend anybody. But (she continued, brightening her words with a smile and the mock menace of a finger) I have a bone to pick with Lord Ewald myself— I'm not at all sorry he's come here. Yes, yes, I've had a few ideas of my own about what's been going on around me for these last three weeks! In a word, I've something on my mind! You gave me something to think about today, something you said that was very surprising, a real enigma . . .

And she added, in a manner that she intended to be dry and lofty, but which gave the lie to her grave and thoughtful beauty:

—Will you allow us to take a stroll in the park, Lord Ewald and myself? There's a particular matter that I have to clear up with him . . .

—Very well, said Lord Ewald, rather crossly, after exchanging a glance with Edison; but (he added) I too have some things to discuss with Master Thomas this evening, and his time is precious.

—Oh, we won't be long! cried Alicia. Come, now; we must preserve the proprieties. I simply can't talk about this in front of him.

She took her lover by the arm. They passed through the doorway and a moment later were strolling toward the Avenue of Oaks.

Lord Ewald, in a fever of impatience, was thinking of the enchanted caverns where, within an hour, he would be facing a new Eve.

But immediately after the departure of the two young people Edison's face took on an expression of deep concern and uneasiness. The engineer seemed to be afraid that, in her foolishness and absurdity, Miss Clary might draw her lover into an untimely confidence; he drew aside the curtains before the window and stood watching them narrowly as they walked into the darkness.

Then he stepped briskly to a table on which rested a pair of marine binoculars, a microphone of a new design, and an electric rheostat. The wires of these two last instruments passed through the walls and stretched away to lose themselves in an electronic network which covered every part of the avenue, stretching from one tree to another on both sides.

He was evidently anticipating a scene of quarrel and perhaps breakup, which *he was bound to hear before presenting Hadaly.*

—What was it you wanted to tell me, Alicia? asked Lord Ewald.

—Not just now, please, she replied; let's wait till we're into the avenue. It's darker there, my dear, and we can't be seen. The problem is nothing but an obscure little worry which occurred to me today, for the first time in my life; I'll explain it in just a moment.

—Just as you please, was the reply of Lord Ewald.

The evening was still troubled; long lines of glowing fires stretched from the aurora borealis to the horizon; a few early stars dotted the dark blue intervals of sky between the clouds; above their heads as they strolled down the avenue, the dry leaves rustled; borne on a soft breeze, the odor of the flowers and grass was fresh, moist, and delicious.

—How beautiful it is tonight! said Miss Alicia with a little shiver.

Lord Ewald, preoccupied, hardly heard her.

—Yes, he said in a constrained tone, that was tinged with bitterness and almost derisive; but tell me, Alicia, what have you got to say to me?

—My dear lord, what a hurry you're in this evening! Won't you come over here and sit on this mossy bench with me? We can talk better, and in any case I'm feeling a little tired.

She leaned on his arm as they walked to the bench.

—You're not feeling ill, Alicia? he asked.

She gave no answer.

It was very curious, but she too seemed to have a lot on her mind this evening.

Was it perhaps some feminine instinct, warning her of a vague danger ahead?

He did not know what to make of the young woman's hesitation. She twisted the stem of a flower, culled at random, and her entire being seemed to glow with a transcendent beauty. Her silken gown brushed the flowers of the lawn; she bent her dazzling features toward the shoulder of Lord Ewald, and the charm of her lovely tresses, flowing loosely under her mantilla of black lace, was both melancholy and intoxicating.

When they reached the bench, she sat down first. Lord Ewald, long accustomed to hearing her mouth platitudes either inane or selfish, waited patiently for her to produce some new specimens.

And yet, another idea danced before him: perhaps this magician Edison had managed to dissolve somewhat the layer of sticky wax obscuring the sullen spirit of this still lovely creature. After all, she was keeping her mouth shut; and that was already a good deal.

He sat down beside her.

—My friend, she said suddenly, it seems to me that you've been depressed for the last few days. Haven't you something to tell me yourself? I may be more your friend than you imagine.

At that moment Lord Ewald's thoughts were a thousand miles from Miss Alicia Clary; he was dreaming of the strange flowers in that secret bower where Hadaly was even now waiting for him. And so when he heard the young woman's question, he was made profoundly uneasy by the thought that perhaps Edison had betrayed their secret!

But after a moment he ruled out that possibility. No; even on that first night, Edison had taken command of her too masterfully, had plied her with too many sarcasms, most of which had passed over her head. And besides, he had had too much time to listen to her since, ever to be deluded by these childish hopes of improving her moral character.

And yet he was surprised by this gentle expression of concern for his feelings. It was the first generous impulse he had noted in Alicia; her instincts must surely have been aroused by the sense of something grave about to take place . . .

A much more reasonable and much simpler notion replaced these first suspicions.

The poet was roused within him. He considered that the evening scene on every side of them was one of those in which it's hard for two human beings, in the glow of youth, beauty, and love, not to feel themselves lifted out of this world. He reminded himself that the mysteries of the feminine soul lie far beyond the reach of reason; that the most clouded hearts, subjected to sublime and serene influences, can grow instantly radiant with a light previously unknown to them. He reflected that such a hopeful development would be encouraged by the fostering influence of this quiet and shadowy twilight; and finally he thought that his wretched mistress, even if not consciously aware of these heavenly promptings, might yet be subject to their subconscious influence. Well, then, on this night of all nights, it was up to him to make a supreme effort at resurrecting the soul—hitherto deaf and blind, stillborn, so to speak—of the woman he loved so agonizingly.

—Dear Alicia, he said, what I have to say to you is only to be expressed in joy and silence, but a deep, contemplative joy, and a silence more marvelous even than that which enfolds us now. Alas, oh my beloved, I love you; you know it! And that means it is only in your presence that I can truly live. For us to be worthy of this shared happiness, we must reach out our minds to everything that is immortal about us, cherish those sensations, enshrine them in our minds. There, in the sphere of our entwined thoughts, no more disillusions, ever again! A single moment of that love is worth more than a century of any other sort.

Tell me, dear, why does this manner of love appear to you so strained and unreasonable? To me it appears perfectly natural, and indeed the only sort that leaves behind neither distress nor remorse. All the most ardent caresses of passion are multiplied in that sphere, a thousand times more intense and more real; everything there is noble, transfigured, liberated! What pleasure can you possibly take in forever disdaining the best part, the eternal part, of your own being? Ah, if I didn't fear the cruel sound of your laughter—so delicious and yet so hopeless—there are a thousand other things I might tell you, or rather a thousand divine experiences that we might share in silence!

Alicia still remained silent.

—But, Lord Ewald resumed with a gloomy smile, everything I've said is like Greek to you, isn't it? Then what is your question for me? What can I tell you—and what words, after all, can speak as eloquently as a kiss?

It was the first time in a long while that he had spoken to her of a kiss. Impressed no doubt by the magnetism of the surroundings and the situation, the young woman seemed ready to abandon herself to the enchanting embrace of Lord Ewald.

Had she actually understood the rich and subtle invitation of his passionate words? A sudden tear rolled down her dark, downcast lashes and over her pale cheek.

—How you suffer! she said softly. And all because of me!

At this emotion, this expression, the young man felt himself transported by a veritable access of amazement. He was in ecstasy. He no longer gave a thought to *the other*, the terrible new creation. A single human word had been enough to touch his heart, and to rouse in it indescribable hopes.

—Oh, my darling! he murmured, almost beside himself.

And his lips brushed the lips which had at last restored and consoled him. He forgot the long arid and despairing hours he had undergone; his love revived. The infinite delights of pure joy bathed his soul, and the ecstasy of his joy was as sudden as it had been unhoped for. A single word had dissipated, like a gust of wind from heaven, all his gloomy and irritated thoughts! He was reborn! Like ghosts from an enchanter fleeing, Hadaly and her empty mirages disappeared completely from his thoughts.

For several moments they remained silently entwined. The breast of the young woman heaved, and he was aware of her intoxicating fragrance; he caught her in his arms.

Over the heads of the two lovers the sky had once more become clear, and the stars twinkled down through the branches of the trees; the shades deepened, the night became transfigured. His soul lost in ecstasy, the young man felt himself reborn to the beauty of the world.

At that moment, the obsessive notion returned to him, that Edison was even now waiting in his lifeless caverns to show him the black monstrosity of the Android.

—Ah, no, he said to himself, was I out of my mind? I was dreaming of a sacrilege, a plaything, a puppet, the mere sight of which would have made me laugh, I'm certain! A ridiculous, senseless doll! As if, in the face of a living young woman as beautiful as this one, all that madness wouldn't vanish on the spot! Electricity, hydraulic pressure, cylinders, and so on—ridiculous! Really, when we go back, I will thank Edison for his trouble and think of it no more. I must have been under a spell even to think of such a possibility; though he's a good man and a wonderful scientist, he simply over-persuaded me.—Oh, my darling! I know you, you exist, truly, as a creature of flesh and blood, like me! I feel your heart beat! You wept for me! Your lips stirred under the pressure of mine! You are a woman whom love can render as ideal as your beauty! Oh, dearest Alicia, I adore you! I . . .

He never finished the sentence.

As he raised his ecstatic eyes, wet with tears of joy, to the eyes of her whom he held trembling in his arms, he saw that she had raised her head and was looking fixedly at him. As his kiss melted on her lips, he caught a vague scent of amber and roses. A deep shudder shook his frame from head to foot, even before his understanding was able to grasp the thought· which had just struck his mind like a thunderbolt.

At the same time Miss Alicia Clary rose from the bench and, placing on the young man's shoulders her hands *glittering with their many rings*, she said to him in a melancholy voice—in that unforgettably melodious, supernatural voice that he had heard before:

—Dear friend, don't you recognize me? I am Hadaly.

# THE ANDROSPHINX

I tell you that, if these should hold their peace, the
stones WOULD IMMEDIATELY CRY OUT!
—The New Testament

A T THIS WORD THE young man felt as if he had been directly insulted
by Hell itself. If at that moment Edison had been present, Lord Ewald in
defiance of all human consideration and gratitude would certainly have
murdered him on the spot, coldly and expeditiously. The blood rushed to
his head and he seemed to see things through a thin red curtain. The
twenty-seven years of his existence passed before his eyes in a flash.
Aghast at the horror of the trap sprung on him, he stared at the Android.
His heart, gripped by a frightful sense of bitterness, burned within him
like a lump of ice.

Mechanically he adjusted his monocle and looked her up and down,
from head to toe, from both sides, and then directly face to face.

He took her hand; it was the hand of Alicia! He breathed her perfume;
his eye measured the curve of her bosom; it was certainly Alicia! He
looked deep into her eyes; they were the very same eyes . . . only her
expression was sublime! Her dress, her style, even that handkerchief
with which she silently wiped away two tears that coursed down her lily
cheeks—it was the woman herself . . . but transfigured! Become at last
worthy of her own beauty, her real identity finally brought to life!

Wholly incapable of controlling himself, he closed his eyes; then, with
the palm of his feverish hand, he wiped the drops of cold sweat from his
temples.

He had just experienced, all of a sudden, the sensation that comes over
a traveler when he is lost on a mountain pathway, hears his guide say in
an undertone, "Don't look to your left," then carelessly does so—and
suddenly sees, right beside his foot, one of those perpendicular drops so
deep and steep that its bottom is hidden from him in the mists, but
which, as it returns his horrified look, seems to be inviting him over the
precipice.

He stood up, blaspheming inwardly, pallid, in silent anguish. Then just
as abruptly he sat down, without saying a word, as if all action were
impossible for him at that moment.

So he had been stripped of his first impulses of tender passion, of hope,
of intimate adoration; they had been snatched from him. He had been
made the victim of this inanimate mechanism, the dupe of this masterpiece of illusion. His heart was confounded, humiliated, thunderstruck.

His eyes measured heaven and earth, while his spirit was capable only
of an immense, sardonic, sneering rictus which rejected to the outer
limits of the void the unworthy insult inflicted on his soul. And that
thought returned him to full self-control.

Then he felt a thought flare up at the dark depths of his understanding, a sudden idea, more surprising all by itself even than the recent phenomenon. It was simply this: that the woman represented by this mysterious doll at his side *had never found within herself the power to make him experience the sweet and overpowering instant of passion that had just shaken his soul.*

Without this stupefying machine for manufacturing the Ideal, he might never have known such joy. The words proffered by Hadaly had been spoken by the real actress, who never experienced them, never understood them. She had thought she was "playing a part," and here now the character had taken her place within the invisible scene, had not only "assumed" but *become* the role. The false Alicia thus seemed far more *natural* than the true one.

He was drawn away from these reflections by a gentle voice.

Hadaly whispered into his ear:

—Are you quite certain *that I was not there?*

—No, replied Lord Ewald. Who are you?

# FIGURES IN THE NIGHT

Man is a fallen god who remembers the heavens.
—Lamartine

LEANING OVER THE young man, Hadaly spoke to him with the voice of the living woman:

—Many a time back there, in your ancient castle, wearied by your long day's hunting, many a time you rose from the table, Celian, without having touched your lonely supper, and following after that light which could do nothing but weary your heavy eyes, you retreated to your bedchamber in search of the dark oblivion of slumber.

There, after a thought raised to God, you soon turned out the lamp and fell asleep.

And yet disturbing visions rose from the shades of sleep to harrow your soul!

You awoke with a start, pallid, staring into the darkness around your bed.

Then it was as if shadows or forms appeared before you; here and there you could distinguish a human face, staring at you with fixed solemnity. At once you tried to deny the evidence of your own eyes and explain away what you were seeing.

To dispel these images, you relit the bedlight, and then you realized, rationally, that these faces, forms, or phantoms were merely a result of nighttime shadows, reflections of remote clouds on the curtains, ghostly images strangely animated by the shades of the night, suggested by nothing more than your own clothes tossed hastily over the back of a chair just as you went to bed.

Smiling, then, at your recent distress, you put out the light again, and with perfect satisfaction at this new explanation you went peaceably back to sleep.

—Yes, said Lord Ewald, I remember, that's how it was.

—Oh! Hadaly resumed, it was all very rational! And yet you forgot that the most certain of all realities—you know perfectly well, it is that in which we are lost and which exists within us in purely ideal form (I speak, of course, of the Infinite)—that reality is simply not accessible to reason. On the contrary. We have so dim an impression that no reason, even though conceding its unconditional necessity, could form any conception of it except through presentiments, dizzy ecstasies—or desires.

Well, then! At these moments when the spirit is still half-veiled in mists of sleep, and has not yet been fully caught up in the weary toils of Reason and Sense, it is particularly susceptible to these rare and visionary experiences of which I speak. And then every man in whom the seed of a further election is already living, who already feels his acts and inward thoughts weaving the stuff of his future rebirth, or, if you prefer, of his continuance, such a man becomes aware of a new and inexpressible dimension of space all around him, of which the apparent and accepted space in which we are trapped, is *merely the metaphor.*

This living ether is a region without limits or restrictions within which the privileged traveler, as long as he remains there, feels able to project within the intimacy of his temporal being the shadowy harbingers and dark anticipations of the creature he will someday become. An affinity is thus established between his soul and those beings, still in the future for him, of the occult regions bordering on that of the senses. The path joining these two kingdoms leads through that domain of the Spirit which Reason—laughing and exulting in those heavy chains of hers, which triumph here though but for an hour—calls, in hollow disdain, MERE IMAGINATION.

That is why your spirit, wandering on the frontier between dream and waking, experienced those impressions so vividly and disturbingly, and that is why your original, intuitive impression was no deception. *They were really there in the room around you, those who cannot be named—* those disturbing precursors who during the day appear only in the flash of an intuition, a coincidence, or a symbol.

Oh! When these presences venture through this infinite substance of Imagination to enter our darkened beings (and what could be more favorable to such an event than these shadows that surround us, this silence unbroken), then by a kind of reciprocal and mediating action they reflect their presence—not *in* the soul, that is not yet possible, but *on* a soul disposed to welcome their visit. Such a soul, its Reason laid gently to rest, can come very close to their world, can almost escape its bonds and be mingled with their essence, already—oh! if you but knew!

And through the dark, Hadaly clasped the hand of Lord Ewald.

—If you but knew how they struggle to appear, how hard they try to reach their worldly mate and augment his faith, even through the Terrors of the Night! How they strive to dress themselves in all the available opacities which may reinforce tomorrow the memory of their passage! Are they deprived of eyes to see? No matter; they look at you through the stone of a ring, the decoration of a lamp, a gleam of starlight in the mirror. They have no lungs with which to speak? But they make themselves heard in the voice of the plaintive wind, in the creaking of an old chair, in the rattle of a decorative spear falling in a hallway (for there is a Foreknowledge which permits all these things). Do they have no material forms or visible features? They invent one for themselves in the fold of a drape; they materialize in the leafy pattern of a bush, or in the outlines of an everyday object, using the shadows of everything that surrounds you, I say, to become incarnate and to intensify to the utmost the impression they want to leave of their visit.

And the first *natural instinct* of the Soul is to *recognize* them, in and through that same holy terror which bears witness to them.

# STRUGGLES WITH THE ANGEL

> Positivism consists of forgetting as useless this absolute and uniqe truth—that a straight line passing under our nose HAS NEITHER BEGINNING NOR END.
> —Someone

AFTER A MOMENT'S SILENCE, Hadaly, more and more deeply stirred, went on:

—Suddenly everyday Nature, alarmed by these approaches of the enemy, rushes up, leaps forward, and reenters the heart, by virtue of her formal title, not yet abridged. Rattling the loud logical rings of Reason in order to frighten you, as one shakes a baby's rattle to distract him, she reasserts herself within you.—Your anguish? She causes it, she *is* it. She alone, aware of her own wretched poverty before that other, immanent world, struggles to make you wake up—that is, to make you discover yourself in her, as your organism still in fact belongs to her—and in that very act dismiss your marvelous guests not only from your presence but from her gross domain entirely! Your "Common Sense"? Why, that's nothing but the spiderweb in which she catches and holds you while she paralyzes your luminous will to flight! That's how she preserves her own being and recaptures you, at the very moment when you are trying to get away! That knowing smile of yours, once you've recognized the walls of your prison cell and shaken off the obscure appearances, is the token of her momentary triumph, when you've re-persuaded yourself of her paltry reality and plunged yourself back into narrow walls of her rat trap.

Then, as you go to sleep again, you are relieved because you have dismissed from your mind the precious presences who beseech you, your future intimates, whom you will inevitably know, whom you have already recognized! You have banished from your side all the sacred and reflexive realities of your Imagination! You have renounced your own holy Infinitude. And what is your reward for this? Oh, now you can sleep in peace!

You have planted your feet anew on the Earth—on this temptress earth which will always deceive you, as she deceived your predecessors. Back on "solid ground," you can revise your memories and correct your thoughts by purely rational considerations until these marvelous prodigies seem to you idle and empty phantoms. You tell yourself: "These are nothing but dream visions, hallucinations! Who knows?" And thus, placating yourself with a few fuzzy words, you mindlessly diminish in yourself the sense of your own supernatural being. As you get up next morning and lean out the open window to the fresh breezes of morning, your heart is full of joy, you're at peace with yourself; in the distance you hear the sound of living beings (beings just like you!) who are also getting up and going about their business, drunk with Reason, wildly excited by the box of toys possessed by a Humanity grown ripe already, and now turning to the sere and yellow.

In exchange, then, for that priceless birthright of yours, you choke down every last lentil on the paltry plate offered you with ironic and mocking smiles by those perpetually deceived martyrs of Well Being, by those who have turned their backs on Heaven, those who have cut themselves off from Faith, those who have deserted themselves, those who have cauterized out of their minds the idea of a God whose infinite holiness cannot be reached by the lies of their mortal corruption. And now you too end up surveying, with the delight of a child dazzled with a new toy, this glacial planet which still circulates the renown of its ancient punishment through Space! Now it seems to you foolish and useless to recollect that, after a few more circles around this sun of ours, which is already mottled with the leprous signs of death, you are bound to depart forever from this sinister lump of round mud, just as mysteriously as you arrived on it! That is the one stunningly clear destiny out of all those you can foresee for yourself.

And so, not without a skeptical laugh or two, you conclude by hailing this Reason of yours—you, who emerge from a grain of wheat, hailing the tottering and unstable creature of an hour—you propose to see it as the unquestioned "Legislator" of the *incomprehensible, shapeless, inescapable* INFINITE!

# ANGELIC AID

Resurrection is a perfectly natural idea; there's
nothing more astonishing about being born twice
than once.
—Voltaire, *The Phoenix*

Extraordinary though his feelings were, Lord Ewald listened patiently to the Android without any sense of how her argument bore on the question he had addressed to her.

But the radiant priestess continued, as if she had just raised some shadowy curtain within her.

—Thus, increasingly forgetful of your true origin, your true destination, in spite of all the warnings both of night and day, you were about to choose self-destruction—and all because of this unhappy and trifling passerby whose voice and face I have assumed. Just like a child who wants to be born before the necessary development that makes him possible, you resolved to anticipate your hour—and you did not even wince at the impiety of the act, or the thought that you were closing off all the most sublime actions involved in overcoming your troubles.

But here I am now, I who come to you from those you will someday know to be your own sort! From those you have many times cast out, those who are uniquely in harmony with your thoughts! Oh, my forgetful beloved, listen a little more, before you decide to die!

I am an envoy to you from those limitless regions whose pale frontiers man can contemplate only in certain reveries and dreams.

There all periods of time flow together, there space is no more; there the last illusions of instinct disappear.

You see the evidence in me; at the cry of your despair, I agreed to dress myself hastily in the radiant forms of your desire, in order to appear before you.

I called myself into existence in the thought of him who created me, so that while he thought he was acting of his own accord, he was also deeply, darkly obedient to me. Thus, making use of his craft to introduce myself into this world of sense, I made use of every last object that seemed to me capable in any way of drawing you out of it.

Then Hadaly, smiling and placing both hands on the shoulders of the young man, spoke to him in an intimate whisper:

—Who am I? A creature of dream, who lives half-awake in your thoughts, and whose shadow you may dissipate any time with one of those fine reasonable arguments which will leave you, in my place, nothing but vacancy, sorrow, and heartache—the fruits of that truth to which they pretend.

Oh! Never awake from me! Never cast me out on some pretext such as those that treacherous Reason is already whispering to you in an undertone. Recall that, had you been born in other countries, your thought would take other forms, and that there is no other truth for Man than that which he chooses for his own out of many thousands—all of them just as doubtful as the one he chooses: choose then the one that makes you a god. You ask "Who I am"? My being in this low world depends, *for you at least*, only on your free will. Attribute a being to me, affirm that I am! Reinforce me with your self. And then suddenly I will come to life under your eyes, to precisely the extent that your creative Good Will has penetrated me. Like a true woman, I will be for you only as you desire me. You still think of the living woman? Compare! Already your passion for her has grown so weary that you cannot even accept the Earth; for me, the Impossible, how could you ever think I would weary of recalling you to Heaven?

Here the Android grasped the two hands of Lord Ewald, whose amazement, mournful uncertainty, and admiration were reaching an indescribable climax. Her warm breath, like a summer breeze blowing off a field of flowers, lulled his mind. He said not a word.

—Are you afraid of interrupting me? she resumed. Take care! You forget that only through your choice can I be either living or inanimate—your misgivings may be fatal to me. If you question my being, I am lost, and that means that you lose in me the ideal creature whom you might as easily have called into existence.

Oh! What a marvelous existence I may yet be granted if you have the *simplicity* to believe me! If you will defend me against your Reason!

It's up to you to choose between me and that ancient Reality which every day lies to you, tricks you, betrays you, drives you to desperation.

Have I displeased you? What I've said may seem too solemn, its imagery too subtle, perhaps? I am very serious and very subtle; my eyes have really penetrated into the realms of Death.

Think of it, and you will see that this manner of thinking is the only one that can be perfectly simple for me. But would you rather be with a joyful woman, one whose words resemble the song of birds? It's perfectly easy; put your finger on this sapphire which glows on the right side of my necklace, and I will be transformed to a woman like that—and you will miss the one who is gone. I have so many women in me, no harem could contain them all. Desire them, and they will exist! It's up to you to discover them within me.

But no! These other feminine potentials that live in me should not be roused. I despise them a little. You had better not touch that deadly fruit within this garden! You would be amazed—and my existence is still so slight that astonishment would wipe out my being, and hide it behind a veil! What can you expect? My hold on life is even more fragile than that of living beings.

Accept my mystery just as it appears before you. All explanations (and they are oh! so easy) would probably turn out, after a little analysis, to be even more mysterious than the first one, but the sure thing, alas, is that they would be my annihilation within you. Wouldn't you prefer that I exist? Then never reason about my being; experience it joyously.

If you could understand how sweet is the night of my future soul, and through how many dreams you have been expecting me! If you knew how many treasures of desire, melancholy, and hope are hidden behind my impersonality! My ethereal flesh, which awaits but the breath of your spirit to become living, my voice within which the soul of harmony lies captive, my undying constancy—is that all nothing by comparison with this empty "reason" of yours, which will prove to you that I don't exist? As if you were not free to REJECT that empty, mortal evidence, as itself doubtful—since nobody can define or explain that EXISTENCE of which it talks, nor say what the idea or the essence of it really is. Is it reason for regret that I'm not in the class of those women who betray? Or those who in their vows accept beforehand the possibility of being widows? My love, which all but equals that with which the Angels burn, has seductions more captivating perhaps than those of the earthly senses, within which always slumbers the spirit of ancient Circe!

Hadaly paused for a moment, considering the young man whose stupefied gaze was fixed on her, then broke into a ripple of laughter:

—Oh, what absurd clothing we're wearing! Why do you put that bit of glass in your eye? Don't you see perfectly well, even without its help?

But . . . here I am asking you questions, just like a woman; and a woman is what I must not become: I should change!

Then, without any transition, and in a hollow voice:

—Oh, take me away with you, into your own country! To the dark castle! Oh, I yearn to lie down in my black silken coffin, where I shall sleep while the Ocean bears us off toward your country! Let the living shutter themselves in by their narrow firesides, and hide themselves behind words and smirks! What matter? Let them consider themselves, if they want, more "modern" than you—as if, long before the Creation of worlds and worlds, the times were not just as "modern" as they are this evening and as they will be tomorrow!

Take advantage of those massive walks, captured and solidified by the blood of your illustrious ancestors in the days when they were forging your nation!

Believe it and never doubt that there will always be solitude on earth for those who are worthy of it! We shall not deign even to ridicule those you leave behind, though we could easily turn against them, and with interest, their silly sarcasms, their bored and blinded observations, their judgments drunk with a pride that is never anything but ridiculous and childish and absurd.

And shall we take the time to think of them? You know one always participates in the things of which one thinks; preserve us then, *from becoming such people, even in the least degree, by thinking about them!* Come. Once we are within the enchanted groves of your ancient forests, you will awake me, if you wish, with a kiss at which no doubt the Universe will shudder, aghast! But the will of a single individual outweighs the whole world.

And in the darkness Hadaly brushed with her lips the shuddering brow of Lord Ewald.

# REVOLT

What matter the bottle, when one is high on the wine?
—Alfred de Musset

LORD EWALD WAS NOT just a man of courage, he was intrepid. The spirit of his family motto, *"Etiamsi omnes, ego non,"* had been instilled in him by the action of the centuries, and it coursed even now in his veins; yet at these last words a long shudder ran through him. Then he arose, proud though haggard:

—So that's how it is! he murmured to himself. Miracles like these seem designed more to terrify the soul than to console it! What man ever supposed this sinister robot would be able to play on my mind with such a collection of paradoxes inscribed on metal plates! Since when has God permitted machines to usurp the right of speech? And what laughable arrogance for these electric phantoms to dress themselves in the form of a woman and then pretend to take part in our existence! Ha, ha, ha! But I was forgetting; this is a theater, I'm watching a stage show! I'm bound to applaud. The last scene was really good—strange, indeed, but strong! Bravo, then! Well done, Edison! Encore! Encore!

And, having adjusted his monocle, Lord Ewald lit a confident cigar.

The young man had just spoken up in the name of human dignity and even of common sense, both outraged by the marvel of Hadaly. No doubt what he had just said was not beyond reach of a riposte, and no doubt if he had been brought before some formal tribunal his position might have drawn down on him a quick counterattack that wouldn't have been very easy to parry. When he asked, for example, *"Since when has God permitted machines to usurp the right of speech?"* a short answer might have been: "Since He saw the foolish uses to which you put it!" As for the phrase, "I was forgetting; this is a theater," someone might have retorted:

—"Yes, and Hadaly is simply reduplicating your actress, with considerable improvements!" And that wouldn't have been altogether off the mark.

So true it is that even a superior man, when under great stress and touched in his essential vanity, may with the best will in the world, and even while defending admirable causes, compromise truth and justice—by a little "too much zeal." His essential vanity makes him try to conceal his vanity.

By now Lord Ewald could not fail to be aware that he was involved in an adventure far darker and more serious than he had anticipated.

# INCANTATION

—Your eyes—clear pools, smiling stars in which was reflected my sacred love—now I must close them!
—Richard Wagner, *Die Valkyrie*

THE ANDROID HAD BOWED her head and, hiding her face in her two hands, was silently weeping.

Then, lifting the divine features of Alicia, but transfigured now and drenched in tears:

—So that's it! she said. You called for me and now you reject me. A single thought from you could give me life, and yet, like a prince unaware of the world's energies, you dare not exercise your power. You prefer before me a consciousness that you despise; you hide from your own divinity. You are terrified of the Ideal made captive. Common Sense has reclaimed you; as if enslaved to your own species, you yield to it, and so destroy me.

Creator doubtful of your own creation, you destroy it the instant it is called into being, before you have even finished your own work on it. Then, taking refuge in an arrogance both treacherous and "natural," you will allow yourself to pity the ghost you have destroyed with a condescending smile.

Yet, considering the use that the creature I represent makes of life, what was the point of depriving me of it? As a woman, I would have been one of those who can be loved without shame; I would have known how to grow old! I am more than human beings were before a Titan stole fire out of heaven and bestowed it on these ingrates! Now that I must destroy myself, nobody will ever redeem me from the Void! There is no longer a man on earth who, to give me a soul, will set at defiance the beak of the undying vulture! Oh, how I would have come to weep with the Oceanids over his heart! Farewell, you who drive me into exile!

As she finished these words, Hadaly rose; then, heaving a heavy sigh, she walked to a tree and leaned there with her hand on its bark, as she looked out over the moonlit park.

The pale features of the enchantress glowed in the dark.

—Night, she said, speaking as familiarly as a child to her mother, here I am, the sacred offspring of living creatures, a flower of Science and Genius sprung after a history of six thousand years. You recognize in my veiled eyes your own pale light, as from stars that will perish tomorrow; and you, souls of virgins dead before the nuptial kiss, you who float in holy awe about my presence, have no fear! I am the obscure creature whose disappearance is worthy not even of a moment's regret. My wretched breast deserves not even the dignity of being called sterile! The Void alone will receive the charm of my lonely kisses, the wind my lofty words. Let shadows and thunder accept my bitter caresses, and lightning alone will venture to pluck the false flower of my vain virginity. Driven out, I depart for the desert without an Ishmael; I shall be like those sad mother birds, blinded by cruel boys, who live out their melancholy cycle of maternity brooding on the bare ground. Oh, my enchanted park! You mighty trees who bless my brow with the shadow of your foliage! You charming plants on whom the dewdrops glisten, and who are yourselves greater than I! Bright streams whose drops glisten against the snowy foam more brilliant and clear than the gleam of tears on my face! And you, skies of Hope—alas, if I could but live! If I possessed the gift of life! Oh, how lovely it is to live! Happy those who live and breathe! Oh, Light, the joy of beholding you! Murmurs of enchantment, the pleasure of hearing you! Love, the ecstasy of being lost in your delights! Oh! To breathe just once, as they sleep at my feet, these roses, so young and lovely! Only to feel the night wind blowing in my hair!

Beneath the stars, Hadaly twisted her arms in anguish.

# NIGHT IDYLL

Ora, Illora, De palabra
Nace razon; Da luz el son
O ven! ama! Eires alma,
Soy corazon!
—Victor Hugo, *The Song of Dea*

S UDDENLY SHE TURNED on Lord Ewald:

—Farewell! she said. Rejoin your fellow creatures and tell them all about me as "the strangest thing in the world." You have every *reason* to do so, much good may it do you.

You lose as much as I do. Try to forget me; but no, that's impossible. The man who has looked on an Android as you looked on me has killed the woman within him; for the Ideal when violated never pardons, and no man mocks the divinity unscathed.

I return to my glittering caves. Farewell to you, who can no longer live.

Hadaly touched her handkerchief to her lips and moved slowly, waveringly away.

Now she turned and passed down the walk toward the lighted doorway where Edison was waiting. Her form, blue and shadowy in the dusk, floated past the great tree trunks, and as a moonbeam fell on it through a clearing, she turned toward the young man. Silently she lifted her two hands to her mouth and, with a frightful gesture of despair, blew him a last kiss. Then, overwhelmed, beside himself, Lord Ewald leaped toward her, reached her, and flung his arm around a waist that yielded, half-fainting, under the strength of his embrace.

—Phantom! Phantom! Hadaly! he cried, we must not part! Little credit to me for preferring your amazing miracles before that dull, deceptive, cold-hearted friend whom fate picked out for me! But let heaven and earth take it as they will, I shall bury myself with you, my shadowy idol! I resign from the human race—and let the age go about its business! For at last it's clear to me that set one beside the other, and it's the living girl who is the phantom!

Hadaly, at these words, seemed on the point of collapse; then, with a gesture of infinite abandon, she flung her arms around the neck of Lord Ewald. From her panting breast, as she pressed it against him, came the odor of asphodels; and her long hair, falling loose, poured down her back and over her dress.

A new grace, which was effortless, languid, and profound, softened her severe and classic beauty; she seemed unable to speak! Her head resting on the young man's shoulder, she looked up at him through her lashes, smiling a secret and radiant smile. Half-goddess, half-woman, a sensual illusion, her beauty irradiated the night. She seemed to drink in the soul of her lover, as if to make it her own; her half-open lips, trembling and alight, quivered in ecstasy as they met those of her creator in a virginal kiss.

—At last, oh my beloved, she said in a hollow voice, at last I have found you!

# PENSEROSO

Farewell till the dawn of the day I foresee,
The day which will once more unite me with thee!
—The music of Schubert

A MOMENT LATER Lord Ewald stepped back into the laboratory, still clasping Hadaly by the waist. She walked uncertainly; her expression was grave, her face pale and drawn, and she still rested her head against the shoulder of her companion.

Edison was standing, arms crossed, before a long and splendid coffin of black ebony. Its two covers stood wide open, revealing an interior of black satin which exactly modeled a feminine form.

One would have thought it a modern improvement on an Egyptian coffin, suitable for the burial of a Cleopatra. To the right and to the left in compartments of the walls were ranged a dozen strips of magnetic tin, like funerary scrolls, a manuscript, a ring of glass, and various other items of equipment. Edison, standing against the intricate control panel of a giant accelerator, watched fixedly as Lord Ewald came toward him. As if suddenly returned to her senses, the Android remained motionless and apart.

—My friend, said Lord Ewald, Hadaly is a gift such as only a demi-god could bestow. Never in the bazaars of Baghdad or Cordova was such a slave displayed before the caliphs! Never did a magician evoke such a vision! Scheherazade, in her *Thousand and One Nights,* would never have dared to imagine her, lest doubt seize on the Sultan Shahryar. No treasure would suffice to buy this masterpiece. If at first it forced me into a moment of anger, admiration soon overcame me.

—Do you accept her? the electrician demanded.

—Truly, I should be a madman if I refused!

—DONE! said Edison solemnly. He held forth both hands, which Lord Ewald grasped warmly.

—Will you dine with me tonight, *both of you, as we did the other time?* said Edison with a smile. If you like, we can pick up the other conversation; you will see that Hadaly's remarks will be . . . different from those of her model.

—No, said Lord Ewald; I'm in haste to be the prisoner of this sublime mystery.

—Farewell, Miss Hadaly, Edison addressed her. Will you remember, over there, your underground room here—where sometimes we used to chat about the man who would wake you to our pallid existence as living beings?

—Oh, my dear Edison, the Android replied, bowing before the inventor, my resemblance to mortals does not extend to the point of forgetting my creator.

—By the way, Edison asked lightly—what about the living lady?

Lord Ewald started.

—My word, he said, I'd quite forgotten her.

Edison spoke casually.

—Well, as a matter of fact, she just departed, in a fit of pique. You two had barely gone out for your stroll when she came in here, quite recovered from her hypnotic influence, and subjected me to such a flood of words that I couldn't hear a single thing of all that you must have been saying to one another in the park. And yet I had some new contraptions arranged so that . . . well, never mind. I see that Hadaly, freed for the first time in her life to the promptings of her own nature, has showed herself worthy; future ages will be proud of her. And, to tell you the truth, I never doubted her for an instant. As for the other lady, who has just passed out of your life forever, Miss Alicia Clary just now told me, loud and clear, that she would have nothing to do with these new roles. Their language, she said, was unintelligible, and she couldn't remember it; and the *long passages* made her head ache. So that from now on, she said, "after thinking it all out," she would content herself by making her debut "in certain comic operas that she knew pretty well"; their success, *"which was quite definite already*, was bound to bring her to the attention of men of taste." As for her statue, she said you would be leaving Menlo Park tomorrow, and all I would have to do would be "to send it to him in London." She was even kind enough to add that "as for my expenses, I could *get a stiff price* out of you, since she understood one didn't haggle with artists." And on that note Miss Alicia Clary said farewell, asking me to remind you (in case I saw you again) "that she was expecting you over there, to make the arrangements." Well, that clears the air. Once at London, my dear fellow, all you need do is let her follow her career in peace. A letter, accompanied by a "princely" gift, will inform her that it's all over—and that will do it. Swift put it simply: What is a mistress? A belt and a cloak, no more.

—I had something like that in mind, said Lord Ewald.

Hadaly, gently raising her head from Lord Ewald's shoulder, gestured at the inventor and said in soft, pure tones with an inward smile:

—He will come to see us at Athelwold, won't he?

At this simple and natural request, the young man repressed a start of admiration and amazement; he replied with a consenting nod of the head.

But, oddly enough, it was Edison who started at these words and looked fixedly at Hadaly.

Suddenly he smote his brow, smiled broadly, knelt before the Android and, pushing away the hem of her skirt, began making some adjustment on the toes of her two slippers.

—What is it? said Lord Ewald, bewildered.

—I am disconnecting Hadaly! replied Edison—isolating her, in a word, since she no longer belongs to anyone but you. In the future she will respond only the the rings and the necklace. On the various points of her operation, the Manuscript will supply you with the most precise and explicit details. Very soon you will come to understand how the sixty basic hours engraved within her can be enriched with infinite complexi-ties. It's like the game of chess; or rather, it's altogether limitless, like a woman. She also has the two other major feminine types, various subdi-visions of which can be easily obtained merely by "mingling their dual-ity." The results are irresistible.

—My dear Edison, I personally believe that Hadaly is a true phantom, and I have no wish to explain or explore the mystery animating her. I hope soon to forget the little you've taught me on the subject.

Hadaly pressed tenderly the hand of the young lord, and said softly and quickly into his ear, while the engineer knelt at her feet:

—Don't tell him what I just said to you a little while ago; it's for your ears alone.

Edison rose, holding in his hand two little copper terminals which he had unscrewed, attached to strands of copper wire so slender that, even with their insulating material, they had remained invisible wherever the

Android walked. No doubt they were linked, somewhere in the distance, with hidden generators.

The Android now seemed to shudder in all her limbs; Edison touched the clasp of her necklace.

—Help me! she said.

And supporting herself with a hand on the shoulder of Lord Ewald, she smilingly entered her beautiful coffin, moving with ghostly grace into its dark recesses.

Then, having drawn her long wavy hair around her, she lay down gently within it.

She slipped over her brow the linen bandage intended to hold her head in place, and keep her face from touching either the sides or the cover of the coffin; then she fastened tightly about her body several wide bands of silk, so that no jolt or tilt could cause her to move.

—Dear friend, she said, crossing her arms over her breast, you will wake the sleeper when we have made our crossing; until then, we shall see one another . . . in the world of dreams.

She closed her eyes, as if asleep.

The two halves of the cover closed over her gently, hermetically, noiselessly. A silver plaque inscribed with a coat of arms was fixed on the coffin above the word HADALY, written in Oriental characters.

—The coffin, said Edison, will be placed at once in a larger square chest with a convex lid; the interior is tightly packed with thick stuffing. We take this precaution simply to keep curious outsiders from indulging in speculations. Here is the key of the coffin, and this is the invisible mechanism which opens the lid.

And he pointed to a little black star, almost imperceptible, at about the level of Hadaly's pillow.

—And now, he added, offering a chair to Lord Ewald, how about a glass of sherry? We still have a few words to exchange.

Edison, turning a crystal switch, lit the lofty lamps which added their light to the softer glow of the oxyhydric bulbs to produce the effect of bright sunshine.

Then he turned on the red signal-light above the laboratory and, having closed all the curtains, returned to his guest.

On a sideboard stood glittering Venetian glasses and a bottle of old sherry.

—I drink to the Impossible! said the engineer with a grave smile.

The clinked glasses; and a moment later, they faced one another for a final accounting.

# EXPEDITIOUS EXPLANATIONS

There are more things in heaven and earth, Horatio,
Than are dreamt of in your philosophy.
—Shakespeare, *Hamlet*

AFTER A LONG SESSION of silent thought:

—This is the only question I would like to ask you, said Lord Ewald. You spoke to me of a female assistant, a certain person called Miss Anny Sowana—who, it appears, undertook to model, measure, and trace limb by limb that tiresome living original, during the first days at least.

From what Alicia told me, I gather she was "very pale, *between two ages,* very taciturn, always in mourning, appearing to have been once very beautiful. Her eyes were almost always closed, to the point that it was impossible to tell what color they were; yet she saw everything very clearly." And Miss Clary added that once, when she was on the platform, this strange sculptress massaged her for a full half-hour, from head to foot, silently, as if she were an attendant in a Turkish bath. She only paused occasionally "to scribble figures and draw lines on bits of paper, which she immediately handed to you.

"And all this while a long 'streak of fire,' focused on the nudity of the model, seemed to follow the icy hands of the artist as if she was drawing with light."

—Well, then? asked Edison.

—Well, then, Lord Ewald took him up, if I judge of her by that first and wonderfully *remote* voice of Hadaly, this Miss Anny Sowana must be a strange and remarkable creature.

—Good! said Edison, I see you've been thinking things over, of an evening in your cottage, and that you've tried to reach an explanation of the process on your own. Excellent. You've guessed, I'm sure, some of the preliminary stages; but who could ever imagine the accidental but miraculous circumstances through which I became master of the whole process? The story simply illustrates that all things come to him who searches.

Perhaps you recall the tale I told you, formerly, of a certain Edward Anderson? What you are now asking for is the end of that tale; and here it is.

Pausing a moment to regroup his thoughts, Edison resumed:

—After her husband's bankruptcy and miserable suicide, Mrs. Anderson found herself dispossessed from her house and thrown penniless upon the world with her two boys, aged ten and twelve. Her only hope was the very uncertain charity of a few common commercial acquaintances, and the stresses of this catastrophe were simply too much for her. She was stricken with a disease that reduced her to complete inactivity—one of those complete neurotic collapses which are known to be incurable. In her case it took the form of a protracted cataleptic trance.

I have told you how much I admired the spirit of this woman, and—believe me, my lord—her intelligence. It therefore occurred to me to help her in her misfortune, as you once upon a time came to my aid! So, in the name of our old friendship (made all the dearer to me by her misfortune), I did my best to get the two children into good homes, and took steps to shelter their mother from all distress.

A considerable period passed without any change.

Often, in the course of my too infrequent visits to this invalid, I had occasion to observe these strange and *persistent* sleep-like trances, during which she spoke to me and answered me without ever opening her eyes. There are a number of such cases of sleep-like lethargy (they have even been catalogued nowadays) during which individuals sometimes remain three months on end without taking any food. At last, perhaps because I have a fairly well developed faculty of attention, I determined to cure, if it was humanly possible to do so, the particular affliction of Mrs. *Anny* Anderson.

Noting the emphasis placed on that first name by the engineer, Lord Ewald started in amazement.

—Cure her? he murmured. Transfigure her, rather. Wasn't that what it amounted to?

—Perhaps, replied Edison. Oh, I saw the other evening, when in less than an hour I reduced Miss Alicia Clary to a state of hypnotic trance, and you showed no surprise—I saw then that you were familiar with these new experiments undertaken by the leaders in this particular field of psychology. As you know, they have demonstrated that the science of Human Magnetism—it is both very ancient and very new—is an actual, indisputable field of knowledge. In a word, the various currents of nervous influence are no less a fact than are currents of electricity.

Well, I don't recall exactly when the idea struck me of making use of hypnotism for whatever advantage this wretched sufferer could draw from it. Perhaps her physical lethargy could be overcome in this way. I studied the most effective methods; then I began to practice, and with some persistence, working at the problem every day for about two months. Finally, when I had been able to produce all the known phenomena, one after another, certain other phenomena began to appear. Science, not knowing what to make of them, was in some difficulty, but I think that uncertainty will dissipate before long. We began to get crises of clairvoyance, apparently without any special reason, at the darkest point of these long unconscious spells.

Then Mrs. Anny Anderson *became my secret.* Because of the state of vibrant, high-strung torpor in which she existed, I was soon able to exercise one of my abilities which is perhaps innate, that of projecting my will into another. With practice, this gift developed, until now, given certain natures, I feel able to exert enough nervous energy to dominate another person almost completely, at a considerable distance—and this in a matter, not of a few days, but of a few hours. I was thus able to

establish a connection between this rare sleeper and myself, so subtle
that I could make the following use of two metal rings, specially founded
by me, and impregnated by me with a certain quantum of magnetic influence. (Didn't I tell you it would be a story of pure magic?) Then it was
enough for Mrs. Anderson—or, rather, Sowana—to put on one of these
rings while I was wearing the other, and instant, occult communication
was possible. She not only received, instantaneously, impulses from my
will, but found herself mentally, sympathetically, actually in my presence, to the point of hearing my voice and obeying my orders—even
though, physically, her body might be twenty leagues away and apparently fast asleep. She could be holding the speaker of a remote telephone,
and would answer instantly questions which I sent her by means of thought
transmission. How many conversations we have carried on in this way,
to the actual contempt of space! As you can see, she's a pretty sensitive
spiritual receiver.

I said *Sowana* just now. You're doubtless well aware that most of the
great hypnotic patients wind up referring to themselves in the third person, like little children. They see themselves from outside their own
organisms, outside their own sensory systems. In order to get further
outside themselves and help them escape their physical personality (call
it "social" if you will), some of them, once in the state of trance, actually
rebaptize themselves. The dream name comes to them, no one knows
whence, and by this they INSIST on being called as long as their luminous
dream endures—to the point of refusing to answer to any other name.
Thus it happened that one day, quite suddenly in the middle of a completely different sentence, Mrs. Anderson spoke to me with perfect, almost terrifying simplicity, these unforgettable words:

—My friend, I remember Anny Anderson, who lies sleeping down there
where you are; but *here* I remember another *me* whose name for a long
time has been Sowana.

—What frightening things I'm learning this evening, the young man
murmured, after a moment of stunned silence.

—Indeed: one would say we are on the outer limits of a field of human
experience verging on the Fantastic. Still, whether it was sensible or
absurd, this wish of hers had to be satisfied—so that in all our long-
distance conversations I no longer call Mrs. Anderson by another name
than the one she has claimed.

And I do so the more readily because the moral quality that I recognized in Mrs. Anderson before her illness, and that which I discover at
the depths of her hypnotic slumber, seem to me absolutely distinct. She
used to be a simple woman, perfectly honorable, even intelligent, but,
after all, of very limited views—and so I knew her. But in the depths of
her slumber another person is revealed to me, completely different, many-
sided and mysterious! So far as I can tell, the enormous knowledge, the
strange eloquence, and the penetrating insight of this sleeper named Sowana—who is, physically, the same person—are logically inexplicable.

Isn't this duality a stupefying phenomenon? And yet this same duality, though lesser in degree and not quite so striking, is a regularly observed, a recognized phenomenon in almost all the subjects treated by trained investigators. Sowana is exceptional only as an abnormally perfect instance of a very common event—and this abnormality is due simply to her particular variety of neurosis.

The moment has now come for me to tell you, my lord, that after the demise of the adorable Evelyn Habal, the artificial girl, I felt obliged to show Sowana that collection of burlesque relics that I carried off from Philadelphia as trophies of war, so to speak. At the same time, I gave her a fairly distinct outline of my plan for Hadaly. You can't imagine the gloomy delight, the vengeful excitement, with which she accepted and encouraged my plan! No time to be lost, I must go to work at once! And so I began the task, then became absorbed in it to the point that for two years it took me away from my work on electric power and new light bulbs for which Humanity was waiting. No matter for that, nor for the few million ridiculous dollars I lost! For at last when all the complexities of the Android's organism were completed, I put them all together and showed her the ghostly creature, the youthful figure in its animated armor.

Once having seen it, Sowana, as if subject to some demonic spirit of exultation, forced me to explain all its most hidden secrets—until, when she had studied every last detail, she was able, *occasionally,* TO INCORPORATE HERSELF WITHIN IT, AND ANIMATE IT WITH HER "SUPERNATURAL" BEING.

Struck by this strange relationship, I quickly worked out with all the ingenuity I could a complex system of controls, involving invisible inductors and some completely new condensers; I added to it a controlling Cylinder exactly corresponding to that controlling the motions of Hadaly. When Sowana had learned all about it, one day she sent me the Android without any advance notice, sent her right here while I was just finishing another job. I tell you that the sight of that vision caused the most terrible shock I ever felt in my life. The workman was aghast at his own work.

And my first thought afterward was this: "When this phantom has become the exact duplicate of a woman, what sort of effect will she have!"

Henceforth all my thoughts and plans were calculated on this one point, of finding a bold soul who would someday attempt what you and I together have this night made a reality. For, I must make this point very clear to you, *not everything about this creature is an illusion!* It is really an unknown creature, it is actually the Ideal, in real truth it is Hadaly who has appeared to you, though behind these veils of electric machinery, beneath this silver armor which imitates a human woman. You must always recall that, though I know Mrs. Anderson, *I swear to you on my soul* THAT I DO NOT KNOW SOWANA!

Lord Ewald shuddered at this solemn phrase from the engineer; the latter continued thoughtfully:

—Stretched beneath the shady trees and flowered groves of our cave, Sowana lay with her eyes shut and her mind wandering far beyond the heavy materiality of any physical organism; and in that state, she incorporated herself, like a fluid vision, within Hadaly! Within her hands, like those of a dead woman, she held the metallic controls of Hadaly; she walked in the footsteps of Hadaly, spoke within her in that strangely distant voice which also vibrates from her lips during her long sleep-like trances! And all I had to do was repeat, *but silently,* what you said, to have this spirit, unknown to both of us, hear what you had said, and then reply to it through the phantom.

Where did she reply from? Where did she hear? Whom had she gradually become? What is this unquestionable force which, like the legendary ring of Gyges, confers on its wearer ubiquity, invisibility, a complete new intellectual character? In a word, whom are we dealing with?

Questions, crying aloud for answers.

Recall, if you will, that response of Hadaly's—so natural!—to the enlarged photograph of Alicia that I projected on the wall. Or, down below, her interest in the machine for measuring the heat of rays from the stars, her improvised explanation of the whole process; or that remarkable scene with the purse! Do you recall the precision with which Hadaly described the exact costume worn by Miss Alicia Clary as she sat in the railroad car, reading by lamplight your telegram sent just that night? Do you see, can you imagine by what subtle, almost incredible means that feat of clairvoyance was achieved? Listen. You are imbued, you are saturated with the nervous energy of your adored and detested beauty. But at a certain moment, if you recall, Hadaly *took you by the hand* to draw you toward the box containing those awful relics of the stage star. Well, the nervous energy of Sowana, *thanks to this pressure of Hadaly's hand,* found itself in close proximity to yours. At this moment, in spite of the apparent distance between you and your mistress, her mind was able to fly forth on the wings of your thought and reach the center toward which your ideas were tending, that is, Miss Alicia Clary in the railway carriage that was bringing her to Menlo Park.

—Is it possible? said Lord Ewald in an undertone.

—No, it is not, Edison replied. But it's a fact nonetheless. So many other things that appear impossible happen every day now, that I can't be too tremendously surprised at this, especially since I'm one of those who can never forget the immense quantity of Nothing that was necessary to create the Universe.

In any case, my restless dreamer was stretched out on cushions thrown over a large sheet of plate glass supported on insulators; she held her hands on a series of switches which electrified the Android and maintained a delicate current of communication between the two. And I may add that there is such an affinity between the nervous and the magnetic currents that I'm not at all surprised at the success of the clairvoyant experiment—especially in the present surroundings.

—Just a minute, said Lord Ewald. I'm sure it's already a remarkable thing that electric current can now transmit energy to great heights and over enormous, almost limitless distances. Indeed, if I'm to believe the reports that flood in from every direction, there's no doubt that tomorrow it will be used to spread through a thousand different networks the enormous blind energy, which always hitherto went to waste, of cataracts and torrents—and, for all I know, of the tides, perhaps. This trick is perfectly comprehensible, given the use of tangible conductors—magic highways—through which the powerful currents flow. But this INSUBSTANTIAL transmission of my living thought, how can I imagine it taking place, at a distance, *without conductors or wires, even the very thinnest?*

—In the first place, replied the engineer, distance in these matters is nothing but a kind of illusion. Besides, you overlook here a number of facts recently verified by experimental science. For example, it is not just the nervous energy of a living being that can be transmitted over a distance, but the simple *virtue* of certain substances. Such substances can influence the human organism from afar without *ingestion, suggestion, or any sort of material transmission.* Here is an experiment that has been witnessed by a number of distinguished and very skeptical observers. A certain number of crystal jars are hermetically sealed and placed in envelopes; each contains a different drug, the name of which is concealed from me, the experimenter. I take one of them at random and hold it ten or twelve centimeters behind the head of . . . let's say, a hysteric. Within a few minutes the subject is seized with convulsions, vomits, sneezes, shouts aloud, or goes to sleep, according to the specific drug held behind his head at that distance. In fact, if it is a deadly poison, the patient will display all the symptoms of that particular poison; they may even lead to his death. If it's a particular electuary, he will promptly fall into a religious ecstasy of a very precise character; his hallucinations will *always* be religious, even if he's a devotee of a very different religious cult. If I hold a chloride compound near him, you will see that the mere *proximity* burns him to such a degree that he emits cries of pain. Where are the conductors causing these responses? And before these unquestionable facts, which strike experimental scientists with well-grounded stupefaction, why shouldn't I hypothesize a third sort of current, a mixed current, which combines the electric and the nervous energies, halfway between that which moves the magnetic needle to point at the North Pole, and that which paralyzes a bird placed under the beating wings of a hawk?

If some sort of *inductive affinity* can carry the vibrant influence of various drugs through the pores of the glass and the thicknesses of paper, to influence a patient in a state of hysterical supersensitivity, this is no more than a magnet does when its power passes through glass and through cloth to attract distant molecules of iron. And if *even vegetables and minerals* have an obscure sort of magnetism which without material connectors can cross distances and pass over obstacles to imprint their virtue on living beings, why should I be surprised if among three individuals of the same species, held together by a common electro-magnetic center, the various currents should so coincide as to produce telepathic communication?

To conclude, from the moment when the hidden sensibility of Sowana showed itself susceptible of secret influence from electric current—from a very slight shock, for example, administered down here to Mrs. Anderson—I sensed that the two sorts of current were linked by some sort of affinity. In other respects there was no connection; in the cataleptic state, Mrs. Anderson could have been burned alive without influencing Sowana in the slightest. But the connection of electric current with psychic current was evidently a fact, and consequently I began to suppose that to some extent various of their properties might be synthesized to create a third power of unknown nature and characteristics. The man who could discover this current and manage it like the two others would be capable of performing feats to shame those of the Indian yogis, the bonzes of Tibet, the snake charmers of Coromandel, and the dervishes of central Egypt.

After a moment's reflection, Lord Ewald replied:

—Though I agree that I probably shouldn't ever see Mrs. Anderson, Sowana I think deserves to be a friend; and if, in this magical environment, she can hear me, I hope this wish reaches her, wherever she is! But one last question: is it true that the words Hadaly spoke just now in the park were all recited—"declaimed," so to speak, by Miss Alicia Clary?

—Absolutely, said Edison, and you know it, since you must have recognized both the voice and the gestures of the original. She was only able to recite the speeches so well (particulary since she didn't understand a word of them) because of the patient and powerful suggestions of Sowana.

Lord Ewald was totally confounded by this reply; and this time, in fact, the explanation made no sense. The fact that all the different phases of the scene could have been anticipated (and yet the voice suggested that they *had* been anticipated) was simply inconceivable.

He was about to protest, and prove to the engineer that his explanation was radically and absolutely impossible, when he bethought him, suddenly, of the strange request that Hadaly had made of him, in a whisper, just before she closed herself in her artificial tomb.

And that was why, keeping all his thoughts to himself, as well as the odd sensation of vertigo he was experiencing, he said nothing. But he did cast an uneasy glance or two toward the coffin; he had just caught a distinct glimpse of a shade from beyond the tomb, within the Android.

Edison, however, never noticed this glance and continued his lecture:

—The state of constant spirituality and supreme visionary insight at which *the real life* of Sowana unfolds, confers on her intense powers of suggestion, especially with subjects already half-hypnotized by me. The effects of her will, even on their intelligence, are instant.

It was only because she was under this influence that your actress submitted for days on end to rehearsals on this stage, where she was surrounded by my invisible cameras and recorders. She performed every last detail of the various scenes that Hadaly possesses and that character-ize her. And this down to the least of her intonations, gestures, and glances, all of which were called forth, inspired, you might say, in this beautiful innocent by Sowana. Hadaly's meticulous golden lungs, guided by the skillful hands of Sowana, recorded only the one perfect vocal nuance out of twenty—that happened sometimes. Meanwhile I, with a micrometer in my hand and my strongest magnifying glass in focus, devoted myself to chiseling on the Android's central cylinder none but the perfectly coordinated movements, none but the most subtle glances and joyous or serious expressions of Alicia. During the eleven days that this work demanded, work on the Android's other physical characteris-tics—except, of course, for the chest—proceeded apace under my scru-pulous instructions. Would you like to see the several dozen photochromic pictures on which are marked the points (precise to several thousandths of a millimeter) where the grains of metallic powder had to be placed in the flesh for the exact magnetic implementation of Miss Alicia Clary's five or six basic smiles? I have them right here, in these boxes. Naturally the various expressions on the features are coordinated with the sense of the words—just as some five different adjustments of the eyebrows mod-ulate the ordinary expressions of this very interesting young lady.

At bottom, all this work, which in its entirety is bound to seem so complex and so difficult of accomplishment, reduces itself to analysis, attention, and perseverance. The whole thing amounts to so little that, once I was sure of my general formulas (based on a bit of calculus, and not altogether easy to formulate—I stayed up nights, working on them!), the close, detailed work of refraction was neither painful nor difficult. Everything worked itself out! Several days ago, I was closing up the plas-tic mediator and applying, little by little, first in the form of powder, then layer by layer, the artificial flesh which was to cover all those thousands of infinitesimal wires emerging from imperceptible openings in the ar-mor. And just then Hadaly—still lost in her dream world—repeated for me, without a single slip, every one of the various scenes which consti-tute the mirage of her mental state.

But today, all day, both here and in the park, her final rehearsal—at which I stood between her, dressed as she was like her model, and Sowana—that confounded me!

She was Humanity at its best—minus that which is unnamable in us, minus that intangible element whose absence at moments like that can hardly be censured. I was, and I admit it, as enraptured as a poet. What melancholy incantations, embodying the voluptuous vision of the dream! What a voice, what a penetrating depth in those eyes! What songs! What a beauty, as of a forgotten goddess! What bewitching withdrawals of fem-inine modesty! What unknown invitations toward an impossible love! With a mere touch of the rings, Sowana transfigured this poetess of en-chanted dreams. Indeed, as I told you, her amazing and overwhelming scenes were created for her by the foremost among the most brilliant poets and thinkers of this century.

Over there, when you wake her up in your ancient castle—after the first cup of pure water and banquet of lozenges—you will see what a talented phantom will appear before you! As soon as Hadaly's habits and presence have become familiar to you, you will become her sincere spiritual companion. For if I have furnished the physical basis for her illusions, a Soul which is unknown to me has passed over my work and, incorporating itself there forever, has laid her hand on the slightest details of those superb and inspiring scenes, imposing on them, believe me, an art so subtle that it surpasses, in all truth, the reach of human imagination.

Within this new work of art a creature from beyond the reach of Humanity has insinuated herself and now lurks there at the heart of the mystery, a power unimagined before our time.

# FAREWELLS

The hour of parting, when each one goes his way.
—Victor Hugo, *Ruy Blas*

—AND SO, EDISON CONCLUDED, the work is finished, and I can conclude that it has not resulted in an empty or lifeless imitation. A soul has been added to it, or so we may say, giving its own qualities to the voice, the gestures, the intonations, the smile, the very pallor of the living woman who was your love. *In her* all these qualities were dead, deceptive, degraded, because enslaved to vulgar, selfish reason; beneath their veils now lurks a feminine being who is, and perhaps always was, the true and rightful possessor of this extraordinary beauty, since she has shown herself worthy of it. In this way she who was the victim of the Artificial has at last redeemed the Artificial! She who was abandoned and betrayed by love turned degrading and obscene has grown into a vision capable of inspiring love at its most sublime! She who was blighted in her hopes, her health, and her prosperity by a wretched suicide has prevented another suicide. Speak your final judgment now as between shadow and reality. Do you think such an empty illusion as the departed creature can hold you in this world, or is worth the struggle of living?

As his only answer, Lord Ewald arose and drew out of its ivory case a small pistol which he handed to Edison:

—My dear enchanter, said he, permit me to leave with you a little souvenir of this extraordinary adventure! You've gained the day, and I surrender my weapon to you.

Edison, rising also, accepted the gun, played thoughtfully with the action, then pointed it out the open window and into the night.

—Here's a bullet, he said, that I send to the Devil, if he exists—and if he does, I rather suspect he's somewhere in this neighborhood.

—Ha, ha! Just like in the *Freischutz!* laughed Lord Ewald, struck by this prank of the great man.

The pistol sent a bullet into the dark.

—A hit, a palpable hit! came an extraordinary shout from the park.

—What's that? asked Lord Ewald, taken aback.

—Nothing. Just one of my old Phonographs, having his joke! Edison replied.

—I'm depriving you of a masterpiece such as no man ever knew! said Lord Ewald after a moment.

—Not at all, Edison replied, since I still have the formulas. But . . . I shall make no more Androids. My underground caves will be used to house secret laboratories in which I will work on other discoveries.

And now, my lord Celian Ewald, a last glass of sherry, and farewell. You have chosen the world of dreams; take with you the high priestess of it. My destiny keeps me chained to the pale "realities" of this world. The traveling chest and carriage are ready; my workmen, well armed, will escort you to New York, where the captain of the transatlantic liner *Wonderful* will be expecting you. We shall meet again perhaps in Athelwold Castle. Write to me. Your hands! Farewell!

There was a final handclasp between Edison and Lord Ewald, and a moment later the Englishman was mounted on his horse beside the carriage, surrounded by the torches of his formidable escort.

The cavalcade got under way, and within a few minutes the strange procession was out of sight on the road toward the little station of Menlo Park.

Alone in the brightly lit center of his cluttered laboratory, Edison walked slowly toward some impenetrable black drapes hanging in one corner of the room. In response to his hand, they slowly parted.

Before him was a woman of elegant appearance, dressed entirely in black and no doubt sleeping on a large couch which rested on glass insulators. Her face was still youthful, though her rich dark hair was touched with silver around the temples. Though severe, her beauty still retained much charm, and from the pure oval of her face radiated a kind of supernatural tranquility. Her hand, resting on the carpet, held the mouthpiece of an Electrophone, but muffled as if set into a thick mask, so that when she spoke into it nobody could hear her, even if he were standing right beside her.

—Ah, Sowana, said Edison jovially, this must be the first time that Science showed it could cure a man, even of love!

But the visionary seer made no answer. Edison took her hand; it was icy cold. He shuddered and bent over her; her pulse no longer beat, her heart had stopped.

For a long time he continued to make the hypnotic passes of awakening and revival over the head of the sleeper; but in vain.

After an hour of anxiety and vain efforts to rouse her, Edison sensed at last that she who seemed to sleep had definitely left the world of living men.

# FATE

And it repented the Lord that he had made man
on the earth, and it grieved him at his heart.
And the Lord said, I will destroy man whom I
have created . . .

—Genesis

About three weeks after these events, Edison, who had received neither letters nor cables from Lord Ewald, began to worry.

One evening about nine the engineer was seated alone in his laboratory, turning the pages of a major American newspaper, when his eye caught the following item, which riveted his attention till he had read it twice over in total shock and amazement.

Lloyd's.—Dispatch. Maritime news.

The loss of the steamer *Wonderful,* which we announced yesterday, has just been confirmed, and we are now in a position to supply the following details of this unhappy accident.

Fire broke out in the rear hold about two o'clock in the morning; it began in a cargo compartment where several barrels of turpentine and gasoline were ignited by an unknown cause, and soon exploded.

Seas were heavy, the steamer was pitching stiffly, and a sheet of flames quickly spread into the baggage compartment, with the help of a strong west wind. So swiftly did it move that there was hardly any warning from smoke before the fire itself was on the crew.

The three hundred passengers, wakened from their sleep, rushed to the bridge in panic, having quite lost their heads. Many scenes of horror were enacted.

Before the advancing flames women and children shrieked in helpless terror.

The captain having announced that the ship would sink in five minutes, the lifeboats were launched immediately. Women and children embarked first.

During these scenes of horror, a strange incident occurred below decks. A young Englishman, Lord E****, seized a capstan bar and tried by main force to rush into the flames where the chests and boxes were already burning fiercely.

Having knocked down the lieutenant and one of the boatswain's mates who tried to stop him, he had to be restrained by no fewer than six sailors who rushed on him and wrestled him to the ground. He seemed to be in an absolute frenzy to throw himself into the flames.

In the middle of his struggles, he shouted that he wanted to save from the flames a chest containing an object so precious that he offered the enormous sum of *a hundred thousand guineas to anyone who would help him save it from the inferno.* But that was absolutely impossible, and would have been useless in any case, since the lifeboats were barely adequate to hold the passengers and the crew.

Because of his extraordinary strength, he had to be bound hand and foot, and carried, unconscious, into the last of the lifeboats, whose occupants were picked up about six in the morning by the French packet *Redoubtable.*

The first lifeboat, filled largely with women and children, unfortunately capsized, with a loss of seventy-two lives. The following is a partial listing of these unhappy victims.

(Followed an official list, one of the first names of which was that of Miss Emma-Alicia Clary, lyric artist.)

Edison flung the paper violently aside. Five minutes passed, while he brooded in silence. With a rough gesture he abruptly turned off all the lamps and began to walk restlessly up and down in the darkness.

Suddenly a bell rang on the telegraphic receiver; at once the electrician switched on the light standing beside it.

Three seconds later, snatching the message from the machine, he read the following words:

LIVERPOOL TO MENLO PARK, NEW JERSEY, UNITED STATES. 17.2.8.40. EDISON, ENGINEER: *My friend, only the loss of Hadaly leaves me inconsolable—I grieve only for that shade. Farewell.*

—LORD EWALD.

Throwing aside the telegram, the great inventor dropped to a chair beside his apparatus. As he looked idly about, his glance encountered, not far from him, the ebony table; a beam of moonlight fell whitely on that charming arm, on the pale hand with its enchanted rings. And the melancholy dreamer, losing himself in unknown thoughts, lifted his eyes to look through the open window, out into the night. There for some time he listened to the indifferent winds of winter, whistling and howling through the bare branches—then, raising his eyes even higher toward the ancient luminous spheres which still shone, unmoved, through the gaps in the heavy clouds, and sent their glints forever through the infinite, inconceivable mystery of the heavens, he shivered—no doubt, from the cold—in utter silence.

# APPENDIX: VILLIERS' EPIGRAPHS

I    1. Giles Fletcher, Jr., "Christ's Victory on Earth," stanza 42.
2. E. T. A. Hoffmann, "The Sand-Man."
3. A creative quotation consonant with the *Ethic*, Part IV, prop. 2.
4. A popular abbreviation of a known Stoic position.
5. First line of "Solvet Seclum," LXXXI of *Poésies barbares*.
6. Matthew 13:43.
7. Perhaps Hugo Lubliner, author (1879) of *Die Frau ohne Geist*.
8. A commonplace.
9. Balzac, *La Recherche de l'absolu*.
10. Cham = Amédée de Noé, French caricaturist (1819–79).
11. Lord Byron, "The Dream," lines 91-93, cited very inexactly, though the theme is appropriate.
12. Lord Byron, *Hebrew Melodies*.
13. A commonplace.
14. Goethe, *Werther*, II, Oct. 26.
15. A mythological commonplace.
16. Remotely from Byron, *Don Juan*, canto 3.
17. Perhaps M. F. P. A. Marrast (1801–52), official and publicist, noted for his crisp prose.
18. Creative quotation based on *Inferno*, canto 23.
19. *Essais*, I, xxi, "De la force de l'imagination," quote not quite exact.

II    1. Unlikely to be found in the Kabbalah, but assigned to it for the aura of occult and mysterious knowledge it implies.
2. A commonplace.
3. Schiller's ballad, "Das verschleiertes Bild zu Sais."
4. J. Moleschott (1822–95), perhaps *Kreislauf des Lebens* (1852), a strongly materialist book.
5. Untraced; he sounds like a figure in a caricature.
6. Approximately, from the *Roman de la momie*, prologue.
7. *Thousand and One Nights*.
8. Creative quotation based on several of the *Pensées*.
9. A mythological commonplace.
10. Creative quotation based on "Des femmes" in the *Caractères*.
11. From the so-called Litany of Loreto.
12. Ptolemy Hephaestion is unknown; Claudius Ptolemaeus was the Alexandrian geographer; but the phrase probably derives from Baudelaire, "Le Voyage," vii: "Nous nous embarquerons sur la mer des Ténèbres."

III  1. Goethe, *Faust* II, Act I, lines 1668–69.
     2. Flaubert, *Salammbô*, Ch. XI.
     3. Milton, *Paradise Lost,* very inexactly remembered from Book III, invocation.
     4. Probably compressed from *Recherche de la vérité,* Book V.
     5. Milton, *Paradise Lost,* Book III, invocation.

IV  1. Not the biblical book of Proverbs, but proverbial wisdom.
     2. Adapted from Balzac, *Cousine Bette,* Part II, Mme de Marneffe to Crevel.
     3. Matthew 7:16.
     4. In line with the "Eloge du maquillage," in *Le Peintre de la vie moderne,* but not word for word.
     5. Catullus, 3.
     6. "La colère de Samson," in *Les destinées.*
     7. Diderot, *De l'interpretation de la nature,* sect. xxiii.

V   1. Conceivably Tertullian, but much more likely the epigraph to Part III, Book VIII, Ch. 13 of *Les Misérables.*
     2. Ecclesiastes.
     3. Virgil, *Aeneid,* I, 409.
     4. Lord Byron, *Cain,* Act V.
     5. A commonplace.
     6. Not the book of Proverbs, but proverbial wisdom. See also Baudelaire, "De l'essence du rire," II.
     7. Poe, "The Man of the Crowd."
     8. Hugo, *La légende des siècles,* II, iv, "Le sacre de la femme."
     9. A popular advertisement for mouthwash.
   10. Marceline Desbordes-Valmore (1786–1859), elegiac poetess.
   11. *Lélia* is full of stars, but the particular phrase has eluded me.
   12. Baudelaire, "Les yeux de Berthe."
   13. A commonplace.
   14. Loosely from Ovid, *Metamorphoses,* II, 413.
   15. Tristan L'Hermite, "Le promenoir des deux amants," in *Les amours de Tristan* (1638).
   16. Goethe, *Faust* II, Act V, lines 551–53.

VI  1. Horace, *Odes,* I, 37.
     2. A commonplace.
     3. A popular saying by/about Edison.
     4. Poe, "Morella."
     5. Luke 19:40.
     6. Lamartine, "L'homme," #2 of *Méditations poetiques.*
     7. A commonplace.
     8. Voltaire, "Le phénix," Ch. IX of *La Princesse de Babylone.*
     9. Musset, "Dedicace" (to M. Alfred Tattet) of *La Coupe et les lèvres.*

10. Approximately from Wagner, *Die Valkyrie*, Act III *ad finem*.
11. From *L'homme qui rit*.
12. Perhaps very loosely from "Abschied," #7 of the sequence *Schwanengesang*, D. 957.
13. Shakespeare, *Hamlet*, Act 1, scene 5, lines 165–66.
14. Hugo, *Ruy Blas*, Act I, scene 3.
15. Genesis 6:6–7.